SILVER TONGUE

CHARLIE FLETCHER

Hodder
Children's
Books

a division of Hachette Children's Books

Typeset in Palatino by Avon DataSet Ltd,
Bidford on Avon, Warwickshire

Printed and bound in Great Britain by
Clays Ltd, St Ives plc

The paper used in this book is a natural recyclable product made from
wood grown in sustainable forests. The hard coverboard is recycled.

Hodder Children's Books
a division of Hachette Children's Books
338 Euston Road, London NW1 3BH
An Hachette UK company
www.hachette.co.uk

For Molly with love,
in memory of her mother, Kate Jones.

CONTENTS

The tongue of the just is as choice silver.
The heart of the wicked is little worth.

Proverbs 10:20

THE STORY SO FAR...

In *Stoneheart*, George breaks a carving on the front of the Natural History Museum. This wakes an ancient force imprisoned in the London Stone hidden deep in the City. A vengeful carving of a pterodactyl peels off the side of the museum and chases him. When all seems lost a statue of a World War One soldier, the Gunner, steps off a war memorial and saves him.

So begins George's ordeal trapped in a layer of London, an unLondon, in which the two mutually hostile tribes of statues, the human spits and the inhuman taints live in an uneasy truce, a truce that George's action has thrown into jeopardy.

No one else can see what is happening to him, except Edie Laemmel, a glint. Glints are women or girls who have a gift of touching stones and experiencing past events recorded in them. George, Edie and the Gunner set off on a journey to make amends. But unknown to them the Stone has alerted the Walker, one of its servants, who stalks them with the help of his own servant, the Raven.

On this journey George discovers he has special powers. The Black Friar identifies George as a maker, someone with a special gift for sculpting things from stone or metal. The Friar also tells them to find the 'Stone Heart' and put the broken dragon carving back to make amends for the damage George has done. But on the way the Gunner has sacrificed himself to try and save Edie, and ultimately falls into the clutches of the Walker. It is left to George to use his new-found gifts as a maker to rescue her. In so doing he sacrifices his own safety and is fated to take 'The Hard Way', remaining with her in this dangerous unLondon.

In *Ironhand*, the Gunner is imprisoned below the city in an old water tank. At the moment George and Edie set off to try and rescue him they are separated, as George is snatched into the air by the cat-faced gargoyle named Spout. Edie sets off on her own.

George is seemingly rescued from Spout by Ariel, a spit who is also an Agent of Fate come to ensure he takes The Hard Way. She takes him to receive the challenge issued by a statue called The Last Knight. He has to fight three duels: on land, on water and in the air. He is rescued from certain death on the end of the Knight's lance by the timely arrival of Spout who snatches him into the sky. George mends Spout's broken wing, and the two form a bond. Spout calls George Ironhand, which he pronounces as 'Eigengang'. Although he has cheated death, the legacy of The Hard Way is inescapably carved into George's flesh, as three veins of marble, bronze and stone twine up his arm, each representing a duel to be fought. Each one will only stop moving fatally towards his heart as he fights the duel it represents.

Edie meanwhile has gone back to the Black Friar for help but, helped by an urchin-like statue named Little Tragedy, tries to escape the pub when it appears the Walker has come to the door. Only when they arrive at their destination through the mirrors does it become apparent that Tragedy has betrayed her to the Walker, since they are now in a past London, the London of the Frost Fair where she once glinted herself being killed. Meanwhile the Gunner has discovered that the Walker has killed many glints and stolen their sea-glass heart stones in his search for power. He escapes the water tank by crawling through London's underground rivers, taking the stones with him. He expects to die at midnight (turn o' day) but survives because George stands his watch on his plinth in his stead.

While he does this, he experiences what the Gunner and his brother soldier, the Officer, experience every night, an hour in the trenches under bombardment during an artillery duel in World War One (this is his first duel). While he does this he meets a soldier with his own dead father's face and, though the soldier dies, George is able to heal his guilt at his father's death and realize he was both loved and known to love him back.

The Gunner and George and the Officer are reunited, along with the Queen (Boadicea) and her daughters who have taken an interest in saving Edie. They travel through mirrors into the past to try and rescue her.

Edie escapes briefly from the Walker but is recaptured, after she has buried her sea-glass heart stone to save it. He takes her to the Frost Fair, where, despite having foreseen it, she is unable to prevent her own death beneath the ice.

George fights the Walker on the ice (his second duel) while the Gunner retrieves Edie's body. The Queen takes them all through the mirrors in her chariot but, at the moment they almost run down the Walker, he escapes into the Outer Darkness beyond the Black Mirrors. Unseen by any of the others, but felt as an icy blast, an Ice Devil enters our world as he exits it and follows them back to the present.

Edie is revived by the power of all the stolen heart stones the Gunner saved from under the city, and she finds, among them, her mother's own stone. This is doubly shocking for Edie – she knows her mother didn't realize she had been a glint, and the fire remaining in the stone suggests her mother, believed dead, may actually be alive.

George has one more duel to fight before the last stone vein twines into his heart and kills him. The arrival of the Ice Devil has frozen time and the city, which is disappearing under a heavy snowfall. And the ordinary people seem to have disappeared, leaving George and Edie the only normal humans in a city now only populated by warring statues.

And now the story continues . . .

PROLOGUE

THE ICE DEVIL

The Ice Devil swirled in over the City, revelling in this new otherworld it had found. It sensed the lines of power and the old places of magic buried beneath the thin skin of the modern streets and buildings, and as it rose higher it tried to make sense of what it was experiencing.

The first thing it noticed as it crashed into this unfamiliar dimension was the dark pulse just barely contained in the London Stone. The Stone, set behind a wrought-iron screen in the side of an undistinguished building on Cannon Street, looked like nothing important. Only the tiniest percentage of the thousands of normal people who walked past it every day actually noticed it, and of those who did, none sensed the malevolence imprisoned within the rough block, or realized that the flaking iron cage was there to protect them from the Stone, rather than the other way round. But the Ice Devil was not normal, nor was it by any stretch of the imagination 'people': it was 'other'. It had come through the Black Mirror from a dimension wholly and implacably different to ours, and was attuned to a very different register of forces. To the Ice Devil the Darkness in the Stone blazed out like a flaming beacon on a starless night, and that was why it made straight there to get its bearings.

What it hadn't expected was the effect of its sudden arrival: the ice that it had made its shape out of was in fact only half as cold as the otherworldly chill that was its

5

normal state, and when the Stone met the shocking sub-zero blast that attended it, it cracked. And when it cracked, the true power and depth of the Darkness within made itself apparent. If the Darkness had been light, then it would have been as if someone had tossed magnesium into that fiery beacon, releasing a blinding flare of whiteness. The Darkness revealed through the crack in the stone was the purest, most malevolent gloom, a fell dark pitched far beyond mere black. It was not a darkness made from the mere absence of light and hope, it was the Darkness that actively sucked light, hope and life into it and obliterated them.

The Ice Devil recoiled from the Darkness, surprised at the power it had released by cracking the stone. It soared up and away into the night, and came to rest on the highest perch it could find: the black block-house structure on top of Tower 42, a tall triangular skyscraper on Old Broad Street. It was on this bunker in the sky that the Ice Devil waited as it surveyed the City beneath and got its bearings, never forgetting to keep part of its consciousness on the Darkness below. And the Darkness also waited, looking back out of the crack in the Stone, waiting to take shape, in no hurry now that the doors to its long prison stood open.

And then their looks met.

What passed between them was nothing more cataclysmic than a nod and a tiny flicker of kinship. And something as delicate as laughter dropped cold and soft from the Ice Devil and joined the heavy snow starting to fall into the city below.

One command, pitched below sound, but audible to every stone-servant and taint in the city boomed out through the night: 'COME!'

1

CHINSTRAPPED

'Where have the people gone?' said Edie, voicing the question in George's head. 'Why's everything frozen?'

George tried to ignore the insistent twinge of pain in his arm where he knew the vein of stone was inexorably twisting towards his shoulder, and looked at the unmoving traffic curving round the uphill bend of Hyde Park Corner. The cars and buses were empty of drivers or passengers, and a riderless police motorbike was stuck leaning forty-five degrees into the turn behind them as if kept upright by invisible strings.

'And why's it snowing?' asked George, looking round at the Gunner.

The Gunner shrugged snow off his shoulders and looked at the Officer. The Officer cleared his throat and looked up into the sky at the fall of thick, fluffy flakes tumbling straight down on them out of the sodium glare that ceilinged the City.

'Well. Ahem. I should say it's, ah . . .'

'Gack,' said Spout, hopping down off the stone howitzer above them, landing in the snow already stacking up at their feet.

'Exactly,' finished the Officer. 'I don't know.'

'How can you not know?' asked George. 'You must know!'

He followed the Officer's gaze into the night sky and then turned slowly, scouring what he could see of the city for anything reassuring like someone hurrying home along a pavement, or people moving in the lighted windows of the hotel opposite. There was nothing.

'We don't,' said the Queen.

'You don't?' said Edie shakily.

'No,' replied the Gunner. 'This hasn't happened before.'

George stopped turning and looked at the statues standing around him in the increasingly white cityscape. The two World War One soldiers had snow massing on their tin helmets, and the Warrior Queen and her two daughters looked entirely underdressed for the eerily sudden winter tumbling down around them. The horses attached to her chariot nickered in the background and tossed white flakes from their manes, eyeing Spout the winged gargoyle with suspicion. Even without the snow, it was a strange sight.

'Great,' he sighed. He knew three things with equal conviction and clarity.

He knew they were in deep trouble.

He knew that whatever that trouble was, they had somehow brought it with them through the mirrors from the Frost Fair.

And he knew he was in no shape to begin to be able to figure it out. The white stone vein twining up his arm was not just counting off the time he had left to face the unavoidable doom of his third and final duel but was also remorselessly draining his remaining energy, drip by tiny drip.

'I'm knackered,' he said.

'Knackered?' shot back the Queen in surprise. 'What is knackered?'

'Chinstrapped,' said the Gunner.

'Exhausted,' explained the Officer. 'As in the only thing

holding him up on his feet is the chinstrap on his helmet. It's not surprising.'

Edie looked round at them, and then down at her mother's sea-glass earring clenched in her hand. She felt a deep and private pain, one that she'd never allowed herself. It was the pain of hoping against hope, a confusing ache of elation and fear spreading through her so fiercely that she almost couldn't breathe. It felt like she was drowning in 'maybes', because the light in that little fragment of glass shouted that maybe things were not as she had thought them to be, that maybe she had been lied to, maybe the great hole in her heart would again be filled with the thing she thought had abandoned it and maybe, just maybe she would not have to carry the pain alone and for ever.

'We can't just go to sleep,' she said. 'We've got things to do . . .'

'The thing about having things to do,' declared the Gunner, 'is that before you start, it's a good thing to have some idea about what they are and how you're going to do 'em.'

'I'm going to find my mother,' retorted Edie, jutting her chin as if daring him to say no.

A look ricocheted from the Gunner to the Queen to the Officer.

'Er,' said the Officer.

'Fair enough,' cut in the Gunner. 'But how?' He thumbed over his shoulder at the empty streets. 'Right now I'd say, bar you and George, there ain't any other bugger in this whole city, let alone your mum.'

Edie shivered and gripped the earring tighter. She caught another look flying between George and the Gunner.

'She *is* alive,' she exclaimed.

No one said anything.

'Edie?' began George.

'She IS,' she said, eyes burning as fiercely as the heart stone in her hand. 'She is. Otherwise why would her heart stone still be alight when all the others have gone out?'

She pointed at the loose scrabble of sea-glass pebbles quickly being covered by the falling snow at her feet. They were dull and sparkless now.

'I thought she was dead. He told me she was. My stepfather. The people, the official people, they told me she was. But she *isn't*. The bastard lied about that like he lied about everything. And I never, I never—'

George – horribly – realized she was on the brink of crying, and suddenly he knew he didn't want her to cry, not because he minded her crying, but because *she* would mind, mind terribly if anyone else saw her with tears running down her face.

'Edie,' he cut in sharply. 'Look. I'm cold. You're cold. I'm exhausted. You're exhausted. I can't think straight. And nor can you.'

'Don't tell me what I can't do,' she said, her spirits kindling.

'You can't do anything until you're properly dry and rested.'

'And fed,' said the Queen. 'Children need to be—'

'I'm not a child,' rasped Edie. 'I can look after myself.'

The Queen knelt in front of her and gripped her shoulders, bringing her eye to eye. Edie tried to shrug out of the grasp of the bronze hands, but they just gripped tighter.

'Let go,' she gritted into the calm face of the Queen.

'No.'

'I mean it,' said Edie, squirming harder, to equally little effect. 'Let go or I'll glint you.'

The shadow of a smile passed across the Queen's face, so fast that if you'd blinked, you'd have missed it. She fixed Edie with her eyes until she stopped trying to wriggle free.

'The fire inside you has brought you a long way, child.'

'I'm not a ch—'

'You are. I don't call you child to belittle you. I call you child to honour you. What you have survived, what your heart and courage have enabled you to endure would have beggared the strength of a grown man long since. Indeed, some grown women might have been able to outface the pain and hurt you have sustained, but precious few. You have a wild and rugged heart, child. And its fire has brought you a long way. But right now the fire you need is not of the heart, but one to banish the cold in your bones, a warmth that will let you sleep and ravel up the tattered threads of your energy so that we can face whatever tomorrow brings.'

'If the people have all disappeared there's a perfectly good hotel opposite with deep beds and thick blankets,' interjected the Officer. 'Be a snug place to billet for the night, until this snow stops.'

'It's ridiculous,' said George, shaking the flakes out of his hair. 'It's like being stuck inside a snow globe.'

'Gack,' said Spout, shuffling forward and flexing a wing above them. The stone membrane stretched and umbrellaed overhead with a sharp snapping noise. Edie flinched, but George held her arm.

'It's OK,' he said. 'He's sheltering you.'

'What's he called?' she sniffed, looking up at the wing arching over her head.

'Spout.'

'That's a stupid name.'

'I know,' smiled George. 'I gave it to him.'

'You named him?' said the Queen, raising an eyebrow. 'You. A maker. Named him. Named a taint?'

'Yes,' he replied.

The Gunner whistled in surprise.

'No wonder he's following you,' he said. 'He's your pet.'

'Gack!' said Spout, eyeballing the Gunner frostily.

'Yes,' said George. 'He's not a pet. He's a friend. He saved my life.'

'Did he now?' said the Gunner. And he grinned into the gargoyle's snarling face. 'Then I reckon he's my friend too.'

And he punched him on the wing.

'Good job, Uglynuts.'

'Gack,' replied Spout, losing the snarl and looking confused.

Edie's teeth were chattering. The Queen stood and pointed across the road.

'Inside, warm bed, now.'

'Come on, little 'un,' said the Gunner. And before she could protest he'd hoisted her into his arms and was striding across the street between the cars.

The hotel had a portico over a driveway that looped in and out off the street, and they stood for a beat looking into the warm, softly lit interior.

'Nothing but five star for you, my girl,' grinned the Gunner, and took a step up into the doorway – just as a high-pitched whistle pierced the night above

12

them. He froze.

'What's that?' asked Edie.

'The Quadriga,' said George before the Gunner could answer. 'It's a warning sign, right?'

'Right,' said the Gunner. 'Well remembered.'

His eyes scanned the sky above them. The Officer cleared his throat.

'Quadriga's a statue. Up on the arch. Boy in it, driving a runaway chariot. He can see stuff coming.'

'What kind of stuff?' said Edie.

There was a sudden flapping noise as Spout looped in under the portico, flexing back on the pillared columns so that he was hidden under the roof along with them. He knuckled George with a talon and then pointed it urgently into the sky to the west of them, where there was a low but insistent rumble.

'Gaings, Eigengang, genny gaings!'

'What kind of . . .?' began Edie.

'Taints,' translated George. 'Many taints!'

'Don't move a muscle!' hissed the Gunner urgently, as he and the Officer instinctively stepped in front of George and Edie.

And then the rolling thunder in the sky hurled through the snow in front of them, and revealed itself to be a phalanx of stone pterodactyls, just like the one that had chased George at the beginning of his adventure. The great stone dinosaurs flapped past, long toothy beaks pointing east, their unblinking saucer-like eyes looking neither right nor left.

George found that his hand had somehow picked up his hammer on the way here, and he squeezed the handle, ready to fight for his life if one of them broke formation and noticed them. He felt the flat metallic tang

13

of fear in his mouth, and tried to ignore it. And then the pterodactyls were followed, somewhat higher and more indistinctly by a flight of stubby-bodied creatures with bat-like wings, also heading east.

'What are they?' whispered Edie.

'Gargoyles. Born ugly an' built to last. No offence,' said the Gunner with a nod to Spout.

'Taints. Gathering and flying together,' murmured the Queen. 'Heading east.'

The spits looked at one another. Edie looked at George.

'What's east?'

'The City.'

'And . . . oh.' She stopped and looked at the Queen. The Queen nodded slowly.

'The City is in the centre of London. The Stone is in the City. And if the taints are gathering at the Stone . . .'

'It's War then,' finished the Officer. 'A bloody meat-grinding war. And we're going to be in the middle, damn it.'

'War's damned without you needing to curse it, my friend,' sighed the Queen, eyes fixed on the now empty sky to eastwards. George looked over the road at the dark tree-shrouded park. The snow was now deep enough to reach the bottom of the hubcaps on the cars frozen in the middle of the street.

'Nothing worse than war,' replied the Officer.

The Queen turned and looked at him. The smile at the edge of her mouth was entirely without humour.

'You couldn't be more wrong, sir. There are many things worse than war. Some of them live in the Outer Dark that lies beyond the Stone Mirrors the Walker

14

escaped through. I fear one of them followed us back here, and now things long feared, things that have never happened, will happen, and there will be hell to pay.'

2

TOUCH NOT THE CAT

Gough Square is a narrow space, too small really to qualify as a proper square, especially if the word 'square' conjures up images of a tree-filled green area surrounded by buildings. It *was* surrounded by buildings, low Georgian brick-built houses in the main, but where a larger square might hope for green there were cobbles, and while there were trees (in the strictest interpretation of the word) they were stick-like things of no age or consequence, significantly and disappointingly outnumbered by the thin metal bollards that surrounded the cobbled rectangle at the centre of the square.

The cobbles were quickly being obscured by the falling snow. At one end of the open space stood an empty plinth, snowflakes beginning to fill up a small bronze oyster shell that lay on its top.

Dictionary Johnson, a bulky bronze statue in knee-breeches, sat on the steps of one of the houses, twisting and fidgeting with something he was trying to work gently inside his close-buttoned coat. Whatever he was trying to force inside the protection of his clothing was less than keen on the whole idea, a lack of enthusiasm manifested in an aggrieved mewling, muffled by the wide lapels of the coat. The big man in the bun-shaped wig hushed and cooed to it as he endeavoured to engulf it within his garments.

'Hodge shan't be cold; no, no, Hodge shall not be cold,' he promised.

There was a slight jingling noise off to one side and he froze, eyes peering into the dark mouth of the alleyway to his left.

'Who's there? If you mean us harm, I warn you that I shall box your ears! And my friend Hodge, he shall rake you. By God, sir, he shall bite and rake you most grievously if you mean us harm . . .'

The jingling resolved itself into a tall figure. As it approached, it was apparent that the noise came from a mass of small tools and instruments hanging on strings and ribbons from a much repaired tail-coat. The thin man, now clearly recognizable as the Clocker, bowed politely.

'No need for fisticuffs, Dictionary. Lord no. Mean no harm. Have greatest respect et cetera. As you know. Friend not foe. Looking for you.'

He paused and waved generally at the falling snow amid the stillness of the square around them. The light glinted off his complicated glasses, rigged out with a bewildering selection of watchmakers' magnifying lenses ready to hinge down over either eye.

'Feel this to be unworldly. All my clocks stopped. All clocks in city stopped. Extraordinary. Do not even have word for it . . .'

His hands tried to pluck the right expression out of the air. Dictionary harrumphed and jerked his head sharply as if shaking loose a couple of forgotten words that might fit.

'Disadventurous? Ominatory?'

The Clocker's hands stopped grasping the air and traced a faint and elegant bow of thanks.

'Precisely. Knew you the very fellow to ask.'

A low yowl of feline disapproval emerged from within Dictionary's garments.

The Clocker cleared his throat.

'Excuse impertinence. Intolerable curiosity. Is that cat?'

Dictionary rose from the step, visibly swelling with something between pride and embarrassment.

'Cat, sir? This is Hodge, sir. More than a mere cat. A boon companion whom I should rather starve and perish than see suffer the vicissitudes of such unchancy and inclement weather.'

'Ah,' ventured the Clocker.

'He abhors the cold, sir, as I cannot abide a Frenchman or a papist,' rumbled the great man in explanation.

Hodge, a cat statue whose normal home was the empty plinth with the oyster shells, took this as his cue to turn himself upside down and claw his head clear of the enfolding coat. Two well-formed bronze ears flattened on his head and he showed his fangs in a moment of displeasure.

'Very fine cat. No doubt,' said the Clocker, bravely reaching a hand forward to stroke the cat, who immediately reared up and swiped a claw at the tentative gesture of friendship. The Clocker jerked back, and as he did so his glasses bounced off his face and clattered to the ground.

'My apologies,' said Dictionary. 'Hodge is more catamountain than fireside puss.'

'He is a fearsome mouser no doubt,' said the Clocker, looking down at the thin half-inch of blood striping the back of his thumb.

'Hodge is the scourge of tittle-mice, the nemesis of rats and the creeping doom of sparrows, Clocker.'

'Sparrows?'

'Birds in general. I believe he takes feathers and flight as personal affronts. I have wasted many a minute watching him stalk the birds in this square. He sees a bird as a challenge, does Hodge. He is, if nothing else, a cat with ambition . . .'

He looked more closely at the Clocker as he stooped to pick up his glasses. He pointed a questioning sausage-finger at the thin man's face. There was an unblinking beam of blue light emerging from one of the Clocker's eyes, an eye that had a miniature clock-face instead of a normal eyeball.

Dictionary stared at it. The hour and the minute hand pointed straight up at midnight, and the second hand was unmoving, perhaps half a second after midnight.

'. . . your eye, sir.'

The Clocker's head bent in agreement.

'Indeed.'

'It does not pulse. It did pulse, if I am not mistaken?'

'It did. Regularly. Marked the passing seconds.'

'I remember it well, sir. And yet . . . it pulses no more.'

The Clocker nodded and licked his lips.

'No. As said. All clocks stopped. Believe time itself stopped. If not stopped, out of joint. Have no idea what happened. No word for what this is. Thought you might.'

'No, sir,' said Dictionary, shaking his head. 'But if time has stopped ticking, then I believe we are in the after-hours. And what that portends I have no means of knowing.'

Hodge suddenly stiffened and hissed at something in the sky above. The two men looked up and saw a flight of distinctively shaped creatures flapping slowly eastwards over the square.

'Pterodactyls?' said Dictionary.

'From façade of Natural History Museum,' agreed the Clocker. 'Almost certain. Never seen flying in pack before.'

'Time's never been out of joint before,' growled Dictionary, eyes scanning the sky for more silhouettes. 'It's the boy and the girl, isn't it? The maker and the glint. They've done something—'

'Or something done to them,' cut in the Clocker. 'Boy was chased by pterodactyl. Liked boy. Girl plucky too.'

He watched Dictionary bend and pick up a battered hat from the step and brush a thick layer of snow from it.

'You have plan?'

'No, sir. But I venture if you were to join me on a fast perambulation towards the Gunner's monument we may have news of them.'

They walked out of the square, side by side, the tall gangling figure of the Clocker crow-stepping through the snow alongside the barrel-shaped Dictionary who bulldozed along beside him. Only Hodge looked back and noticed the square was not left quite empty. High on the roof opposite a lone bird looked down at them, a dark bird. A Raven.

Hodge hissed.

The Raven didn't blink.

It waited until they had turned the corner before pushing off into the night sky and flapping over their footsteps in the snow, keeping its distance . . . almost as if it was stalking them.

3

A FIRE IN THE DARK

'George,' said Edie very quietly.
   'I know.'
They were frozen about ten paces inside the warm lobby of the eerily silent hotel.
'You feel it too?'
George nodded slowly, his face tight with tension.
'Yes.'
'We can't . . .'
'No. We can't.'
The Gunner looked at them, then at the Officer and the Queen. 'You got any idea what they're on about?'
The Officer shook his head. The Queen's eyes were fixed on Edie, who was looking up at the ceiling as if something unpleasant was about to drop through it.
'No,' said the Queen, 'but if she's sensing something, it's here somewhere.'
'It's *everywhere* in here,' whispered Edie, looking at George.
He tried to control the strange sense of nausea and fear building in his gut. He couldn't put it in words, not in a way that would do justice to the oddness of what he was experiencing, but ever since they'd walked into the building, ten long paces ago, he'd felt wrong, wrenchingly wrong, out of place in a way that was like a kind of vertigo, except instead of the fear of falling down, he felt like he was in imminent danger of losing his grip on where and why and who he was, and just

falling in every direction at once.

'It's the people who aren't here. The ones who disappeared. They're . . .' Edie flailed for an explanation.

'They're still here. Just not "here" in a way we can see,' finished George. 'Right?'

Edie grimaced and took a step back. She looked so tired and cold and wet that George thought if she got any paler he'd start being able to see through her like a—

'Ghost. Ghosts. It feels like ghosts,' he blurted.

'Exactly,' said Edie, turning to look at the Queen. 'It's like when people say you walked through a ghost. The people who aren't here, they're *almost* here, and they're like . . . frozen too. Stuck between here and now.' She wiped her hand across her face, then rubbed it hard, trying to scrub the exhaustion away. 'It's like walking through a silent scream. Being in here with all of them, the ones who are here – but not here.'

She eyed George. He nodded, and she began backtracking carefully across the well-polished floor. 'We can't sleep in here. This stillness, this silence . . .'

'It's too loud,' he said.

'Exactly,' said Edie, still backing up to the door. 'If we sleep in here we'll go—'

'Doolally,' finished George.

The Officer shook his head.

'You need sleep, you need food, you need warmth. We'll take turns to stand watch over you. It'll be fine.'

'No,' said George, looking at Edie's face. 'No. We're not sleeping inside. Maybe you lot can't feel it, but we can. We sleep outside.'

'Outside? It's bloody snowing, pardon my French,' exploded the Gunner, tipping an eye at the Queen. 'Not a night to be playing Eskimos.'

22

George turned on his heel and headed for the door. He must have walked through someone who wasn't there, a doorman perhaps. Anyway, he was ambushed by a sudden cold lurch in his guts as if he wanted to retch. He took Edie's shoulder and walked them both out of the door and into the street.

'We'll sleep under the arch. Under the Quadriga.'

'You're both nutty as a fruitcakes!' snorted the Gunner, hot on their heels. 'It's warm indoors!'

'There's heat and beds and blankets and food . . .' began the Officer.

George was so exhausted he felt that if he stumbled the ground would just open up and he'd fall into the black maw and never be seen again. 'So bring them out. Duvets, blankets, whatever. We'll make a fire . . .'

'Dry clothes. Coats. Hats,' said the Queen. Her daughters nodded and ran off soft-footed into the depths of the hotel.

'What are we going to make a fire with?' asked Edie as George steered them both back towards Hyde Park Corner and the great protective stone arch in the middle.

'That,' he said, pointing at a builder's truck loaded with what looked like the smashed wooden debris of a recently gutted kitchen. 'That'll burn nicely.'

'Couple of suicidal pyromaniacs now!' grumbled the Gunner, but he angled off and scooped up a big armful of wood off the truck anyway.

One of the Queen's daughters came running out of the hotel with an armful of coats that she'd obviously just lifted straight out of the cloakroom. She tossed George a couple and then lobbed him a mad-bomber hat with long ear-flaps.

He put the hat on first and grinned.

'Cool.' He smiled, the ear-flaps dangling down on each side of his face like ears on a cartoon dog.

'Not really,' said Edie.

The daughter handed her a long black fur coat.

'Warm,' she said simply.

Edie nodded and put it on without slowing down. The hem skimmed the ground as she walked.

'Yeah,' she said, pulling it around her. 'Warm.'

4

NIGHT PATROL

As in the rest of London, snow was falling heavily outside the pillared façade of The Royal Exchange. Two World War One soldiers stood at ease, back to back on either side of a tall war memorial. They wore peaked caps instead of tin helmets, and one was noticeably older than the other.

To their right was an impressive equestrian statue. A martial Duke sat astride a noble stallion, a cloak falling off his shoulders, a marshal's baton clenched in one hand.

'Oi, Uncle – it's snowing,' observed the Young Soldier.

The older soldier looked at the Duke. The Duke was watching a pair of stone gryphons flying overhead. He didn't let anything like worry play across his impressive brow, but the Old Soldier noticed that he unobtrusively pushed the baton inside his waistcoat, freeing up a hand to rest casually on the pommel of his sword.

'Oi. Uncle. You there? I said it's snowing,' said the Young Soldier, craning round the end of the monument to see the Old Soldier on the other side.

'You know what you are, young 'un. You're the Grand Bloody Panjandrum of the Painfully Bleeding Obvious,' scowled the Old Soldier.

'I was just saying. It's snowing. And everything stopped.'

The Old Soldier blew out his cheeks.

'I dunno, son. Sometimes I wonder if you got both blades in the water. Or was you asleep when the clock struck thirteen?'

'It never!' The Young Soldier sounded impressed.

'You're as much use as an inflatable cheese-knife,' sighed the other, then stiffened. 'Watch out, Hooky's having an idea.'

The hook-nosed Duke ran a hand over his face and squared his shoulders as if making a large decision. He cleared his throat and pointed at the two soldiers.

'Right. You two, at the double.'

The two soldiers stepped off their plinth and hurried over to the Duke. He didn't take his eyes off the sky.

'See that?'

'Flight of taints, sir. Up to no good, I shouldn't be surprised,' said the Old Soldier.

'Up to mischief,' said the other.

'No doubt,' said the Duke. 'Very well. I think a little reconnoitring would pay dividends. Don't like not knowing what the enemy's up to.'

'Want us to go have a shufti, sir?' volunteered the Old Soldier.

'No.'

The Duke kneed the horse and clicked his teeth. The great animal stepped off the plinth and crashed to the ground. The Duke wobbled alarmingly but stayed on.

'All right, sir?' asked the Young Soldier innocently. The Old Soldier kicked him while the Duke wasn't looking.

'Me, sir? Sound as guns. The sickening artist johnny who made us omitted any damn stirrups,' barked the Duke, steadying himself. 'But everything else has gone for a ball of chalk, I'd say: people disappeared, time

26

frozen, snow bucketing out of nowhere. Damn queer straits we're in.'

And without a backward glance he led them off into the street of trackless snow leading away from the square.

'Keep your muskets primed and your powder dry.'

5

DEATH BY DROWNING

Edie was drowning again. She had felt the horrible ache of exhaustion in her leg muscles as she tried to run in the snow covering the ice beneath her. She had winced at the burning pain in her lungs as she rasped for breath in the cold night air. She'd heard the Walker chasing her down, his breath coming in harsh ugly counterpoint to the crump of his boots pounding heavily through the dense snow-pack behind her.

Despite herself she'd turned again to see him, just enough to see his silhouette backlit by the flaming torches of the Frost Fair spread on the ice behind him, fire reflecting off the gutting-blade that he held low to his side as he ran. And as she'd looked back, knowing she shouldn't but not quite remembering why, she had felt the sickening lurch once more as her shoe plunged down into nothing, where the treacherous hole in the ice was lying in wait for her unseeing foot.

Knowing what was happening, she threw her arms wide, trying to stop herself on the sides of the ice-hole, but as time slowed and she fell into the dark water she realized with another jolt that the Walker, the Frost Fair and London itself had mysteriously disappeared entirely.

She twisted as she plunged into the water in a treacly slow-motion and saw that there was suddenly no ice at all, and that the only hole was the one she was making in a gunmetal sea that stretched to the horizon all around her.

She had enough time to note the way the small waves caught the moon, their interlocking surfaces like a wilderness of knapped flint heaving slowly in the moonlight – and then her face hit the water and the shock of the cold slapped her back into normal speed, and she was fighting to get back to the air with a mouthful of salt water.

She struggled to swim up through a skirl of bubbles, but no matter how hard she kicked and pulled for the surface the black water pulled her down and down, until there was nothing left to make bubbles with and only the sound of her blood pounding in her ears. Her lungs ached with the effort of keeping the last breath inside her as they burnt every last bit of oxygen. And this time there was no Gunner to rescue her, or drop a heart stone through the hole in the ice to light her way, only death closing in all round her.

Her last thought was to reach into her pocket and pull out her mother's heart stone, which she did with numb fingers, thickened and made clumsy with cold. She held it in front of her eyes, but it had ceased to blaze forth any inner fire and was as lightless as the water around her. She caught only the reflection of her own staring eyes and the long hair ribboning across her pale face like tendrils of seaweed binding her to the blackness that surrounded her.

She opened her mouth to scream 'No!' as the last air in her lungs burst for the surface far above and the icy water entered in its place and started drowning her. Then she woke.

She gasped for breath, and tried to sit up, but a firm hand pushed her gently back amongst the pillows and the blankets as her mind came out of the dream and returned to a world no less strange, but – in this moment and this place – better and safer.

The Queen smiled down at her. Edie saw the comforting curve of the wide stone arch above, the large square-cut stones uplit by the flames from the fire burning at her side.

'A dream, child. A bad dream, no more. Sleep. You are safe. For now.'

Edie remembered her mother's heart stone. She scrabbled it out of her pocket and was relieved to see it still had the spark of fire at its core. It had only died in her dream. She clenched it in her fist and lay back in the cocoon of stolen hotel duvets and pillows.

'I was drowning.'

The Queen smiled and smoothed Edie's hair from her face, in a mother's unconscious gesture that Edie felt like a sharp pang of something from her past.

'We are all drowning, child. The world is drowning. And there are other ways to drown than in water. But you shall not die tonight. You are among friends.'

Edie looked round. The weird romance of the scene struck her. Maybe it was the fire and the stone and the snowstorm beyond, but it was both otherworldly and ancient. The Queen's daughters stood over the flames, talking quietly in the red glow. Beyond them the Gunner leant on the stone at one side of the arch, relaxed but alert, looking out into the night, his large hands unconsciously playing with the two small mirrors they'd used to travel back from the Frost Fair, like a man practising a coin trick. And when she moved her head she could see the Officer on guard on the other side, his long coat belted round him, collar up. The crackling fire threw bright sparks swirling into the air and illuminated the snowflakes falling just beyond the warm glow of the arch.

There was a grunt and a snuffle from beside her, and she looked over to see George fast asleep in his own cocoon of white duvets, the mad-bomber hat pulled low over his eyes. Edie smiled as he snored.

They had sat up late before going to sleep and Edie had been touched, although she hadn't shown it, by the horror he had showed as she told him about her misadventures with the Walker and her drowning at the Frost Fair.

'You like the boy,' said the Queen.

'Yeah. But not like that,' said Edie without thinking. 'He saved me. He's . . . like . . .' She stopped, searching for a word she couldn't quite put her finger on. It was a word she didn't use much, which made it all the more surprising when it found itself and popped out without her being able to control it, or the need it revealed.

'. . . family.'

The moment the word came out she knew it was right and she wished she'd had the sense to bite her tongue to stop it escaping. Somewhere inside she knew she'd betrayed herself.

'You trust him?'

'Much as I trust anyone, yeah, suppose I do,' she said, staring up at the curve of firelit stone high above her. And then she shivered as a chill passed through her.

'You're cold, child. Let the girls warm you.'

Edie looked over at the two girls standing close to the fire as their mother waved them over.

'You feel the cold?' she asked.

'We feel it. We just don't mind it as much as flesh and blood does,' smiled the Queen. 'Besides, the girls aren't warming themselves for themselves. They've been warming themselves for the both of you. Bronze absorbs heat well.'

The daughters lay down on either side of Edie and grinned at her. She felt the warmth coming off them in waves.

'Like radiators,' she smiled.

'We've been called many things before,' said the girl on her left.

'But a radiator is a new thing,' laughed the one to her right.

Edie felt she'd said something rude, and though saying rude things was not anything she normally gave two hoots about, she didn't want to be impolite to these girls or their mother. After all, they'd saved her too. And more than that, she liked their quietness. It was a very strong kind of quietness. They made no fuss, but they were obviously tough and fearless and very brave. Edie wasn't used to seeing people she wanted to be like, so she didn't know how to behave.

'It's not a bad name. I mean, I don't mean it like that. I reckon it's like radiant, right. And radiant means, you know . . .'

And here she found herself blushing and hating herself for it.

'. . . beautiful,' said the Queen.

'Yeah. But. I mean, that sounds soppy. I don't know, sort of weak,' Edie fumbled on.

'There's nothing weak about beauty, child,' snapped the Queen. 'The only weakness in it is if you think it means anything important. The ugliest thing in the world is a beautiful woman without the brains or courage to know that it is nothing more than an accident.'

Edie kept quiet.

'Now sleep. We will watch over you from without, and within may Andraste guard you in your dreams.'

The warmth from the two girls at her side was making Edie finally drowsy again. 'Who's Andraste?' she murmured.

'She is the goddess of the Iceni, moon-mother, maiden, thread-cutter, Lady of the Silver Wheel and Victory herself. May her far-seeing eye watch over you in the blackness of sleep, and may her wings of comfort heal you.'

'And who is the Iceni?' asked Edie, her eyes closing.

The Queen spoke very softly.

'We are, child. My daughters and I are the last of the Iceni, one of the greatest tribes of this island, made to stand again long after our true memories had faded from the earth.' She smiled and shook her head. 'Once I was Boadicea, Queen of thousands. Now we are but three. But once? Once we were something.'

'You're still something,' mumbled Edie. And then she fell asleep.

The Queen watched her with a slight smile on her usually austere face until her breathing became regular. Then she stood decisively.

'She's asleep.'

'Good,' said the Gunner, squinting back into the light as his eyes adjusted from watching the outer darkness.

The Queen's face had lost all traces of the smile, and her voice was low and urgent.

'Wake the boy. Things are worse than we feared.'

6

THE DARK HORSE

Long, long ago, before history started and the wildness of the world was tamed, there was a great struggle between the Light that gave Life, and the Darkness that walked the earth spreading ignorance and hatred, feeding off the terror it left in its wake. Only after a long and brutal fight did Light win this struggle and pen the Darkness deep in the rocky heart of the world.

Ages later, but still long before the time of the Romans or even the Druids that came before them, the people of the island needed a sacred stone. And the place where they went to hack that stone from the living rock was the place where the Darkness had been defeated. They went there because they knew it was a sacred place, but they had forgotten why, or they would have chosen a different spot and a better stone. But because the struggle between Light and the Darkness had happened so long before their distant ancestors had even been born, the memories of precisely why the place was sacred had been lost. And so the Stone was carved from the earth, and when it was moved to its new place, the Darkness went with it.

And the Darkness stayed imprisoned in the Stone.

And waited.

It waited close to a crossing-place, where a broad slope of wooded land latticed with streams met the broad river to its south. It waited through the long fall of centuries and watched those virgin woods retreat as the men built a hamlet, then a village, then a bridge and a town. It waited while the town spread all around it, stealing more and more of the woods and the hidden green spaces within them. It waited and watched as the town rose and fell, was burnt and rebuilt, and grew more bridges on either side of that first crossing. It waited while the town grew to a city as wood and thatch gave way to stone and brick. And it watched brick and stone in their turn give way to steel and glass as the quiet river-crossing that had become a great growling beast of a city ran out of land and rose up to steal the sky in its stead.

It waited because it knew that one day it would again walk free, and it also knew that while stone itself does not last for ever, it lasts much, much longer than people or their memories do, and it knew that one day something would happen to release it.

And then, in the moment when the Ice Devil came to the city, stopping time so violently that all the people disappeared and permanent winter came on its tail, it knew the long wait had ended.

It knew it even before the Ice Devil passed over its stony prison and frost-shattered it open.

But still it waited. It didn't wait because waiting had become its habit over the aeons it had been pent in the Stone. It had simply forgotten the shape in which it had once moved in the world, just as someone confined to a hospital bed for a long time forgets how to move their legs.

It waited because now that the long imprisonment was over, it needed just a fragment, the tiniest mote of extra time to start remembering.

Snow and silence filled the anonymous stretch of Cannon Street. The only place the flakes did not stay was on the ornate grille in front of the Stone. When the flakes landed on the hot metal they melted instantly in a tiny hiss.

And then the Stone caught the scuff of hooves and the cautious tread of hobnailed boots. And the Darkness coiled within it, a great fiend, ready to spring.

'I'm only saying,' grumbled the Young Soldier, 'that my boots is hurting.'

'Your boots is always hurting,' replied his older companion. 'Give it a rest and keep your eyes peeled. If old Hooky up there hears you whining, there'll be merry hell to pay.'

They were following the hook-nosed Duke as he slowly moved his horse forward, cautiously snaking his way through the snow-covered cars frozen in the middle of the street. His sword was drawn and held at his side. He looked calm but ready for anything that might surprise him.

He stopped alongside a double-decker bus, raising himself a little higher in the saddle, as if sniffing something on the wind.

''Old up,' said the Old Soldier.

'If he's the general,' said the Young Soldier, scratching himself, 'what's he doing out front, up the sharp end?'

The Old Soldier sighed and took advantage of the pause in their forward progress to pull a battered pipe from the chest pocket in his battledress. He stuck it in his mouth and sucked on it reflectively.

'Well, young 'un. It ain't like we haven't had this conversation before, is it?'

'I'm just . . .'

'You've just got a memory like a bleeding sieve is what it is. First off, he's cavalry, see, and in his day cavalry went

36

out in front and done the forward scouting. Secondly, he don't quite trust us, which looking at you I can't help thinking he's half right about. And finally, he's a hundred-per-cent copper-bottomed writ-up-in-the-history-books kicked-Boney-in-the-arse-at-Waterloo fire-eating hero, isn't he?'

'But ain't we heroes?' whispered the Young Soldier.

'I dunno,' said the Old Soldier, 'but I do know we're mincemeat if he hears you rabbiting on like this, and that's a fact.'

He nodded towards the Duke, who was leaning forward on the horse, craning for a view round the front of the bus. Something on the other side of the street was getting his full attention. He reached back and silently waved them forward.

'Come on,' said the Old Soldier, gripping his pipe between his teeth in a grimace of unwelcome anticipation. 'Keep your cake-hole shut and stay low.'

They ducked below the snow-laden roofs of the cars and low-ran quickly forward to the bus. The Duke backed his horse a couple of paces and leant down to talk quietly to them.

'Something's got my horse spooked,' he said as he smoothed the neck of the large stallion. The soldiers could see it was trembling, and it pawed skittishly on the ground as the Duke continued. 'Something over there.'

They all peered through the windows in the bus, trying to see across the street.

'Nothing what I can see,' began the younger soldier, looking round. 'Where are we anyway?'

'Cannon Street,' replied the Old Soldier.

'There's nothing in Cannon Street,' said the Young Soldier. 'No taints what I can think of, nothing except . . .'

'London Stone,' said the Duke calmly, nodding across the street on the other side of the bus. 'Over there.'

The Old Soldier peered through the frost-rimed glass of the bus window. He couldn't see much and what he could see was bleary and indistinct. He turned to find the Duke looking at him. One of the things that made the Duke such an uncomfortably good leader – if you were a follower – was that he seemed to be able to give orders without actually speaking them. The Old Soldier nodded and cleared his throat quietly.

'I, er, could crawl over and have a look-see ...'

'Ah, if you'd be so kind,' nodded the Duke. 'I'd be much obliged.'

The Old Soldier pocketed his pipe, dropped to his knees and crawled around the rear of the bus. He edged forward through the snow, his zigzag route dictated by the need to keep cars between him and the Stone until he could get close enough to get a better look.

Only once did he pause and look back, and as soon as he saw that the others could still see him he gave them a thumbs-up, put his finger to his lips and then continued on until only a taxi stood between him and the strip of pavement in front of the London Stone's cage.

He tried to look under the taxi, but the snow was already too deep. So he quietly propped his rifle against the side of the vehicle and reached up to the passenger door handle.

'What's he doing?' breathed the Young Soldier, voice suddenly cracking with tension. The Duke put a hand on his shoulder.

'He's doing a damn fine job, youngster. Using all available cover, if I'm any judge ...'

The Old Soldier quietly opened the passenger door

and crawled inside the taxi. The only thing between him and the three metres of clear air separating him from the Stone was the thin glass of the side window. He calmly turned the peak of his cap backwards, and lifted himself off the floor just high enough for his eye to sneak a peak over the lintel of the window.

'Bloody hell,' he whispered.

Maybe something heard him. Or maybe it was just coincidence, but at that moment there was a noiseless detonation and everything seemed to jump, just a millimetre or so, and then all was still again.

'What was that?' said the Young Soldier nervily.

'Steady,' whispered the Duke, raising his sword.

Because the rest of the city was so silent they heard the snow moving before they saw it.

The Young Soldier looked down at his boots.

'Er . . .' he began.

The Duke reined in his horse, which had skittered sideways.

'I see it . . .' he breathed. At their feet all the snow was moving. Because there was no wind, the effect was not of the flakes being blown, but more like them being sucked beneath the bus, towards the Stone. '. . . I see it, but I'm damned if I know what it is.'

The Old Soldier crouched in the back of the taxi, staring in disbelief at the Stone. From where he was watching he could see that snow was being pulled into it, or more precisely, into a thick black crack that had split it from top to bottom. The blackness emerged like a slow-motion gush of oil that came out as the snow was sucked across the ground into the crack, as if to take its place. Where the darkness met the ornate iron cage guarding the Stone, it simply dissolved the metal.

The blackness flowed across the pavement towards the cab. Indeed, by the time the Old Soldier had noticed this he couldn't see if there was still time to get out and escape.

'God 'elp us!' he swore, and started to back out of the cab.

He looked down before he put his foot on the road, which was lucky. A thickening stripe of blackness, darker than oil, was now moving purposefully across the ground, sucking in all light and reflecting nothing back like a tear in the fabric of all that is, through which could be seen the Outer Darkness. It had already flowed beneath the taxi and was moving steadily onwards towards the bus as if it had a mind of its own.

Perhaps the Old Soldier already sensed the Darkness flowing beneath him did have something like a mind, because he hesitated an instant before shouting across to the others.

'Oi,' he shouted. 'Move yourselves. There's something coming under the bus!'

'What?' said the Young Soldier. 'What kind of something?'

'Move back now!' ordered the Duke, tugging on his horse's reins. The horse responded instantly, dropping slightly on to its powerful haunches and beginning to corkscrew round and leap away, when it suddenly jerked to an abrupt halt.

The Duke kept on going. He slid off the saddle and tumbled down the flank of the horse, dumping into a snowdrift in a very un-ducal jumble of cloak, boots and flailing sword.

'Bedamn and blast the blockheaded booby that made me stirrupless!' he exploded, stumbling to his feet with the reins still held tight in his hand.

The horse shrieked, and the Duke was nearly yanked off his feet as it reared in terror.

'Steady boy . . .!' he cried, instantly forgetting his own recent indignity as he tried to calm the frightened animal.

'It's got it by the hoof!' shouted the Young Soldier, pointing in horror.

The Duke stepped back, narrowly avoiding a flailing foreleg as the horse attempted to break free from the Darkness spiralling up its back legs in fast-moving black tendrils. The tendrils did not wind round the skin of the animal. They seemed to leach into it and replace its very substance, as if Darkness was replacing the metal body and taking its shape, like ink filling a bottle. He stared in a mix of horror and outrage as the clean bronze curves of his horse were devoured from within by a black darker than coal.

'By God it shall not have him!' roared the Duke. He leapt to the rear of the animal and slashed his sword at the thickest tendril of darkness reaching out from under the bus, joining the horse to the split in the Stone across the street.

The sword stuck fast in the Darkness with an impact that all but jarred it out of the Duke's hand, and then a side tendril sprouted from the main one leaching into the horse and moved up the blade.

'No, sir, you shall not have my damn sword either!' spat the Duke in cold fury as he jerked at his blade, snapping it cleanly two-thirds of the way down, where the darkness met the untainted metal.

CRACK CRACK CRACK CRACK. He heard the sound of rifle fire from across the street. He took one last despairing glance at his horse – now Darkness all the way to its heaving neck. It lashed its head from side to side in panic, was if it as drowning in the rising tide.

Then he ran to the sound of the guns.

He slid round the corner of the taxi, kicking up a flurry of snow, in time to see the two soldiers firing into the Stone.

The Old Soldier spun and then put up his gun as he recognized the Duke.

'All I could think of doing, sir,' he panted. 'Not a blind bit of good.'

There was another shot as the Young Soldier reloaded and pumped a new round into the stone to no discernible effect.

'Save your ammunition,' barked the Duke.

The horse's frenzied shrieks suddenly stopped dead. There was a beat of silence. And then they heard a snort and the sound of hooves slowly clopping nearer, then a single hoof pawing the ground.

They all turned slowly.

The horse stood behind them. The bronze horse had become a black horse, made out of pure Darkness, from the bottom of its hooves to the tip of its ears.

It seemed bigger.

Dark smoke drifted from its eyeballs.

The Old Soldier raised his rifle. The Duke reached out a hand and pushed the gun aside slowly.

'No,' he said simply. 'I don't know what in Hades this is, but I know a fight when I see it, and I know this kind of battle will be close-work, blades not bullets.'

The Dark Horse pawed snow backwards as its sable eyes smouldered at them.

'And I intend to start by getting my damn horse back . . .'

'That's not your horse, not any more . . .' said the Old Soldier.

'Looks black as the devil's horse,' added the Young Soldier.

'That's what I'm afraid of,' said the Duke. 'Some bloody devil anyway. Whatever was in the Stone has got out.'

He looked at the horse, at the strip of blackness joining it to the Stone. The tendril was thinning out, as if the Darkness in the Stone was nearly all gone. And as the flow of Darkness dwindled, so the split in the Stone was closing up.

'What do we do?' said the Old Soldier.

'Warn people,' said the Duke. 'You go now, go fast and don't look back. Warn them so they can try and find a way to put whatever this cursed genie is back in its damned Stone.'

'Right,' said the Young Soldier. 'You heard the man, off we go . . .'

The Old Soldier wasn't in such a hurry to leave.

'What about you, sir?'

'Me, sir?' smiled the Duke, looking from the horse to the split in the Stone. 'I don't know, sir. But I think we must stop that crack closing or we shall not have even a sword's-breadth of hope left . . .'

The Old Soldier knew what he was going to do the instant before he did it, and greatly to his credit tried to jump between the Duke and the Stone.

'No, sir!' he shouted.

The Duke sprang past the Old Soldier and plunged his sword into the crack in the Stone, right up to the hilt.

There was another silent detonation and a great blast of heat pulsed out of the Stone. The horse reared high on its back legs and snorted in rage, and the Duke . . .

. . . the Duke melted into a frozen gout of bronze. The only thing left to show where the human statue had been was the point where this curve of liquefied metal was held to the Stone by his hand, still clenched unflinchingly to his unmelted sword handle, the blade of which was held fast by the crack.

The two soldiers looked at each other. The young one opened his mouth to speak.

The old one just grabbed his shoulder and ran.

Behind them the Dark Horse pawed the snow and felt the power in its limbs, recalling how it felt to move, because the Darkness had remembered one of the ways it had walked the earth all those aeons before its imprisonment.

It had walked the sleeping hours of men on four strong legs like this.

It had ridden through their dreams, spreading terror.

It was the Night Mare.

7

DEATH AT THE BEACH

Death came for Edie on the beach, but he didn't come immediately. To start with she was alone, and she was running, not a panicked run, but a solid and unrelenting jog across the shingle.

The beach was divided by groynes, long barriers of weathered wood marching down from shore to sea at thirty-metre intervals. She knew she could run better if she got off the beach and ran on the track along the shore, but some kind of repellent magnetic force kept her as far from the track as possible. The tide was out, so every now and then the pebbles gave way to hard sand, ribbed by the current. When she hit these patches she picked up speed, but the ribs made it painful and uneven going, and she was always in danger of turning her ankle. Whenever she came to a groyne, she scrambled up and tumbled over it and kept on running.

As she ran something gnawed at the back of her mind, not a thought so much as a lack. She was missing something, but she couldn't spare the time or the energy to figure out what it was. She knew it was important, but not as important as keeping on running.

As she thumped down on an unexpected stretch of sand on the other side of a particularly high barrier her ankle did, finally, turn, and she stumbled and fell.

Something small and powerful and grey was surprised by her dropping out of the sky and started running at a fast lope up the beach away from her. It was a hare. She watched it crest the pebble ridge where it stopped and stared back at her, long ears outlined against the sky. For a long moment the world seemed strangely still and silent as she stared back at it. Then there was the sound of a distant bell, tolling once only, and the hare twitched its tail and was gone. Edie hauled herself to her feet and made herself keep going.

The sea to her left was the same expanse of dark, flint-knapped water she'd drowned in before. It lapped back and forth gently and relentlessly at her side and though she was, somewhere at the back of her mind, apprehensive about it, she was less scared of the water she could see than whatever it was that she couldn't quite catch sight of up on the shore to her right.

Because of course although she couldn't see it, she knew that it was death she was running from.

On the edge of her vision a great grey seabird flew parallel with her on the seaward side, as if keeping distant company. Other than that the beach, the sea and the shore were empty.

The groynes were, she realized, getting taller. Each one was higher and harder to get over. And they were increasingly covered in limpets and seaweed and ever sharper barnacles that scratched and cut her legs and hands.

But she climbed them all.

And still she ran.

Strangely she was both exhausted and yet never exactly tired enough to stop. She felt every lurch from leg to leg, and her feet were sore, but there was also something comforting and familiar about the rhythm of running and breathing hard. She knew she was sobbing for breath, but that didn't hurt any more either, not in any important way.

She seemed to be able to run and run for ever.

The sobs of breath were also a strangely reassuring counterpoint to the smack of her feet on the sand and the lap of the water at her side.

And just when she felt she really would go on like this for ever – she couldn't.

The next groyne was an unscaleable cliff of vicious shell-shard barnacles and treacherously slippy bladderwrack. To her right the beach slanted sharply in an upsweep of pebbles, shortening her horizon so that she could no longer see the shore behind it. The groyne looked climbable at the top of the incline, but anything could be waiting for her up there, just lurking over the lip of the slope. She decided to wade round the seaward end of the groyne rather than risk meeting it.

As soon as she was ankle-deep in the inky water she knew she'd made a bad mistake.

Her foot was sucked into the beach beneath the water, and when she pushed with the other one to get her leg free, it just went deeper and held fast. She struggled against the suck of the quicksand, but within seconds she was knee-deep. She had a horrible feeling exactly as if hands had grabbed her ankles and were pulling her down. She knew this was just fear and too much imagination, so she reached for the end of the groyne to try and haul herself out, but it was just too far away. Her hand caught a trailing tendril of bladderwrack, but when she tugged at it, it just came loose and tumbled into the sea beside her.

She bent over one knee and pushed on it with both hands, trying to lift the other foot even an inch. Nothing happened, but the sea seemed to rise a little. She stared at it in horror.

'Help!' she shouted, and looked up.

And there he was, in the water.

Striding towards her.

Smiling and reaching out a helping hand.

'Edie. It's OK. I've got you.'

George.

George stood there with a sudden wind blowing his hair back off his face, smiling into the light.

Smiling into her face.

She felt suddenly giddy with relief and happiness.

'Grab my hand. If I come further it'll get me too.'

Their fingers reached for each other. She missed on the first attempt and nearly fell.

'Come on, it'll be fine. I'm not going to hurt you,' he said.

And as she looked up from the water she caught the glint of the little blade held in his other hand. And then her gaze continued up his arm and took in his face and the appalling thing that was happening to it.

His face was melting and shifting so that it was George and then it wasn't George, not completely, not very, not really, not hardly and then . . . not at all.

It was her mother's partner. Her stepfather. The smiler with the knife, right down to the streak of blood across his face where she had scratched him with her nails as she made her escape from the beach hut and the horrors she had glinted within.

It was death on the beach, a death delayed, a death from what seemed a lifetime ago.

'Don't be silly. I'm not going to hurt you,' he wheedled, a smile curdling across his red face, and she caught the rank bar-and-tobacco smell on his breath. 'Why would I hurt you?'

'I killed you!' she yelled into his face.

He laughed.

'Didn't kill me, love. Sticks and stones may break my bones but girly can't never hurt me, eh?'

When he laughed his eyes fluttered, and she remembered how creepy she'd always known he was, creepy from the first moment her mother brought him home to the last time she'd seen him, after he'd told her about her mother dying. After they'd gone for the walk on the beach and he'd tried to be nice to her.

Before he'd tried to make her go into the old beach hut where she'd seen the full horror of it all.

He lurched deeper into the water and grabbed at her. She couldn't dodge much because her feet were caught fast, and he quickly got her.

As his hand grasped her upper arm and pulled her, something else happened. A blast of wind hit them, a blast from the sea, followed by another and another, building in strength. And then she saw it was not wind but the downdraught from the wing-beats of the huge bird that she'd seen keeping level with her as she ran. Close to, she saw it was an owl. And for a reason that she neither understood nor questioned, she knew it meant her no harm.

The man saw it at the same time.

His mouth crumpled into a loose 'o' of shock, then widened into a scream as the bird screeched at him. The power of the noise blew the tops of the wavelets around them flat. Maybe because the screech wasn't aimed at her, Edie's ears only rang with the force of it, but the man seemed suddenly maddened by the sound. His hands bunched over his ears as the great grey bird hung in the air between him and Edie, staying in place with great thunderous wing-beats.

The man slashed desperately at the owl with his knife.

Edie saw the blood ribbon across the gap in the air between them, and spatter into the water.

'No!' she gasped in horror for the bird and the damage it had just sustained for her.

'Get off with you or there's more of that!' shouted the man, suddenly elated by his success. 'I'll have you! Get away!'

The bird stayed in its place, between Edie and the knife. It screeched, but this time the man both flinched and lunged. Edie saw the knife blade come through the wing, and then the man screamed even louder than the owl's screech.

The owl's talons gripped his head on either side and the great wings dragged him out of the water and up into the air. He shrieked again and it lifted his kicking body higher and higher. The screaming got less and less as the bird lofted him deeper into the sky and further out to sea.

Edie stood in shock, the waves lapping above her knees as the bird and the man got smaller and smaller.

Her face didn't change when the owl dropped its prey and the distant man-shape rag-dolled its way through the great gulf of air between the bird and the sea. Because of the distance, the smack of impact that cut off the screaming arrived a beat after she saw him hit the water.

She still didn't change her expression.

She watched the great owl's slow wing-beats as it flew back to her. She saw the blood on its breast, red against white, and then it dropped into the sea and was gone.

Edie gave a startled half-cry of disbelief.

Once more she was alone.

And then the sea's surface burst open in a mighty wing-beat and the owl resurfaced, all traces of the blood washed clean away.

Edie allowed herself a smile of relief, and then it hovered overhead and powered its wings up and down without moving, and the water moved instead.

Somehow the owl was forcing the water back, making a kind of bowl around Edie's legs. The water dropped below her knees, and then she saw her calves, stuck in the sand, and then the owl screeched and the sand began to blow away from her legs, revealing her calves and then her ankles, and the hands that were holding her.

They were hands made from sand, women's hands, and they gripped her ankles tighter as they were exposed. Edie knew that all she had to do was reach down and brush them off, but something within her rebelled at the idea of touching them and she hesitated.

The owl screeched again, a deeper noise, and Edie knew it was telling her to do it. She tried to touch the grasping sand hands, but just couldn't make herself do it. Her skin crawled at the thought of touching them. Although they were made of sand, she knew they were a dead woman's hands.

'I'm sorry. I can't,' she murmured, her voice low and gravelled with shame. 'I just can't . . .'

The owl roared. It wasn't a screech. It was a deep thrumming noise, rumbling with age and power and primeval fury. It was such a profound and implacable sound that all Edie's fear suddenly seemed irrelevant and petty by comparison. It was a roar that resonated through her bones and straightened her back and when it stopped her face was set and she felt washed clean by the noise that had just blown through her.

She looked at the owl.

It held her gaze long enough for Edie to notice how large and pale and moon-like its eyes were, then it blinked and looked away, as if uninterested.

Edie bent and rubbed at the sand hands tugging at her ankles.

And as she had known, they just disintegrated into a scrabble of shell granules beneath her palms. She stepped out and looked back. As the water filled the depression in the sand, something gleamed and rose out of it.

When she saw it was another hand, she stepped back a half-pace.

The owl turned and looked at her pointedly. Edie watched the hand rise above the water and open out, revealing something small and familiar that blazed light at her.

Her sea-glass.

The thing she had felt the lack of while she was running away.

The thing she had forgotten to remember.

Her heart stone.

The owl hooted low and insistently, and Edie stepped back and took the sea-glass. The hand disintegrated and dropped back into the sea, leaving a momentary grey swirl in the water before all evidence that it had ever been there was gone.

The moment she held the heart stone in her hand, Edie knew she was whole again.

She looked up to the ridgeline of the land ahead of her and saw the silhouette of the hare against the pale sky. It seemed to sense her gaze, because it twitched its ears, dropped its head and was gone. She walked out of the waves and up to the top of the shingle bank where it had been and sat leaning against the smooth wood of the groyne, looking back out to sea with no care or worry about what might be behind her on the shoreland any more.

After a bit the owl came and sat on the groyne next to her.

Other than staying close, it gave no sign of any particular interest in her. Edie sat gazing out at the dark water as the light changed.

'Thank you,' she said.

8

DARK HORSE, BLACK TOWER

Nature abhors a vacuum, so when the Walker used the Black Mirror to escape into the Outer Darkness, something from the Outer Darkness escaped into our world to take his place. In the same way that the old Darkness in the London Stone had needed to take substance and shape in order to move in the world, and so had taken over the Duke's horse to become the Night Mare, so the new Darkness had taken the first substance it had met as its own: that substance was the ice crystals thrown up in the wake of the Queen's chariot. This is why it became the Ice Devil.

The shape it took was that of the being who it had swapped dimensions with, which meant that the Ice Devil pacing back and forth on the top of Tower 42 was a Walker-shaped figure whose slightly stretched and twisted body was made from permanently whirling ice crystals.

It had already recognized the presence of the old Darkness, a force with powers akin to its own as it overflew the London Stone, and it had felt that power watching it back. It had acknowledged the kinship, and had been acknowledged in turn because of course the old Darkness had itself once escaped into this world from the same Outer Darkness.

In the exchange that had occurred between the two

Darknesses was also communicated the idea of the taints: the fact that the taints were useful hands and wings and claws with which to move upon this world. And it was for this reason that the Ice Devil had called them to him.

It had sent out the command 'Come' and they had. Throughout the night, flight after flight of gargoyles and phoenixes and pterodactyls and all manner of winged stone creatures had arrived and perched wherever they could find claw- or foot-hold at the top of the skyscraper.

Wingless taints had also heard the call and run, trotted or shambled through the snow to the foot of the tower. Those who were equipped to climb had begun the long ascent on the outside of the building, and those who couldn't waited in a tormented rabble of misshapen creatures below.

The clean straight lines of the tower's top had gone as the arriving taints had bloomed all round it like a parasitical fungus. The new and increasingly crowded eyrie of monstrous creatures were also affected by the proximity of the Ice Devil, and froze up, catching the falling snow in their various hooks, folds and hollows. Giant icicles began to form on the more pronounced extremities of this outer flange, and every now and then a shifting gargoyle would send ice and snow tumbling slowly through the night air to explode on the ground at the tower's foot, to the consternation of the earthbound taints congregated below.

The intense icy temperature at the apex of the tower caused cold air to fall down the sides of the building in what looked like an unendingly slow cascade of smoke, or dry ice.

The Ice Devil had cordoned itself behind a living wall of taints encircling its fortress in the sky, and it walked the unlikely parapet of this aerial stronghold, mapping the other lines of power that it could sense criss-crossing the jumbled urban landscape beneath. There were lines of power it understood, and others that it sensed but did not know the nature of, and there was nothing as strong as the brother power it had felt in the Stone. But when it returned to the façade of the building from which it had looked down and exchanged unseen nods with the Darkness in the Stone, it was gone, almost completely.

The Ice Devil loped around the high perimeter of the tower, trying to sense where this power had gone, and then its attention was taken by a disturbance in the crowd of terrestrial taints beneath. They had parted in order to let something through, and the moment the Ice Devil saw it, it knew it for what it was. The dark horse shape of the Night Mare stood looking up, and this time there was more than a nod.

There was a connection.

The Darkness smouldering out of the horse's eyes slowly circled its way up into the night sky, and met the falling ice smoke, and where the Darkness met the ice a third thing was formed, a kind of thick and unwholesome grey miasma that billowed outwards from the tower in all directions as it filled the roads and alleys, enveloping the surrounding buildings in a light-leaching cloud of freezing Ice Murk.

In the moment of connection the Ice Devil and the Darkness realized they both came from the same place outside this world, and that they could conquer the world by joining forces. The Ice Devil also learnt that the obstacle to this was the moving points of power and light it had sensed, called spits. And it agreed with the

Darkness that the first order of the day was to destroy them, them and the two other powers that moved with them.

The Ice Devil watched the Dark Horse turn and walk into the Ice Murk, towards the edge of the City.

9

IN SHTUCK

'She said thank you,' said George. He sat wrapped in a blanket looking over at Edie in the firelight. She was fast asleep.

'The goddess Andraste looks after her in her dreams. She is safe for now,' murmured the Queen.

'For now?' said George, rubbing the sleep from his eyes and wishing the Gunner hadn't just shaken him awake, especially by gripping his shoulder. The pain of the stone vein twining up his arm had been rekindled and immediately reminded him of the clock ticking down to the moment when he would have to face the final duel with the Last Knight of the Cnihtengild, a duel that he felt was more death sentence than fair fight. He shivered despite himself. 'It doesn't feel like any of us are particularly safe right now. Doesn't feel like any of us even know what's happening. Which is pretty harsh.'

'We're all in shtuck, right enough,' growled the Gunner. 'But her majesty here reckons Edie's in deeper, because of having been dead and all.'

'But she—' began George.

'The girl drowned. She was dead. We all saw it. And yet she came back. The heart stones of the dead glints, the ones the Walker killed, they brought her back. But she was, make no mistake, boy, dead,' said the Queen emphatically.

'I'm not saying she wasn't. And my name is George,

not "boy",' he said. 'What does having been dead mean?'

'It means the barrier between life and death is weaker for her now that she has crossed it twice. It means death will come further into life looking for her than it will with you, for example. She is a fearless girl, but too little fear can be as dangerous as too much.'

'So we'll keep an eye out for her then,' shrugged George.

'It's more than that,' said the Queen sharply. 'It means she'll be changed. It means she'll favour the darker side of herself, because compared with the real death that it is a pale reflection of, it holds fewer fears now. She may harm herself by the choices she makes.'

'OK,' said George slowly. 'No offence, but that just sounds like stuff the school shrink says when he doesn't know what else to say. Edie's a fighter, not suicidal.'

'School shrink?' said the Gunner with a questioning tilt of the head. 'What's that mean?'

George scrabbled quickly for a way to explain this, trying not to think about how bizarre it was having to translate the modern world to a bronze statue in the middle of a snowstorm.

'When my dad died I didn't cope with it that well. Not well at all in fact. I thought it was my fault. My mum had me see the school shrink. Psychologist.'

George was surprised at how he was able to talk so matter-of-factly about the great unspoken pain in his life. He remembered the soldier with his father's face and the firm grip he had taken on his arm across the horse's neck. He remembered his smile and what he had said. And then he almost gasped as he realized that a locked door in his heart had opened somewhere back there, only he hadn't had time to notice it. And now where there had been a black treacly darkness he felt clean air and light flowing through.

He knew he'd never stop being sad about his dad. But he now knew that he wouldn't ever have to be chained or made less than himself by that sadness.

He grinned.

'What?' said the Gunner.

'Nothing,' said George. 'It's all right.'

'No it isn't,' said the Officer, tensing and aiming his pistol out into the night. 'Gunner. We've got company.'

10

DARK KNIGHT

As George feared, the Last Knight of the Cnihtengild was slowly quartering the City, looking for him. He was in no hurry, since an Agent of Fate, such as he was, knows things will come to their inevitable end at some stage. So he doggedly criss-crossed the wandering maze of streets in the Square Mile looking for George.

He didn't really notice the clocks striking thirteen, nor the way all the people faded out of the City as that last chime dwindled to nothingness.

He was aware of the snow, but thought little of it.

In his mind he rode with his great ghostly company of fellow knights on either side of him, their hacked and battle-worn armour creaking and jangling as they searched the streets with him.

He thought little of the snow because, in truth, he didn't think much about anything. He didn't have much of an internal life, indeed he didn't have much internal anything. He was precisely what he had been made to be: a Hollow Man.

He was constructed, as was his horse, from curving sheets of metal, welded together at certain points, showing the gaps in his construction in a way his maker had intended. He was an armoured man on an armoured horse. The horse's surcoat was made from interlinked wavelets of metal set with circles of blue glass, and jangled as he rode forward, seeming louder and louder as the clop of its hooves became increasingly deadened by the falling snow.

His one thought was to find the boy and end the duel they had begun. He had no hatred for the boy. He had no rancour about this. He just had a job to do and was going to do it.

It was just the way things were fated to be.

He had no fear of losing the coming fight, not because he felt himself invincible, but because the duel itself was the point, not the victory. It was a fight that had to be had, and would be had, and he would throw himself into it without holding back one ounce of his strength or his battle-skill.

That's what it took, being an Agent of Fate. Unswerving commitment to the 'how?' the 'when?' and the 'who?' of things, and very, *very* little reflection on the 'why?'. That's what it took, that and being unstoppable.

He was riding across Holborn Viaduct when his horse whinnied and snorted at something in the roadway ahead. The Knight had been looking to his side and vaguely wondering where the statues of the ladies who normally adorned the bridge balusters had gone, so he didn't initially see what had unsettled his horse.

He turned his helm, and the two glowing eyes behind the slit in it burnt a little brighter as he peered ahead through the thickly falling snow. All he could make out was the slow white blur of the falling flakes greying out the deeper darkness beyond. And then something detached from the wider dark and walked towards him.

It was a horse.

The Knight stopped.

'Who goes there?' he bellowed.

The Dark Horse did not speak, but the Knight heard the answer in his head.

THE DARK OF THE SUN AND THE FEAR THAT WALKS AT NIGHT.

His horse whinnied and tried to walk backwards. He tugged the reins and dug his heels in.

'Halt!' he thundered, dropping his lance point and aiming it at the approaching animal. Now it was closer he could see it had a shadow-figure on its back, an indistinct shape made from the same darkness as it was, a hazy rider whose edges and shapes were cloaked in a shifting cowl of black smoke.

WHAT MANNER OF THING ARE YOU?

The question echoed in his head, though again he couldn't exactly hear it.

'I am Fate's Champion and the Last Knight of the Cnihtengild, and no man or thing may stop me on my Quest, so stand aside!'

He shook his lance to show he meant business. The Dark Horse kept right on coming through the endlessly tumbling veil of snow.

WHAT IS YOUR QUEST?

'I seek the Boy Maker, the bearer of the Light.'

The Dark Horse still walked towards him.

WHY DO YOU SEEK HIM?

'He has chosen the Hard Way. I must fight him. I must kill him, if I may. So must I kill any who stand between me and my purpose or try and stop me. Stand aside!'

The Dark Horse didn't falter a fraction as it bore down on him.

I DO NOT WANT TO STOP YOU . . .

'Then stand aside!' roared the Knight, jabbing his lance forward.

. . . I WANT TO BE YOU.

And with that the Dark Horse walked straight on to the sharp point of the lance, and as it did so the Knight's horse shuddered and bucked and turned to flee, despite his attempts to stop it. And the Knight was twisted right round in his saddle as he kept his tenacious, unstoppable grip on the haft of his weapon, and so he saw exactly what happened as it happened, and what that was is this:

The lance pierced the Dark Horse and the Horse kept on coming, and as it came the lance blackened as the Darkness leached into it ahead of itself. And he could not tug the weapon free, and his horse became frozen as a tendril of Darkness dropped off the lance and poured inside the horse through one of the curving gaps in its metal plates. And then very quickly other tendrils enveloped the horse and the Knight like black creepers and wound and twined their way inside the gaps in them, filling the hollow within with the Darkness.

And when he spoke, it was not just with his own voice any more.

I TOO SEEK THE BOY. AND NOW I AM YOU.

It was the voice of Darkness and the Knight.

WE ARE THE DARK KNIGHT.

11

THE COLD LIGHT OF MORNING

Spout sat on top of the arch on Hyde Park Corner watching things. Not that there was much to watch. Nothing moved anywhere. Throughout the night he'd seen occasional taints flying past, but he'd kept very still and not joined them. Now in the cold light of morning the skies were empty. Even the snow had stopped abruptly as the dawn rose. The city remained unpopulated, and no birds sang. In fact the birds seemed to have gone too, except for one large black one slowly picking its way along the spiked top of the palace garden wall far below. Maybe all the other birds were still roosting. Maybe it was the cold.

Edie felt a hand gently shaking her shoulder, and woke instantly. She looked up to see the giant wings of the owl spread wide above her, and then she really woke and saw the wings were not wings at all, but the smooth sweep of the massive stone arch over her head.

George was squatting beside her with a ham sandwich in his hand and a big smile on his face.

'Edie. It's morning.' He held out the sandwich. 'Room service.'

She sat up and pulled the duvet round her shoulders. She noted sadly that her hand no longer held her own sea-glass heart stone as in the dream, but only her mother's smaller earring. Still, it was better than nothing.

And the little flicker inside it was not just flame, but hope, the hope that said, 'She's alive.'

She took the sandwich and munched down on it. It was just bread and butter and ham, but because she had not really eaten in a long while, it tasted like the best thing she'd ever had.

She surveyed the scene. London was covered in snow. In fact it was more than covered. It was buried. The fire was still blazing beneath the centre of the arch but out beyond the red and orange of its flames, and below a crisp blue sky, the city had gone monochrome.

It was no longer snowing, but given the size of drifts all around them this was maybe because all the snow had run out.

Beyond the arch all was white punctuated by grey buildings and black tree trunks. It would have been magical if it hadn't been so still. The absence of people or movement made it a sad sight, somehow. The snow deadened everything. It hung in great cornices from the tops of the buildings, and lay so thick on the ground that cars were buried up to their windows, and wore thick snow-caps on their roofs. The cold made her breath plume.

The Queen crouched in front of the fire, holding a hotel teapot directly over the flames. She looked over at Edie and smiled. Edie heard a loud sneeze and a 'Gah' from the other side of her.

She stopped chewing and turned to look at the source of the explosion.

'Dictionary!'

The big man twitched and ducked his head in a half-bow that would have been more effective had it not dislodged his wig and slid it dangerously askew.

He stood and straightened it up with a surprisingly shy smile.

'Ah. I give you joy of this fine fresh and unworldly morning, my dear. And I am told that you whom I wrongly called a mannerless sprunt have turned out to be a doughty nonpareil after all!'

'Doughty what?' said Edie, looking at George who just shrugged, equally baffled.

A thin figure with complicated glasses, one eye obscured by a dark lens appeared from behind the great man's shoulder.

'Brave heroine. Or somesuch. Dictionary wordy man but means well. Introduce self. Am.'

'Clocker,' said Edie, realizing who he must be. 'George told me about you. You gave him chocolate for me. It was good.'

'Obliged,' said the Clocker, beaming at her. 'You asleep last time we met. Or didn't. But inordinately happy to see good self safe. And well. Indeed am,' said the Clocker with a nervous bob that made all the instruments hanging off his coat jingle at once. Combined with his rusty green coat and the snow they gave him the look of an amiable – if spindly – Christmas tree.

'They come out of the dark last night, and me and him nearly blew holes in them,' said the Gunner, thumbing in the direction of the Officer who was still looking alertly out at the wintry scene. There was still nothing moving in the snow-clogged landscape. Even the solitary bird perched on the spikes topping the wall round Buckingham Palace Gardens seemed frozen into stillness.

The Queen pushed past Dictionary and the Clocker and knelt in front of Edie with the smoke-blackened metal teapot and a china mug.

'Warm milk. Drink it,' she ordered, pouring from the pot.

'So what's happening?' Edie asked George.

'We don't know,' he said. 'Clocker and Dictionary passed loads of taints heading east on their way here last night.'

'Into the City,' interrupted Dictionary. 'No doubt in my mind that something is afoot, something inimical to us brewing within the Square Mile. 'Tis plain as a pikestaff that fell days attend us. All people erased from the city at a stroke, this unseasonable and unnatural snow, all portend evil. Not a word I use lightly, but I am muchwhat confirmed in my apprehension that a new devil walks the earth and this snow is his footprint.'

A beat of silence followed as everyone absorbed his gloomy words.

'Still, we've been talking about what to do,' said George, rallying. 'We've got a plan.'

In the distance Edie saw movement, but it was just the bird gliding off the wall and landing nearby.

'I just want to find my mum,' said Edie. And as she said it a horrible thought came to her, cloaked in the memory of a dream and the sandy hands pulling at her feet, and she scrabbled in her pocket. She pulled out her mother's heart stone, and was relieved to see it still shone from within. Seeing the fire also kindled the pain of hoping against hope again, but she didn't mind.

She held it up.

'She's still alive, see? I thought she wasn't, but she is,' she explained to Dictionary and the Clocker.

'Edie,' said George quietly. 'This might be a bit bigger than that. If we can't stop what's happening, it won't matter where your mother is or why you thought she was dead . . . there won't be any *when* for her to exist in.'

'What do you mean *when*?' snapped Edie, drinking off the last of her milk and standing in one motion. She stamped her feet to get the circulation going and reached down for the fur coat. She glared at George as she pulled it on. 'Saying "there won't be any *when*" doesn't make sense!'

'Actually,' coughed the Clocker, 'makes complete sense. Precise definition of predicament. Time out of joint. Stopped dead. No when. No then. Just now. Imperative put time back in joint or all stuck here frozen in time for ever.'

He grimaced apologetically.

'And how do you put time *in* joint?' she said, lip curling. 'Sounds like a big job. What do you do? Find time and then just kick it and bang it on the side? Or is there a button you push? Reboot, reset, off we go again?'

'No,' said the Clocker. 'Have to go to Queen of Time. She will know.'

'Fine. You go to the Queen of Time. I'm going to find my mum.'

'How?' said the Gunner, looking her straight in the eye.

Edie had no idea, and that made her all the angrier at the question. Her jaw jutted forward. Dangerously.

'By trying, for a start,' she snapped. 'I can't just not try, can I?'

'Edie,' said George with a glance at the Queen. 'Why are you getting so angry? We're all in this together. Last night you were . . . happy. Now you . . .'

The Officer stepped between them, decisively ending the exchange.

'If the girl's got out of bed the wrong side, so be it. Expect she'll get over it once the food's kicked in and the day progresses. We don't have time for nannying, sorry, but there it is.'

'Nannying?' said Edie incredulously. 'You think I need *nannying*?'

'It's not about what you need. It's about what we talked about. What we all need to do. We're burning daylight as it is.'

'It stopped snowing as it got light. Pretty uncanny. We think it'll start again when it gets dark,' explained George.

'And another snowfall like this and we won't be able to move at all,' continued the Gunner.

'Here's the plan,' said George. And over his shoulder Edie noticed the big black bird hop closer to them, right into the shadow of the arch. It cocked its head.

'The Clocker is going to find the Queen of Time. He says if there's anything to be done, she'll know what it is. You, me and the Queen here, Boadicea, are going to go with the Officer and the Gunner to see the Sphinxes . . .'

'*Sphinxes?*' Edie choked in disbelief. 'Why've I got to go back to the sphinxes? They don't exactly like me, do they . . .?'

'That's why we need you,' said the Queen calmly. 'Glints are the only things we know of that the Sphinxes are wary of. And when things are awry, or need clarifying between the spits and the taints, it's the Sphinxes who are most likely to come up with an answer.'

'Not that their answers are the acme of clarity,' grunted Dictionary. 'So having someone like you who disconcerts and possibly affrights them may enable us to put their feet to the fire in case of obscurity or obfuscation.'

'It's not just them that aren't clear,' said Edie darkly. She snaked the belt out of the loops in her jeans and used it to cinch the fur coat tight around her.

'If there is anything to be done, it is the Sphinxes who will know. It is likely that many other spits will come to ask them. It is a good place to marshal our forces, anyway. There is safety in numbers, and we should look to defend ourselves in case this massing of taints is aimed at attacking us,' said the Queen.

'Well—' began the Officer, but what he was about to say next never got said, because there was an explosion of activity behind them, everyone spun, and those who had weapons drew them and aimed them at a furious whirlwind of snow and feathers and yowling bronze feline at the foot of the arch.

The black bird – who on closer inspection of course revealed itself to be the Raven – was a big bird and a feisty scrapper, but the cat Hodge was just as fierce and much, much heavier. After a few flaps and a lot of aggrieved squawks the Raven found itself pinned to the snow with a metal forepaw across its neck. The cat hissed in victory, showing its teeth, in no hurry to kill the bird while there was still fun to be had from it. The Raven went limp, hoping the cat would lean lower and try and bite it, so that it could then give it a good hard peck in the eye. It had died and gone to Hel so many times before that death itself had no fears for it. What it never enjoyed was the journey back. It always reappeared in the world with its feathers in a shocking state of disarray. Pecking the cat wouldn't do a bit of good to anything except the Raven's self-respect.

'It's the Walker's bloody bird,' said the Gunner. 'Either the cat kills it or I do . . .'

He cocked the pistol in his hand.

'NO!'

The vehemence of the voice surprised everyone. Including Edie, whose voice it was.

'No. Don't kill it . . .'

The cat hissed again and raised its free paw to swat the bird in the head. Cats don't like being told what to do.

They also aren't particularly in favour of ferocious girls diving across the snow, grabbing their tails and flinging them into a snowdrift.

Which is exactly what Edie did.

The cat rolled and turned back with its claws out, ready for bloody revenge.

'Hodge!' bellowed Dictionary. 'No!'

Hodge stopped and looked at the girl and the Raven.

The Raven lay on its back and looked at the girl.

Part of its natural instinct was to flip over and fly away to safety. But the Raven had seen everything, both through its own black eyes and the ones it had borrowed, and forgotten none of it. And one of the things about remembering everything about the past is that it can all get a bit stale. The Raven carried the past with it all the time. What it was particularly interested in was the opposite of the past, the bits it didn't yet know about or remember.

Its job was the past.

But its hobby was the future.

What it enjoyed, and one of the things that kept it – and many other beings – in the world was the simple pleasure of seeing what happens next.

So it ignored the instinct to fly, and waited to see what the glint would do.

What she did was reach forward and move the feathers at its neck.

And now the Raven was so interested it didn't move a pin-feather.

'It's still alive,' said Edie. 'But there's blood . . .'

She suddenly pulled her hand back in surprise.

'It's not blood. It's a thread . . .' She leant back in and moved the oil-black feathers apart. The Raven didn't dare blink.

'It's a red thread . . .'

'Don't touch it!' said the Queen and both of her daughters at the same time.

'It's part of the old magic: *"Red Thread to bind, Red Thread to catch dreams, Red Thread to make the wearer not what she seems"*. It must be part of the binding spell the Walker put on the bird,' the Queen continued. 'Meddling with the old magic if you don't know what you're doing is a very, very . . .'

Edie leant down and neatly bit through the red thread.

'. . . very bad idea,' finished the Queen.

12

LOST IN THE MURK

It wasn't daylight everywhere in London. Inside the Ice Murk, the grey freezing miasma that slowly billowed out from the Ice Devil's tower it was still dark. Anyone flying above the city would have seen that at the centre of the whiteness covering everything the Ice Murk was a starkly contrasting cloud of near-black fog. It bloomed slowly and inexorably, now a massive black growth two hundred metres high and nearly a mile across that swallowed buildings and exuded into the intervening streets, filling them with its icy and impenetrable gloom.

Somewhere in the middle of this the Old Soldier was trying to light his pipe. The Young Soldier stood behind him, barely able to see his companion at arm's distance. The fog was so thick that even the flare of the match as the Old Soldier struck it only showed as a brief frosted globe of hazy light against the side of his face, before sputtering out.

'It's a ruddy pea-souper and that's a fact,' mumbled the Young Soldier.

'Pea-soupers weren't this cold. And they weren't this thick,' replied the Old Soldier. He held out his arm. He could barely make out the pipe-stem in his hand.

'You don't know where we are, do you?' said the Young Soldier.

'Nah. We're poor little lambs who've lost our way, baa baa baa . . .' said the Old Soldier. 'Little black sheep who've gone astray . . .'

He unlooped his belt and fumbled for the Young Soldier's hand.

'Hold this end, don't let go, at least that way we'll both stay lost in the same place and won't get split up.' And he walked slowly forward, feeling along the side of the building like a blind man. The Young Soldier followed, clinging on to his tether. It was painfully slow going.

'He was all right, Hooky was,' he said after a bit.

The unseen figure on the end of the belt ahead of him just grunted.

'I never seen nothing like that,' continued the Young Soldier. 'It done my nut in, I don't mind telling you.'

'You was made with your nut done in, youngster,' growled the other. 'Now keep your trap— hello.'

The youngster stopped. The belt went tight between them.

'What?' he said nervously. 'Oh blimey . . .'

And he dropped the belt and quickly unshouldered his gun.

'Why'd you do that?' said the Old Soldier's voice. 'You dropped the belt. I said hold on, didn't I?'

'I thought there was trouble,' admitted the Young Soldier. 'I'm sorry.'

He reached ahead with his hand, swiping it back and forth, trying to find the Old Soldier in the Murk. Now the panic started to rise.

'Oh bloody hell,' he whined. 'I've been and gone and done it this time, haven't I?'

The Old Soldier stood watching the Young Soldier's hand with a grin of enjoyment as he lit his pipe. He was not in the Murk. He was two paces ahead of the Young Soldier and standing knee-deep in the snow under a bright blue sky, a wide swathe of clear air that cut through the Ice Murk like a firebreak in a forestry plantation. The Murk rose up on either side, so that he was in a canyon between two sheer walls of dark fog, walls that were so flat and smooth that it seemed as if the roiling gloom within was being held back by giant sheets of glass.

It was out of one of these flat walls that the Young Soldier's hand was waving.

'Just stay where you are,' said the Old Soldier. And he calmly stuck his pipe in his mouth and took the time to strike a match and get it going properly this time. He took several deep happy puffs.

'You still there?' he said to the shaking hand sticking out of the fog-wall in front of him.

'Yes,' came the quavering reply.

'Right,' said the Old Soldier, grabbing the cuff of the Young Soldier's jacket.

'Oh thank God,' said the relieved voice from inside the Murk.

And then the Old Soldier yanked him forward, and his face and then his whole body stepped out of the wall of Murk and into the clean air.

The Young Soldier stared around him, blinking.

'Hang on. You been standing in the clear all that time? While I was in there?' he asked querulously.

'Had to get my pipe going,' explained the Old Soldier, smiling innocently. 'Now come on. Looks like St Paul's down there . . .'

'Right,' said his companion. And they walked towards the south elevation of the great cathedral partially emerging from the fog-wall in which it was embedded.

'Blimey,' said the Old Soldier. 'We ain't near where I

thought we was. That fog come down and we got turned around good.'

'Well, I'm glad we're out of it,' said the young one. 'As long as we don't meet that blooming horse . . .'

The soldier in front froze and raised a hand. They both stopped and crouched, weapons ready.

'What?' whispered the young one.

'Cover me,' said the Old Soldier without looking round. He loped forward through the snow and stopped in front of the cathedral, or at least the corner of it that wasn't eaten by the Murk. He looked down at something lying in a jumble at his feet. He shook his head, turned to the Young Soldier, put a finger to his lips and beckoned him forward.

As the Young Soldier hurried through the snow towards him, he kept alert, gun shouldered, panning around for dangers that might be approaching him from any direction.

He was at a point where the clear avenue between the Murk that he was in intersected with four other ones. He was at the centre of a star that radiated ten separate different directions to go in. He checked each one in turn.

The Young Soldier gagged when he saw what he was standing guard over.

'I know,' said the Old Soldier. 'They went hard.'

Fragments of bronze bodies lay around them. Something had ripped apart the Blitz memorial that stood in front of the cathedral. Heads in tin helmets lay apart from torsos that were missing arms and legs. The other limbs were spread about in the snow.

'They was just firemen,' said the Young Soldier. 'They wasn't soldiers.'

'They was spits. Reckon that's all that matters now,' said the Old Soldier, gathering up body parts.

'What you doing?' said his companion.

'Put 'em back on their plinth. For turn o' day,' said the Old Soldier. 'You ain't got the sense you was made with.'

'Right,' said the other, reaching for a sightless head. And then he went very still, his eyes widening at something over the Old Soldier's shoulder. The Old Soldier caught the look and froze.

'What?' he mouthed.

The Young Soldier just pointed with his chin. The Old Soldier turned in time to see a huge bronze lion's body, about the size of a large elephant as it followed its head into the sheer wall of the Murk. Neither spoke until the tip of the lazily twitching tail had been swallowed up.

'What was that?' breathed the Young Soldier.

'Dunno,' said the Old Soldier. 'But if it's as happy to walk in the Murk as in the light, it's up to no good.'

13

RED THREAD

Edie looked down at the red thread between her fingers. It didn't seem very magic. It was just thread.

The Raven jerked and flapped to its feet and then just stood in front of her, pecking and preening its ruffled feathers back into some kind of order, keeping its eye on Hodge who was very still, watching from the edge of the drift into which Edie had flung him.

'Why did you do that, child?' asked the Queen.

Edie didn't know why she'd done it, not in a way she could explain. Her mind was still half jumbled with sleep, a tangle of too much exhaustion and too many 'maybes' again: maybe she'd done it because she had to, maybe because it felt like the thing to do. Maybe she knew what it was like to be imprisoned – although maybe she wasn't kind, maybe she was just clever. Or maybe she'd done it because she knew the moment she felt it that the Walker had placed the thread there and she instinctively wanted to undo everything he'd ever done. Then again, maybe she just liked birds.

'A bird saved me,' she said.

'What bird?' said George.

'In my dream,' she said, beginning to get irritated. 'Look, I don't know, an owl saved me in my dream, and I didn't think about it much, it just seemed like the thing to do.'

'An owl?' said the Queen. 'In your dream? An owl watched over you?'

79

Edie looked at her in surprise.

'Yeah. A grey owl.'

'Andraste,' said one of her daughters, coming closer.

'Or Arianhrod,' said the other.

'Who?'

'Different names for the same White Lady. The moon goddess,' explained the Queen. 'You see, you are wrong. You're not on your own. No one ever is.'

'Goddess?' snorted Edie. 'There's no such thing as goddesses. It was an owl. In a dream. That's all . . .'

'A goddess comes to you in a dream and you think it's nothing?' hissed the Queen in disbelief.

'I don't believe in goddesses. Or dreams. Or magic,' Edie said flatly. 'I believe in me and what I can see and what I can do.'

'What about your power? What about your glinting?'

'Not magic, is it? It's just what I do. I can feel the past in stones like dogs can hear high-pitched noises humans can't. It's not magic. It's just a thing.'

Edie balled the red thread and stuffed it in her pocket.

'You don't make sense, Edie,' said George. 'After all that's happened to us, you can't . . .'

'Yes I can,' she said. 'I can do what—'

And at that point Hodge leapt for the Raven and the Raven lofted into the air and came to rest on Edie's shoulder, so neatly that the cat got nothing but a face full of snow and embarrassment.

Cats hate looking stupid more than anything else in the world, so Hodge twisted in a fury and prepared to spring up at the Raven again.

'NO!' shouted Edie.

And Hodge stopped dead. He looked at the girl. He looked at the Raven. And then he slowly walked away, as if suddenly bored by the whole affair.

'Takes one catamount to know another,' said Dictionary, stooping to pick the cat up and stroke some dignity back into the affronted animal.

The wind, which had been entirely absent until now, picked up a light skirl of snow and blew it across the empty space between the arch and the war memorials.

'You don't believe in goddesses?' repeated the Queen, voice no warmer than the ice crystals dancing across the top of the snow around them.

'No.'

'Or gods?' asked one of the daughters.

'No,' said Edie. 'Sorry. I believe in me. And what I can see, and what I can touch.'

She cinched the belt round her fur coat tighter, as if that finished the discussion.

'Fine,' said the Queen, standing. 'You see that Raven on your shoulder?'

'Er, yuh . . .' grunted Edie, as if it was the stupidest question in the world.

'There was another god, a one-eyed god, a hanged god. He was called Odin and he came to this island with the Vikings. He had two birds. One was Thought, one was Memory.'

'And?'

'They were Ravens.'

'So?' said Edie, suddenly not liking where this was going.

'So I suppose you don't believe in that god either?' said the Queen.

'No.'

'Interesting,' smiled the Queen. 'But complicated. Because you've got his Raven on your shoulder.'

'It's the Walker's bird,' said George looking at the Gunner, who shrugged.

'It is Memory, the Raven whose name is also Munin. The Walker was a mage before he was cursed by the Stone. He enslaved the bird with a spell, the spell that appears to have been broken when your friend broke the red thread and made the bird her own,' explained the Queen.

'It's not my bird, it's free to go,' declared Edie. 'Seriously . . .'

She shrugged her shoulder as if to dislodge the bird. The Raven rode the rise and fall without turning a feather or going anywhere.

'It has seen everything and forgotten nothing that it has seen. It certainly has seen enough to know that a favour left unthanked and not repaid will always come back to haunt you. It knows how the world balances accounts. I think Munin is with you until you are done with it, child, like it or not,' said the Queen.

'I don't mind it. I just don't like animals and birds tied up or caged. Or people,' muttered Edie, thinking of the woman with the sewn eyelids in the House of the Lost.

The wind buffeted again, whirling the powder off the top of the surrounding snow and dancing it past them. George looked across at Edie as the gust whipped her long dark hair into a rippling flag behind her. Silhouetted against the snow and lit by the wind-kindled blaze, wearing the black fur coat with the Raven perched on her shoulder, she didn't look modern at all. She looked just for an instant like something out of time.

Edie, George thought, may not have believed in the old myths, but she suddenly looked like she'd just stepped straight out of one.

The Queen was also looking at her appraisingly. The sternness and outrage in her face was so strong that George wasn't sure whether she was going to shout or hit her.

She took a deep breath and did neither.

She went down on one knee so that she was eye to eye with Edie, and gripped her chin firmly. Edie tried to escape the implacable bronze grip, but couldn't.

The Queen spoke very calmly. It was clearly a great effort not to lose her temper.

'The goddess that you don't believe in and the magic you are so sure doesn't exist had power on this island so long ago that the island itself went by another name. It was Albion, the white land, the white of the moon. The goddess had the power of the moon, and she took the shape of an owl, the moon bird, and owls and certain other creatures like the hare were sacred to her and the—'

As soon as the Queen mentioned the hare Edie knew she had to stop the conversation.

'Look,' she interrupted. 'It's all rubbish to me. Sorry. Means a lot to you, I can see that, but that's not my world, is it?'

In her mind's eye she was unable to stop the replay of the dream, the bit where the hare watched her from the ridgeline on top of the pebble slope.

'I just want to find my mum. It's not about gods or Old England or Albion, see? It's about me thinking she was dead and now having a chance to find her.'

The Queen opened her mouth to speak. Edie went on, fast, because she was only telling half the truth.

'You'd do the same if you were me. And if they were me, so would your daughters. They'd rip the world apart looking for you. Wouldn't they?'

The Queen was, as Edie had hoped, temporarily unable to speak or deny the truth of what she was saying.

The Officer filled the silence.

'We need to get south to the Sphinxes. Time may have stopped but night will still fall soon enough.'

'And I go north. To see Queen of Time. See what we can do,' interjected the Clocker. 'Best of luck to all.'

And he turned and strode off into the snow, his long thin legs crow-stepping through the drifts. There was something brave and sad about the sight of him setting off into the whiteness on his own, thought George. Dictionary must have thought so too, because he harrumphed and called out after him.

'Clocker. Dear fellow. I would be inordinately gratified if you would do me the great unmerited honour of allowing me to accompany you. I should admire to make acquaintance of the lady sovereign of things temporal.'

Dictionary turned to the others and lowered his voice.

'Look at him. No meat to his bones, the icy blast must blow right through him. I must admit that I have taken a liking to the poor jingling spindle-shanks. I should feel a great indolent booby were I to let him venture off alone into this icy vastness. So, I give joy and success of the day to you, my friends.' He bowed jerkily then beckoned the cat. 'Come, Hodge . . .'

And with that the broad figure bulled his way through the snow towards his lanky companion, the cat leaping through the drifts at his side.

'Jack Spratt and his wife,' said the Gunner, looking at the mismatched pair walking away from them. 'Come on. I've already seen other spits heading south through St James's Park over there. We ain't the only ones'll have thought about consulting the Sphinxes. Don't want to miss the party.'

They turned their back on the homely fire and walked across to the park, led by the Gunner. The Queen's daughters led the horses and the chariot, which was too low to the ground to be able to surmount the snow where it had drifted deeper.

George walked beside Edie, but every time he turned to say something to her all he got was the side of her face, jaw jutting forward, and an appraising look from the deep black eyes of the bird riding her shoulder.

He felt a hand on his arm, and turned to find the Queen walking beside him. She pulled him back a couple of paces, out of earshot, and spoke low.

'The glint may not wish to hear it from me, boy, but the truth of things is this: there is something in you, one or both of you, something that has scraped through to the forgotten layers of old England, before it was England even, when it was Albion. Whatever is happening, whatever has followed you here in your quest, is connected with that wilder world, the world of the ancient magic. It goes deeper than I can fathom, but in the depths are black things that are calling to that girl. And if she listens to them and forgets the light, she is lost. And I would have no more girls lost because I failed to speak out and warn them.'

George looked over at Edie. Now even the Raven was avoiding his eyes. Not a good sign.

'We are in a place I have never been, boy. And though I know nothing of it, I do know it will be darker, before it gets better.'

'If it gets better,' said Edie without turning.

It was then they heard the screaming.

14

LOVE LIES BLEEDING

'Someone's hurt!' shouted George.

'Sounds like a boy,' said Edie, pushing past him and staring eastwards.

They all stood frozen, listening to the distant screams, trying to figure out exactly where they were coming from.

'Somewhere on Piccadilly,' barked the Officer, starting off in that direction.

'No,' snapped the Gunner. 'South of there. In the park. Look . . .'

And then, just for an instant George saw it, above the snow-laden treetops of Green Park. At this distance it looked like three birds fighting, but only for a moment, until his eyes adjusted to the scale of the winged creatures, and he realized he was seeing two bat-winged gargoyles swooping and tearing at the third winged human figure, like crows mobbing an owl.

The human figure was flying lopsidedly. He was swatting at the gargoyles with a bow held in his left hand as they lunged at him. His right arm dangled loosely, somehow bent the wrong way.

Then one of the gargoyles folded its wings and dropped like a stone, using all its weight to hammer the boy out of the sky. They dropped below the top of the trees and were lost from sight. But not from hearing: the sound of the impact reached them, followed by a cry of agony and terror, and the sound of something like a terrier snarling and worrying at its prey.

No one gave an order.

Everyone ran at once.

'It's the Bow Boy. From Piccadilly Circus,' shouted the Queen.

The statues outran the two children, but even with their added strength and size, running through the thick snow was like running in a dream, the kind of bad dream where however hard you try, you're never quite running fast enough.

George knew those dreams.

He also knew how they ended.

He knew they were going to be too late.

He turned and looked back at the arch. Spout sat on the cornice of snow, quivering like a dog. George saw there was just one chance to save whoever was screaming in the unreachable distance.

'Spout!' he yelled. 'Go! Help the boy!'

'Taints won't just do what you tell them, they ain't b—' began the Gunner.

And then there was an eruption of snow as Spout leapt into the air, his wings unfolding with a sharp decisive whip-crack. He powered through the air, accelerating as he went, great wing-beats kicking up the snow around them as he passed over, and disappeared into the trees ahead of them.

'Blow me,' said the Gunner. 'Never seen that before . . .'

'He's not going to get there in time . . .' panted Edie, chopping her way through the snow a couple of paces behind George.

'He'll still get there before us,' gasped George. Although he seemed to have been hurtling through London ever since he broke the carving at the Natural

History Museum, this new sensation of running in snow made him tired in entirely new and more painful ways.

The screaming stopped dead.

The sudden silence was shocking in itself, so much so that the Queen and the Officer came to simultaneous halts, and stood straining to hear any more noises.

George heard the Officer curse under his breath as he ran past him.

'Damn and blast.'

George kept plunging ahead in the wake of the Gunner who hadn't slowed one bit as he ran in under the trees, unholstering his pistol as he went.

'Look out!' shrieked Edie as something large came crashing through the branches in their direction – an angular jagged shape getting bigger with startling rapidity as it spun straight at them. The Gunner ducked and George swerved, and then the thing hit the snow and cartwheeled between him and Edie in a savage series of impacts before embedding itself in the trunk of a tree.

They stared at it.

'Your gargoyle,' said Edie, deflating.

It was a stone wing, torn off at the root. George looked at it for an instant longer, and then threw himself forward into a lurching snow-hobbled sprint.

'Spout!' he yelled.

'I'm sorry . . .' shouted Edie, trying to keep up.

George said nothing more. He needed all his breath to keep running. The extra surge of energy was not despair, because Edie was wrong.

The wing wasn't Spout's.

He heard the crack of the Gunner's pistol ahead of him, and then he burst out of the trees, crashed through a hedge and stopped dead.

Spout was fighting two gargoyles at once. Or rather, he was fighting one intact gargoyle with the other one whose wing he had obviously just torn off, swinging the damaged one by its undamaged wing, using its truncated body like a hammer.

The intact gargoyle yammered in fury and pain as Spout stood astride the broken-winged figure of the boy, cutting huge swathes of air with his gargoyle-hammer, trying to keep it at a distance and prevent it darting in to rip at the unmoving figure on the ground.

As Spout's improvised bludgeon whirred past its snarling face it pounced in and latched on to the boy's outflung leg with its teeth, worrying at it with the growling terrier noises George had heard from a distance.

Up close there was something truly horrible about the inhuman fury and malice in the taint's onslaught. It seemed to want to hurt the boy even if it meant putting itself in greater danger, a danger that manifested itself almost immediately as Spout caught it a bone-crunching blow with its partner. The intact gargoyle was knocked head over heels. There was another sharp crack as the gargoyle-hammer broke, leaving Spout with a second dismembered wing in his talon.

He tossed it over his shoulder and leapt for the undamaged gargoyle, who took to the sky just too slowly to avoid Spout catching it by its foot. Spout stayed on the ground, one talon hooked round a park bench, anchoring his desperately flapping adversary and stopping it escaping.

Spout was panting with exhaustion. George could now see how much the uneven fight had taken out of him. He had a great gouge across his chest, and one of his brows was now lopsided, having been sheared off by a blow from his attackers.

'Eigengang! Gow, Eigengang!!' he howled hoarsely at George.

'Shoot it!' George yelled at the Gunner.

BLAM. The Gunner's first shot knocked the gargoyle out of Spout's grip. It stuttered in mid-air, nearly fell, but then flapped away. Spout launched himself after it.

'Again!' roared Edie, who had caught up with them.

'Your bloody pet's in the way!' snarled the Gunner in frustration, running after the disappearing gargoyles, leaving George alone with the injured boy.

'Spout! Leave it!' George shouted. 'SPOUT! GET DOWN.'

Spout swooped lower, exposing the gargoyle. The Gunner stepped sideways and rested his gun-hand against a tree, steadying his aim.

BLAM.

The gargoyle flew on.

'Too far for a pistol . . .' he growled, squinting along the gun's sights.

BLAM.

He shook his head in frustration.

'. . . what I need is a bloody—'

CRACK. CRACK.

The sound of two distant shots smacked flatly across the snow. The gargoyle suddenly tipped in mid-air and cartwheeled into the very solid side-wall of the Ritz hotel in an impact they felt as much as heard, even at this great distance.

For an instant it stayed there, as if embedded in the masonry, then it plummeted straight down out of sight, unmistakably dead.

'. . . rifle,' finished the Gunner wonderingly. And he raised his head from his point of aim and squinted across the snow towards the sound of the other gunshots.

'Who the hell was that then?'

As if in answer to his question the Old and the Young Soldier broke out of the distant trees, waving and running towards them.

George relaxed a fraction, which was a mistake, because just as he did so, something hopped towards the still figure of the Bow Boy and leapt on him, sinking its teeth into his ribs and starting to shake him from side to side. It was the now wingless gargoyle.

George didn't think, he just leapt, throwing his arms round the barrel-chested creature and wrenching it off the boy. The gargoyle kicked at George with its feet, winding him enough so that he loosened his grip. The thing twisted and reared its head back to strike: he had a sickening impression of stone fangs and angry eyes blurring at him, and just managed to jerk his head sideways so that the rough granite skin of the creature painfully grazed his cheekbone as it struck, instead of pulverizing his skull.

He latched on to the taint with an even tighter grip, to prevent it being able to head-butt him again, keeping his own head buried in its shoulder, like a boxer riding out a flurry of blows while he figures out what to do next.

'Shoot it!' yelled Edie.

The Gunner spun to see what was happening behind him.

'Might hit George!' he spat in frustration. He dropped his gun on its lanyard and ran back towards George and the snarling gargoyle. He was too far away. It was forcing its head back, ready for another blow, and George's grip was weakening.

'GIRL!' shouted the Queen. She was running towards them, also too far away to be able to help in time.

And then she stopped.

Edie stared in shock.

The Queen cocked her arm and threw her spear. It flew through the air and landed a yard in front of her.

'GIRL!!' roared the Queen. 'You . . .!!'

And Edie understood and was moving before the Queen got to the next word. She ripped the spear from the ground, reversed her grip as she spun on her heels, and as the gargoyle broke George's grasp and snarled in victory before slamming his head to pulp and oblivion . . .

. . . Edie struck.

The bronze spear entered under the monster's jaw and came out the back of its head, effectively stapling its mouth shut as she continued her forward momentum, vaulting over it, snapping its neck backwards and ripping it off George. It lashed out a savage back-kick with a sickle-sharp talon, but she twisted out of the way without letting go of the spear. She gritted her teeth and used all her strength to jerk it even further backwards.

The taint's head snapped off with a sharp cracking noise, and its body twitched and was still.

She looked down into George's eyes, still wide in surprise.

'That,' she said with a dark and somehow terrible smile, 'felt good.'

Inside herself the ache of hoping against hope was suddenly a little less painful.

15

ANTEROS

The Old Soldier and the Young Soldier wasted no time in telling the other spits what had happened to them and all about the Ice Murk within the City. There was a shocked silence at the fate of the Duke. And then the silence was shattered by a spasm of coughing which made them all look down to where Edie and George crouched on either side of the Bow Boy who lay in the snow, unmistakably broken.

His bare torso was heaving for every breath, each of which looked more painful than the previous one. A head-dress like a wreath made of feathers lay at his side. The Gunner bent and picked it up.

'You know who he is?' he said.

'Cupid,' said Edie.

'Eros,' said George.

'Same thing,' said Edie. 'Poncier name.'

'You're both wrong,' said the Queen. 'Mind you, so is everybody. He is not Eros. He is Anteros, his brother. The opposite of Cupid. Cupid is god of the loved. Anteros is god of people whose love is not returned. He is the god of the unloved.'

'He doesn't look good,' said George.

The Bow Boy opened his eyes. His normally handsome face was stretched tight with pain and fright. His words came out ragged and thin with desperation.

'Nothing good . . . nothing good going to be safe, not safe or good ever now . . .'

'What's he saying?' said the Officer.

'Darkness walks again,' coughed the boy. 'Darkness is calling.'

He coughed some more and got his breath, his eyes rolling upwards to look at Edie. She smoothed his hair. He closed his eyes. She saw George looking at her.

'Darkness is calling,' she said. 'That doesn't sound great.'

'Not unless you're a Goth,' he said, trying to find a smile.

'Goths,' she snorted quietly. 'They don't know the first thing.'

The boy's eyes opened.

'I'm broken,' he whispered.

'Get you back on your plinth, by turn o' day you'll be right as rain,' said the Gunner cheerily.

Edie felt a tremor go through the boy.

'What happened?' she said softly.

When the boy spoke, he stared straight up into the sky, as if the blank clouds above were somehow carrying a projection of the past that only he could see. His voice was so thin and ragged that every now and then it just wasn't there, as if a hole had been worn in it.

'It was a normal midnight. The lights were on, the people were out. The cars and taxis were all going past like usual . . . then it struck thirteen and . . .'

'And everything stopped. And the people disappeared,' filled in Edie.

He nodded and licked his lips as if he was parched. George scooped snow into a ball and held it to his mouth. He swallowed some and smiled thanks.

'Nothing happened. Anywhere. I've never seen anything like that before. So I just watched, and I waited . . . and it was all quiet and still, and the snow started to fall. It was . . .' He smiled again. 'It was . . .'

'Nice?' guessed Edie.

He shook his head.

'It was peaceful. It's never peaceful in the Circus. There's always noise and people and something happening, hurrying or shouting or . . .' He coughed. George offered him more snow but he shook his head.

'It was quiet. And the neon lights looked so . . . they never look pretty, not to me, just bright and flashing, but in the snow, in the silence with no people . . . just for a moment it was lovely.'

He smiled at the image only he could see.

Then his face dropped.

'Until it started.'

'What started?' asked George.

'The calling. The Darkness calling. Not like a noise, not exactly, more than a noise. A pull.'

'What kind of pull?' asked Edie.

'Just like a word you can't hear that gets inside your head and stops all your other thoughts and words. Just a word . . . just "COME".'

'Come?' said George. 'Come where?'

'Just "COME". But I knew if I started flying I'd know where to go. It was like a magnet, pulling me to the east. To the Darkness in the east. And then they started flying overhead . . .'

'The gargoyles?' said Edie.

'Taints. All the winged taints. They all must have heard it too. I saw them flying past.' He looked at the other statues. 'You felt it too, yes, the pull?'

The statues looked embarrassed. George and Edie both noticed.

'No,' said the Gunner. 'No. We didn't feel it.'

'Ah,' whispered the boy. 'I see. I always wondered . . .'

He was shaken by another spasm of coughing. The Gunner leant in and put his winged wreath gently back on his head.

'Well, you know now, don't you?'

The boy nodded. A tear rolled out of his eye.

'What does he—' started George.

The Gunner cut him off.

'Later. He ain't got much more in him, and this is important.' He turned to look down at the boy.

'Two taints came back. This morning. Those two . . .'

The memory seemed to trigger a panic attack. He started hyperventilating. The Gunner put a big hand on his chest and rubbed it like a man calming a horse.

'S'all right. Why did they come back?'

The boy's eyes closed.

'To punish me,' he breathed. 'The Darkness punishes everything.'

'They attacked you because you wouldn't answer the Darkness's call?' said George.

The boy nodded, eyes bright.

'I did hear the call. But I stayed. I just knew it was not for me. Not for who I *really* am . . . I'm not one of them, you see?'

'No,' said the Gunner quietly, keeping his wide hand on the heaving chest of the boy. 'No, son. You're one of us.'

And the boy began to smile and then his chest stopped moving and his eyes rolled back in his head as his leg kicked a couple of times.

And then he was gone.

'Right,' snapped the Gunner, rising to his feet in

one decisive move. He pointed at the two soldiers. 'You two, bearer party, put him back on his plinth, keep your eyes peeled, meet us at the Sphinxes, double time. Move now.'

'Why do we—' began the Young Soldier.

'It's not a debate, it's an order. Stow it and catch hold of his legs,' snapped the Old Soldier, stashing his pipe in his breast-pocket and slinging his rifle across his back. He bent and took hold of the Bow Boy's shoulders and lifted. His companion took the legs and they moved away.

'Let's crack on. We're burning daylight,' said the Gunner, and led the rest of them off at a trot.

Spout lofted off a distant tree from where he had been keeping an eye on the sky and flapped after them.

'What was that all about?' said George, trying to keep up.

'The Darkness is calling the taints to itself,' said the Queen.

'Not that,' said Edie. 'We get that the Darkness is a bad thing. He meant the other thing . . .'

'The "now you know" thing you said to him. To the Bow Boy. About not being able to hear the call or being able . . .' agreed George. 'What was that about?'

'He's human shaped, but he's not a real person,' said the Gunner. 'There's spits and taints and then there's the ones in between. We're spits, because we're made to be real people, right? Taints is made to be frightening imaginary creatures, yeah? And in between . . .'

'In between there are the ones we're not sure of,' finished the Queen.

'You're not sure because they're not sure,' said Edie, suddenly having a memory flash of Little Tragedy, betraying her with sadness in his eyes.

97

'Yeah,' said the Gunner, turning to look at her with a keen eye. 'The Bow Boy didn't know. But he heard the call. And he refused it. And so now I guess we all know which side of the line he is. And what it cost him to find out.'

'I think we're all going to be asked to pay that price, sooner or later,' said the Queen. 'I think this Darkness would claim us all.'

16

THE GATHERING

As the strange party worked its way through the snow-choked streets towards the Embankment, they discussed what the Old Soldier had told them of what he had seen within the City and the Murk in the night. The Queen and the Gunner were particularly horrified at the death of the Duke. The Officer stayed silent and trudged ahead of the group, stamping a path that the children could follow in the hip-high snow.

'I knew there was Darkness in the London Stone,' said Edie. 'I felt its pull worse than any stone I've glinted, even though I never even touched it.'

The silence that followed was broken only by the clump and squeak of their feet compacting the fresh fallen snow as they walked on.

'Wonder what would have happened if—' began George.

She turned and interrupted him with a snort.

'If I HAD touched it? If I had touched it I'd have, I probably would have, you know . . .'

'. . . lost her mind,' finished the Queen. 'The Darkness pent in the Stone would have burnt out her sanity and cored her mind like an empty husk. She'd have been left a haunted, dribbling idiot.'

George and Edie watched her cloak swirl around her shoulders as she turned back to plough ahead of them in the Officer's wake.

'Nice,' said Edie.

'Especially the dribbling bit,' agreed George, hoping for a smile. But her face was as wintry as the snow-blanketed buildings on either side of them.

'Anyway,' he went on, 'that wasn't what I was going to say. What I was going to say was I wonder what would have happened if I HAD put that broken dragon's head on the Stone.'

'You mean if you hadn't stayed because of me?' Edie said. 'You'd have gone back to your layer of London and wouldn't have remembered anything or known about any of this, would you?'

'No. It's not about you. Not always anyway,' he replied, suddenly irritated. He had woken with an itch on his upper arm, and that itch had now become a sort of dull pain, the kind you get from being punched hard on a muscle. He didn't need to look to know that the third and last twining vein of stone was again moving slowly towards his shoulder, marking the duel he had yet to fight before he was done with the Cnihtengild's challenge. He'd forgotten about it as he slept in the night, and all the unfamiliar events occurring around them had pushed it to the back of his mind. Whatever Edie's problems were, they didn't involve the fear of the Knight on his eerily hollow horse being out there somewhere, slowly riding towards a fight that George had no confidence in surviving. Then he looked over at her and saw she was looking down at her hand, which held the earring heart stone that had been her mother's. The moment she saw him looking at her she reflexively closed her hand and pocketed the stone, and there was something in the unguarded protectiveness she showed in doing it that touched him and made him remember the rollercoaster of hope and disappointment she was on.

He caught the Queen watching them both, and remembered what she had said about Edie's extra vulnerability, having been taken over the line into death and back. He felt suddenly ashamed of the irritability he'd let escape. He was tired and worried. And as annoying as Edie could be with her defensive spikiness and her willingness to fight and argue with anyone and everyone, their predicament and the icy blight that was being visited on this layer of London was not her fault.

'I didn't mean . . .' he continued, trying to make eye contact through the long sweep of dark hair she'd let fall forward, obscuring the side view of her face.

'. . . I meant that I was wondering if this is all getting worse because of *me*.'

She didn't turn her head. The only response George got was from the Raven, who was riding her far shoulder and had him fixed with its unblinking shiny black bead-eyes over the top of her head. The fact that she had acquired this supernatural companion somehow made him feel both worried and a little jealous. He couldn't put his finger on why, but the way she had instantly and easily accepted the fact that this bird chose her – as if it was nothing, as if having a Raven ride your shoulder was the most natural thing in the world – perturbed him. He didn't trust the bird. That was what it was.

'Look—' he began.

'What?' she cut in, way too fast for politeness.

'Put a sock in it, you pair of moaning Minnies,' growled the Gunner, coming up behind them and putting a great hand on their shoulders. 'It ain't the time for a competition about whose fault any of this is, but if it was, I'd say if I hadn't broke my oath and let the Walker take me, we wouldn't be in Queer Street now. So stow it, or you'll start making me feel all guilty and wobbly and then I'll be needing one of these "shrinks" of yours, and then where will we be?'

He stopped abruptly as they turned a corner on to the Embankment.

'Bleeding Nora . . .'

George and Edie stopped too. The dark obelisk of Cleopatra's Needle had been guarded by two Sphinxes the last time they had been there. Now it was girdled by a great jumbled throng: figures on horses stood out above the heads of other statues of all ages and types, bound by the one common thing which was that they were all human. It was a great gathering of the spits, and even as they approached from a distance, two things were apparent: firstly there was a debate in progress, and secondly, a ring of soldier statues at the edge of the crowd faced outwards, their backs to the debate, rifles and muskets with bayonets fixed, swords drawn, eyes watching the sky and the approaches to the Needle.

'I've never seen a gathering like this,' murmured the Queen.

'I've never heard of one. I think this is the first time so many of us have been in one place,' agreed the Officer.

'Oh well. In for a penny, in for a pound,' said the Gunner with an attempt at cheeriness, and led them onwards.

George turned to Spout.

'Better stay back here,' he said. 'In case they don't know you're one of the good guys.'

'Goog gai,' agreed Spout, and jumped up to perch on a tree in the shadows.

The rest of them walked slowly towards the jumbled

mass of spits bunched at the river's edge, ahead of them.

'I can't see the Black Friar,' muttered Edie.

'Yeah, but you can see everyone else,' said George in a voice tinged with wonder.

And the closer they got the more intense the strangeness ranged round the obelisk became. Once the eye adjusted to the fact that this seething knot of humanity was made from stone or bronze, the smaller details began to stand out: firstly their clothes were an extraordinary mishmash of ages and professions – men in armour argued with men in suits and ties, and elaborately bewigged heads bobbed next to crowns and steel helmets and bearskins and tricornes, while at the centre of one of the most vehement knots of debate a bear-like man with a great bald head atop a large shambling frame swathed in a long overcoat swapped terse words with a tight-britched figure who buzzed round him like a wasp, cutting great swathes in the air with his hands as he tried to make his point. And this was the second detail that became immediately apparent: a lot of men – and a few women – from all ages of Britain's history were gathered in this crowd, and they all appeared to be talking at once. The reason the noise level was so high was that they didn't seem to be complementing the talking by doing much listening, which only encouraged the people they were talking at to speak even louder.

It did seem as if every spit in London was here: in the water beyond the embankment wall George could even see a statue of a Boy on a Dolphin that he recognized from further down the riverbank in Chelsea, now jumping and diving in the river.

The outer ring of bayonets and blades relaxed and parted a little as they reached it. Two grey stone seamen, each armed with nothing more than sailors' knives, made a gap for them. The taller one grinned thinly.

'Gunner.'

'Jack,' smiled Gunner in greeting, and nodded at the other sailor with his oilskin coat tied round his middle with a piece of string. 'Bosun. Strange days.'

'Aye, and worse weather to come, I'd say,' said the one the Gunner had called Jack.

'Strange days and strange shipmates,' said the Bosun, nodding at George and Edie.

'Boy's a maker, the girl's a glint,' explained the Gunner, making the introductions. 'George, Edie, these matelots is mates of mine from the east end of town. Jack Tar and the Bosun. Their normal billet is Trinity Square. They're—'

George interrupted with a grin.

'Merchant Seamen. From the memorial. My dad took me to see them once, when we went to the Tower next door. He was a sculptor,' he explained. 'He liked you. I mean he liked what you were. Are. As statues.'

Memory flashed and he saw his dad on a bright spring afternoon. He had his sketch-book out and was doing a quick pencil drawing of the two statues. They had a similar square-jawed heroic quality in their making as the Gunner did, but like him they were somehow more than just idealized caricatures of heroes. They looked windswept and used to the weather in all its guises, and instead of uniforms they wore the kind of working sea-gear that real sailors assemble through years of experience. He remembered his dad commenting on the Bosun's choice of belt, for example. George pointed.

'He liked the string round your middle.'

'So do I,' grunted the Bosun. 'Keeps my trousers up.'

The Queen pushed in close behind George and Edie and peered into the hubbub surrounding the Needle.

'What's happening?'

'Jaw bloody jaw,' said Jack Tar. 'Too many kings and dukes and generals and not enough sense if you ask me. They're all used to getting their own way, see, and nobody's got a firm hand on the tiller.'

'We'll see about that,' said the Queen, nodding at the Gunner. 'What have the Sphinxes said?'

The Gunner dived into the inner throng, pushing great men to left and right as he made his way to the Needle itself. The Queen looked at Jack Tar, waiting for an answer.

'There's a problem with the Sphinxes,' he said. 'First off she says we're asking the wrong questions and she'll answer the right people when they ask it. And secondly . . .'

'. . . There's only one Sphinx,' said Edie, looking round for the second one. George saw that she was right. They were one Sphinx short.

'Yeah,' he said, suddenly wanting to be close to the Gunner as more and more eyes nearby began to notice them and stop talking. 'Come on . . .'

The Officer pushed a way through the crowd for them. The noise of chatter was still very loud and sustained, and every now and then voices rose in anger and turned into bad-tempered shouting.

A king wearing chain mail blocked their way as he stood in the stirrups of his charger and started jabbing his sword in emphasis at another lavishly wigged nobleman on a smaller horse.

'Oi!' said Edie, stepping back sharply to avoid being trampled by the charger. She stuck two fingers in her mouth and whistled shrilly to get the rider's attention. 'Coming through, mind your back . . .'

'That's Richard the Lionheart,' said George, recognizing the statue from the edge of Parliament Square.

The king spun on his horse and glared down at them with such an intensity that the first thing you noticed was 'angry' and only then 'king'.

'I know very well who I am, boy, but who, *pardieu*, are you, girl, to be whistling at a king as if he was some hound to be called to kennel at your whim?' he bellowed, raising his sword.

Two loud gunshots cracked through the clamour and reduced it to instant silence as all the statues tensed and looked round for where they had come from.

They saw the Gunner standing at the shoulder of the Sphinx, who snarled and shook her head as if disturbed by the explosions from the smoking pistol the Gunner was pointing into the sky.

She slowly got to her feet and towered over the crowd, stretching like the giant cat that she partly was. And then she looked straight at George and Edie.

'They are the *right* people,' she purred in a slow dreamy voice.

17

THE RIDDLE
OF THE SPHINXES

At the words of the Sphinx, perhaps underlined by the warning glare from the Gunner at its side, the Lionheart backed his horse up with an ill-natured dig of his stirrups, and the crowd parted for George and Edie. They felt the weight of every eye in that immense, strange crowd turn and strain for a look at them as they moved forward on to the plinth next to the Sphinx. Edie looked at the side of the great lion's body before she looked into the finely modelled human face she bore beneath its elaborate Egyptian head-dress. She saw there were no shrapnel holes punched in the animal's flanks.

'It's the nice one,' she breathed to George.

'I hope so,' he answered. 'Because I wouldn't like to meet one angrier-looking than this.'

The Sphinx's normally impassive face was twisted into a very dark and unpromising scowl.

'I am not angry at you, child. I am out of sorts.'

'Where's your sister?' asked Edie.

The Gunner cleared his throat.

'Er, you remember what the Bow Boy said about the call, and how he heard it but didn't go, and now we know which side of the line he's on . . .?'

'Yes, and I remember you saying the Sphinxes were somewhere between spits and taints, half animal, half human,' said George. 'So I suppose . . .'

'We both heard the call. Only one of us answered it. I have always seen the human side of things but my sister had become too taintish of late,' said the Sphinx, her tail lashing behind her in a slow flick of irritation. 'I did not think we should go. I did not like the call. I do not like being told what to do. I do not like that whatever is doing the calling thinks it can call us to heel as if we were a common house pet. We are not dogs, after all.'

The Sphinx arched her back in a decidedly feline stretch, and then lay back down in her usual position. Her eyes remained on George and Edie.

'What is calling?' said George.

'A voice from the Outer Dark. From the Darkness before time. Something unknowably powerful and dangerous. Someone let it through.'

The Sphinx was not looking at George as she said this, but sometimes you can not look at something just as pointedly as you can look at it. And he knew she was talking about him as surely as he knew the great icy blast that had shot past them as they returned to this layer of London from the Frost Fair was the source of that dark voice. A voice he had let into this world.

'How do you know?' said Edie, staring at the Sphinx with a gaze as unblinking as the Raven's on her shoulder. 'If it's unknowable, how do you know? It doesn't make sense.'

'Ah, little rainsplash, there you are,' sighed the Sphinx. 'And still asking such interesting questions.'

George could tell how much Edie disliked being called a rainsplash by how fiercely she jutted her jaw at the giant cat with the human face.

'And you're still giving such unhelpful answers,' she retorted. 'How can you know all this if it's unknowable?'

'Because it has happened before: the old Darkness imprisoned in the London Stone came from the same place long, long ago. It is only the strength and exact nature of the power of this new Darkness that is unknowable, not the fact of its existence,' replied the Sphinx. 'This kinship explains why the two Darknesses are working together and combining their strengths.'

'How—' began Edie, but George stepped in front of her. He knew she irritated and perturbed the Sphinx in a way he didn't, and while she seemed to be answering questions without needing a riddle answered first he didn't want her provoked.

'What has happened?' he said quickly. 'Exactly?'

'The new power comes from the Outer Darkness, a dimension beyond and without time. Coming here, it has sent a shock through all the layers which has cut this layer of London off from the present, or the future.'

'That's stupid,' said Edie. 'We're in the present, aren't we, I mean this is all happening . . .'

'It's not the real present. It's just now,' explained the Sphinx. 'The real present is a living thing through which time flows from the past into the future, like blood through a vein, keeping the body of the universe alive. This "Now" we are trapped in is disconnected from that Present and can not flow forward into the Future. And like a vein through which the blood cannot pass, it will eventually die.'

There was a great rumble of shock at this news, and so many of the spits started shouting questions at once that it was impossible to distinguish any one voice or make sense of it.

Another shot cracked flatly into the air and silence again returned abruptly, this time everyone turning to see the Officer pushing through the crowd with the Queen. Once more their way took them past the Lionheart, and once more he bridled as one of the Queen's daughters pushed at his horse in the tightly packed crowd to make a space for her mother to pass through.

'Unhand my horse!' snarled the Lionheart, as he jerked his reins and made as if to cuff the daughter, only pulling the blow as he realized it was in fact a girl he was about to hit.

In an instant the Queen had her spear-point parked dangerously under his chin.

'She whom you would strike is of as royal a blood as you, boy, and I, her mother, was Queen and conqueror centuries before you were whelped! Bar our way one moment longer and I shall take your sword and thrash you with it until you bawl like the great baby you show yourself to be!'

Regal eye met regal eye, and in very short measure the male eye blinked first. The Queen removed her spear-tip from its uncomfortable proximity to the Lionhearted Adam's apple and leapt up on to the dais next to the Sphinx.

A faint growing rumble of discontent began to well up again, and she quelled it with a look as she started to speak.

'Of everyone here I am the only one ever to have destroyed this city, and having washed my anger in blood once I shall not see it happen again. To the victors may go the spoils, but only a destroyer knows the true cost of the destruction they have wrought, and only then too late.'

In the crowd a few of the generals nodded, including two who looked like other Dukes of Wellington.

'She's right,' said a spit in a World War Two

RAF uniform, a statue that George remembered Edie commenting on a lifetime ago as they had begun their quest, by St Clement Danes. She had said he had a lot of death about him.

'What has happened before shall not happen again!' continued the Queen, turning to the Sphinx with a great flourish of her cape. 'What can we do?'

There was a small groan from the crowd. The Sphinx shook her head from side to side.

'That is the wrong question.'

'We already asked her that,' said a voice from the crowd.

The Queen looked unexpectedly deflated to see her grand gesture go so flat so quickly.

'Been like that all morning,' said the RAF Officer to the Gunner. 'Too many kings and generals, not enough bloody common sense.'

'Well, that's easy for you to say, Bomber,' retorted a periwigged figure, waggling an enraged sceptre at him. And with that the crowd of spits started arguing and bickering amongst themselves louder than before.

George found Edie looking at him, something between despair and disgust spreading across her face. The Raven was gone, he noticed.

'I know,' he answered.

And in a sick lurch of his stomach he realized of course that he did. He knew exactly what to do. He knew exactly what the question was, and he knew that there was only one person who could ask it. So amid all the argumentative din rising round them like an angry sea, he turned and put his hand out to steady himself against the Sphinx's great fore-paw.

He looked up into her eyes, to find they were waiting

for him. He couldn't say whether the smile in them was friendly or hostile, but that, he supposed, was one of the things that just went with being a fabled enigma. He cleared his throat and spoke quietly but steadily.

'What can *I* do?'

The Sphinx jerked to her feet. The sudden movement in the huge spit was enough to get the attention of the crowd, and George sensed once again that all eyes were on his back.

'That,' said the Sphinx with a purr like honey, 'is exactly the right question.'

18

THE QUEEN OF TIME

Oxford Street was if anything blocked more solidly by snow than the roads the Clocker and Dictionary had taken to get there. The Clocker led the way, his long legs high-stepping through the drifts, while Dictionary seemed to barge rather than walk through them, yet he puffed and grumbled his way forward with such doggedness that he kept pace with his taller friend.

The Clocker turned to check on his progress.

'Snow a particular hindrance. Perhaps a rest before continuing?'

'Nonsense. It may be a particularly discommodious and unobliging oberration, but I'll warrant the unfortunate Highland denizens of the Far North endure worse without complaint. And what a Scotsman may do with composure, I shall not be baulked by . . .'

And with that he ploughed ahead with such determination that the Clocker had to stretch his legs to keep level with him.

'Ah,' he said. 'Oberration?'

Dictionary allowed a momentary smile to betray his satisfaction at the Clocker's question.

'Oberration, sir, is a much underused word meaning "perambulation" or, in more common speech, "walking about". It is both an activity and a word I am very fond of, though I will admit this unnatural snowfall does make the current exercise of the activity

113

less than normally joyful to me.'

'Many thanks,' panted the Clocker as he forged slightly ahead through a deepening drift of snow that had blown across the street and stacked up next to a long bus. 'Your acquaintance both a pleasure and an education. Most obliged.'

'Pleasure all mine, sir,' puffed Dictionary, looking up at the façade of the great department store they were approaching on the north side of the street. 'And almost as great a pleasure to note we have arrived.'

The Clocker looked directly up at the canopy jutting over the main entrance to the block-long shop.

'My lady,' he said simply, and as far as the snow permitted, executed a graceful bow.

'Clocker,' replied a gentle, golden voice with a barely audible undertone that sounded like a myriad of tiny bells chiming through it. 'I wondered when you would come. I wondered when you would notice . . .'

'When clocks struck thirteen, lady.'

The Queen of Time stepped out from beneath the great golden globe above her head, a globe that was also a clock with both its hands pointing motionlessly straight up towards the due north of midnight.

She was a golden angel, her beautiful face framed with thick hair topped with a diadem inlaid with blue enamel. Her outspread wings steadied her as she lifted the knee of her gown so that she could kneel on the edge of the canopy and look down at the Clocker more closely. The gown itself, and the girdle that snugged it to her waist, were also inlaid with a startlingly deep blue enamel, and the gold from which she was made of seemed to intensify and shine from her eyes like sunlight.

'Time stopped when the clocks struck thirteen, and yet only now do you come to me,' she murmured. 'But is it not your curse to keep an eye on the time, as it is my joy to see it wing its way from day to day?'

'It is, my lady. Or rather, was,' nodded the Clocker, and he lifted the black lens over his clock-eye and revealed the clock-face, and the fact that it no longer pulsed. Dictionary noted that the blue of the Clocker's eye was exactly the same blue as that counterpointing the gold clothes and wings of the Queen of Time.

'Believe curse was to keep eye on time until time stopped.' He pointed at the clock above her head.

'Believe time now stopped.'

She looked hard at his eye, and then smiled. The smile seemed to light up the grey and white street as she took a small step off the canopy and descended to the Clocker's side in a delicate swirl of her wings.

'I believe it has, my old friend. And I am very happy that the one good thing that seems to have come of it is that you no longer toil under your curse. You have not failed in your duty . . .'

He smiled and bobbed his head in embarrassment.

'I, on the other hand, seem to have failed in mine . . .' she went on, face darkening as her head bowed in something like shame.

Dictionary found the sight suddenly unbearable, and pushed off his lamppost.

'No, dear lady, no indeed . . . we are in the grip of unparalleled and unanticipated circumstance, and one cannot be blamed for that.'

'Yet I am the Queen of Time, and Time is out of joint,' she sighed. 'And if I am Queen of a broken thing, then it is my job to mend it. Otherwise I am a fair-weather

Queen, am I not? A mere ornament. My duty is to mind the Clock of the World here above me.'

She looked up at the golden globe set above her gilded plinth.

'I sense a great disruption in the east, but have been loath to leave the Clock unattended in case time should restart in my absence, and for fear that some of the taints I have observed flying towards the City should return and interfere with it.'

'That would not be good,' concurred the Clocker.

'Indeed not,' she said. 'You have always understood Time as I do. As I have watched it, you have monitored its unbroken passage through the ticking watch-mills of the city's clockwork. Though I must admit there is a part of me that fears what I may find in the east, and I wonder if I make too much of my guardianship of the clock in order to excuse a reluctance to go and confront it out of cowardice . . .'

'Nonsense!' erupted Dictionary. 'I've never seen anything or anyone less possessed of the cowardly vices. Why the very—'

Clocker interrupted him.

'Not coward. Prudent. We also have seen taints flying east. Fault mine. Should have gone east myself, reported back to you. Delay intolerable, cowardice mine. Apologies. Will go immediately.'

'But you are no longer cursed to watch Time . . .' began the Queen.

'But am aware time out of joint is fatal to all of us here in end. Shall report back.' He turned and started to head off towards Oxford Circus.

'No,' said the Queen in a harder voice. 'You shall stay and watch the Clock of the World, for if time

116

starts and the Clock does not run fast to catch it up again, it will be a disruption as great as the present one afflicting us.'

'But . . .' he said.

'No. No buts, my friend. My wings will get me there faster, and if there is anything to be done, it's better it's done without delay. You can aid me by watching the Clock.'

The Clocker looked at Dictionary and then nodded, accepting the rightness of her words.

'If I may,' said the Queen, and put her arms round him, launching into the air with a mighty downbeat of her wings. She flew up to the canopy and placed him on it next to two reclining maidens who smiled at him.

'They do not talk,' she smiled. 'They are the silent witnesses to Time's passage. But they have sharp eyes.'

And with that she lofted into the sky and flapped east. Somewhere ahead of her there was a low rumble like distant thunder. She didn't falter, but flew towards the noise in a straight line, disappearing quickly from view over the snow-topped roofs of the buildings on the far side of the street.

'Clocker,' said a gruff voice from below. 'I have a grave foreboding about this. I like it not a jot or a tittle that the lady goes into harm's way unescorted.'

'Agree. But in press of circumstance, sometimes all ways forward perilous,' said the Clocker. 'Lady knows time like no other.'

'Mayhap you're correct,' snorted Dictionary. 'But she knows nothing of a martial or self-defensive nature, and unless I misguess our situation, some power with dark intent has cried havoc and let slip the dogs of war.'

Another far-off rumble of thunder broke over the buildings towards the City.

'Thunder in the snow, Clocker. A never-heard-of thing. It bodes ill.'

19

THE WRONG
QUESTION

The rumbling squabble of the crowd dropped away as all eyes turned to look at George and the Sphinx.

'What was the right question?' shouted a voice from the back of the crowd.

'Couldn't hear,' answered another. 'But the boy asked it.'

'What did you ask, boy?' bellowed the first voice.

'He asked what HE could do about it,' rumbled a new yet familiar voice from behind them, a voice with a deep purring undertone.

The other Sphinx walked across the street, her tail swaying lazily as she clove a path straight through the crowd of spits. A thin covering of hoar-frost had turned her normally dark bronze body silvery grey, one effect of which was that the shrapnel holes in its side stood out more obviously than before.

George felt Edie step closer to him.

'That's the nasty one,' she breathed quietly.

The silvery Sphinx looked at her sharply, as if she could hear everything she said.

The bronze Sphinx stood and took a step forward.

'And where have you been, sister?'

'I have been where I have been and seen what I have seen,' murmured the other.

'You answered the call.'

'I heard the call as you did. I did not *answer* it. I went to see what made it. I went to see how the balance has shifted. I went to see the thing that has come.'

'And why was that?' said the Gunner. George noticed that his hand rested very casually on the holster he kept under his cape. And when he saw that, he then noticed that the Officer had his hand on his gun, and that several of the other soldier spits were responding to slight movements of the Officer's head and casually moving round the silvery Sphinx with their weapons ready.

'Because a cat may look at a king,' smiled the Sphinx. And for the first time George noticed that the Sphinxes' human heads were only human on the outside: inside their mouths the sharp incisors and fangs were much more in keeping with their lion bodies. Perhaps he hadn't noticed it before because the Sphinxes hadn't done much smiling, only enigmatic grinning with their mouths closed.

'What's it got to smile about?' whispered Edie, as if she could read his thoughts.

'Perhaps you like this new "king" that you have seen,' said the bronze Sphinx at their side. 'Perhaps this new power appeals to your . . . anger.'

The other Sphinx shook its head slowly.

'My anger is at men and what they have done to me, the holes they have blown in my perfect body, the contempt with which they walk past us day in and day out without realizing our ancient place in their history and their lives. And as you see, there are no men here, none anywhere in the city. Just these children. Not men at all.'

Edie started to say something, then appeared to bite her tongue as she thought better of it. The Sphinx raised an eyebrow at her and then smoothly continued.

'I went into the night City because I was curious.'

'Yeah well, curiosity and cats ain't a great combination, are they?' said the Gunner.

The creature's face turned on him, the smile thinning out into a narrow line of icy malice.

'It is hardly time for clever word-games, Gunner. I would have thought you would all have wanted to know what the night held and what manner of things have happened in the City.'

She shrugged past him, stepping back on to her plinth. She stretched and lay down, as if unconcerned by the crowd staring at her.

'What did you see then, sister?'

She opened one eye, yawned, and then closed it again. She spoke sleepily, as if what she was describing was obvious, as if having to remember and then explain it was slightly annoying and beneath her dignity.

'I saw all the taints flocking to a great high tower in the east. I saw a new Darkness atop that tower, a power that has taken an icy shape and brought this snow to fill the city, and I heard its call as you did. I saw the great citadel in the sky it has made for itself, ringed by flying taints at the top, guarded at its foot by a horde of walking taints that could swallow this gathering in a heartbeat. I saw the London Stone cracked open and I saw the old Darkness walking again. I have seen statues shattered and destroyed in the city, spits that shall not walk again unless this war is won by turn o' day.'

'What war?' said George. The Sphinx yawned again.

'The war that we have always avoided. The war we have always feared. The war between the spits and the taints.'

Her eyes snapped open, and George found himself

caught in their very awake, very unsleepy gaze, like a deer in the headlights.

'The war YOU started,' she said with icy satisfaction.

George actually stepped half a pace back and gasped as the words hit him like a gut-punch.

'He didn't start this,' exploded Edie from George's side. 'Spits and taints have always been fighting. We've seen that, you know that . . .'

'Spits and taints have always been hostile to each other, but it has been a balanced hostility. The boy has thrown the balance out.'

'Rubbish,' said the Gunner. 'You just said, it's this new Darkness that's come here that's got things stirred up!'

'Would the Dark power have come here had the boy not used his making hand to mar, to break the carving at the museum? Make no mistake, it is his fault.'

George felt a kind of growing vertigo as all the spits looked at him, their eyes filling with the growing realization of the truth that had been slowly metabolizing inside him all morning.

Of course he was to blame.

'That's a load of tosh,' said the Gunner decisively. 'It ain't his fault. He didn't know he was a maker, he still don't really know what it means, and he can't be guilty if he didn't know what he was doing.'

'And he's done more than any of you to try and make it right!' exclaimed Edie from George's side. 'So don't look at him like that or I'll come down there and glint every last one of you!'

'The trouble is,' said the silvery Sphinx with a calm smile, 'that everything he has done to make it right led to the moment the door between the Outer Darkness and this world was opened and the new power got in.'

'No,' said Edie.

'Yes,' said George, stepping up to the silvery Sphinx. 'You're right. So what do I do about it?'

'Is that your question?' she purred in a familiar way that made all the hairs in George's body feel like they'd just been stroked in the wrong direction.

'Careful,' said the Gunner.

George thought if there was a better question, he didn't have it in his head.

'Yes,' he said. 'That's my question.'

'Then this,' murmured the Sphinx, hiding her cat's teeth behind a tight-lipped half-smile, 'is my riddle.'

'Sister,' said the other Sphinx flatly.

'It is our way. For the important questions, an answer for a riddle.'

'Right, and a riddle for an answer often as not,' said the Gunner.

'It's not time for games, is it?' interrupted George, looking up into the Sphinx's eyes. 'You said it. I'll answer your riddle, but only if you give me a straight answer.'

'Straight as a die. Straight as an arrow. Straight as the road from cradle to grave,' it replied. 'The riddle is—'

The other Sphinx cut in before she could begin.

'I am not amused when confused with a stony stare,
With a lifeless head but lively hair,
Wise men twist their faces from me,
Or stand frozen in their track
My nemesis outfaced me by the turning of his back.'

'Too easy,' hissed the Icy Sphinx. 'Too, too easy.'

'It doesn't have to be hard,' said her sister. 'It just has to be a riddle.'

123

They stared angrily at each other. The crowd of spits began to rumble and discuss the riddle amongst themselves. George looked at Edie, who returned the look expectantly.

'You did it last time,' she said encouragingly.

He tried to slow his mind. He had done it last time, but somehow the stakes hadn't been as high. Or maybe they had, but he just hadn't known enough to be as panicked as he felt inside.

'Calm down,' said the Gunner, leaning in. 'And breathe slower.'

Only then did he realize he had started to hyperventilate. He closed his eyes. Last time he had thought of his dad and the crosswords he had loved to waste time poring over with a stub of pencil. He thought of how his dad had explained the way things worked in cryptic clues.

This riddle was a cryptic clue, full of hooks and minefields he was sure: words that didn't mean what you thought they meant, hidden in clues that had other clues in them. Or words that meant two things at once. And no wasted words, not in the clues. All there for a reason. He thought about what the Sphinx had said. 'Not amused,' he thought and blurted the first thought that came to his head.

'Victoria. Queen Victoria.'

She had not been amused. She was famous for it. He looked at the Sphinxes.

'Is that your answer?' said the icy one.

'No,' said George. He didn't know why, but he knew he'd spoken too fast and hadn't checked it with the rest of the clue. He closed his eyes and let the words of the clue wash through his mind again, seeing which ones flashed extra bits of meaning at him, like someone panning for gold. 'Not amused . . . confused . . . stony stare.' Why was everything about stones? Well, he supposed it had to be. 'Lost my head . . . lively hair?' What was that about? Why talk about lively hair? It was an odd thing to say. And losing your head meant losing control, or falling in love, or going doolally . . .

'He answered Victoria,' hissed the Icy Sphinx. 'He got it wrong.'

'SHHH,' hissed back her sister. 'He said that wasn't the answer.'

Maybe it was the hissing, but something unlocked in George's head and he saw the answer in a oner.

'Snakes,' he said.

'What?' said Edie.

He opened his eyes. Even though he hadn't said the answer he could see the Icy Sphinx's eyes cloud with disappointment and he knew she knew that he had it now.

'Lively hair – snakes, who had snakes for hair?'

'I don't know,' said Edie. 'Oh. Stony stare, wossname . . .'

'Exactly,' he said. 'Not amused but confused.'

George felt a kind of savage elation; often things in riddles didn't mean what they said, but sometimes they meant exactly what they said and just looked like they meant something else. And in this case 'lost her head' meant exactly what it said.

'Have you got it or haven't you?' asked the Gunner. 'Because you might as well be talking Greek, far as I'm concerned.'

'Bang on the money,' said George triumphantly, silently thanking his dad for reading him the Greek

125

myths when he was a little kid. 'Greek it is. Confuse "amused" meaning jumble up the letters in "amused" and you get what?'

'A headache?' said the Gunner.

'Medusa,' said Edie.

'Medusa: hair made of living snakes, turn you to stone with her stare. Had her head cut clean off by the Greek hero Perseus, and carried away in a bag,' finished George, grinning at the Sphinxes. One turned away in disgust, but the kind one nodded calmly.

'You are right. It's a good answer.' And here the Sphinx did something strange. She leant low and spoke quietly. 'And you'd do well not to forget it.'

'OK,' said George, baffled again. The Sphinx meant something, but he had no idea what.

'Your question was what you can do,' continued the Sphinx. 'Am I right?'

George nodded. The Sphinx's eyes rolled back a little in her head and she answered in a kind of sing-song monotone that George remembered from the first time she had answered his question what seemed a lifetime ago.

'There are two things to do, and by you they must be done, and in this order. First the old Darkness must be defeated and penned back in the Stone from which it came. Only you can do this, for only a maker can mend the rent in the Stone through which it escaped. Only once the old Darkness is vanquished can you have a chance of fighting the Ice Devil back into the Black Mirrors and putting time back in joint.'

'How can we fight an Ice Devil?' said George, hopelessness suddenly rising round him like a cold dark tide.

'Take the way of the dragon, and by the Knight of Wood who lies all alone you may find kin you can call your own. Find your kin, and within the hour the dead stone's tongue will be in your power,' intoned the Sphinx.

'That's it? I don't understand. What then?' asked George.

'You ask the dead stone,' shrugged the Sphinx, as if it was obvious.

'What stone?' exploded George, tipped over the edge by the cat-like disinterest. 'What dead stone? There's always a stone!'

'As there is always a George, and there is always a dragon,' purred the Sphinx. 'That is how the world and all that is stays in balance. The dead stone is a Stone Corpse. And now I think I have given more than enough answers . . .'

'Wait, what's the Black Mirror?' he gabbled desperately, beginning to lose the thread in all this talk of Ice Devils and Darknesses and dead stones and Black Mirrors.

'I know about the Black Mirror,' said Edie, 'I just don't know where it is . . .'

'Great,' said George. And then a bigger thought hit him and put the next question he was going to ask about the mirror clean out of his mind.

'What if we put time back in joint first,' he blurted, the image of the Clocker and Dictionary pegging off through the hip-high snow to find the Queen of Time and try to do that very thing flashing into his mind's eye. 'What if the Queen of Time succeeds in restarting time?'

'To attack the Ice Devil while its brother Darkness joins forces with it is suicide. You must halve their power, and finishing your business with the old Darkness must happen first.'

'What do you mean finish . . .?' started Edie. 'He hasn't . . .'

'He chose the Hard Way,' said a light airy voice that came tinkling out of the sky above them.

George looked up and saw a golden girl holding on to the sheer sides of Cleopatra's Needle above them.

'Ariel,' he said.

'Hello, boy,' she smiled, and dropped so delicately to the ground between him and Edie that she didn't seem to disturb the snow as she landed.

'Who's she?' asked Edie, looking at him over a golden shoulder that was draped – just about – with a very filmy piece of equally gold cloth that seemed to be held on to her body with nothing more than an invisible wind that blew her hair back around her face at the same time.

'I am a Minister of Fate as surely as you are a glint,' said the golden girl. 'And the boy has unfinished business. He has a third and final duel to fight . . .'

'Yeah,' said George, 'but that's with the Cnihtengild, not the old Darkness that was in the London Stone.'

Ariel laughed.

'They are now one and the same: the Hollow Knight is hollow no more. The Darkness has taken him. He rides the Night Mare within the shell that was empty, and the duel that must be fought, the duel neither on land nor water, must be resolved first. Darkness has a prior claim on you, a claim underwritten and guaranteed by fate. And even you, boy, even a maker cannot mis-make the fabric that fate has woven around you.'

George was painfully aware that every spit around the Needle was looking at him.

'OK.' He swallowed, looking back at the Icy Sphinx. 'But you're saying that if the Queen of Time tries to restart time without the old Darkness being dealt with . . .'

'She will fail. She will die.'

Edie looked at George. At the Gunner. At the Queen.

'But they've already gone to try . . .' she said.

'Then it's a suicide mission,' interjected the bronze Sphinx. 'You must stop them.'

'But we can't get to them in time,' said the Gunner, 'not pushing through this bloody snow.'

George looked at Spout, who was perched on the railings across the street, being looked at with great suspicion by the soldiers guarding the outer ring.

'I can,' he said.

'But you have a duel to fight, boy,' exclaimed Ariel, as if he'd suggested something shockingly improper.

'If the people who can start time again are killed because they try before I've fought that duel, then it's pointless anyway, isn't it?' he snapped. Anger was what he found to get him through the wave of fear that was threatening to rise up and engulf him.

'I'll stop them jumping the gun, then I'll get to the bloody duel.'

'But how can you get there in time?' asked Edie.

George looked at Ariel, remembering his experiences in the London sky with her. His stomach rebelled at the memory, but it was the memory that gave him the idea he was now committed to.

'I can fly there,' he said.

'I will not help you, boy. I cannot help you avoid or delay your fate,' said Ariel.

'I know,' he said grimly. He turned to Edie and the

Gunner and the Queen. 'You've got one more riddle and one more question with the other Sphinx. See if you can find out how to put the Ice Devil back in his box. I'll be back as soon as I can.'

And he stuck his two fingers in his mouth and blew hard, a piercing whistle that he had almost forgotten he knew how to do. His dad had taught him, one long summer's evening, sitting in a field, watching the pigeons flock as they headed to their roosts.

Spout lofted off the bridge above them. Soldiers raised their weapons.

'He's with me!' shouted George. 'He's going to fly me to warn the others.'

Spout swooped low over the heads of the assembled spits. He neatly grabbed George's outstretched hand and swung him up on to his back as he punched air beneath his wide stone wings, climbing into the lowering sky above.

'He's got guts, the boy,' said the Gunner.

'Yes,' said the Queen, watching George disappearing over the rooftops. 'The kind that get you killed.'

20

DOGFIGHT

The last time George had flown with Spout, he had been gripped in the gargoyle's talons, both the right and the wrong way up. Even being held the right way up had been uncomfortable, so this time George found their new way of flying infinitely more comfortable and even exhilarating. The only discomfort came from the ridges along Spout's spine, but as long as he sat between them and didn't slip, he was fine. Being perched between the two stolidly flapping wings, with an unobstructed forward view over the creature's head gave him a feeling of the power and majesty of flight itself.

Spout still flew as if every next beat of his wings might suddenly fail to defeat the insistent tug of gravity, jerking himself through the sky by main force rather than natural aerodynamics, but George had enough time and confidence to feel both the pleasure of being airborne and the unusual view of the city that it gave him: white shrouded everything as far as the eye could see, and the rounded cornices of snow on all the roof edges softened the hard lines of the buildings, making everything less regular and ordered than it normally was. London had started to look more and more like a fairytale. The white roads were largely trackless and bumped by the snow-laden shapes of cars that were now well buried up to the door handles. Here and there were footprints in the snow, made, he guessed, by statues walking towards the Sphinxes, but mostly the narrow alleys and broad streets unfolding below him were like unblemished pages in a new book.

He was enjoying the view and the sensation of flight when the revealed vista of a road stretching east took his eye. When he saw what was at the end of it, all that pleasure and enjoyment died at once.

It was the Ice Murk. The great dark wall of mist rose sheer from the ground to hundreds of feet above the rooftops. It was a shock to see its looming presence overhanging the clean snow like a stain. At its very edge a white stone steeple stood out in stark contrast to the turbid gloom roiling slowly behind it. And then it was swallowed. The Murk was moving slowly.

He'd seen old slow-motion footage at school of the mushroom clouds of atomic explosions, and this reminded him of that, not just because the snow and the Murk had the monotone look of those ancient black and white films, but because those slow explosions had carried with them a deep and indefinable air of threat and menace, made all the worse by the slowness with which they unfolded their deadly bloom. The Ice Murk had the same air of threat to it.

'Gack!' screeched Spout. 'Gainger, Eigengang, gag gainger.'

'Yes,' said George. 'I see it. Bad danger, and lots of it.'

He wondered whether the Murk would get to Cleopatra's Needle before he could get back and alert the spits, and was trying to work out the geography of London over in that direction, when they were attacked.

Something leapt up at them from below and behind, erupting from the snow covering a roof beneath. It hit Spout like a snarling missile, and for the first couple of seconds it was all George could do not to fall off.

He had a fast fuzzy impression of a savage dog-faced gargoyle trying to rip out Spout's throat in a series of snapping bites, and then Spout dipped in the air, unable to carry the weight of George and the dog-gargoyle at the same time. Spout kicked at the attacker with his foot-talon, and the dog yelped in pain and fell off, snarling with renewed anger as it twisted and turned round on itself in mid-air, trying to get its wings in the right shape to curb and control its downward plummet.

Spout pulled them higher in the sky, panting as he did so. George was able to let go with one hand and get a grip on the hammer that had hung uselessly from his wrist throughout the short aerial tussle. He looked behind them and saw that the dog-gargoyle was on their tail, flying much faster, gaining on them.

'Left!' shouted George as the creature snarled in for another attack, snapping at Spout's trailing leg.

'Gack?' squawked Spout, to whom left and right were clearly new concepts.

'This way!' yelled George, reaching out and yanking the gargoyle's ear to the left.

Spout angled in the air and broke left, just in time to avoid the dog who underflew them, fangs clashing on nothing but cold air.

'Good,' shouted George. 'That was left.'

He tugged the ear the other way.

'This is right! Go right!'

Spout followed his lead, and the dog rocketed past them again, missing his target but just clipping Spout's wing. It had a dangerously fast turn of speed, and was much nimbler in the air than the cat-gargoyle. George wondered if the intense terrier-like ferocity of its attacks had something to do with the dog's natural hatred of cats, but before the thought had time to really take root the dog had found another lurching hairpin bend in the clear sky and was dropping on them. This time George saw that the dog had slowed its attack, making it less likely to be fooled by a sudden jink from side to side.

In fact this attack was disconcertingly leisurely, as the dog calmly matched its speed to Spout's and simply edged closer, easily following the bobbing and weaving of its more heavily laden adversary.

As it closed the gap in the air between them with a horrible inevitability, George could see its sides heaving for breath, and the tongue lolling out of the great fanged mouth. It was covered in a rime of frost, so that the rough stone it was made of had a white sheen on top of it. He could also see the intensity in its eyes and, worse than that, he was pretty sure that it was now not looking at Spout, but him.

As if to confirm his fears the dog chose that moment to lunge at him. George just had time to duck as the gnashing teeth passed overhead, and then the world tipped and lurched as it hit Spout's wing instead in a crunching collision of stone on stone. The impact spun Spout on his axis, so his wingtips were pointing straight up at the sky and down at the ground as the skyline pitched from horizontal to vertical in a gut-wrenching roll that threatened to capsize them.

George threw his weight against the direction of the roll, desperately trying to stop them tipping over completely, and Spout grunted explosively as he clawed with one wing only, grabbing air on the other side and forcing them the right way up. It would have worked if the dog-gargoyle was not able to turn so sharply at the end of each of his attacks. It stood on one wingtip, pirouetted gracefully, then hurtled back in, this time ignoring George and aiming for the much bigger target of Spout's flailing wing. It didn't snarl or try to bite; it just hit the wing and put all its inbound weight into cancelling Spout's attempts to right himself.

It hit him so hard that Spout spun like a propeller, once, twice, nearly three times round. The world and the sky above it cartwheeled past George's eyes as all he could do was hold on.

As Spout nearly went over for the third time George got his grip sorted out well enough that he was able to try and counter the spin by once more throwing himself in the opposite direction. It wouldn't have worked anyway, because his weight was so much smaller than the spinning mass of stone, but what it did was worse than failure.

By leaning out from the body of the cat-gargoyle he exposed himself.

The dog barked victoriously, then swooped in and neatly picked him off Spout's back with a savage snap of its jaws.

George had time to feel the impact on his upper arm, a deep crushing sensation just below his armpit, and then he could see Spout dropping away below him as the dog soared higher into the sky, growling in victory.

The pressure where the dog had him in its jaws was immense. It got worse as the dog started shaking him like a terrier worrying a rat. He stared in horror at his arm, knowing that it could not withstand the stone fangs, and was about to be torn off at the armpit. He scrabbled for the hammer on the thong round his other wrist, trying with a last and desperate reach of his flailing fingertips to get a grip on the one weapon that might save him, but before his hand could find the wooden handle, he heard the sickening crunch on his arm and knew that the dog had bitten through the bone.

The dog stopped worrying at him, and he had a glimpse of his arm in its mouth, and then the dog yelped and grabbed him with a talon as it shook its head and spat something out. For a moment George couldn't work out what it was, and then he saw the gap in the dog's teeth and realized that the tiny grey nub of stone falling to the ground far below was one of the dog's front fangs.

The crunch he had heard had been the tooth breaking, not his arm being shorn off.

He stared at his bicep, and through the shredded sleeve saw grazed skin and the thing that had broken the tooth: the dog had bitten down on the vein of stone twining up from his wrist, and the stone vein had saved his arm, and probably his life.

Relief seemed to add another two inches to his fingertips, because in the moment that he realized he was not going to die yet, he found the hammer hanging off his wrist, clenched his fist round it and brought it up in flailing roundhouse blow that ended in a bone-shaking thwack on the dog's chest-bone. It woofed out a lungful of air, winded by the impact. As it lowered its head, trying to hunch itself over and get a next breath that wouldn't come, George struck again. Right at the limit of his swing he managed to reach high enough to land the heavy steel hammerhead just off-centre in the middle of the gargoyle's forehead.

Stone split and a large chunk of the monstrous head sheared clean off and tumbled away, ear-over-eye towards the deserted white streets below. George looked at the dog-gargoyle's head and found he was looking at a flat plane of newly exposed stone, dark in contrast to the ice-skin that covered the rest of the creature. Then the head turned and he saw he had shattered the head at an angle, leaving one eye and one ear – and all the jaw – looking at him in shock.

Bearing the teeth still in the jaws in mind, he cocked his arm for another blow. As if the pain and the injury had hit it in a shocked delay, the dog suddenly yelped and cowered away from him. It flung him off, out into the clean empty gulf of air, tucked a spiked tail between its legs and flew away as fast as it could, leaving nothing but a high keening whine of enraged pain trailing behind it.

George saw none of this, and if he had, he wouldn't have had the time or the stomach for any kind of satisfaction. He was too busy falling earthwards with a velocity that left his stomach far behind.

He didn't even have time to wonder what sort of mark he was going to leave in the clean white expanse of snow rushing up to meet him.

21

EDIE'S QUESTION

All the spits seemed to be looking at the rooftop over which George and Spout had just disappeared. Edie was the first to look away. The truth is she was scanning the sky for the Raven. She didn't find it. Instead she found the steady gaze of the Icy Sphinx.

The spits around her all erupted into more talking and questions, and the sound of old arguments being re-kindled left Edie in a strange cone of silence, alone with the great creature.

'You have a question so big that keeping it within makes you feel like you will split and burst, is it not so, child?'

Edie stopped herself reacting reflexively to the indignity of being called child, and nodded.

'But it's not mine to ask,' she said. The Sphinx was right. The question growing and growing inside her was so big that she had to keep a grip just so that she didn't scream it out all the time.

'Why not ask?' said the Sphinx, so low that none of the arguing spits could hear it. 'It would be easy to ask. It would be easy to answer . . .'

'Yeah,' said Edie. 'But you know what?' And she lowered her voice and stood her ground, so low that the Icy Sphinx had to bend close to hear her. 'I don't trust you, not any more than I did last time. In fact a lot less. There's an Ice Devil out there, calling taints to it, and you've been gone all night. And now you're back, covered in ice . . .'

'Ice is just ice. It's very cold,' purred the Sphinx dangerously quietly.

'Right,' said Edie. 'But your sister isn't covered in ice and I think you want me to ask my question so that the other question, the question about how to defeat the Ice Devil gets unanswered. At least until tomorrow, when it'll be too late . . .'

The Icy Sphinx hissed quietly at her, a strangely threatening sound at the back of its gullet. Edie stood her ground.

'I remember your rules, see?' she said. 'One question each a day. And you're trying to make me waste the one we've got left.'

'Why would I do that?' breathed the Sphinx.

'Dunno. Maybe you answered the call. Maybe the cat looked at the king and found something it liked. Maybe the Darkness sent you back as a spy, to give bad advice or to lie or something.'

The snarl that greeted this last was loud enough to stop the talking all around them.

'I cannot lie,' seethed the Sphinx. 'And I call no man king!'

Edie felt a firm hand grip her shoulder. Without looking she knew it was the Queen.

'What's happening, child?' she said. Edie took strength from the statue at her back and jutted her chin at the Sphinx.

'Trick answers,' said Edie, 'seeing as how this Ice Devil isn't a man . . .'

And in the microscopic pause that followed, Edie saw the Sphinx's eye twitch, and she knew she had just stopped herself blinking, and she knew she had touched a raw nerve and the creature was trying not to show it.

She could feel the tension building inside the elephant-sized bronze body standing over her.

'Sister?' rumbled the other Sphinx over Edie's shoulder.

The four things that happened next happened so fast that for Edie they appeared to be simultaneous.

The Icy Sphinx smiled.

And then lashed out a giant paw at Edie with unimaginable speed.

The Queen's hand ripped her out of the way, so nearly too late that the sphinx's claw caught in the welt of her boot and tore it clean off her foot.

And the other Sphinx pounced.

The good Sphinx hit the bad one with an impact that all the spits felt through the soles of their boots. It was like two lorries colliding head on, except the moment after the impact the difference immediately became apparent, since colliding lorries don't then roll into a yowling ball of fury and bite and tear at one another like two great cats locked into a life-or-death fight.

The Sphinxes were of course perfectly matched, and each gave as good as she got as they tumbled and rolled off the plinth and across the road in a yowling ball of bronze fury that sent spits leaping out of the way as it whirled past. They seemed to have latched on to each other's throats as each one tried to disembowel the other with great tearing movements of their hind paws. It was an ugly and brutal fight as it rolled under the wide railway bridge, kicking up clouds of snow.

They hit one of the solid bridge supports with such an impact that they broke apart for an instant. Snow avalanched off the bridge above them, creating a curtain of whiteness between them that almost immediately exploded outwards as the Icy Sphinx leapt through and knocked the other on to her back. She pressed forward her advantage by jumping on to the prone body and pinning its neck to the ground with one paw, raising the other in preparation for a wicked slash across the exposed throat.

At that moment the raised paw sprouted a lance straight through its middle as the Queen threw hard and straight from the edge of the watching crowd.

The Sphinx screeched in pain and turned on her new assailant, which gave her sister just enough time to roll out from under her grip.

There was a sudden clatter of metal on metal as rifles and pistols were cocked and aimed at the Icy Sphinx, but before the first shot could be fired the good Sphinx had thrown herself in front of her.

'NO,' she roared, so loud that the top layer of snow seemed to be blown off the ground towards her would-be rescuers. 'This is between me and her, and no others!'

Behind her the Icy Sphinx gripped the lance with her teeth and pulled it out of her paw, spitting it contemptuously back at the Queen. She looked at her sister.

'Come with me,' she panted. 'The Darknesses will win.'

'Maybe,' said the other hoarsely. 'But that is not enough reason not to fight them.'

'Spoken like a human,' hissed her sister contemptuously. 'You always were too much with people and their paltry hopes and fears.'

'I find there is much to be said for hope,' replied the other simply.

'There is only one thing to be said about it.'

She raised her head and looked over the other's shoulder directly at Edie.

'Are you listening, glint? Are you thinking of your question? Because yes, what you hope for is true . . . but hope seduces with a silver tongue, double-edged like a dagger that cuts both ways . . .'

And with that the great cat body suddenly flexed and sprang right over her sister's head and neatly clawed its way up and over on to the railway bridge, and before anyone could do anything about it, it was gone.

'What question were you going to ask?' said the Queen quietly.

'Come on,' said Edie, holding out her mother's heart stone. 'It's obvious, isn't it? I want to know if my mum's alive and where I can find her. Only now's not the time, not if we've just got one more question and a whole world to save, not to mention putting time back in joint or whatever.'

She knew what she was saying was the right thing to say, but she ached to ask the question anyway. It was almost worth the world to her.

The Sphinx walked stiffly over to her and looked down.

'You do not need to ask the question, child, or answer any riddle: the answer is within you.'

'Is it?' said Edie bitterly. 'Jolly good. That's the sort of answer you get in crappy kung-fu films. I'll just sit down and wait for enlightenment, shall I? Or maybe do some chanting . . .'

The Sphinx opened her mouth to reply, then shrugged and walked on, her eyes becoming blank and unreachable as she curled back up on her plinth and looked at them and the spits beyond.

'Do what you will, my answer stands. What is the question you *would* ask?' she said wearily, examining a long jagged gash in her side, scraped there by her sister.

Edie looked at the Gunner. The Gunner spoke.

'Where do we find this Black Mirror to banish the Ice Devil through?'

The Sphinx took a deep breath and looked away from them, over their heads.

'The mirror sleeps on a bed neither here nor there,
Not beneath the ground, nor under the air,
It cannot be seen, not by you or by me,
But can be found where the boy felt it to be.'

There was a silence as everyone absorbed what had been said.

'Is that the riddle or the answer?' said Edie, exhausted and wishing George was there to put his mind to the conundrum.

'It is both,' said the Sphinx and closed her eyes. 'For I am tired and must rest before I go hunt my sister.'

22

CATCHER'S MITT

George dropped head first through the sky, legs bicycling, hands reaching downwards, reflexively trying to cushion the inevitable impact as the wide sweep of road round the south end of Hanover Square rushed up to meet him with blank white finality.

He opened his mouth to yell, but the wind forced the words back into his throat, so the 'No!' he was shouting at the world only echoed inside his head.

All he heard was the wind rushing past and the blood pounding its last in his ears. And one word, screeched out of the cold morning behind him.

'Eigengang!'

Spout swooped in below, and tumbled himself on his back. George had no time to think – all he saw was that the stone wing unfolded itself beneath him like a giant outflung catcher's mitt in a game of baseball. And then he hit it, and though the impact was hard enough to jar the air out of him, it also spun Spout the right way round, which cushioned the blow. Spout grabbed him and lurched to a stop, having hooked the claw at the end of his other wing on to the gutter of a building on the side of the square. George smacked into the wall between two windows and just hung there, getting his breath and enjoying not being a splat mark in the snow below.

'Nice catch,' he said as soon as his lungs had recharged with oxygen.

He patted the stone wing draped protectively over him.

'Very nice catch. Thanks, Spout. You saved me again.'

'Gack,' agreed the gargoyle, sounding rather pleased with himself in a way that George, in the circumstances, felt was entirely justified.

They hung there for a long moment, and George stared in to the window in front of him. It was an office full of workstations and computer monitors. His eyes slowly skated over the mundane jumble of each desk. Each one was fundamentally the same space, but strewn with different personal items – mugs, photographs, the odd figures that people stuck to the top of their screens. It was just everyday stuff, the things working people let silt up around their workplace in an unconscious attempt to make the blankness homely and specific to them. His eye rested on a quartet of wild-haired trolls that someone had arranged on the windowsill in front of him. They lined up next to a paperweight, a thick circle of clear glass embedded with a photo of a laughing woman and child.

The sight of it made him feel suddenly very alone.

They made the city seem emptier.

They made him suddenly and sharply miss people.

He thought of his mother. He wanted her to be safe. He hadn't thought of her much in the past few hours, but now he did, and he desperately wanted her to be there and laughing and telling him the stories of her day, the ones where she couldn't help acting all the people she'd been with at once. He knew she wasn't going to be a perfect mum, because she wasn't built like that. She would never give him all the attention he wanted, because she always had at least one eye on herself to see what she looked like and how others were reacting to her. That was because she was an actress. Or maybe it was why she was an actress. But whether it was the chicken or the egg, he didn't mind now. He realized that whatever he'd found out when he saw the soldier with his dad's face had not only made him feel OK about his death, it had let him feel OK about his mum. Only now that he didn't have the black treacly feeling of anger inside him did he realize that a lot of it came from what he felt about her – but could never say. Where he'd felt angry with her, he now felt worried.

The weight of knowing that this layer of London might never be full of bustling people with their novelty mugs and framed family photographs and pointless troll collections bore down on him.

It was his fault.

He'd better get going.

'Come on, Spout,' he said. 'Let's get to the Clocker before something happens to the Queen of Time.'

Spout unhooked his talon from the roof-edge, and flapped hard. In a couple of wing-beats they were cresting the buildings across the square and angling across Oxford Street towards the great store.

Because his eye was taken by the familiar bulky figure of Dictionary stumbling out from under the canopy and waving at him, he did not at first notice that he was too late. It was only when the Clocker raised an arm in greeting from beneath the Clock of the World that George noticed the Queen had gone.

Spout came to an untidy landing and George stumbled towards the front of the store.

'Where is the Queen of Time?' he gasped, pointing up to the elaborate plinth.

'Never fear, my young friend, the lady has flown east to discover what has obstructed time's smooth passage and if possible remedy it!' boomed Dictionary.

'No!' exclaimed George 'She must not go yet . . .'

Dictionary looked at Clocker. They both looked at George. George looked at his feet. They looked at Spout.

'Gack,' he said helpfully.

'Why "No", if I may ask?' said Dictionary.

'Because the Sphinx said so,' explained George. 'That's why I came. To try and stop her going before we'd had a chance to put the Darkness back . . .'

Again the two figures exchanged a look.

'Put what Darkness back . . . where?' ventured the Clocker.

'And why?' added the man of letters.

So George got to his feet, took a deep breath to drown his rising disappointment and fear of the futility of the course they were embarked on, and told them everything that had happened with the Sphinxes. They remained silent as he spoke, and neither looked anywhere but his face.

'So you see,' he finished, 'we can't fight the Ice Devil before we deal with the Darkness.'

'But the lady has flown east,' said Dictionary.

'And not returned,' said the Clocker, who stiffened and held up his hand. They watched him as he stood on the canopy above them and listened, his eyes closed, his face straining into the air, the concentration on it so intense that he almost seemed to be trying to smell and taste as well as listen.

'What?' whispered George. 'What is it?'

'Listening,' said the Clocker, eyes still shut. 'Listen hard enough, can hear almost everything that is. Can hear fault in clock before even see it lose time. Can hear individual cogs turn, springs unwind, ratchets move. City is like a clock . . .'

His eyes opened. He looked deflated.

'Something has changed. Cannot hear her.'

'Wait,' said George, incredulous. 'Are you saying you can normally hear her?'

'She is one of the great cogs in the city. Can hear the great cogs if I try.'

Then, just on the edge of hearing, George caught a flap of wings. Spout heard it too, because he spun in the snow and looked east.

'What?' said Dictionary.

'Wings,' said George.

Dictionary's face cracked in a smile and his shoulders relaxed.

'Why, see, Clocker, all is well, your fears are unfounded, the great lady is . . .'

The words died on his lips as the flying figure flared its wings and came to rest on a parapet, looking down at them.

'. . . a dog,' finished Dictionary.

The dog-gargoyle stood looking unconcernedly away from them, silhouetted against the sky, its tongue lolling out of its jaws. It looked precisely like a bat-winged dog until it turned to look at them head on, and then the lopsided, one-eyed and one-eared shape of the head was instantly recognizable as the creature Spout and George had just fought.

'Gaing gack,' said Spout.

'Yeah,' agreed George. 'He came back.'

The dog barked at them.

Something squirmed beneath Dictionary's tight coat buttons, and Hodge stuck his head out and responded with a hiss of pure feline fury. Spout looked impressed. He turned and emitted a similar noise at ten times the volume right back at the dog.

The gargoyle lurched to its feet and started to patrol back and forth with a stiff-legged gait, snarling and barking at them.

'Why's it come back?' said George.

Dictionary waved a disgusted hand at the roofline.

'Because the canine intellect is greatly inferior to the feline, part baying braggadocio, part craven yelping when the master's hand is turned against it. In short, it is stupid . . .'

The dog turned its back on them and lifted its hind leg in an unmistakable gesture of contempt.

'It can't be . . .' began George.

'It is,' said Dictionary as a stream of liquid arched out over the street and spattered the ground in front of them.

'Didn't know they could do that,' said George wonderingly, impressed despite himself

'They are rain spouts. Channelling water is what they do on a normal day,' said Dictionary, stepping back. 'I told you it was stupid.'

Spout launched into the air in a flurry of snow.

'Why else would it make a spectacle of itself with all this showy micturation?' finished Dictionary as the dog flapped out of sight, pursued by Spout.

George didn't have an answer for that.

And almost immediately, as soon as Spout had disappeared from view, he didn't need one.

The dog-gargoyle had not been beaten by George. Even with half its head sheared clean off, it had gone for reinforcements.

And then it had come back as a decoy.

And it had drawn off Spout and distracted George and his companions so effectively that they only heard

149

the two dragons that had been quietly circling round their backs when they burst out of the snowdrifts right behind them.

And then it was too late.

23

A MATTER OF
LIFE OR DEATH

The time for listening and thinking had clearly passed. Now the Sphinx had given her answer all the spits started talking at once, and the more they talked, once again, the less any of them seemed to listen. Even the Queen and the Gunner waded in and started trying to out-shout the others. The gist – if there was a gist – seemed to be a great discussion about whether they should all stay here, or find somewhere to better defend themselves if the taints attacked en masse, or even pre-empt the possible attack by mounting one of their own into the heart of the City.

Edie thought they should be trying to find ways to help George, if he was the one who had the key to ultimate victory, but this key point seemed to be drowned in the rising tide of the argument.

As often happened when she was in a crowd, Edie began to feel very solitary. She walked off to the edge of it to retrieve her boot, hopping as she went to keep her sock from getting soaked by the snow.

She leant on the stone wall curving along beside the river to keep her balance as she put it back on. When she was done, she looked across the black water at the distant bank and thought about what the nasty Sphinx had said. She had certainly not said what she did to make her feel any better about her mum. Or had she? Edie had always sensed her hostility, right from the moment she had glinted the Zeppelin raid that had mutilated her. So why had she said it? To make Edie feel worse.

If that was the case, she had succeeded perfectly. She pulled the earring made from her mother's small heart stone out of her pocket and looked at the pale light shining inside it, the flicker that said 'She is alive'. She felt the sharp treacherous swoop of hope in her stomach again and tried to ignore the pain that came after it. The Sphinx was right. Hope was double-edged. If you stopped hoping and expected the worst, you were in Edie's experience much less likely to be disappointed. Every time she looked at the heart stone something in her soared into cleaner, clearer air, but she had a horrible feeling that the higher you went with it, the further you'd fall.

She had just decided to put the stone away and not look at it again until George got back, when someone tapped her on the shoulder. She turned, to find nobody there. Instead the tail of her eye caught a flutter of oily black feathers darting round the other side of her, and then she felt a tug at her fingertips, and by the time she'd turned back she discovered the Raven had returned, and had pecked her mother's stone out of her grasp.

It landed on the top of the stone wall a metre away, and cocked its head at her, the stone dangling and twisting at the end of its long beak.

'Hey!' gasped Edie, stepping forward and reaching for her stone.

The Raven hopped backwards along the wall, not too far, just enough to make her take another step.

'Please . . .' she cried, the prospect of losing this last link with her mother and all the vulnerable possibilities it had opened up being suddenly more than she could bear.

The Raven hopped back again, just out of reach.

'Come on,' said Edie in desperation. 'I freed you . . .'

The Raven's beady eyes bored in to hers. It ducked its head twice, then hopped back another metre.

'Seriously . . .' said Edie. 'Don't make me . . .'

She didn't know what to do, but she did know that it was going to be whatever stopped the Raven flying off with her mother's stone. She had a memory hit of the Fusilier shooting the Raven, blowing it to a cloud of slick black feathers.

That recollection triggered the next flash, when it had been tugging George's boot-lace at the top of the Monument and the Gunner had shot it, and it had spun round George's foot like a propeller before dropping to the ground and dying again.

She turned and looked for the Gunner in the crowd behind her. All she saw were backs, and then she spotted his tin hat and was about to call him when something tapped her shoulder.

It was the Raven again. At first her heart jolted horribly when she couldn't see the heart stone in its beak, but as it flew back up the stone wall she saw the glass winking at her on the top of it.

She was about to shout for the Gunner when the Raven, as if reading he thoughts, picked up the earring and held it out beyond the edge of the wall, high over the water slapping the stone embankment below.

It didn't drop it, but it definitely looked at her pointedly.

Edie looked back. She was pretty unbeatable in a staredown, but the Raven had millennia of practice on her. Edie blinked first.

'OK,' she said.

The Raven brought the stone back from the drop, and awkwardly twisted and ducked its head, exactly like it was beckoning her.

She stepped forward.

It hopped back.

She took another step.

It hopped back again, keeping the exact same tantalizing distance between her outstretched fingertips and her mother's stone.

'Please don't play games,' she said. 'It's not a toy . . .'

The Raven nodded and hopped backwards.

'. . . it's important. To me. Please.'

She wasn't used to telling people what was important to her. It felt too much like giving them a tool to use against her. It felt dangerous and unguarded to be saying it out loud. It felt odd.

It felt even odder to be saying it to a bird.

The Raven looked at her as if it was again reading her mind. And unless that mind was going and she was losing it completely, it rolled its eyes at her.

Then it very slowly, very deliberately nodded, one, two, three times. Then it hopped round and jabbed its beak up the Embankment, away from the crowd, towards the City. It was definitely pointing.

'You want me to follow you?' she said. Talking to birds was not something she was going to get used to any time soon.

It nodded again. She looked back at the crowd of spits. Even the soldiers who had been facing outwards when she arrived were now facing inwards, joining the great roiling argument. No one was seeing her go. She should tell them . . .

The Raven slid into view, between her and the crowd.

It hung in the air in the disturbing way it sometimes did, treating all three of Newton's laws of motion with equal and eerie contempt. It shook its head very deliberately.

'Why not?' she said, and then noticed it wasn't carrying the stone in its beak.

''Cos they'll stop you coming. 'Cos they don't understand,' said a scratchy little urchin's voice from behind her. ''Cos they don't want what you want, do they?'

Edie turned.

There was the earring.

And the hand that was holding it belonged to the one living person – after the Walker – who she trusted least in the whole world.

Little Tragedy.

He smiled a very complicated smile at her and twisted her mother's heart stone in the light.

Then he held his finger to his lips, pointed at the crowd that was suddenly too far away, and then crooked it in a beckoning gesture.

'Mum's the word, and step lively,' he whispered. 'I 'spect you'll want to see this . . .'

24

DOUBLE DRAGON

The taints would have crushed George if they had hit him on that first rush as they came barrelling out of the snow, but Dictionary, who was a pace closer to them, turned with surprising speed and shoved him out of the way. They were two squat City Dragons, the kind usually stationed at the boundaries of the Square Mile, blocky mass-produced statues, painted with silver except for their barbed tongues and wing ribs, which were picked out in municipal fire-engine red. What they lacked in individuality or fineness of modelling they more than made up for with ferocity and strength.

George went sprawling into the plate-glass window on the side of the building. It shuddered but did not break, and because it didn't shatter he saw what was happening behind him in a blurred reflection in the glass.

One of the dragons hit Dictionary, who – in saving him – had left it too late to save himself, and the big man was knocked brutally down the pavement. The other dragon stopped itself by sticking its arm out sideways and clawing on to a lamppost. With shocking agility for such a heavily built assailant it allowed its forward momentum to swing it round the anchored talon, neatly reversing the direction of its onslaught by one hundred and eighty degrees. It slammed to the ground opposite George with an impact like an anvil falling out of the sky.

George spun to face it.

He saw it kink its neck left and right, like a prize

fighter eyeing its opponent, and then it hissed and fanned its wings behind it. Fierce hostile eyes seemed to pin him to the glass.

He felt the scar in his hand twinge, and the vein of stone circling his upper arm throbbed in sympathy. The pain in his hand reminded him of the Temple Bar Dragon who had marked him with the livid scar slashed across it. He remembered the savage intelligence of that dragon's piercing eyes. He looked into the eyes of the taint opposite. They were fierce, no doubt, but just as its body was more lumpen and blocky than the Temple Bar Dragon, so its eyes were different. They were angry and burning and . . . stupid.

Sometimes when you're out of choices, the oldest tricks in the book are all you have to work with.

'Behind you!' shouted George, pointing.

The dragon turned to look.

George sprinted for safety.

The dragon may have been stupid but it wasn't slow. It turned back with a roar of frustration, and blasted flame out of its mouth – not the multicoloured wildfire that had spiralled out of the Temple Bar Dragon, but a workman-like white flame, more like a blowtorch than anything magical. It jetted into the window and spread out wide, but George was gone.

He was sprinting down the pavement beneath the canopy. He felt the blast of heat behind him, turned his head for a snatched look backwards, saw the dragon stop flaming and start after him with a roar, so just dug in and ran faster. Unfortunately the first thing he saw when he turned back to face front was the second dragon charging head-on at him from the other direction.

'George!' cried a voice above him.

He saw the Clocker leaning down off the edge of the canopy, reaching a long arm straight down, hand wide.

George had no time to think, not if he was to avoid becoming a very squashed and messy filling in a heavy metal dragon sandwich, so he leapt. His hand slapped round the Clocker's forearm, and he felt the Clocker grip on and swing him up into the air like a pendulum just as the two dragons met in a head-on collision in the space where he had just been.

The thunderous clang beneath his feet was still echoing round the silent street when he started to swing backwards on the down-stroke of his pendulum arc over the two train-wrecked dragons sprawled groggily beneath him. He caught a glimpse of their eyes trying to focus on him, and then he was swinging forwards again. One of them tried a half-hearted slash of its claw at him as he passed over.

'Let go!' he shouted. The Clocker released his arm and he flew a short way forward and tumbled into the snow.

Dictionary was sprawled in a drift ahead of him. Hodge was at his side, hissing towards George.

'Run, boy!' shouted Dictionary.

Hodge was not hissing at George, he was hissing at the Dragon unsteadily lurching after him.

A dragon that was stupid but fast. And resilient.

George jinked over a road-menders' barrier, just avoided falling into the trench on the other side, and ran across the street, bobbing and weaving round snow-buried cars.

The dragons didn't weave. Nor did they bob. They jumped. And not round anything. Over everything. In a straight line. A rapidly shortening straight line at whose end was George. He grabbed another quick look back and saw the two of them springing over the roofs of cars, hot on his trail. They were gaining on him much too quickly.

One of them landed with a thump painfully close on his heels, and he knew he wasn't going to make it to safety on the other side of the street. In fact he couldn't see any safety there anyway. And then he was face to face with a long estate car, and he didn't think at all, but ripped open the door and dived in, slamming it behind him. He had enough time to slam the door locks down, and then the side of the car was rocked by the impact of the dragon hitting it. Snow cascaded off the roof, and then the car was, for an instant, still.

He could hear the dragon's snuffling outside the car. He scooted into the back seat, looking round for a weapon. There was a nearly full litre of bottled water and something that squished in his hand as he grabbed it.

'Great. A banana,' he muttered, and then the side window blew in as one of the dragons smashed its head through the glass, and he was staring straight into the wide snarling mouth, so close that he could see the tongue of fire deep in its throat as it inhaled, ready to fill the inside of the car with flame.

George rammed the bottle into the gaping maw, thinking it might plug the throat and make the dragon choke, then he squirmed over the back of the seat into the cargo area, which was both a bad move, because he realized as soon as he got there that he couldn't open the back door from inside, and a good move, because it got him out of the way of the dragon's blast.

It didn't fill the inside of the car with a ball of incinerating fire. The flame belched up the dragon's throat, met the plastic bottle George had shoved down it, melted the plastic and thus hit the water within.

Water hit the flame and turned to steam, and the dragon choked and spluttered, coughing out the now empty top – and unmelted – half of the bottle so hard that it ricocheted off the window on the far side of the car and hit George in the back of the head as he scrabbled for any other weapon on the floor of the boot. The bottle-rocket shot out, not on a gout of flame, but on a steam-jet. The inside of the car suddenly became very, very hot and impossible to see through. As the steam rapidly cooled, it also became very wet.

George's hands found a curved plastic handle underneath him, attached to a spindly shaft wrapped in material and even spindlier ribs of metal. He knew instantly what it was, and as he made out the dragon's head coughing and spluttering and turning to look for him through the steam cloud, he pulled it free and stabbed it between the dragon's teeth, straight down into its throat.

The dragon stumbled back, jerking its head out of the door. It staggered into its partner, short arms reaching for the handle of the umbrella George had just choked it with.

One of the very useful things about an umbrella in this situation is the fact that the ribs of the canopy act like a lot of tiny barbs, so that when the dragon tried to rip it free, they caught in its gullet and made it choke even more. It thrashed its head from side to side, making increasingly desperate coughing and hacking noises as it continued to try and pluck the spiny obstruction from its throat.

George couldn't see any of this clearly, because the

windows of the car were obscured with condensation from the steam, but he knew this was his moment to try and escape. He scrambled over the seat back and fumbled with the rear passenger door handle. As he did so the door on the other side of the car was tugged and shaken as the other dragon tried to wrench it open, and then suddenly there was a great screech of protesting metal ending in a sharp crack as the door was torn clean off its hinges.

For a moment there was nothing but light and snow in the empty doorway as the dragon stumbled back and tossed the door to one side, and then just as George got his door unlocked, the empty space was rammed full of a different but equally snarling dragon.

George felt the door at his back open and he tumbled out of the car as the second dragon bulled his way inside, trying to reach him across the wide bench seat. George's feet were almost clear of the car as he crabbed swiftly backwards into the snow when something red darted out of the dragon's mouth and wound itself around his ankle like a whiplash.

The dragon's tongue tightened and tried to pull him back into the car. His hands found the raised edge of the kerb, and he flexed his fingertips round it, trying to anchor himself.

The dragon meanwhile just kept trying to barge its too-large body through the width of the too-small car. The velour seat was ripped to shreds as its talons dug in and endeavoured to shove it further forward and the thin sheet-steel of the roof buckled and split as it tore and wrenched after George.

George's fingers weren't strong enough to fight the dragon's pull. And then, just as they were ripped free of their tenuous purchase on the lip of the kerb, the dragon smashed its way out of the door by snapping the door pillar and emerging in a hideous pop of destroyed metal.

Its tongue loosened for an instant as its body lurched forward, and George tried to throw himself out of the way. A foot-talon stamped down, missing his ankle by a millimetre but jagging through his trouser leg, pinning it to the ground. He was stuck, but desperately hoping the material would rip and free him, he pulled against the impaling claw as if his life depended on it. Which it did.

The dragon cocked its head, to spit fire at him . . . and then something small and furious leapt on to its head, sharp bronze claws slashing at its eyes.

The cat Hodge clung on to the taint's head, obscuring its vision and using every ounce of feline fury to tear at the vulnerable eyes. The dragon tried to shake it off, but four sets of claws gripped its head and refused to be dislodged. For extra grip, Hodge sunk his teeth into the dragon's ear and held on, yowling wildly as he did so.

Dictionary lurched between George and the dragon and ripped his trouser leg free of the claw.

'Quick, boy . . .' he puffed, unused to the exertion, 'while Hodge remains under the happy misapprehension that the dragon is a big bird . . .'

He grabbed George and they started to run across the pavement towards a narrow alley when something sprang over their heads, twisting in the air as it went, a trailing foot knocking Dictionary flat on his face. It landed on the turn, wings still swirling round it like a matador's cape as it blocked the alley and gagged angrily at them. The dragon would have been a purely terrifying sight but for the small imperfection of the umbrella handle sticking out of its mouth. As if conscious of this fact it reached up, gripped the handle and gave a final almighty wrench, tearing the umbrella inside out as the barbed ribs bent back on themselves and came free of its throat.

George didn't wait to see what it did next; he turned and started to run.

Before he got half a step the dragon had grabbed his hand and yanked him back. And now there was nowhere to hide or run or do anything to save himself, because the metal claw gripped him like a cuff and he was forced to look once more into the dragon's mouth. He again saw the inhaled breath and flicker of ignition in the back of the throat as the dragon prepared to burn his face off.

He instinctively put his free hand up to ward off the inevitable, only to have it numbingly smashed aside as Dictionary threw himself between them, his meaty hands grabbing the dragon's muzzle and chin and forcing the mouth shut. As he did so Dictionary caught sight of something gold and blue trapped in the dragon's claw, jammed in the gap between skin and talon. It looked familiar, but just as he realized what it was the dragon jerked its head violently, trying to shake itself free, and all he could think about was holding on.

'By God NO!' he gritted, as the dragon tried to open its jaws.

A short brutal trial of strength followed between them. Smoke started to curl from the sides of the dragon's mouth as the build-up of fire found a way to escape between the gaps in its teeth. George tried to get free of the grip on his wrist, but the creature just yanked him closer.

'Must free yourself . . .' panted Dictionary. 'Cannot hold . . . much longer.'

George could see the big man's hands shaking with the effort of fighting the dragon, but he was stuck.

The dragon punched Dictionary. A vicious uppercut with a hooked talon hit him in the stomach and jerked upwards, ripping open his coat and waistcoat. George heard the 'unh' of surprised pain from the man shielding him, and then the dragon shook its muzzle clear of the hands holding it shut.

George saw its eyes find him, zero in on him, and ignite with a fire as hot as the one it was about to jet into his face.

'No, sir, you shall NOT!!' roared Dictionary, looking up from where he was bent over the pain in his stomach.

The dragon spat flame in a jet like a fire-hose. As the world went fatally slow, George saw the jaws fill with a ball of fire that grew as it headed for his face only feet away, and then the ball of fire was eclipsed as Dictionary lunged between them again. Using the last of his energy he did the only thing that could possibly save George. He used himself to shield the boy from the fire.

The fire hit him in the head, but he didn't move. Instead he stood four-square, hands trying to keep George behind him while the dragon tried to pull him clear.

'You . . . shall . . . not . . . have . . . him!' bellowed Dictionary as the hose of fire hammered into his eyes. George saw him trembling with the effort to hold his ground, and when he looked up was horrified to see the top right-hand quarter of the bronze head was being melted off, the velocity of the fire-jet working it into an outflung splash, like a frozen wave of metal sloughing off the face.

The dragon exhausted its breath, and the flame

stopped as it filled its lungs for a second blast.

'You must get free, boy,' murmured a strange raw voice. 'I fear I cannot hold him for ever . . .'

It was only when Dictionary turned to look blindly at him, and George saw the terrible erasure that the fire had wrought across his eyes and forehead, that he realized the voice was his.

'Dictionary,' George cried involuntarily.

The dragon roared, cocked its head confidently for the *coup de grâce*, and then jerked it violently sideways once, twice, three times.

It coughed and looked at George, a question in its eyes, as if it didn't know why it had done that, and then *BLAM*.

. . . a fourth shot rang out and knocked the head limply back on the scaly neck, and George realized he had heard three earlier shots but had been too busy preparing to die to work out what they were.

The dragon pitched backwards, its twitching tail sweeping Dictionary off his feet as it went down.

'What happened, boy?' he said hoarsely.

There was a strange noise building to their right – a low rolling thunder of hooves with a high-pitched yipping in counterpoint, like someone shouting 'Hi – hi – hi!' over and over. George's eyes followed the sound waves back to their source.

'I don't know,' he breathed, 'but whatever it is, it's still happening.'

25

A TRAP WORTH WALKING INTO

Little Tragedy scampered ahead of Edie along the Embankment, heading east.

Towards the Ice Murk louring over the City.

Edie didn't notice the cloud. All she saw was her mother's stone bobbing along in Little Tragedy's hand. She sprinted after him and grabbed his shoulder.

'Hey,' she said, spinning him round and bunching her fist.

'Don't . . .'

She punched him. The pain in her hand was instantaneous and numbing. He stumbled backwards.

'. . . hit me,' he finished, getting his balance.

'Give me that stone,' she growled, holding her throbbing fist and deciding not to look at it, no matter how broken it felt.

'I'm made of metal,' he said, backing up as she advanced on him. 'It's stupid to hit me . . .'

She kicked out and hooked his legs out from under him. He smacked down on his back with a satisfying thud.

'Ow!' he yelped.

'Give me the stone!' she repeated, bunching her fist again. She tried not to show how much just bunching it now hurt.

'All right all right, keep your hair on,' he grumbled,

and held up the stone. 'I was just trying to help . . .'

As she reached for it the Raven swooped in and picked the stone from his hand, so close that her fingers brushed the feathers on its back as it passed between them.

'You're pulling my leg,' she said.

The Raven hung in the air and beckoned her.

'Don't start that again,' she sighed. 'I'm really not in the mood.'

'He's trying to 'elp an' all,' said Tragedy. 'Can I get up or do you want to hurt your hand some more?'

'You betrayed me. You took me to that house, that prison with the woman with the sewn-up eyes!'

She couldn't begin to explain the scope of his treachery or the depth of her disgust and hatred for him. It rose in her throat like a black column of bile.

'You lied, you stole, you stole the broken carving, the one George broke. And you handed me to the Walker. He hurt me. You hurt me. You worse than hurt me: you got me killed!'

'If I had it to do again, I wouldn't,' he whined.

'Yeah, well, if I had a gun. I'd shoot you,' she spat. 'In fact, I'm going to get a gun right now . . .'

And she turned away and started to call out to the Gunner.

'Wouldn't do that if I was you, girly. Not if you want to see your mother again . . .'

Edie's heart gave that treacherous lurch skywards.

'What?' she gasped.

'Your old mum. You want to see her, right?'

The best of all possibilities was being laid before her by the worst of messengers. She took a deep breath, then another. Tried to think straight. Gave up.

'Yes,' she said.

'Well, then, that's why Old Black sent me,' he said, as if she should have known this.

'The Black Friar sent you?' she said, trying to catch up.

''Course he did. This 'ere bird flapped in, all of a twitter, an' clacked away in Ol' Black's lug 'ole, and Ol' Black, 'cos he understands the bird, sends me to get you. The bird wants to show you something . . .'

'Where,' said Edie.

'In the pub, where else?' sighed Tragedy. 'Blimey. You sure you didn't bang your 'ead as well as your knuckles?'

Edie was well aware her heart was still fluttering somewhere above her head, ready to be dashed to the ground and crushed by the familiar iron heel of disappointment. As far as she had experienced life, which was further than most people three times her age, when things were too good to be true, they usually weren't either good or true.

It had to be a trap, at the very least.

What changed her mind was what happened next.

The Raven swooped really close to her, eyeballed her, and then dropped the stone into her hand. Then it nodded and flew off towards the distant lights of the Black Friar's pub.

'Ol' Black said it owes you one. Said you freed it from the Walker,' said Tragedy.

Tragedy had betrayed her. He had maybe betrayed other glints before her. She had no reason to trust him. He had got her killed.

The Friar, on the other hand, had initially seemed suspicious to both her and George. But then he had saved her life, shielding her from a bomb-blast and rescuing her from the Blitz.

Caught between a traitor and a saviour, Edie decided it was a trap worth walking into, and set off after the bird. She walked fast and then broke into a jog. Once she had made up her mind to do something, she never wasted time getting it done, for good or bad.

Little Tragedy hobbled along after her, wincing.

'You hurt my leg,' he snivelled. 'Look. I can't walk proper. I landed funny . . .'

'Good,' she said, without turning. 'Does the Friar know you betrayed me to the Walker?'

'No,' he moaned. 'You think I'm soft or something? 'E 'ates the Walker.'

After a few more steps he obviously decided she wasn't going to turn round and look at him, because he shrugged and straightened up and walked perfectly normally, all hint of a hobble gone.

The whine had also miraculously been cured when he next spoke, just as they were jogging up and across the intersection at the end of Blackfriar's Bridge.

'You ain't going to tell 'im?' he said.

'Why not?' she said, looking up and noticing the Murk for the first time. It hung above and behind the white pub like a slow-moving thundercloud.

'Because you don't know why I done what I did?' he said, and the air of hopefulness in his voice made her gorge rise, and she spun and grabbed a handful of his collar in her fist, so angry again that she ignored the pain in her split, bruised knuckles as she did so.

'Oi . . .' he said.

He was still protesting when Edie booted open the door of the pub and threw him in ahead of her. He pancaked on the floor in an ungainly spread-eagle, coming to rest against the legs of the Black Friar.

The burly monk looked down at him, and then up at Edie, his normally cheerful smile lost in an expression as thunderously ominous as the cloud outside.

'Please,' said Tragedy, turning to Edie. 'You don't have to tell him . . .'

'Indeed she doesn't,' boomed the Friar, bending down and hauling Tragedy to his feet in one powerful move.

The Raven flapped in and took a perch on one of the pump-handles on the bar. The door slammed shut behind it.

The Friar looked straight into Edie's eyes.

'I know exactly what you did.'

26

BUFFALO GIRL

George was torn between his horror at what had happened to Dictionary and wonder at the apparitions who had saved them both.

Three figures were approaching at a run, spread across the width of the street. The bronze one on the left had the unmistakable helmet of a World War One soldier like the Gunner, but even at this distance George knew it wasn't the Gunner because he carried a rifle and a scarf fluttered around his neck as he ran.

The bronze one on the right seemed to shamble speedily instead of actually running, but this was because he was swathed in an extraordinary collection of clothes – a thick woollen balaclava, a long garment that seemed at this distance to be half anorak, half smock and huge woollen mittens that seemed to hang from some kind of strappy chest-harness.

But as extraordinary as he looked he was nothing like as strange as the third one charging up the middle of the road at a faster clip than either of the two bronze statues. It was in fact two figures carved out of marble as white as the cloud of snow they were kicking up behind them. The larger one was an immense white buffalo, hooves pounding into a full gallop. The smaller figure was riding on its back, just behind the muscled shoulders, the fingers of her left hand gripping the woolly hump instead of a bridle. She wore only a thin cloak that rippled in the wind behind them like a battle-flag, and she held a businesslike lance in her right hand, ready to throw. On her head a warbonnet of eagle-feathers was blown flat by the speed of the charging buffalo, and lest there be any doubt that she was a warrior, bent on warrior's business, she carried a tomahawk clenched between her teeth.

The high-pitched yipping 'Hi's were coming round the handle of the war-axe, and her eyes were fixed in steely concentration on the dragon ahead of her.

The dragon ripped Hodge off its head and hurled the mewling cat into a snowdrift, turning its one remaining good eye on the source of the yipping, at the very moment the warrior raised herself on the buffalo's back and threw the spear.

It flew through the air and hit the dragon in the shoulder, so hard that the tip came a foot out of its back.

The dragon roared in outrage, so loud that cornices of snow fell off the surrounding buildings, but the buffalo just lowered its head as the rider snatched the tomahawk from her mouth with her newly empty hand – and then they hit the dragon smack-on dead centre, the buffalo's horns going each side of the taint's breast as it knocked it backwards in a mighty collision. The buffalo trampled right over the dragon and slewed round for a second charge.

The dragon pushed itself up, using a wing as a temporary crutch, but the impact had stunned it so badly it couldn't avoid the woman as she leant far out from the side of the passing buffalo and smashed the tomahawk into the side of its head in a blow that spun the head almost a full one hundred and eighty degrees.

Again the buffalo lumbered in a curve and came back for a third run. This time the warrior threw her tomahawk, which whirred end-over-end, thocking home in the centre of the taint's chest, just below the point where its neck rose up. Thick fire bled out of the wound like lava, because she had hit it right in the fire-crop, and it dabbed at itself in horror as its own fire began to eat into its scales.

As the buffalo passed on the other side the dragon took a last despairing swipe at the warrior woman riding it, but missed. She leant out and gripped the spear sticking out of the dragon's back and neatly pulled the whole length through the taint's body.

As it roared in pain and frustration behind them, she scissored nimbly off the side of the buffalo in a galloping dismount, not even stumbling a fraction as her bare feet hit the ground. And then she ran back in close behind the turning dragon and killed it stone dead with one decisive thrust through the centre of its back. She jerked her spear free as it fell on its side, and rolled the taint over with her foot, yanking her tomahawk out, while neatly avoiding the thick fire pooling round it.

'Doe-nada-go-huh-ee, do-way-gah!' she said, spitting on the twitching corpse. And then she looked up at George and grinned.

'Ah-see-you,' she said, eyes still wide in elation at her kill.

'Right,' he said. 'Er. I see you too.'

'No,' said a deep voice from behind him. The man in the balaclava was striding up. 'Ah-see-you is "hello" in her language.'

'Yes. Hello,' she barked as she ran past and dropped to one knee next to Dictionary, who was trying to get up. She put a gentle hand on his shoulder and made him lie down as she leant over and examined the damage.

George went to join her, but the man in the balaclava

gripped his shoulder and stopped him.

'Let her see to him, sonny. She knows as much about healing as she does about harming,' he said in a voice that was English, with a lilting hint of something else in the background. The slightly clipped ends to some of the words made George wonder if he was a bit Irish, perhaps. He knew he'd seen him before, on the side of a red-brick building by the park.

'You're Shackleton,' he said.

'Friends call me Shack,' said the spit with a smile, sticking out his hand to shake George's. 'You'll be George, the boy maker. We heard about you. This is the Railwayman . . .'

He nodded towards the soldier reloading his rifle as he jogged across the street to join them.

'And who's that?' breathed George, looking back at the warrior woman leaning over Dictionary, while her buffalo nosed the snow, as if hoping to find a few buried blades of grass on the pavement beneath.

'Well,' said Shack, a hint of amusement glimmering in his eyes, 'the Buffalo's called Bill, for obvious reasons . . .'

'No,' said George. 'Her. Who's she?'

'Oh, her?' said the soldier. 'Sitting on a buffalo, head full of eagle feathers? 'Oo do you think she is? S'obvious . . .'

He snorted and rolled his eyes at Shack.

'She's the Queen of America.'

27

THE MACHINE OF
TIMES AND PLACES

It is my fault, indeed it is,' repeated the Friar, scowling at Little Tragedy.

'You knew what he did?' said Edie incredulously.

'That he tricked you, that he spirited you through the mirrors to a place of detention in London Past, no – I did not know that until it was too late. Indeed, until the Raven here came to me I knew nothing of it, or of the fate you and the boy arranged for the Walker. You are to be congratulated, my child, my word yes, you are,' he said, his stern face relaxing for a moment as his more usual smile made a brief appearance, his eyes all but disappearing in creases of mirth. Then he turned back to Tragedy. 'But that this imp was partial to another, that the Walker had him in his thrall, using him as a common kitchen-spy and tattle-tale? That I did know. My failing was to believe, while he may have been capable of mischief and tale-bearing, he was not capable of evil.'

Tragedy carefully got to his feet and looked at the Friar. He couldn't hold his gaze for longer than a second and looked away.

'I ain't evil. I was just . . . I been made wrong, ain't I? Like there's something in me what ain't quite right. It's not my fault.'

He glanced pleadingly at Edie.

'I thought the Walker 'elped glints, see? He was always looking for 'em. And 'e said one day when 'e was free of the Stone and its curse, 'e'd make me better inside.'

'Bumblepuppy! One liar should see another's lies for what they are,' roared the Friar.

'Yeah, but you talked to 'im,' shot back the small boy, in a sudden cringing counter-attack. He pointed a thin finger. 'You talked whenever he was past here . . .'

'You talked to the Walker?' Edie said, horrorstruck.

'Frequently,' the Friar replied instantly.

She tried to get her bearings in a tilting world that seemed to lurch from one side to another every time she thought she had it straight.

'But he was bad, I mean worse than bad, he was a murderer and a . . . and you just TALKED to him! Why???'

The Friar spread his arms wide, his voice bouncing off the marble and mirrors and rattling the glasses on their shelves.

'Why? WHY??? Why would I talk to any man, any woman, any waif or stray who found their way to my door? Because it is my lot to bring cheer and succour to any that seek it!'

Edie tried to protest, but he silenced her with an imperious sweep of his hand.

'Close your mouth, child, and hear me out. An open mouth is a great obstacle to an open mind, indeed it is. I talk to the Walker because I am a priest, and a priest must talk to all men who wish to talk. And who but the darkest souls have the most need of the light a listening heart can bring? And then I am also a landlord and a host, my house a free-house, open to men of every stripe and colour.'

'The Walker wasn't a man. He was a *monster*!' she protested, unable to keep in her outrage any longer.

The Friar hoicked up his cassock and knelt on one knee, coming eye to eye with her. His voice lowered and he spoke as if he was talking to her alone.

'He is a man. You know it to be so, because you know as I do that, slice the world how you will, it is men and men alone who make the very worst monsters.'

There was a long beat. Then Edie nodded, despite herself.

'And then there's the other reason . . .' he said, reaching out a hand to one side. The Raven flapped off the beer pump and came to roost on his outstretched finger. 'It is good to keep your friends close, but better to keep your enemies even closer.'

And with that he winked and bounced to his feet, suddenly invigorated.

'I am a man who needs to watch his enemies, child, and what better way to do so than to appear to be all things to all men, and if that is a crime then every landlord who was ever worth his salt should swing for it!' he said, clapping his hands in sudden mirth. 'And why need I watch my enemies? Because I am three in one and one in three, Priest, Landlord . . . and Guardian.'

'Guardian?' said Edie. 'Guardian of who?'

His hand swept round the extravagantly decorated room, taking in the reliefs on the walls, the mirrored pillars leading to the barrel-vaulted snug with its mosaic roof, smoky mutton-fat marble and exotic alabaster light-fittings.

'Guardian of *what*, child, not who. Guardian of this. Guardian of the Thresholds, Guardian of the Ways between Here and There, between Then and Now, between what may be and what might be.'

And he snapped his fingers theatrically, and in an instant the light dimmed to a redder and more ancient glow, as if the electric bulbs had become flickering oil lamps. And as his finger-snap still echoed round the room, the alabaster figures that hung beneath the lamps launched off the walls and flew to him.

The beaming black-robed Friar was framed by the four white winged imps with their goat legs and satyr horns.

'This spot, this house, this Machine of Times and Places has always been an uneasy point, balanced between the best and the worst, between monks and devils. It is my duty to maintain the equilibrium. I make no apologies for the way I do it.'

Edie remembered the large figure reaching up to the compass-rose mosaic in the ceiling of the snug and shifting the chequered rings before showing her the past in the mirrors.

'This is a time machine,' she said, feeling stupid. 'This whole building is a time machine!'

'Yes . . . and no, child,' he said, walking back into the shadowy arch between the rooms, standing between the two narrow mirrors facing each other on either side of the pilasters.

'It is a place where the lines of power cross. And where lines of great powers cross you can travel between both Now and Then, and Here and There . . . if you have the knack of it.'

'So I can go to the past? I can change the past!' she said, excitement rising in her throat.

'No,' he said. 'Good lord, no. Changing the past? What

a thought. No, child, if people could change the past where on earth would we be? Certainly not where we are today.'

'But I went back into the past,' she said. 'It doesn't make sense. In the Blitz. To the House of Lost Hope. To the Frost Fair!'

Edie was getting so very excited about the idea of changing the past because she thought she could go back and alter what had happened to her mother. She was sure that this was what the rising elation and frustration she had been feeling ever since she'd been revived and found her mother's heart stone was all about.

It all made sense.

She was going to see her mother because she was going to go back and warn her. She was going to tell her about the—

'No!' he repeated. This time with a voice like a church door slamming. 'You cannot change the past if you were not in it in the first place. If you were meant to be there, you are. Otherwise you just see it. Or rather you are in it but not of it. You can see but not be seen. Like your glinting.'

'I don't understand . . .' she protested. But she didn't go on because she sort of did. She realized that nothing that she had foreseen about her death at the Frost Fair had happened any differently when she had actually been there, being the one being killed. All the air went out of her as her heart dropped.

'. . . yeah. No. Actually I do,' she said grimly, looking at the carpet and the dust-sheets on the floor. 'It's all crap as usual.'

The Black Friar watched her until she lifted her head and swept the fall of hair from her face.

'You thought you would change things for the better,' he said with an unexpected gentleness that ambushed her and made her eyes prickle with the tears they were just managing to hold back.

She nodded, not trusting herself to speak. He blew his cheeks out and scratched the back of his head.

'We have little time, child. Time itself is out of joint. The old Darkness rides again, and the taints have flocked to a new Darkness whose frozen evil is blighting the City. Even now an Icy Murk is billowing over the roof of this building. And yet all is not lost, and kindness that was done can be repaid. And while this Machine of Times and Places may not change the past, what is learnt by it may yet change the future.'

'What do you mean?' said Edie.

'You freed the Raven, Memory. And he would repay your kindness with a gift of his own. Maintaining the balance, you see. And he has much to give, since he has seen much and remembered all.'

The Raven bobbed off his hand and flew on to her shoulder. It looked into her eye. It was too close for her to focus on it, but she could see it was nodding enthusiastically.

'What gift?' she said carefully.

The Raven clacked in her ear.

The Friar tapped the mirrors on either side of him.

'If you will allow him to guide you back into the mirrors . . .'

'What then?' she said, suddenly aware her skin was goosebumping.

'He would take you to see your mother.'

28

STONEARM

'The boy! What of the boy . . .?' cried Dictionary, pushing aside the restraining hands of the Queen of America as he staggered to his feet. '. . . Boy, where are you?'

George ran over to him as he felt blindly around him with increasing desperation.

'Dictionary!' he gasped, trying to hold the stumbling figure up. The ravaged head turned eyelessly towards him as the great legs gave way and Dictionary abruptly sat back down again in the middle of the road.

'Thank God,' the big man said, breathing hard. 'You are alive.'

'Yes,' said George, choking as he looked at the damage to the man's head. 'But . . .'

As if sensing the look of horror that he could no longer see, Dictionary's hands traced the maimed contours of his fire-splashed face, finding the blank sweep of new-melted metal where his eyes had been, pausing as they moved up and over the extravagant curves of the frozen fire-splash.

His opened his mouth to speak, then shut it again, and clenched his jaw in a fierce jut that reminded George of Edie.

'Dictionary . . .' began George, his voice catching.

The big man waved him off, as if he could hear the pent-up emotion about to burst out of the boy and wanted no part of it. He fired off a single burst of harsh laughter.

'Ha! I thought my wig had perhaps become dislodged and was serving the purpose of an unexpected blindfold. But I find, as you see that I am blind, sir.'

His hands waved out in front of him, reaching for something. George grasped one, and it closed on his in a fierce grip. As he did so he saw the Clocker being lowered from the canopy in front of the department store by the Queen of Time's handmaidens and hurrying towards them.

Shack was kneeling by one of the fallen dragons, poking at it.

'I'm so sorry . . .' George began, the words choking awkwardly in his throat. Dictionary shooed them away.

'Not a thought of it, child. Fortunes of war. I have never had cause to exert myself in a martial cause, and I may now admit that when I once said every man thinks meanly of himself for not having been a soldier, the everyman I was thinking of was myself.'

The Clocker put his hand on Dictionary's shoulder.

'Dear friend. Your injury most gallantly won . . .'

Dictionary smiled bravely.

'They have taken my sight, not my mind, Clocker. And yet . . .'

He turned his face round, as if blindly looking at them both and something beyond.

'. . . and yet I shall miss the sight of this great city, and my friends.'

And here he gripped George's hand even more tightly and pulled him in closer.

'And it *is* a great city, child. True, I have not voyaged to Stamboul or the fabled cities of Far Cathay, but I cannot imagine them mightier or fuller of event and majesty. London is the greatest metropolis that ever was. And now I feel in my water that it is up to you to ensure it remains so.'

George found the lump had grown in his throat.

'I don't know . . .' he said.

'I do, child,' growled Dictionary, gripping his hand. 'You will do it or die trying. You have the doggedness and the grit that has ever been the mark of the true Londoner. This is a city of liberty, made by free men for free men. It is not a city that knuckles under easily to oppression. Why 'tis not long since that even kings had to ask leave to enter it. You will liberate it from this time-frozen blight, George. You will free it again.'

The Clocker gasped. George's first thought was that Dictionary had squeezed his hand too hard. His second thought – following the Clocker's eye-line – was that the dead dragon he was looking at had moved and was not actually dead. And then he saw it was still, but that the Clocker had seen something that Shack had just pulled loose from its talon.

'There's a couple of things I don't like here,' tutted Shack.

'Surely not,' cried the Clocker and ran over to the taint's body. Shack handed him the gold and blue fragment that had got jammed in between the creature's claws.

He held it up in horror.

'The Queen of Time. This monster has . . .' Shack took the fragment and handed it to the warrior queen.

'Is her dress,' she said simply.

The Clocker nodded.

'Then the taints got her.'

George rode the empty feeling of despair that welled up inside him.

'It's my fault. I should have got here sooner. The Sphinx said she shouldn't try to restart time until we had penned the Darkness back in the Stone.'

Shack looked at him. He had the kind of eyes that seemed to see everything; not just what was on the surface, but the stuff behind it, with equal clarity.

'Did you come with all speed?'

'Yes,' said George.

'Then it's scarcely your fault. You don't have time to waste being guilty,' he snapped, as if closing the issue.

'We find her,' announced the Queen of America. 'Follow dragon's tracks in snow back to where he got this.'

She held up the fragment of gold and blue.

'We bring her back. At turn o' day she will be revived on her plinth. Is simple.'

She looked at Shack, who nodded. He was about to speak when the Railwayman snapped alert.

'Hello!' he said, raising his gun.

'No,' said George. 'No! He's with me. He's one of us now.'

It was Spout, flying in over the rooftops. He carried something in his mouth. Like a great cat he was bringing his prey home, its haunch gripped in his jaw. As he came in to land he spat the body of the dead dog-gargoyle out ahead of him. It hit the snow like a bag of bricks and lay still. He flared his wings and landed in front of George.

'Gack,' he announced.

'Nice job, Spout,' said George. 'He killed the dog-gargoyle.'

'Good,' grunted Dictionary in satisfaction. Hodge walked up and sniffed the corpse, looked at Spout in approval, and then leapt into Dictionary's arms. The big man caught him on reflex, and held him tight. The cat looked at the terrible scalloped wound flaring out from his owner's head and allowed himself to be stroked. He purred deeply as he did so, and licked Dictionary's hand.

'There you are, you catamount,' he said gently, smiling. 'You dragonslayer. Had I a barrel of oysters, you should eat them all.'

'You know the other things I don't like,' said Shack, pointing to the corpses of the gargoyle and the dragons.

'The taints' bodies are still here. Normally they go to pieces and are winnowed away on the wind,' said George.

Shack nodded and clapped him on the shoulder. 'Good man,' he said, 'but there's the other thing. City Dragons guard the City perimeter. That's their purpose. They keep their station. They don't gang up and go marauding like this.'

'I think all bets are off,' said George. And in as few words as he could, he told them about everything that had happened since coming back through the mirrors and allowing the Ice Devil in after them.

'Well,' muttered Shack, watching George unconsciously rubbing at the pain in his arm, 'if the Dark powers are exerting the kind of pull which makes the taints forget their maker's first purpose, we're in trouble. Though these City Dragons are mass-produced trash really. So the maker's first purpose is probably a little diluted. Now, I think we'd better have a look at your arm.'

'It's fine,' said George. 'I mean it aches a bit . . .'

'Jacket and shirt off, please,' said Shack in a calm voice that said 'I don't believe you' and 'don't you dare disobey me' in equal measure.

George hesitated, and then did as he was asked. He

unbuttoned his coat and the one beneath it, and then lifted his shirt over his head. The cold hit his exposed torso and raised instant goose bumps all over him.

'Wah!' said the Queen of America, impressed.

George looked at his arm.

'Oh,' he managed, then shut up, because had the strong urge to be sick and so needed to keep his mouth closed.

'That is something,' said Shack, whistling in appreciation.

George's arm had disappeared.

Not a scrap of skin remained.

The new arm was made of stone.

The white and gritty limestone vein that had been twining up in tight spirals had thickened and spread, obliterating the strips of skin that had separated them. It had also pushed up and over his shoulder.

He raised it and flexed it in fascinated horror. The stone was stretching down over his wrist and taking over his hand as well. It felt horrible looking at a part of his body that he controlled that was both him and very definitely not him at all.

'You know what a retiarius is?' said Shack.

George shook his head, not ready to risk a word as long as 'no' in case he lost control and threw up right there and then.

'Retiarii were Roman gladiators. They fought with nets and a trident, no protection except for one arm covered in armour, just like that. You look just like one of them.'

Shack smiled, as if the horror on his arm was nothing.

'OK,' George managed to say, and then started clumsily tugging back into his clothes as fast as he could.

It seemed very urgent to cover up this appalling growth as quickly as he could.

Once he was covered up he felt strong enough to tell them about the Cnihtengild and the three veins that had started to twist up his arm, each one representing one of three duels he had to fight. He told them about how he'd fought two duels and had lost the marble and the bronze veins, and how this stone vein that had spread over his shoulder was all that remained, marking the final remaining duel he had yet to fight.

'And you say you have to fight this last duel before the stone spreads across your chest and encases your heart?' said Shack, as if this was the most natural thing in the world and he was just making certain of the details.

George nodded, buttoning one jacket over the other.

'And was stone on your shoulder this morning?' said the Queen of America.

'No,' said George uncomfortably. 'No, I don't think it was.'

'So it is moving,' she said, looking at Shack.

'So it's moving, yes,' said George.

'Right,' said Shack decisively. 'Can't be helped. It is what it is. We should take its example and do the same ourselves.'

He pointed to the Railwayman.

'If you'd be so kind as to lead Dictionary back to his plinth.'

'Sir,' snapped the soldier, his hand tipping his tin helmet as he walked over and took Dictionary's arm.

'We'll find the Queen of Time,' said Shack, watching the Clocker being lifted back up on to the canopy by the waiting handmaidens. 'You go follow the Sphinx's instructions, though they sound like mumbo-jumbo to me. If we succeed, we will meet you wherever the spits decide to make their stand. God willing you will succeed and it will not be necessary.'

And with that he raised a hand in parting and followed the Queen of America as she trotted back along the dragon's tracks. She paused as they were about to turn the corner and raised her spear in farewell, a wide smile on her face, and then she, the buffalo and Shack were gone.

'Come on, guvnor,' said the Railwayman, putting Dictionary's hand on his shoulder. 'Clap on there and don't let go. You talk and I'll walk, eh?'

'A moment,' said Dictionary, turning towards George.

'George Chapman. I know you go with a heavy heart to face an unpleasurable and frightening duty. But heavy though your heart be, find enough space in it to carry a little hope: for the natural flight of the human mind is from hope to hope, and it is in making those great leaps that we most extend our humanity. And heroes, as you have seen from the exertions of this cat . . .' he said, holding Hodge up to view. 'Heroes come in all shapes and sizes. Godspeed, boy.'

And with that he harrumphed and let the Railwayman lead him off, leaving George alone with Spout and a very large lump in his throat. He took a deep breath, swallowed and made himself stand straighter.

'OK,' he said, looking at the waiting gargoyle. 'Let's get this done.'

29

MEAT AND DRINK

It's impossible,' said Edie, looking into one of the two parallel mirrors on the inner face of the central arch leading into the snug. She could see a whole chorus line of Edies dwindling away into infinity in the reflection, all in identical dark fur jackets cinched tight round their waist, each with an identical Raven perched on their shoulder. The Ravens all pecked the ear of their Edies.

'Ow!' she said, flinching at the nip on hers. 'Why'd he do that?'

The Friar stood outside the arch looking at her. The Raven clacked its beak.

'He wanted to get your attention,' he said.

'He's got my attention. I still say it's impossible . . . how's he going to get me to my mum?' she asked, cocking her own head and squinting at the bird. 'I mean, if he's got all the memories in there, how's he going to pick out the ones of my mum?'

The Raven pecked her ear again.

'OW!' she winced. 'Knock it off!'

'He wants to see your stone. Or rather, your mother's,' said the Friar.

'Well, he could have said so,' said Edie, rubbing her ear.

'He did,' said the Friar. 'You just don't know how to hear him.'

Edie pulled her mother's heart stone from her pocket

189

and held it up. They all looked at the small fire still kindled inside it.

'She's still alive, see?' said Edie. 'There's still fire.'

The Friar squinted closer.

'There's still fire,' he agreed.

'So she's still alive,' insisted Edie.

He grimaced.

'There's still fire. What that means is beyond me.'

'Means she's still alive somewhere. And I was told she was dead,' persisted Edie.

She took a deep breath. Whatever was going to happen next was going to knock her world on its ear, she knew that. A heady mix of anticipation and something very close to fear began to flood her system. Her mouth was suddenly dry and she was certain that the Friar could hear her heart pounding.

'So how does this work?' she asked the Raven. 'How do you find my mum in all those choices?'

She pointed at all the slices of time in the mirrors as the reflections banked up and away to vanishing point.

The Raven clacked its beak once, looked at the Friar who nodded shortly, and then nipped the heart stone clean out of her fingers.

And swallowed it.

'You are joking!' said Edie in disbelief.

And as the Friar reached above his head and twisted the great outer ring of the roof mosaic, the Raven flew into the mirror, and Edie leapt after it without thinking, determined not to let it escape with the last memory of her mother.

'No!!!' she cried.

And then she was falling through the layers in the mirrors, a terrible sideways rushing vertigo making her gag into silence. She seemed to fall like this for a long time, and as she fell she had the sensation of the black bird flying raggedly alongside her. She twisted to see what exactly she was falling and flashing past, but all she saw was black strobing a deeper black in a way that made her feel very nauseous, and then she landed.

She landed in the snow, between two cars in a street hard up against the sheer wall of the Ice Murk. She was in one of the ley-line canyons that intersected the fog. It took her a moment to get her bearings, as she looked at the section of church sticking out of the Murk, and the graveyard wall to her right with its gate topped by stone skulls. Then she knew exactly where she was. She stumbled through the gates, following the Raven.

And then he was in the cramped graveyard at Ghastly Grim, the last place she'd been free before the Walker captured her and took her to the Frost Fair. The place where she had hurriedly buried her own heart stone at the foot of an ancient grave marker.

'Aemilia Bowles,' she said, looking at the words carved into the stone tablet, now topped by a toadstool cap of snow.

The Raven dropped to the ground and started scratching away.

'Here, I'll do it,' she said, and swept snow aside, revealing the earth beneath. She tore and scrabbled at it until her fingers found what she was looking for. She pulled her piece of sea-glass from the ground and wiped the mud from it.

The raven clacked its beak.

Edie nodded and closed her fingers round her own heart stone. Something quietly clicked into place inside her, and she felt stronger. Her mother's heart stone had kept her going, but it wasn't quite the real thing. This was.

'Thanks,' she said.

The Raven led her out of the gates and back into the street. It flew eerily straight into the side mirror of one of the parked cars, and Edie took a deep breath and just stuck her hand in after it and jumped.

Again she fell through the strong darkness, wondering as she fell if she strobing was in fact the regular wing-beats of the Raven just ahead of her, and then she landed.

It wasn't a hard landing. It was as if she'd just stumbled on grass. She felt the warm green under her outstretched hands at the same time that she saw it. She stared at the ground in front of her nose, getting her breath.

It was bright and hot, and noisy all around her. After the church-like gloom of the pub and the snow-deadened city, the London she had fallen into was glaring, summery and boisterous with sound.

Perhaps it was the sudden contrast, but she felt painfully sensitive to the sensations crowding in on her all at once. The colours seemed too bright, the heat too hot and the noise . . . the noise was too loud and too various. Cars were passing, people were talking and laughing, and music was bleeding over everything. She could hear a man's voice on a nearby radio, skating over a choppy guitar and a skanking bass, singing insistently about not wanting to go to Chelsea.

There was the thump of a passing lorry, and in the side-wash of air as it went by, some purple foil blew into the narrow green world of grass she was focused on. It was a purple she knew, a distinctive chocolate-wrapper purple, but as it flipped over and caught the sun she saw white curvy writing that spelt 'Aztec' – the name of a bar she'd never seen before. Somehow a memory was kindled, not a visual one, but before she could chase it down a man shouted nearby and the wrapper blew under a bench beside her.

'Oi. Litterbug. Pick it up!'

Edie raised her head and looked round on reflex, thinking the man was shouting at her. It took her a moment to get her bearings before she saw him and the young girl he was shouting at. In that moment she saw a stone building with Tudor windows and a small white-capped clock tower, and then as she continued to turn she saw the old building was just one side of a lopsided square, the other faces of which were hemmed in by much more modern buildings. Then she saw the corner of a huge barn-like structure in a road leading towards her and she recognized it as Smithfield Meat Market. It took her a moment to do so, because although she had walked past it many times as she moved round the City, she had never walked past it thirty years ago.

She reckoned it must be about thirty years from the strangely thin and angular shapes of the cars in the street, painted in non-metallic colours she didn't recognize.

The radio the music was coming out of was in a car parked close to the side of the grassy area. Its door was open and several men were standing round a little clump of beer bottles marching raggedly across its roof. They were burly men, some of whom wore white pork-pie hats. A couple were stripped to the waist. The one who was shouting, the only one who turned to face her was smoking and wearing an alarmingly bloodstained apron.

Butchers, she thought. After work. Having a beer. Cooling off. Or hotting up.

Drunk.

Edie had radar for Drunk. She'd had to develop it to stay one step ahead of her stepfather. Drunk, for Edie, was another way of spelling Danger.

'Go on. Pick it up!' he shouted again, a dangerously fragile smile on his face. And it was then that she realized he wasn't shouting at her, but at a little girl sitting on the bench next to her. The girl looked up from where she was reading a comic. It wasn't the comic that Edie noticed though. And it wasn't her face, not to start with.

It was her hair.

It was a long sweep of aubergine-coloured hair, scraped back from her face in a red Alice band.

It was Edie's own hair.

'GO on then!' said the man, pausing to light a new cigarette from the butt of the previous one.

But the face, when it turned towards the shouting butcher, was *not* Edie's face. Not quite. It was younger, seven, maybe eight, although the dark-ringed eyes looked older, too old for the pinched and suddenly scared face they sat in. It was the eyes that hit Edie low in the gut and made her gasp.

'Yeah, Dad. Sorry.' The girl flinched, and scooted off the bench, reaching for the wrapper, her mouth still working on a lump of Aztec bar.

Edie looked into the face, so close to her own. Her heart hung there, not beating, ripped raw by the realization of who the frightened girl was.

She started to say 'Mum . . .' but immediately knew it was the wrong thing to say. She corrected herself and gasped out her mother's name.

194

'Sue . . .'

She needn't have bothered changing what she said.

The girl couldn't see her. Or hear her. Edie was invisible.

30

LOST GIRL

'Where's Edie?' said the Gunner, looking round the crowd of spits, all still talking at once in a series of more or less heated arguments. No one heard him. So he pulled his pistol and fired a round into the sky.

'Where's the girl?' he said to the sudden sea of faces that all turned towards him.

'Damn,' swore the Officer, looking around. The Gunner met the Queen's eyes over the top of the crowd.

'I thought she was with you,' she said, looking troubled as she scanned the crowd from the higher vantage point of her chariot.

'Why are we worrying about a girl . . . ow!' said the Lionheart, almost completing the question before the Queen caught him a sharp smack on the side of his crowned helm with the shaft of her spear.

'Because she matters, you battle-addled buffoon, she matters in all this!'

'I was just asking,' he mumbled, straightening his crown. 'There's no need to be violent . . .'

The Queen's daughters were running round the perimeter of the crowd, looking at the well-trampled snow.

'Any tracks?' said the Queen.

'Too many,' said the closest.

'Where's the Raven?' asked the Officer.

'What Raven?' said the Lionheart. 'Ow!'

A wigged figure on a horse had smacked the other side of his helmet.

'Who are you that would strike a king!' shouted the Lionheart, turning to see who had dared to touch him.

'Another king, fool,' sighed the other, shaking his gloved finger in his face. 'And if you can't concentrate, for mercy's sake keep quiet.'

The Lionheart noticed several other kings and a couple of very frosty queens glaring at him, distinctly unamused.

'This is an outrage,' he muttered. But only very quietly.

The Queen and the Gunner and the Officer had come together at her chariot.

'If she's gone with that damned Raven . . .' said the Gunner.

'The Raven is not damned,' said the Queen, 'but it is fated. The girl wanted none of this.' She swept her hand around the serried ranks of spits gathered in front of them. 'In truth she only wanted one thing, ever since she found that heart stone.'

'Her mother,' said the Officer.

'Thinks she's still alive,' agreed the Gunner. 'You think she is?'

'I don't know,' said the Queen, 'but all that matters is that *she* does and she must have gone looking for her.'

'Or the Raven's led her astray,' scowled the Gunner. 'George is going to be well bent out o' shape when he finds we've lost her. Right. Search party. I'll go east. She was talking about the Black Friar.'

He pointed up the Embankment towards the City. The Dark wall of the Ice Murk rose in a sinister grey massif above the rooftops.

'I'll go north, my daughters will go east and south,'

said the Queen, jerking the reins on her horses.

The Officer put out his hand and gripped them.

'No,' he said. 'Sorry. You have to stay with me. Send your girls. But I need you.'

'What?' said the Queen, bridling. 'You dare to command me?'

'Yes,' he said. 'Sorry and all that. But someone's got to take charge of this lot, and if I start issuing orders there's just going to be even more bloody chaos.'

'But—' she said.

'No "buts", your majesty. Just a large dollop of the old *noblesse oblige*, I'm afraid. You're the ranking Queen here. You just stand behind me and grip anyone who bloody argues.'

The Queen absorbed this, and then nodded. Her daughters ran off in different directions. The Gunner raised a hand and headed along the Embankment.

'Good luck,' said the Officer, and turned back to the Queen. 'Ready?'

She nodded. He stepped up on to the front wall of her chariot and then they both turned on the crowd, who had started bickering again.

'Right!' bellowed the Officer. 'Eyes front, all of you!'

His parade-ground bark cut through the noise and made every head turn towards him. He drove straight into the moment of silence before it closed again.

'First thing we're going to do is move our position. All of you, up there, Trafalgar Square, round the column, move now.'

'Who are you to give us orders?' barked a king with wobbly jowls and a too-tight uniform dusted with medals and ribbons.

'He is the Officer. A soldier by profession, not by

accident of birth,' said the bear-like bald man in the long overcoat. He jabbed a thick cigar at the king. 'He was made to give orders. Whatever foul axis of darkness we are now facing, we would do well to listen to real soldiers.'

'Well said, Bulldog,' said the Queen, stepping up next to him and looking round at the other spits very pointedly. 'You will all listen to him or answer to me.'

'May I ask why Trafalgar Square?' said the king, trying to regain a little face.

'More room to see 'em coming on the ground, and the High Admiral can be a lookout in the sky,' said the Officer. 'No more questions. Move now.'

31

THE PIT

Edie watched the small girl who would one day be her mother reach under the bench to get the trapped chocolate wrapper.

Even though the child could not see or hear her, the urge to make contact was unstoppable. At some fundamental level of being like was calling to like, and demanding to be heard.

She reached out to stroke the cheek only centimetres away from her.

She couldn't touch it.

Just couldn't. No matter how hard she tried. No matter how desperately she wanted to. Her hand just skated away.

She gasped and tried again. Her hand just reached a point where the forward motion was deflected by a force that felt exactly like the one you feel when you try and push two strong magnets together at the same pole. At a certain point you can't get them any closer. They can't touch. They just slip apart, repelling each other.

Edie watched as the girl reached for the wrapper. She saw her hand touch a stone sticking out of the grass.

And she heard the girl choke.

She saw her face go pale and her eyes jolt open. She saw her start shaking violently, trying to tear her hand away from the stone. And she saw the child's mouth drop open in horror, chocolatey saliva pooling on to the grass in front of her in an unnoticed loop of drool.

'Let go of the stone!' shouted Edie.

The girl of course couldn't hear her, but Edie knew exactly what was happening.

She was glinting.

The girl's breath was coming in shocked sobs now. Her small body was vibrating with the terror of what was flowing through her from the stone.

Edie had never seen anyone else in the grip of what she still felt was her curse. Knowing the agony and incomprehension gripping the small child, and not being able to help it was unbearable.

'Put it down!' she yelled impotently. And then she gritted her teeth and threw her arms round the thin ribcage of the girl and tried to pull her out from under the bench, away from the stone. It was like trying to squeeze a wet bar of soap, or an ice cube. She couldn't get a purchase on her, and the girl just didn't feel her at all. She certainly didn't move. Tears began to streak down her face as she started shouting at whatever abomination she was seeing:

'No . . . no . . . no . . .!'

Edie felt answering tears of frustration in her own eyes. She stopped trying to tug the girl, and dived under the bench next to her, determined that if she couldn't get girl to let go of the stone, she'd take the stone from the girl.

'It's OK!' she gasped. 'It's not you, it's the stone, it's OK!'

She touched the stone.

It wasn't.

A juddering flash sent a skull-splitting knife of pain straight up her arm, over her shoulder and neck, and buried it in the back of her head as her eyes now jolted wide and she glinted what the seven-year-old next to her was seeing.

'Oh God,' said Edie. 'They're all dead.'

The past came at her in the juddering time-slices that it always did when she glinted, and though the scene changed with each burst of pain and the light that punctuated it, the pit didn't.

The pit was a vast hand-dug quarry, intermittently shrouded with smoke from the bonfires that reeked and billowed along its edge. The low roofs of a much earlier London were occasionally visible through the shifting vapours. It was a London of half-timbered houses and stooped, shambling figures in early medieval dress. The figures at the edge of the pit moved and changed with each slice of time, but the pit didn't change.

It didn't change at all.

It just filled up.

Bodies were dropped in in ones and twos, sliding off hand-carts or planks or even doors that were used as stretchers. Great horses pulled solid-looking wagons through the murk, axle-deep in the mud at the top of the pit, loaded down with the dead.

Piles of dead, stacked like firewood and then tipped in. Men, women, children. All shapes and sizes and ages. Some were clothed, some wrapped in shrouds, some grey and helplessly naked. Many had blood streaking from their mouths, and on the naked ones there were great boils clumping in certain parts of the body. All went over the edge, all tumbled down the side of the pit, all landed with a slap or a thump and then lay unmoving on a jumbled layer of earlier corpses. Hollow eyes stared slack-jawed and sightless at the hellish bed on which they'd been carelessly flung for their long rest, until another load dropped into the pit and covered their final indignity with a new blanket of the freshly dead.

Black-cowled priests patrolled the edge of the pit, hurriedly blessing the departed by the cart-load, one hand carving quick crosses in the air, while the other held herb-stuffed rags to their mouths and noses.

Edie's eye caught movement in the pit below, and for a ghastly moment she knew that some poor soul had been thrown in alive and was trying to swim upwards and break into the air from beneath a sea of corpses. And then she saw it was not a person but a dog, and that it was tugging at something, something that looked like a child's . . .

. . . she never got to see what it was because the butcher yanked his little daughter out from under the bench, and the stone was jerked out of her hand as he laid her panicked twitching body on the grass, and the glinting stopped.

'Sue!' he cried. 'Sue!'

His friends clustered round, red-faced and beer-fuddled.

'She's having one of her turns!' he shouted. 'Give her some bloody air!

'She's going to swallow 'er tongue,' warned one of the other butchers. 'Here.' And he pulled a pencil from behind his ear.

The father grabbed it and jammed it in the little girl's mouth. She bucked and tried to spit it out.

'You're choking her!' shouted Edie, but no one could hear or see her either.

'I dunno what to do,' said the father, swearing under his breath. 'It's getting ridiculous . . .'

His hands held the girl flat to the ground. Edie could see he was trying to shake the alcohol out of his head, and wasn't doing anything but try and calm the girl, but she could also see the girl was now feeling trapped on top of the shock of what she had seen.

There was a crunch and a snap as she bit through the pencil and spat the pieces out.

'There was dead people, so many dead people, and I thought I was going to fall in and they were all dead . . .' she choked.

'Shh,' said the man. 'Shh now.'

'But . . .' she said.

'No,' he said, smoothing his hand over her mouth and cheek. 'Get your breath. Don't talk.'

Edie saw what no one but the girl saw, because his face was looking down, and all his friends could only see the back of his head. She saw the flicker of fear and the accompanying flush of embarrassment.

Edie had been where the girl was, and had seen that flicker in other faces. The flicker that meant 'Don't be a loony, please don't let anyone else know you're a loony who sees things. Not yet. Not in front of my mates. Just wait till we get home . . .'

He snatched a cigarette from a pack of ten and stashed it back in his pocket as one of his friends leant in and lit it for him. He sucked nicotine and nodded at the little girl staring up at him with wide, wet eyes.

'Just wait until we get home eh?' said the butcher. 'You had a turn.'

'Too much sun,' laughed one of the men as the others began to drift off now the fit had passed and nobody was going to need to call an ambulance.

'Yeah,' said the father, and he clean-lifted the girl into

his arms. 'Too much sun . . .'

And the last Edie saw of the little girl who would one day be her mother was a tiny hand flopping alongside a ribbon of dark hair as the butcher carried her away, cigarette smoke eddying back round the side of his face.

"Course, there wasn't any sun when she had that barmy fit at Christmas, was there?' said one of the remaining friends quietly.

'Nah,' said another. 'Poor little spazz-ball. She's gonna end up having that electro-shock like her old mum, I reckon.'

'Can't call her a spazz-ball,' said the other one, slapping him across the head.

'Ow!'

'Shut up and get the next round in,' said the slapper. 'You're a disgrace.'

'I know,' laughed the other. 'Mind you, maybe she seen a ghost?'

'No such thing,' said the other.

'I know. But look where we are.' He pointed up at a street sign. 'Charterhouse Square. Biggest plague pit in London under there.'

They both turned and looked at the innocent patch of grass for a beat.

'Everyone round here knows that,' said the slapper. 'She'll have heard her dad talking about it.'

They looked at the green for another beat.

'Yeah,' they both said at once.

And turned away, walking towards the other drinkers at the kerb.

Edie stood alone, feeling that a great salty wave had washed through her, leaving her empty and sad and somehow scoured out and unsure what she would do next.

She felt a tug on her arm. The Raven pulled her away towards an open shop door on the other side of the street. Edie felt so empty that she let the bird lead her. Halfway across the street she turned back and stared after the girl, now a distant burden to the shambling figure of the butcher as he carried her home.

The Raven pecked her insistently.

'I can't,' she said.

It hopped up and pecked her ear, hard.

She hardly noticed, eyes watching the tiny white thing bouncing in time with the Butcher's steps, knowing it was her mother's hand sticking out from under his arm.

'She's so little,' she said, her voice choked with despair and impotence.

It was a hand that would grow and one day try and smooth away Edie's cares and fears in the way she had just failed to do for its owner.

'She's so little . . .'

The butcher turned a corner in the distance and disappeared. Edie turned to the Raven. The Raven nodded twice and jerked its head sideways, as if saying 'Come on then.'

She followed its slow flap into the shop, which turned out not to be a shop at all, but a men's barber shop.

It was a small two-chair barber's. The barber was shaving a customer and talking about football, raising his voice above the tinny red radio propped up on the shelf in front of him next to the combs and scissors pickling in a great blue jar of Barbicide.

Neither barber nor customer could see Edie, or the great black bird that flew in ahead of her and perched on the back of the free chair. Edie sat in the chair, unnoticed. She looked into the mirror and saw it was doubled to infinity in a matching mirror on the wall behind her, the blue disinfectant and the red transistor gently arcing away in ever decreasing versions of themselves like a cheery two-tone rainbow.

The Raven flew over her head and into the mirror and she stood up on the footrest of the barber's chair, reached out after it. And as she followed it, the last thing she noticed was a smooth-voiced man singing out of the red radio about how much he loved the sound of breaking glass . . . especially when he was lonely.

Edie felt lonely as she fell into the mirror.

Lonely.

Sad.

And suddenly and inexplicably doomed.

32

MILE ZERO

George and Spout flew fast and low as they made
their way back to the Embankment. In the main they
flew below roof level, only popping above when the street
they were flying along went too far in the wrong direction
and they needed to take a short cut.

George was flying like this because he didn't want to
draw the attention of any new spits to their whereabouts,
and Spout seemed happy to let him steer them. George
could see he was tired by his two fights.

'You're doing well,' he said, gently slapping his neck.

'Gack,' said Spout, tipping sharply as he chicaned out
of the bottom of Leicester Square, heading for Charing
Cross and the Embankment beyond. George caught sight
of something moving fast across the snow, heading north
past the bookshops on Charing Cross Road. He craned
round to look backwards, and was relieved to see it was
no taint, but one of the Queen's daughters. He was just
starting to wonder what she was doing when Spout
flared his wings and seemed to stop dead in mid-air,
almost standing on his tail.

'Genny gits, Eigengang!'

George snapped his head round and saw the horde
now pouring into the centre of Trafalgar Square.

'Wow,' he breathed. 'Yeah. That's many spits all right.'

The Queen and the Officer were easy to see, even in
the crowd, because firstly they were directing people here
and there, and secondly, there were several horses but

only one chariot. But no Edie that he could see.

'Down, Spout,' he said.

The cat-gargoyle headed for the chariot without any need for George to steer him. As he dropped smoothly and flew along the lower level of the square, between the snow-filled fountains, George scissored one leg over his neck and jumped off in a running dismount. He lurched sideways, pulled off balance by an unnatural weight on his right side. The twinge of pain in his shoulder reminded him that his arm was now stone. He looked down at his hand, and shuddered at the sight. Only the two fingers next to his thumb were still him. The limestone had spread over the rest. He jammed his hand in his pocket and decided to think about it later.

'Did you stop her?' said the Officer as he ran up.

'No,' said George. 'Where's Edie?'

And while the square filled up around them, as spits of all shapes and sizes took up defensive positions, using the balustrades and raised pools and walls as cover, the Queen told George what the Sphinx had said about the Black Mirror, about how it was in a bed not a bed, somewhere where he had felt it to be, and then how they had failed to keep an eye on Edie. The news of her disappearance rocked him, and to hide how shaken he was, he bought time by telling them how he had failed to stop the Queen of Time flying to her doom. But even as he spoke, at the back of his mind an insistent and increasingly loud little voice kept telling him that Edie having disappeared was very, very bad news indeed.

As they talked, Spout became tired of being jostled and given funny looks by the spits bustling around him, and flapped up on to a tall, empty plinth on the north-west end of the square. From this raised viewpoint he watched the spits taking up positions all round him.

'Oi, Puss,' said a voice from below. Spout looked down and saw the four soldiers of the Euston Mob looking up at him. The one called East was grinning up at him.

'You got a nice view up there on that empty plinth have you? Good field of fire and all.'

'Gack,' said Spout uncertainly.

'Jolly good,' grinned East, holding up a hand. 'Give us a hand up, eh?'

As Spout reached his wing talons down and helped each of the four soldiers in turn, there was the sound of a throat being cleared behind George.

He turned to see the armoured king on his horse, looking a little apologetic.

'Not now, Lionheart!' hissed the Queen.

'This isn't a great beginning, is it?' said George, staring pointedly at her. 'You lose Edie and the Queen of Time is missing.'

'The girl lost herself . . .' began the Queen.

'That's just not good enough!' snapped George, finally giving in to the worried voice wheedling away in the back of his head. 'And you're the last person I'd expect to be making excuses. It was you took me aside and told me that she was especially vulnerable now. It was you told me to keep a special eye on her. And the moment my back's turned, it was YOU who lost her! Now we need to stop messing up like this and move fast . . .'

The Queen's eyes flashed in anger at being spoken to so bluntly.

'How dare you—' she began.

George shut her up by ripping open his jacket and showing the stone arm and the almost stone hand.

She swallowed her anger and threw a worried look at the Officer.

'Like this,' he said flatly, looking between the Queen and the Officer. 'I don't know how long until the taints attack this lot, but I'm running out of time. I need to find this Wooden Knight.'

'Ahem,' came the Lionheart's voice from behind him once more. He shrugged his coat back on, quickly hiding his shoulder.

'Not now!' barked the Queen, waving the Lionheart away and turning back to George. 'Does the clue about the mirror mean anything to you?'

'No. The mirror may "sleep on a bed neither here nor there" but I've got no clue where that may be,' he admitted, looking across the square. 'Spout!'

They looked at him as he dropped off the empty plinth and glided towards them.

'What?' said the Queen.

'Spout can cover more ground from the sky, looking for Edie,' said George.

And as the gargoyle landed next to one of the great lions at the foot of the column, George ran over and told him what he wanted him to do.

'Gint,' said Spout. 'Gind gint?'

'Yes,' said George. 'Find glint. Find Edie.'

'Gogay,' said Spout, and launched into the air with a racketing bustle of stone wings punching at the air and sweeping it past him as he headed for the rooftops.

'Look,' said a voice from behind George.

He turned to see the Lionheart leaning down off his horse.

'Before that harridan gets going and tries to shut me up again. I keep an eye on all the gentlemen in armour, and there's a Wooden Knight in Southwark Cathedral.'

'Well, why didn't you say so, you great booby?' snapped the Queen.

The Lionheart rolled his eyes at George.

She whistled for her horses. As the chariot rolled up behind them she turned to the Officer. 'You seem to have this lot in some kind of control.'

He nodded as she jumped on the back of her chariot and held out her hand.

'Come, boy. To Southwark.'

George jumped up behind her, and with a crack of the reins they were racing downhill, through the snow.

33

GUNNER TO
BLACK FRIAR

The Gunner could see several tracks as he jogged east along the Embankment. It wasn't clear which direction most of them were going, and he supposed they had been made by spits heading towards the Sphinxes. He kept on going with his eyes on the snow because he hoped one of them would turn out to be Edie's feet going in the opposite direction. As he approached the traffic island at the end of Blackfriars Bridge he was so deeply focused on trying to decipher the footprints and disentangle who they might belong to that he didn't look up and notice the blank wall of the Ice Murk looming vertiginously above him.

He started noticing one set of footprints that had a shorter distance between them than the others, and a sort of feathered drag mark going along with them. He was hoping it was Edie's long black fur coat brushing the snow as she ran. And when he stopped and peered deep into the snow hole of one footprint he was elated to see it was definitely a small boot-print at the bottom, and that it was heading away from the Sphinxes. He grinned and picked up speed.

It was only when he looked up that the smile died and he hit the brakes. He was six feet away from the uncannily flat front edge of the Ice Murk, a sullen escarpment that soared three hundred sheer feet above his head. He tipped his helmet back and stared up at it.

'Bloody hell.'

He took a couple of paces back and looked down. Edie's footprints – for he was sure now they were hers – led straight into the Murk.

He scratched his head.

'Edie girl. You're in trouble now.'

And then something caught his eye. Something was moving, about fifteen feet up the wall of icy cloud. Something round. Something whirling, like a propeller. As he looked closer he saw three golden numbers below it, just covered by the thinnest layer of Murk.

'One Seven Four,' he said. And then he realized what the whirling propeller was, and he knew what he was looking at. He looked along the wall of Murk and saw where Edie's footprints angled into it, and knew his hunch had been right. He squared his shoulders and stepped into the Murk. If he was right, the door he was looking for couldn't be so far away that he would get lost looking for it. Despite that, the moment the Murk swallowed him, he was disoriented enough to stumble and have to reach out to stop himself falling. He ended up on his knees, feeling blindly in front of himself.

'Come on,' he said, and then he found a wall and crawled along it until his hands found a door. He pulled himself to his feet and twisted it, flinging it open and stepping into the Black Friar's pub.

'Edie?' he said.

'Close the door, you damn fool,' roared the Friar, kneeling in front of the mirrors, his hands trying to shield the candles that were sitting on the floor in front of them like an impromptu shrine as they guttered in the breeze that the Gunner had let into the room.

'Black. What are you up to?' said the Gunner, closing the door behind him. 'The hands on that clock of yours outside, the one that never works, always five to seven, they're whirling round like a bloody propeller. Got to be the only clock working in the City . . .'

'What do you want?' said the Friar, relighting a candle that had been blown out, and then scrubbing at the mirror with his hand.

'I'm looking for the girl. Edie. The glint.'

'She's not 'ere!' said Little Tragedy, his face popping into view upside down from the top of one of the arches.

'I saw her footprints,' growled the Gunner.

'She's in there,' said the Friar. Pointing at the mirrors.

'What do you mean she's in there?' said the Gunner dangerously.

'The Raven took her to see her mother,' replied the Friar. The mirrors he was scrubbing at were becoming frosted with the intense cold brought on by the Ice Murk enveloping the building. Only at the bottom were they clear, where the heat from the candles was stopping the frost riming them completely opaque.

'Her mother's dead,' replied the Gunner.

'You saw the clock whirling,' said the Friar. 'You know this is a Machine of Times and Places. She is not only there, the there where she is is not now, but then.'

'That ruddy bird has taken her back in time?' said the Gunner incredulously.

'He's discharging an obligation,' shrugged the Friar.

'I'll discharge my bleeding pistol up his jacksie if that girl comes to any more harm on his account,' swore the Gunner.

The Friar lit another candle.

'What are you up to?' said the Gunner suspiciously.

'If the mirrors frost up because of this freezing Murk that is enshrouding the building they will not find their way back here,' explained the Friar, moving the candles closer to the mirrors.

'Well, can't you get them back?' asked the Gunner, pointing to the concentric rings of the mosaic on the ceiling. 'Can't you control this thing?'

'I would go in after them,' said the Friar. 'But I cannot quite trust this imp to tend the candles ...'

'Oooh!' squealed Tragedy. 'that's so unfair, I said sorry and I never meant—'

'SILENCE!' roared the Friar. He looked up at the Gunner. 'Perhaps you could watch the candles while—'

'No,' said the Gunner, hitching up his belt and pulling his pistol. 'You watch. I'll go.'

34

CLUB DEATH

Edie and the Raven fell into a dark cavern, lit by a thousand points of light that cascaded across the ceiling and walls from a giant glitterball turning slowly on the ceiling. A heaving crowd of dancers bobbed and wove on the dance-floor beneath as a singer complaining over a drum-studded riff about someone twisting his melon (man) punched into them at more than a hundred and twenty beats per minute.

She was about to follow the Raven when something clumped to the ground behind her with an impact like an anvil dropping out of the sky.

She turned to see the Gunner looking round, disoriented and scowling.

'Hey!' she called.

He saw her and smiled in relief.

She felt two contradictory emotions at once. Pleasure at seeing him. And rebellion.

'I'm not coming back!' she shouted.

He waved his hands round his ears.

'This is worse than a bloody artillery barrage!' he yelled back.

'It's a club,' shouted Edie.

'I'm sure it is,' he roared back, 'it's certainly giving my ears a right old pounding. Come here . . .'

And before she could twist away he caught her arm and pulled her close enough to talk into her ear.

'Calm down,' he said as she tried to escape. 'Let me

explain. You don't have to go anywhere you don't want. Only things have changed back there in the pub . . .'

She relaxed a fraction as he spoke into her ear, telling her what had changed and how things were now more dangerous. And then she turned her head and shouted into his ear in her turn, telling him what she had seen. And why she had to keep following the Raven.

When she finished he gently gripped her by both shoulders and held her at arm's length. All around them the world was in motion, bouncing and writhing and flailing its arms in the air to the music, but in this one place, in the matrix bracketed by his two strong arms, there was stillness in which an understanding was born as she looked back into his eyes.

'Please,' she mouthed. 'She's my mum.'

He took a deep breath. Looked at the pounding mayhem around them. And then nodded.

'But not on your own,' he shouted, pointing at himself. She nodded back. Almost smiling.

They had no more time to talk, because the Raven flapped across the dance-floor, so low that his wingtips seemed to brush the raised hands of the dancers.

Then the DJ hit the strobe machine – and for a moment Edie thought she was glinting as the world suddenly stopped flowing seamlessly and all the rhythmic movement around them was chopped into frozen flash-frames. Then she realized she was touching no stone or metal and had her hands bunched deep into the pockets of her coat.

She followed the Gunner through the strobe-lit dancers, who appeared to move miraculously out of his way just enough for them to move forward, then close in behind them as soon as they passed – all without seeing them.

The Gunner, she noticed, had his fingers in his ears. She could only see the back of his helmet reflecting the wheeling pin-spots above him, but she knew his face would be wrung into a tight scowl.

They passed through a thicket of jumping girls waving luminous glow-sticks in the air, and then found themselves trailing the Raven as he dipped lower and led them along a green-painted passageway to one side of the dance-floor. Above him a blocky air-conditioning duct twisted and jinked along the roof like the body of some great man-made snake.

The noise was less oppressive here, the top notes getting lost in the distance, and only the deeper thump of the bass following them down the passage. The Gunner took his fingers out of his ears and took a moment to grimace back at Edie.

'People pay money to come in here and have that row fired at them? Could stick your head in a bucket and whack it with a hammer for free . . . hello . . .' he said.

The Raven had banked and turned into what was undoubtedly the ladies' toilet.

'I think I'll stay . . .' He pointed at the wall opposite. 'Here.'

Edie walked past him and into the room.

Apart from the Raven the only person in there was a girl in a short neon-pink mini-skirt and a cropped white T-shirt, across whose back was a green day-glo smiley face that looked a bit sick. The girl had her hair plaited on both sides of her head and tied up with neon-green and pink scrunchies. The hair was dark, almost black, and it was only when Edie moved forward and saw the girl's

219

face stretched wide in horror that she realized it was her mother, ten years or so older than when she'd last seen her. Now she was recognizable as the mother Edie had known ten years further on down the line.

She was leaning against the brickwork, hand spread wide against it for support, staring in to one of the cubicles. Edie steeled herself to look in and see what it was that had so terrified her.

She looked in and saw nothing, just a lavatory bowl and a paper dispenser.

'Oh God,' whispered her mother. 'Make it stop . . .'

Edie looked at her. She looked at the hand spread on the wall.

'It's OK,' she said. 'It's not really there. You're seeing the past . . .'

Her mother couldn't hear her. Edie couldn't leave her there alone, and she couldn't help her. So she did the one thing she could, which was just to be there next to her and witness what she was witnessing. It didn't make any sense she could have explained to anyone. But it did make the other kind of sense, the kind that you just feel in a place beyond words.

She put her smaller hand on the brick below her mother's.

The past sliced at her like the strobing lights had done on the dance-floor. And what they showed wasn't violent or full of action. It was just desperate and still. It was another girl, twisted on her back, jammed between the toilet bowl and the wall. Her eyes were wide, the pupils irissed down to pinpricks, her face so drained of colour that the white powder on her nostril was almost unnoticeable.

Her chest rose and fell with irregular movements

in time with occasional rattling gasps from deep within her throat.

The breaths came slower and more intermittently, each gap between them getting longer and longer, and the rattling inbreaths, when they came, more strangled and desperate.

She was dying.

And the slow inevitability of it made it all the more horrible and sad.

When the legs started to spasm, Edie tore her hand off the wall.

Her mother slumped back against the sinks, sobbing silently.

'I don't know how to stop it,' she said, and for a soaring moment Edie thought that she was speaking to her. Then she turned and realized she was talking to another young woman who was standing in the doorway.

'Stop what?' said the woman. 'Sue? You having one of your turns?'

Edie could see her mother struggling. She'd struggled with the same thing herself, so she knew exactly what was going on and the precise nature of the conversation going on inside her mother's head. If you told people what you could see and they couldn't, you were telling them you were a loony. On the other hand, glinting was too heavy a burden to carry on your own. So in the end you found other ways to take the pressure off. Edie had tried running away and getting angry a lot more often than normal girls of her age.

'I need a drink,' said her mother heading for the door.

'But you don't . . . I mean, you never drink . . .' said her friend. 'I mean, I thought . . . because of your . . . you know . . .'

Edie's mum stopped in the doorway and looked back for a second. She shrugged.

'Yeah,' she said, voice flat and lifeless. 'My mother. Maybe she had the right idea after all.'

Edie walked after her. She sort of knew what was going to happen, but she needed to see it. They exited the narrow corridor and walked back out into the dance-floor. Edie stayed close, just aware that the Gunner was hurrying along behind her.

She arrived at the bar a pace behind her mother. She saw her order the drinks, four fingers held up in front of the barman's face. She saw her taste the first glass and grimace, before downing it in two swigs. She stayed watching until she started on the third glass with a look of murderous determination on her face, and then she turned and allowed the Gunner to lead her away.

As they approached the mirrored wall they'd come out of she swung round and took a last look at her mother, now a tiny figure glimpsed through a bouncing sea of dancers. She still stood at the bar, doggedly making herself finish the last glass. You could see in her face that it wasn't a taste she liked.

And then she turned and held up two more fingers to the barman.

'Oh, Mum,' said Edie, her heart breaking again. 'Oh, Mum.'

35

VOICES IN THE DARK

Shack and the Queen of America followed the dragons' trail with ease because the taints hadn't worried about being backtracked as they had crept up on George and Dictionary and the Clocker. The Antarctic explorer jogged along beside the buffalo and the warrior Queen in urgent but companionable silence as the trail unribboned ahead of them.

Only twice did they have to cast about at the end of a lost trace, and that only because the dragons had leapt an obstacle. Both times they found where they had landed very quickly, and kept on a course that led them remorselessly east.

After ten minutes of silence the Queen stopped abruptly.

'Trail go bad,' she grunted, reining in the buffalo and pointing ahead.

Shack, who had been following the dragon's footsteps and the wavy lines between them that he was sure were the marks of their dragging tails, looked up.

The street ahead was abruptly curtailed by the Ice Murk that sheared it off as neatly as a guillotine. He stared at the perfectly flat cliff-face and the slow grey cloud moving within.

'Bad indeed,' he agreed. And he reached out a hand to the mirror-flat surface and looked up at the sheer face of the Murk, and then down at the two sets of dragon prints leading straight into it.

'Colder,' he said, pulling on his great furry mittens.

The Queen dismounted and put her ear to the wall of fog. She stood still as a tree and listened, holding her hand palm-out to keep him silent.

'Voices. Many voices. Women, maybe girls crying,' she said after a minute.

'Nonsense,' he said, freeing an ear from the cowl of his woolly balaclava and pressing it to the wall alongside her.

'Not nonsense,' she said calmly.

He listened. He heard it. And like all good leaders, he didn't pretend he hadn't.

'Right,' he admitted. 'My mistake. My apologies. Not nonsense. You're a better man than I.'

'Yes. But am not man,' said the Queen, remounting the buffalo.

'You stay here,' he said decisively. 'It's going to be a freezing grey-out in there. Too cold for man or beast.'

'Am not man. Am not beast,' shrugged the Queen of America, kneeing the buffalo forward and jamming her hand into the Murk up to the elbow. 'Is not crack-stone cold. We go together.'

'Then take some of my clothes.'

'No,' she said, leaning off the side of the buffalo and following the tracks into the Murk.

Shack jogged to catch up with her, and just caught hold of the buffalo's tail as the white beast was swallowed by the Murk ahead of him.

'You're *definitely* a better man than I am, Gunga Din,' he shivered as he disappeared in after them.

And if there had been anyone left in the light and the

snow outside to hear it, they might have heard a woman's gravelly voice say:

'Am not Gunga Din either.'

36

SOUTHWARK

Take the way of the dragon, and by the Knight of Wood who lies all alone you may find kin you can call your own. Find your kin, and within the hour the dead stone's tongue will be in your power.'

The Sphinx's rhyming answer kept playing through George's head as he rode along the Embankment next to the Queen. His hands gripped the front of the chariot tightly so as not to be thrown out as they bucked and swerved through the thick snow. He tried not to look at his hands now, trying to ignore the fact that one was normal and the other was almost one hundred per cent stone, nearly as white as the streetscape in front of them.

'You think the stuff about the dead stone's tongue speaking to me means I'm going to glint like Edie or something?' he asked the Queen as they approached the roundabout at the end of Blackfriars Bridge. 'Whoa . . .'

What he was reacting to was the unexpected sight of the Ice Murk, a slow rolling slab of darkness that towered across the roundabout at an angle. The thrill of terror he felt was the same as that felt by sailors who look up to find themselves suddenly much too close to the cliffs in a strong wind on a lee shore. The pub on the corner was invisible behind the threatening bluff of icy cloud, as was everything east into the City.

'Edie might be in there,' he shouted, pointing in the direction of the pub. 'She could have gone to see the Friar.'

'Too bad if she is,' shouted back the Queen, skidding the chariot into a sliding turn on to the bridge. 'Mind you, the Gunner was headed this way. Maybe he found her . . .'

George looked back at the sheer face of the Murk, at least three hundred louring feet high. If Edie was in there she was lost. If the Gunner was with her, that was better, but then that just meant they were both lost. As if his arm was reacting to his thoughts, he felt another sharp pain and looked down despite himself. The only pink thing in his hand was now the index finger, and that only upwards of the first knuckle.

Not wanting to look too closely, because he had the nasty feeling if he did he might actually see the gritty stone moving, he looked sideways at the river. Time might have stopped, but the great gunmetal twists and ripples in its surface were still moving, as the unstoppable current cut its way seawards.

He shivered. And then he REALLY shivered.

'Edie,' he said, the word coming out of his mouth on a reflex.

He grabbed the Queen's hand.

'Stop!' he yelled. She leant back on the reins. The horses snorted in protest as their heads came up, and the chariot slowed as he jumped clear.

'What, boy?' shouted the Queen, watching him run back along the double-track made by the chariot's wheels.

'I don't know. I felt something. Like in the hotel when we were walking through people who weren't there . . .' he called back.

'Ghosts?' said the Queen, jumping down after him.

'Yeah,' he said, casting around to left and right, as if

trying to catch hold of something invisible. 'No. I don't know. Like that. It was somewhere round here . . .'

He couldn't find it.

'Why did you shout "Edie"?' the Queen asked.

'Did I?' he said, surprised. 'I must have . . . I don't remember . . .'

He ran across to an alcove in the side of the bridge, jutting out over the buttresses like a section of turret. It was empty, but as he entered the enclosed space and stepped up on to the snow-covered half-circle of bench he shivered again.

'That's it!' he gasped as he put his hand on the scarred stone lintel and looked over the edge.

'That's what?' said the Queen.

George was smiling as he turned and pointed behind him.

'The mirror sleeps on a bed where I felt it before. God I'm stupid. It's there!'

'What's where?' said the Queen, looking over. 'The river?'

'The river*bed*. The mirror sleeps on the riverbed . . . neither here nor there. Not beneath the ground, nor under the air, it cannot be seen because it's underwater, but I felt it there, I did.'

He laughed in elation.

'The first time Edie and I were in the water, I did, I felt something Dark, out there in the centre of the river. It was pulling at me, like a sort of magnet or an undertow . . .' He hit his head in frustration. 'I'm so stupid. Of course. We both are!'

'Thank you,' said the Queen frostily.

'Well, of course we are!' he said. 'The Walker used the mirrors on the ice at the Frost Fair, just over there. We left the ice when he disappeared . . .'

'. . . So the mirrors just stayed on the ice . . .' said the Queen, catching up.

'. . . and then when the ice melted they must have fallen to the riverbed.'

He grabbed the Queen's hand and held it out over the edge of the bridge.

'Close your eyes,' he said, shutting his. 'Can you feel it?'

He felt the same Dark pull from the centre of the river, the one he had thought was a tide, but that he now knew was the pull of the Darkness in the Black Mirrors.

'All I can feel is a stone hand gripping my wrist, too hard,' said the Queen dryly.

He immediately released her wrist and grimaced at his hand.

'Sorry,' he said. 'I'm just happy we found it. Honestly. If we hadn't ridden through that ghost, if we hadn't stopped . . .'

He shook his head.

'Can't believe how lucky we are,' he said wonderingly.

'Yes,' said the Queen. 'Except I don't believe in luck. It was meant . . . and before you get too excited, how are we going to find it down there, under the water?'

'Ah,' he said. 'Yes . . .'

There was a silence as they both looked down at the dark rope-twisted currents swirling below them. His shoulder twinged and he winced despite himself.

'Right,' he said. 'I can't waste time on this. Go and get those sailors the Gunner talked to – Jack Tar and the Bosun. This is a problem for people like them. I need to find this Wooden Knight before I turn to stone or something.'

229

'Does it hurt a lot?' said the Queen.

'It hurts enough,' he replied shortly.

'You take my chariot,' she ordered. 'It will get you there faster.'

She whistled and the horses pricked their ears and trotted over. She whispered in their ears, pointed at George, and then, without waiting to take no for an answer she lifted up the hem of her dress and ran back, spear held low in her right hand, fast and reckless as a young girl.

'Go, boy!' she shouted over her shoulder, without turning. 'And may you stay safe and alive until we meet again.'

It was probably a good thing that George couldn't see the grim look on her face as her legs pelted through the snow.

37

MESSAGE IN A BOTTLE

Edie and the Gunner stumbled out of the mirrors into the night, just a pace behind the Raven.

'Blimey,' said the Gunner. 'Haven't come far, have we?'

They were standing in the middle of Blackfriars Bridge. Edie looked around just as a lorry ground past, almost hitting her. The Gunner jerked her back out of the way. She shivered, feeling suddenly cold.

'George!' she said involuntarily.

'What?' said the Gunner.

The shiver passed. She felt normal again.

'What?' she said a little uncertainly, looking at him.

'You said "George".'

'Did I?' she said, looking at a young woman walking along the other side of the bridge. It was her mother, no doubt about it, a few years older than the girl at the club. As Edie stepped across the street the Gunner followed.

'Who's that?' he asked.

'My mum,' said Edie, speeding up as her mother turned into an alcove in the bridge. There was someone waiting for her, a youngish man more or less her age, but a lot drunker. He was draped over the edge of the turret with a bluey-green bottle resting on the scarred stone.

Edie's mother leant companionably against the wall next to him and lit a cigarette. Edie heard the tail end of what he was saying as she entered the alcove behind her mother.

'. . . said I come from a long line of dead men,' he said, smiling at her mother. Even though he was at least half in the bottle, Edie could see he was a nice enough bloke. 'A long line. Got their names up in that church over there.' He jerked his thumb towards the South Bank.

'Why are you drinking?' said her mother, taking the bottle and sniffing it. She wrinkled her nose and put it back.

'Why aren't you?' he grinned, offering her the bottle again.

'I'm not . . . I'm just having a bit of time not drinking. Why are you?'

'Why do you ask?' he said, swaying a little.

'Because you don't normally, and you're not very good at it,' laughed her mother, holding out a hand and steadying him.

Her touch also seemed to take the smile and the lightness out of the man. He sat down on the bench and looked at his feet. Then, as if they disappointed him, he scowled and looked at her. He didn't look drunk any more. Just very sad. He took a deep breath.

'She's pregnant, and it freaked her out. Freaked her out so much she went off and had an affair with someone else. Said it won't happen again, but . . .'

He shrugged and shook his head, unable to find the words.

'Ditch her,' said Edie's mum brightly. A little *too* brightly.

He grinned without a shred of humour, and took another swig.

'Can't. It's worse than that. I feel terrible. I'm going to do something terrible.'

'How terrible?' she said. Edie could see the effort it took to keep her smile in place as she waited for the reply. There was a long pause as he looked up at the night sky overhead.

'I'm going to forgive her.' Something in the way his voice dropped made the declaration sound like an apology.

'What?' she said, her smile dropping away.

'Yeah,' he said, offering her the bottle and the last half-inch of its contents. She shook her head. Now she looked sad too. He swigged it back and grimaced as it went down. He placed it carefully on the scarred stone lintel of the bridge. 'She's having a kid. My kid. And she's, you know ... I don't think she'll be much of a mum. Kid'll need someone who ...'

'Right.'

'Timing's really ...' He couldn't find the word.

'Isn't it?' she said.

They both looked at the black water flowing under the bridge.

She started to say something. Then stopped herself. He didn't seem to notice. After a bit he shivered, rubbed his face and turned to her.

'What did you want to say?'

She squared her shoulders.

'Not important.'

'You OK?' he asked.

She shook her head. He watched her as her eyes remained fixed on the great volume of water streaming up to and under the bridge.

'Say something, Sue,' he said. 'Swear at me, tell me I'm a complete ...'

233

'Why?' she said. 'You're not. You're a good guy. You're being a good guy.'

'So why does it feel so bad?'

She snorted back a short laugh. Edie saw her forcing the brightness back into her smile with so much effort that it hurt to see it. She stood up on the bench and looked down at the river.

'I like it here. River's always been where I come when I want to escape. All that water. Pulls you, doesn't it? Moving past. Washing everything away. Washing it out to sea. Can't stop it. Just finds its own way. Be nice just to drop in, float out to the sea, never come back . . .'

Whatever it was he had wanted to say, she didn't want to hear. He grinned ruefully and went with it. Like a good sport.

'I don't know. Be a bit cold . . .'

'Yeah.' She sighed. 'Still. I like the sea. New tide every day, start fresh. Always wanted to live there.'

'Why don't you?'

She turned to look at him, showing her own rueful grin.

"Cos I reckon you can only run away once. Once you've run away there's nowhere else to go. So it's easier to stay put and know you always *can* go one day if it all gets too much or you need a special reason to escape. You feel less trapped.'

'Doesn't quite make sense,' he said.

She smiled at herself.

'I don't make sense. Made wrong, see? I'm a loony,' she declared, crossing her eyes for a moment.

'Yeah.'

She picked up the empty bottle. And as she did so, Edie felt a surge of heat in her pocket. She reached in and pulled out her heart stone. It was blazing light, but only round the edges, outlining it. She felt it humming in her hand. Somehow she knew it wasn't a warning sign. Then she looked at the glass bottle in her mother's hand.

'We should put a message in the bottle, send it out to sea,' she said, twirling it in the light from the passing cars on the bridge behind them.

'Oh my God,' said Edie.

'Got any paper?' said the man, patting his pockets.

'What?' whispered the Gunner.

'No,' said her mother.

Edie just pointed. Outlined in light on the bottle was an identical shape to the irregular disc shape of the glass in her hand. Glass the exact same colour as the bottle.

'Bloody hell,' said the Gunner.

Edie couldn't speak. Her eyes were wet and wide in wonder. Her mother smiled too eagerly, too cheerfully at the man. He looked so sad. His eyes, Edie saw, were very nice when you looked closer. His trousers were flecked with different-coloured paint, as were his hands. Maybe he was a house painter, she thought.

'Then let's make it an invisible message. What would you put in it if you could?' said her mother.

'All the good stuff. Hope. Love.' He smiled sadly into her eyes.

'And happiness,' she said, theatrically jamming the cork into the bottle. 'And one day it'll float up on a beach and someone will think it's empty, and not realize it's a magic bottle. And they'll never know . . .'

'. . . never know what?'

'Never know why their life changes for the better.' She smiled, and held out the bottle. He put his hand on it too.

'OK. God bless her. And all who sail with her,' he said mock seriously.

'And all who sail with her,' she echoed solemnly.

There was a pulse in the bottle that only Edie saw, a low flash of light between the man's hand and the woman's. She felt an answering tingle in the glass in her hand. And then her mother took the bottle and launched it up and away and then down, tumbling through the night air to land with an inaudible splash in the river far below.

'You're weird,' he said, looking at her as if he was taking a picture in his mind and trying to fix it before it faded away. 'I'm sorry.'

'Me too,' she said and reached up and kissed the side of his face, just once. He winced like it hurt.

'Another life,' he said. And kissed the side of hers.

'Yeah. Oh.'

She reached in her pocket and handed him a key on a ring that had a sort of metal plane dangling from it. He nodded and put it in his pocket. She sketched a wave in the air and walked away. He watched her, the last of the light draining out of his eyes.

'Hey,' he said when she was fifty feet away.

'Hey what?' she said, turning.

'If you ever get to the sea one day. I hope you find your bottle.'

She nodded.

Said nothing.

And walked off into the night. Edie watched her go.

'She liked him,' she said as the Gunner led her off, after the Raven flapping across the bridge, heading south.

'I reckon he liked her and all,' said the Gunner. 'Just saw his duty calling in a different direction.'

She took a deep breath and said it.

'I thought he was going to be my . . .' she started and then stopped.

'Did you?' he said.

She nodded.

'I thought that was why the Raven was showing me this moment. But it wasn't that. It was the bottle. The bottle that made this.'

She held up the sea-glass.

'She sent this to me, even though she didn't know what she was doing. Even though she didn't know that I was going to be born. That's something, eh?'

'Yeah,' said the Gunner. 'That's something.'

He said it like he meant it. But the way he watched Edie walking across the road to the Raven also said he wasn't sure they were talking about the same something.

38

THE LONE DRAGON

The Railwayman led Dictionary round the edge of the Church of St Clement Danes. The spits who normally stood at the western end were gone, and the snow had piled up on the top of their vacated plinths.

'Tell you what, Dictionary, it ain't half lonely with all the other statues gone,' he said. 'S'like a ghost town.'

'Indeed it may be,' said the burly man, turning the awful scalloped wound in his fire-smelted face to left and right. 'But I fancy I can hear a great multitude behind us.'

The Railwayman stopped moving and they both listened.

'Trafalgar Square, I'll bet,' said the Railwayman. 'Shall we go have a look-see?'

'You go, my friend. Now I am so nearly back at my plinth I feel the need to rest and await whatever balm and cure turn o' day may bring me. I admit that this unheralded exertion has quite debilitated me.'

The Railwayman led him on, a worried look on his face.

'I'm not happy about leaving you alone here, whether it's your home or not, tell you the truth,' he said. 'Blinded and without a guard? Don't seem too clever a plan, somehow. I think I'll stick with you if you don't mind the company.'

'In any other circumstances I should welcome the society,' said Dictionary. 'But if there is a battle to come, you would serve London better by joining our friends than playing nursemaid to an old word-juggler. Besides . . .'

Suddenly Hodge went rigid in his arms and hissed furiously at something to the east of them.

'Bloody hell,' said the Railwayman, and hastily unshouldered his gun.

'What is it?' said Dictionary.

'It's only the Temple Bar Dragon. And it's looking at us like we're lunch,' said the Railwayman, cocking his gun.

The dragon at Temple Bar was a different order of statue to the cruder mass-produced dragon statues that guarded the other entrances to the city. It was not painted the garish silver and red of the creatures the Railwayman and the Queen of America had killed earlier. It was thinner and spikier and much more dangerous-looking, lithe and sharp and deadly where the other dragons were more like blunt sledgehammers. And the sharpest thing about it was not its wicked fangs or its cruelly barbed whiplash tail – the sharpest thing about it were its eyes.

It cocked its head and looked at them.

It opened its mouth.

'I'm going to drill the bug—' began the Railwayman.

'Dictionary?' barked the dragon, a voice as harsh as a shovelful of coals being thrown into a scuttle.

'Wait,' said Dictionary, slapping a blind hand sideways and knocking the Railwayman's weapon down.

'Eyes. Dictionary. Happened. What?' snarled the dragon. Its words didn't quite join up with each other like normal speech.

'It talks!' said the Railwayman, recovering his balance and aiming at its head.

'Of course it talks,' said Dictionary. 'But only when it

has something to say. I wonder why it has not joined the other dragons?'

'Why don't I shoot first and ask afterwards, eh?' said the Railwayman.

'No,' said Dictionary.

The dragon leapt forward off its high plinth. As it flew through the air the Railwayman saw that one of its wings had an uneven rip in it, and when it landed thirty feet closer, it staggered, and when it straightened itself with a hiss of frustration, he saw that one of its ears was torn and hanging at an odd angle.

"E looks beaten up. Like he's been through the wringer,' he said out of the side of his mouth.

The dragon walked forward.

Hodge hissed and stiffened in Dictionary's arms. The Railwayman kept his gun aimed at the taint's chest, and his finger on the trigger. The Dragon ignored him and stopped ten feet away. It pointed a viciously curved talon at Dictionary's face.

'Who. This. Did?'

'Dragons,' spat the Railwayman. 'So you want to step back, eh?'

The dragon ignored him and stepped forward.

'Dictionary?' said the Railwayman.

'Leave him,' said the big man.

The dragon reached slowly forward and ran its talon delicately over the smooth concave wound that had erased Dictionary's face above the nose.

'Why?' it said quietly.

'The dragon was trying to kill the boy. The maker you marked. I could not allow that to happen.'

'Fight. You. Did?'

'I interposed myself.'

'Tchak! Happy. Not,' rasped the dragon, flicking its tail in irritation. 'Day. Bad. Time. Gone. Dark. Calling.'

Dictionary coughed and spasmed involuntarily.

'Why have you not answered the call as the other taints have?'

The dragon leant its face closer.

'First. Dragon. Am. I.' Its eyes burnt hotter. 'To. Guard. City. Made.'

It scowled in irritation, and all the spines on its body bristled as it drew itself to its full prideful height.

'Not. Made. Answer. Call. One. Who. Enslave. City. Would,' it growled, and spat in contempt.

The Railwayman stepped out of the way as a fizzing gout of multicoloured wildfire hissed into the snow. 'Steady,' he said. 'What happened? You look like you been in the wars.'

'Lesser. Dragons. Darkness. Answered.'

It growled, a talon unconsciously trying to smooth its damaged and dangling ear back into place. 'No. Slave. I. So. Fought. We.'

'That's a turn-up for the books,' whistled the Railwayman. 'Taints fighting taints.'

'There are bad spits too, no doubt,' said Dictionary.

'Bad. Darkness,' hissed the dragon. 'Not. Will. I. City. See. Destroyed. Guardian. Am. I.'

Dictionary looked blindly for the dragon's face and spoke just three heartfelt words.

'Then join us.'

39

THE STONE CORPSE

The streets were eerily quiet as George rode the chariot east along the south side of the river. He thought the Thames must be a barrier that the Ice Murk couldn't cross, because he caught flashes of it every time he passed the end of a street heading north, at right angles to the river. If he'd been on the other side of the water, in the City, he would have been lost deep in the Murk.

He was a little lost on this side, he realized as he found himself hitting Borough High Street. It was an area he knew a bit, and he thought he must have overshot the road leading to the cathedral. He pulled left on the reins, and the horses leapt and kicked through the slightly thicker snow heading towards the bridge.

He was looking left for a way into the block in the centre of which he knew the cathedral was, when a sign caught his eye.

'Whoa,' he shouted, pulling back on the reins as he'd seen the Queen do. The horses slowed, and he took a left turn into the mouth of a covered stone walkway, leading into the market beyond. The horses stopped. He turned to see why, and then he noticed that though the chariot might just fit through, the scimitar blades sticking out from the wheels would jam it stuck.

'OK,' he said, climbing down and patting the closest horse's flanks, his eyes returning to the street sign. 'This is the place all right. The way of the dragon. Er, you stay here, OK?'

He had no idea if the horses could understand him, and he wondered if he should tie them up somehow. He decided not to, and ran off down into Borough Market, as behind him the horses stood breathing hard beneath a street sign that read Green Dragon Court.

The market stalls were locked away and the doors to the shops barred, but George still felt a rumble of hunger in his stomach as he hurried through the warren of alleys. This was where his dad used to come and buy things that smelt like a home George now only had in his memories – strong coffee, stronger cheeses, knobbly and delicious fruit and luscious tomatoes exuding an odour of the sun itself. George ran past a shuttered barbecued meat stall and wished he had Edie's gift for conjuring the past out of the stone, because if he did he knew he'd see his dad again, standing with a younger version of George beside him, breath pluming on a cold Sunday morning, ordering delicious roast pork and apple sauce rolls to eat as they walked home along the river.

He banished the memory and angled sharply into the churchyard surrounding the cathedral.

The spire was the only part of the roof that wasn't covered in snow, its almost sheer sides being too steep for the stuff to get any purchase. Deep cornices of snow overhung the edge of the lower roof, and each buttress had its own toadstool-cap of white perched on top of it.

There were no footsteps in the virgin snow, so George had to toil through the thigh-deep drifts by main force alone. He reached the door, knowing it was going to be locked, but he twisted the handle and found, to his surprise, that it swung open.

A cleaner's cart was angled in the entrance way, and a mop stood on its own like the frozen hand on a metronome. George realized a cleaner must have been in the middle of swabbing the floor when the clocks struck thirteen.

He turned to look up the aisle and froze as something jabbed warningly under his chin. He was pretty sure he went 'ulp!' or 'erk!' or made some other undignified noise, but he stopped worrying about it when he saw the daunting figure blocking his way with a sword at his throat.

A wooden sword. But a wooden sword can be almost as threatening as a real one when it's being wielded by a large armoured figure who is himself carved from the same wood.

'Halt!' he said.

'I'm halted,' said George. 'And you're the Knight of Wood, the Wooden Knight.'

'What manner of mortal are you that can see me?' said the Knight.

'I'm a maker,' said George, 'and I'm afraid I'm in too much of a hurry to explain.'

'That is not for you to say,' said the Knight, jabbing the sword into his chest again.

'Er, yes it is,' said George. 'See this?'

And with that he stripped off his two coats and opened his shirt, exposing the stone arm.

The Knight took a step back.

'What ails thee, child?'

'Like I said, no time,' repeated George. 'The Lionheart sent me. I'm looking for the dead tongue of stone, or the dead stone or something. It's important. You see what's happening out there?' He pointed out of the bright windows along the transept.

'We see and we feel,' said a gravelly voice from the

shadows far down the church. 'The ice storm shall sweep away the refuge of lies and the waters will overflow his secret place.'

'Who's that?' said George.

'The Stone Corpse,' said the Knight. 'One that used to be a monk.'

'I need to see him,' said George, taking a deep breath and walking down the side of the cathedral. The wall was covered in memorial plaques, and he could feel the eyes of other statues and bas-reliefs swivelling to look at him. What stopped him taking too much notice of them was the figure slowly getting off a stone sarcophagus that was set in a long niche in the side of the wall.

It wasn't quite a skeleton, but the emaciated figure wasn't a healthy body by any stretch of the imagination. The stomach had withered down to nothing, making the ribcage stand out like the prow of a boat, and the legs and what remained of the arms were little more than bones with a skein of shrunken flesh wrapped tightly round them. One arm was missing below the elbow joint, giving the impression that it had rotted off, with more to follow.

The head was hollow-eyed and sunken-cheeked, and the mouth had the haggard lipless perma-grin of a skull. As the Stone Corpse stood and turned, George saw him shake loose a bunched shroud that had gathered round his head and shoulders, and which now fell over his body like a veil, mottled with cream and brown patches. Although it was stone, the veil was so thin that it both clung to the details of the corpse below, outlining the ribs and joints, and was translucent like alabaster.

As the dead head turned to look down on him, George realized he didn't quite know what he was meant to ask. He tried to keep his mind straight as he circled the Corpse warily.

'What would you, boy maker?' wheezed the Corpse. 'For what would you disturb my rest?'

'I need your help. I think,' said George, trying not to notice the way the shroud billowed out from the face as the Corpse spoke. And as fast as he could, he outlined his predicament and the sudden harm the two Dark powers were visiting on London. He didn't dodge any of the hard facts, and made it clear that it all seemed to be his fault, stemming from his accidental act of vandalism in breaking the stone carving at the Natural History Museum.

As he spoke he heard footsteps and shuffling in the gloom behind him, but he knew it was the other statues and effigies in the church coming closer to listen. All the time he spoke the Stone Corpse just stood over him, the only movement being the regular in and out of the shroud as he breathed in a succession of flinty rattles.

When George was done, the Corpse held out its one good hand.

'And why should I help you? I have no fear of Judgement Day. The problems of the world are but transitory . . .'

'You have to help me because it's not all the people who have disappeared's fault this happened. And they may NOT be ready for Judgement Day, not like you. We should at least give them a chance, you know, to live their lives.' As he spoke the stone in his shoulder smarted badly, and he flinched involuntarily.

'But why should I help *you*, boy?' repeated the Corpse.

'Because the Sphinx said so,' said George, out of other

arguments and beginning to feel the panic rising inside him again.

'What did the Sphinx say?' asked the Corpse, bending closer.

'Something about taking the way of the dragon, which I did – Green Dragon Court which leads here – and then by the Knight of Wood finding kin I can call my own, and if I do that then the dead stone's tongue – that's you I suppose – will be in my power.'

'Have you found kin?' asked the Corpse.

George looked around. There were statues looking at him all round, but none that he recognized.

'No,' he said. 'I don't know where to start.'

'Names,' said a bald trim figure in Elizabethan dress. He stroked a small beard and waved a quill at George. 'I always find it best to start with names when I am stuck for a beginning. Yours, for example.'

'I'm George.'

'Well, we only have one George here, but a first name implies no kinship, and I very much fear that unless he was less saintly than we imagine, he fathered no kin for you to have sprung from,' said the quill bearer. 'Still, a start is a start. Mayhap he can help you . . . he is at your back, behind the altar.'

George turned and stepped back. And there it was, on the wall. Surrounded by a gilded frame of laurels and ribbons, picked out in gold and red and white and a deeply satisfying lizardy green was a George and a Dragon.

'There's a dragon!' he said in surprise.

'Of course,' said the Stone Corpse. 'If you will permit an observation from the other side of the veil: life balances things out. Like for like, ill for ill, good for evil, and for every George, a Dragon.'

'But it's not my kin,' said George, deflating. 'He's a saint, not a Chapman. And you're right, I'm not a saint. All the bad stuff that's happening is my fault! Look. Can't you just answer my question without—'

And here he stopped abruptly, because the St George pulled his lance out of the dragon's mouth, and while the dragon coughed and choked like a cat just having dislodged a hairball, he leant out of his gilded roundel and tapped the long list of names carved into the World War One memorial below him.

George knelt down and traced his fingers over the sharply incised words. And then he gasped.

His finger ran down the column with the 'C's in it, skating over CASEY and CHADWICK and CHALLIS and slowing down abruptly as it hit CHAPMAN. And not just one Chapman, but three of them.

'I didn't know,' he said, staring open-mouthed at his name in triplicate. Maybe it was because two of the Chapmans had the same first initial as his father, or maybe it was because he knew this was a First World War memorial, but he was, for an instant, so powerfully back in the artillery bombardment that he felt the ground shudder beneath his feet and smelt cordite and a horse's fear pressed to his nose, and saw the soldier with his father's face gripping his arm over the horse's neck. And then the moment was gone.

'We oft know little of who we were, only something of who we are, and nothing of who we may be,' said the man with the quill quietly.

'The old blood of this city runs deep in you, boy,' said the Stone Corpse, 'for there have been Chapmans here from its very foundation. I am yours to command.'

'Then please tell us how we can beat the Ice Devil?' said George. 'I know where the Black Mirrors are that we must banish him through, but I don't know how we can beat him first.'

The Stone Corpse's head rocked back on its neck and it looked at the ceiling, and then it began to turn slowly. George had the distinct impression that it was not quite standing on the same ground as the rest of them. It intoned the answer, when it came, just like the Sphinxes.

'As the dragon marked your hand, so a dragon shall be your tool, and flames taint and ice have fanned only spit and fire shall cool.'

George watched it twirling in the air for a moment, while he tried to make sense of what it had just said.

'I don't understand,' he exploded in frustration. He had been so near, and now seemed as far away from a clue as he had ever been. And what's more his shoulder had stopped hurting, but only because the pain had moved across to his chest. He felt under his shirt. His chest was, as he had feared, marked by a distinct gritty ridge, where the stone met the skin.

'This is just like the Sphinx! What does spit and fire mean?'

'To see the flames of Darkness fade will require all the light glint and maker made,' chanted the Corpse, as if it hadn't heard him at all.

George shot out a hand and gripped the stone shroud. It felt thin and slippery, almost so wispy that it wasn't there, like a greasy cobweb.

'What does spit and fire mean?' he repeated.

The Stone Corpse stopped turning and bent its head to look down at him. As he returned the look, it pulled

249

the shroud back and revealed the full horror of the death's head beneath.

'You carry the answer with you, George Chapman. You always have.'

And just as George was about to ask what was meant about the dragon and the tool part of the answer the church was rocked by the sound of a bell.

It was a deep unavoidable tolling, one that George had heard before. He knew in his heart and in his guts and in the sharp pain where the stone arm met his flesh that it was for tolling for him.

As if the Stone Corpse could read his mind, it reached down its one bony hand and gently removed his hand from its shroud. He saw the last pink tip of his fingertip gripped between the dead stone fingers, and then he saw the pink disappear as the white limestone engulfed the last bit of his arm.

The bell tolled again. George's stone hand flexed in answering pain.

'If thy hand causes you to offend, cut it off,' said the Corpse.

'What?' said George in horror.

'Gospel of Mark: it is better to enter life maimed than having two hands go to hell, into the fire that shall never be quenched,' intoned the Stone Corpse. 'Peace be with you.'

George watched it turn and drift back to its alcove.

The summoning bell tolled again.

The Wooden Knight hurried down the aisle.

'Boy? There is a chariot at the door. And a golden girl who says you must go with her.'

George stumbled to his feet and made them walk towards the door. Everything had almost made sense, but now he was going to face the final battle without knowing how to win.

The man with the quill walked beside him, looking at his face.

'The Stone Corpse is of his nature a dark and doomy fellow, but there is often illumination in his words, as a sullen thundercloud may carry the brightest lightning.'

'Er . . . OK,' said George, distracted.

He could hear the horses snorting beyond the door, and could see Ariel's golden reflection on the inside of the arch. He looked down at his open shirt and saw the stone crossing over the centre of his chest.

'Chapman,' said the man, a hand on his shoulder. 'That bible that the Corpse loves to quote has cheerier verses, and I have scarce ever seen a boy more in need of cheer, so I give you Ezekiel as a blither fare-thee-well: I will give them one heart . . . and I will take the heart of stone out of their flesh and give them a heart of flesh.'

'Thank you,' said George. 'But what does it mean?'

'Whatever you make of it, boy,' smiled the man with the bald head and the beard, 'for are you not as I was, a maker?'

'Yes,' said George, looking down at his stone arm. 'I am.'

'Then nothing is yet lost, just as nothing is yet won, and the great globe itself lies beyond those doors waiting to be made anew,' said the man, clapping him amicably on the shoulder and sending him on his way.

George walked out of the dark, into the light, and as he did so, he smiled.

'You're right,' he said. 'Dead right.'

251

40

ON THE BENCH

Edie tripped out of the mirror to find herself in a clothes shop. She was getting used to people not being able to see her, and walked straight past the shop assistant who was straightening already perfectly aligned stacks of sweaters on a shelf by the door, chatting to someone on her phone as she did so.

The Gunner squeezed past and they followed the Raven into the street. The bird waited, hanging unnaturally in the air until he caught up and, casting a backwards glance at Edie, dropped on to his shoulder and clacked its beak animatedly next to his ear.

Edie watched the traffic pour past. They were definitely in London again. A red bus and a line of taxis confirmed that, and as the Gunner led the way across the street towards a mean triangle of thin grass and patchy shade spread beneath a sick-looking plane tree, Edie wondered what would happen if she stepped in front of a car.

She wasn't feeling suicidal or anything like that, it was just that if nobody could see her, did that mean she would just slide off a car unhurt? Or would she get run over?

'What happens . . .?' she began, catching up with the Gunner as he snaked between two cars going in opposite directions without breaking pace.

The Gunner stopped on the edge of the pavement and held up a finger. At first she thought the Raven had flown ahead of him, because there it was, hopping along the back of a park bench, sidling up to a drunk man sprawled across one end of it, his feet surrounded by a small collection of empty beer cans. His head flopped back bonelessly over the back of the bench, so all they could see was the underside of his stubble-mottled chin and a very prominent Adam's apple vibrating as he snored.

Then she noticed the Raven was still on the Gunner's shoulder.

The Raven on the bench was either a different Raven, or . . .

'It's you, isn't it?' she said.

The Raven back-paddled off the Gunner's mountainous shoulder and neatly lofted down on to hers. Out of the corner of her eye she saw it nod its head.

'Why are we watching you?' she asked. And then the Raven on the bench clacked its beak imperiously, and the drunk woke and sat up, his head hingeing back to a normal position with an audible grunt of pain.

'Oh,' said Edie. 'Oh.'

It was him. The stepfather. He leant forward and spat, his phlegm smacking down in a glutinous green ground-burst amid the beer cans at his feet.

'He used to come up to London. Be gone for a week, sometimes weeks at a time. I loved it, left me alone at home at the seaside with my mum, without him ruining everything. She drank less when he was away as well. I hate him.'

The Raven clacked on, and he cocked his head and listened, rubbing his face as he did so.

'Yes,' he slurred. 'Yes, we have seen what you ask about. We have seen such a stone . . .'

'We?' said Edie, tugging at the Gunner's sleeve. 'Who's "we"?'

'Them what choose booze and oblivion instead of real life, leaving their untended minds prey to a creature like the Walker. He's always got a use for their eyes and he knows the spell to conjure them,' rumbled the Gunner.

'You mean he . . .' started Edie, and stopped as the stepfather's eyes opened and she saw them for the first time. The eyes, normally pinched and bloodshot, were pure black from lid to lid, shiny as gobbets of oil. They were eyes she had seen before in another face, counting her at Puddle Dock.

'He's a Tallyman,' breathed Edie in horror. 'And he's talking about my mother's stone!'

'We have seen it,' mumbled the stepfather. 'We can show it.'

Edie whirled on the Gunner, so fast that the Raven on her shoulder was left in mid-air.

'We're going back to warn her!' she snapped.

'You can't change the past, Edie girl,' said the Gunner sadly, reaching out a hand to comfort her. She whirled away, back in the direction she had come from. Her hand snapped out and clamped round the Raven's leg.

There was an undignified squawk.

Edie fumbled in her pocket and pulled out the red thread.

'Tell him we're going back. Tell him we can do it the easy way, or the other way, the one where I put that red thread back on him and choke him with it.'

Ravens don't have much practice at looking long-suffering. Mostly they just endure and look ominous. So the look the Raven sent the Gunner was unusual. It clacked its beak slowly, with an air of strained patience.

It looked down at its trapped leg pointedly.

The Gunner sighed.

'He says he'll do what you ask. Says he was going to do it anyway. But he says you should always be careful what you ask for.'

'Fine,' said Edie, and walked straight across the street. She didn't look where she was going, the traffic didn't slow, and nothing hit her.

Given the jut in her jaw and the fire in her eyes, it probably didn't dare.

41

THE IMPOSSIBLE
BRIDGE

Ariel was waiting for George outside the cathedral, holding the horses' reins in her fist.

'Here,' she said without ceremony, and passed them to him as the bell tolled again and the horses whinnied and shivered.

'They can tell, boy, they hear the bell and they can tell . . .' she began.

'I know,' he said, stepping into the chariot. 'It tolls for me and all that. Let's get it over with . . .'

He sounded braver than he felt, but the pain in his stone shoulder had swept across his chest and he was clear enough in the middle of his fear to know that in the absence of anything else, facing it was the best chance he had.

'Follow me then,' she shrugged, unimpressed by his appearance of stoicism.

She flew ahead of him, as he twisted the horses out of the narrow gate to the churchyard and into what seemed like a series of less and less passable alleys that suddenly opened up into the riverwalk along the south side of the river.

'Hurry, boy!' she shouted back over her shoulder. He snapped the reins experimentally over the back of the horses and they accelerated.

He held on tight as the chariot sped along the side of

the river, kicking up an ice-storm in the wake of its whirring scimitar-bladed wheels. The cold wind in his eyes made him look sideways, and he couldn't help but look over the wind-scalloped surface of the river to the blank wall of the Ice Murk that rose in a solid impenetrable slab on the other side.

They shot under a bridge and back out into the light, and then a railway bridge approached, and as they followed Ariel the ringing definitely got louder and the pain radiating up his arm and into his chest stabbed sharper with each toll. He ground his teeth together and decided not to cry out.

Ariel flashed golden then was gone into the dark arch beneath the railway bridge. The horses cut through the strip of untouched snow, hot on her tail, so fast that when they came back out into the light on the other side George almost missed her.

She had stopped and hovered in the middle of the stretch of embankment between Blackfriars railway bridge and Blackfriars Bridge itself. He pulled back on the reins, and the horses sat back on their haunches, bringing the chariot to a slewing halt in a cloud of snow.

'What?' he said between tolls of the bell, looking up at the golden girl suspended above him.

'Your third and final duel,' she said, and pointed across the river.

'Where?' he asked, staring over the water. The wall of Ice Murk on the other side was sheer and unbroken. He could see no one and nothing between him and it.

The river was flowing past a series of columns that stuck out of the water, marooned between and dwarfed by the two bridges. You could see that they had once been the supports of an iron bridge that was either unfinished or long gone.

'I can't see anything,' he said.

The bell tolled. There was an accompanying muted flash low down in the face of the Murk opposite, like lightning muffled within a thundercloud. And then, to his horror, he saw the uncannily flat surface of roiling greyness darken and bulge and swirl outwards as the emerging bumps resolved into a coherent whole, a Knight on a horse coming out of the fog.

It had the shape of the last Knight of the Cnihtengild, but the Darkness that had flowed into it like a parasite had dimmed the metallic armour, so that it was as matt black as the inside of a soot-blackened chimney. The rider and the horse both had eyes that leaked wisps of black fire and smoke. Only the discs of glass on the horse's surcoat still lanced out their beams of light, no longer a clear blue but a colourless white that was somehow grey at its core, like white noise on a detuned television screen.

'That's not the Cnihtengild,' said George, staring, 'not any more . . .'

The other thing he noticed was that it had started to snow.

I AM THE DARKNESS INVINCIBLE thundered the Dark Knight, his words as clear from across the intervening gulf of black water as if he was standing next to them.

'This new Dark Knight is still enough the Cnihtengild for you to have an undischarged obligation to fight him,' said Ariel. 'Look at your arm if you doubt me.'

George didn't have to. The stone was binding round his chest now, and the constriction and the pain were making it hard to breathe.

The bell tolled once more.

BOY. LIGHT BEARER. WILL YOU STAND?

Despite the pain crushing his arm and chest, George still had enough reflexes left to shudder at the awful tone in the voice and the horror of the challenge it was offering.

'Where are we meant to fight?' he said to Ariel. 'I mean, I fought underground, at least I think it counts as underground, in that bombed-out cellar with the horses, that was below ground. And I fought the bloody Walker on the water, because we were on the ice at the Frost Fair . . .'

'So you must fight the third battle on the ground,' she said, pointing to the middle of the river. 'There.'

'That's a river,' said George after a beat during which the bell tolled again and his chest squeezed painfully in response, jerking the stone arm.

'It's a bridge. A bridge is solid enough ground for a duel,' she said. 'Don't be so picky, boy. It can't matter a jot where you face your death.'

Her cheerful callousness needled him.

'It's not a bloody bridge,' he said, pointing at the columns sticking out of the water. 'It's just some old bridge supports. They're not joined up, are they?'

'Of course they are,' she flounced back. 'Don't be a baby.'

'You're impossible,' he said with a snort of frustration.

'No I'm not,' she said, almost hurt at the suggestion. 'But the bridge is.'

'I know,' he said.

'No you don't. It's the Impossible Bridge. Look . . .'

He stared more closely but still could see nothing but sturdy, unconnected, red-painted stanchions stretching

259

across the river towards the Black Knight. He thought of the Impossible Door behind which he and Edie had taken sanctuary, only two, or was it three long nights back? Either way it seemed like a whole other lifetime ago. That had worked, but this didn't look like it could work, and even if it did, the outcome was going to be the very opposite of sanctuary. It was going to be a fight to the death. And the twingeing in his arm and chest were sending very strong hints as to whose it was likely to be.

As he looked the Knight kneed his horse forward. It stepped up on to the wall of the embankment, and then – to George's amazement – out on to thin air. It didn't fall. It just walked forward on the line where a bridge – if there were a bridge – would lie on top of the columns.

'How . . . ?' began George, and then squinted and looked even harder at what was happening. As the horse walked slowly forward, the snow that was falling started to land. And where it landed it took on the distinct contours of a wide road, pavements and two side-walls around and just ahead of the Knight's progress, as if there had been an invisible bridge there all along.

'It's the Impossible Bridge,' repeated Ariel, again with that insufferable tone as if that explained everything. 'All it requires is a leap of faith.'

And suddenly he thought of Dictionary's last words to him.

He smiled grimly.

'The natural flight of the human mind,' he said.

'What?' said the golden girl, hovering closer to him.

'From hope to hope,' he explained.

He swallowed. This is it, he thought, looking at the approaching Black Knight, who was clearly making the bridge as he came.

This is the moment.

The moment when I find out who I am.

The last possible moment when I can run.

He looked at the empty strip of walkway ribboning away to his left. He tensed. There was nothing and no one in the way to stop him trying to escape this.

Instead – or maybe because – of this, he stepped up on to the wall and faced the Darkness slowly riding towards him on the other side.

'I've done enough running,' he said very quietly to himself.

And stepped out into thin air.

42

BACK TO THE BEACH

They fell out of the black strobing passage through the mirrors into grey evening light, the cold tang of sea air and the sharp sting of wind-blown drizzle in their faces.

If Edie had looked back she'd have seen they had fallen out of the wing-mirror on the side of a parked-up lorry in a residential cul-de-sac. Edie didn't look back, or sideways. One glance had told her where she was, and she knew with a violent twist in her gut exactly where she had to go and how to get there. She'd been this way a hundred times before.

She ran down a narrow alley between two houses, brushing past dripping blue hydrangeas and breeze-blown tamarisk overhanging their garden fences, and came to the sudden light and larger sky at the top of the small bluff overlooking the beach. She hurtled down the cracked concrete steps three at a time, followed by the Raven and the Gunner.

'Take it easy,' he puffed.

'I know where I'm going!' she shouted as she hit the wet promenade at the bottom of the steps and swerved left, nearly falling as she changed direction

She sprinted past the railings on her right. High tide heaved greasily between the wooden groynes, only a narrow shelf of wet pebbles between her and the beckoning blankness of the sea.

She remembered her dream, but there was no hare and no owl to help her here. She was the helper.

The doors of the beach huts set into the base of the cliff jolted blurrily closer as she hammered down the wet cement walkway. They were all closed and padlocked as they always were, all except the one that was open as she knew it would be.

Seeing the blackness within stopped her.

This was her Bad Place.

This is where the nightmares came from.

This is where she had glinted the Worst Thing.

If she was so very, very tired, if she was at the end of her tether because it felt like she'd been trying to escape from something since for ever began, this was where she had started running. And this was what she had been running from. This was the other end of that tether, and here she was.

She hadn't escaped it at all.

She had been pulled right back.

She turned away from the open door and jumped down on to the beach in front of it.

'Edie,' said the Gunner, sliding to a stop behind the metal balustrade and looking down at her. 'You all right?'

'No,' she said flatly. 'No, I'm not all right . . .'

She wiped wetness from her face and realized it was not just the drizzle, because drizzle doesn't taste of salt.

'. . . I'm here.'

She didn't have time to be embarrassed.

She leant down and picked up the biggest stone she could grasp in one hand, and then climbed back up on the promenade, heading straight for the black doorway with a face hard as the flint she was carrying in her fist.

The Gunner reached out a hand to slow her, but she shrugged out of it and kept on going.

It was all as she'd seen it before. The white-painted

brick walls. The dripping ceiling. The Thermoses, the beach ball, the broken deckchair and the two plastic seats with the table between them. The beer cans. The bottles. The sour reek of old cigarette smoke.

Her mother.

Her mother sat in the gloom on one of the white plastic chairs, looking out at the grey seascape beyond. A cigarette had burnt down to a fragile arc of ash in her unmoving hand, ash as grey and burnt out as her eyes.

Edie had always hated it when drink made her mother's eyes lose focus and go flat like that. It was as if she had partly gone, partly left, partly died. It was only when she was drunk that her mother let her sadness take over, only then when she became unreachable.

The stepfather emerged from the shadows unscrewing the top of another bottle of wine. And of course it was always him who poured the wine in the first place, always him who prodded her mum into another glass.

'Come on,' he said, blurring the edges of his words as he sat down with the exaggerated care of the truly inebriated and poured a shaky stream of red into the clouded plastic tumbler at her mother's elbow. 'Misery loves company.'

He cracked another can with a beery cackle and sucked the foam from the top.

Her mother shook her head as if waking up from a long, wide-eyed sleep. The ash fell on to the floor, unnoticed.

'Edie,' she said.

Edie's heart stopped dead. Her mouth made silent shapes, and only the Raven saw her eyes become a drowning pool in which both despair and hope fought to survive.

'Mum?' she whispered.

Her mother looked right through her.

'Got to get Edie,' she mumbled, trying to focus on her watch. 'Get her tea on . . .'

'She's got a key,' said the stepfather, belching. 'S'nice here.'

'It's cold,' shivered the mother.

'Come on,' he giggled. 'I'll give you a little cuddle . . .'

Edie knew this. The drunker he got, the nastier he got. And the nastier he got, the more babyish his language became. The flint felt smooth and hard in her hand.

Her mother pushed his hand away.

'Can't go anyway,' he shrugged. 'Got to meet my mate. You'll like him.'

'No,' said her mother. And she got to her feet. 'I don't know why you like it here. It's creepy. Feels like I'm being watched.'

'You are!' cried Edie. 'I'm here, Mum!'

Edie lurched forward. She couldn't help herself. She threw her arms around her mum, trying to bury her face in the coat and sweater she knew so well. The force-field that protected the past from the future just neatly slid her off to one side as her mother stepped past, a finger twisting her earring.

Edie recognized the gesture. It was a tic her mother had, and only now, now that she knew what being a glint was and what a heart stone meant to one, did Edie understand. She longed to be able to explain it to her mother. She knew it would help, she knew that once she had a chance to explain it the great burden of thinking she was mad would disappear and she wouldn't have to try and lighten it by looking for forgetfulness in a bottle.

'Mum!' she shouted.

The Gunner's hand clasped her shoulder.

'She just can't hear you, girl,' he said softly.

'MUM!' she yelled, so loud that it felt like her vocal cords were tearing.

'I don't want to meet him,' said her mother, leaning down to pick up her shoulder bag. 'I don't know him, why would I want to?'

'He's a laugh, you'll like him,' said the stepfather, putting his foot on the bag. 'Come on, don't be a spoilsport, he's heard all about you, he wants to meet you, he'll be in a right old huff if you go.'

'Who is he anyway?' said her mother. She kept hold of the bag handles with one hand, but reached for her glass with the other.

'John, Johnny something. Like the whisky.' He slurred, his S's skidding all over the place. 'Johnny Walker.'

Edie'd known this was coming, but still the word caught her by surprise. She saw her mother let go of the bag and reach again for her ear, in the way she did when she got agitated, and in that moment Edie saw the sea-glass fragment blaze light.

'NO!' she shouted. 'GET OUT!!! RUN!!!'

''E's a mate from London,' said the stepfather, swigging more beer. 'You'll like him. He's a right cut-up—'

Edie flashed the memory of the Walker coming after her on the ice, the light from a distant brazier flashing redness on the long dagger he held as he came after her, and she was in motion before the Gunner could pull her back.

'NO!' she roared, and hit the stepfather with every ounce of power in her body, slamming the sea-smoothed flint into his temple like a sledgehammer.

The rounded edges of the stone spun out of her tight grip with the force of the impact, but his head didn't move a millimetre. He just kept on smiling his nasty smile as the stone flew into the darkness at the back of the hut. Only when the stone hit the back wall with a clatter did he react, turning towards the sound.

'What was that?' sad Edie's mother, her head coming up in fright.

'Something fell off the roof,' he said, peering backwards.

Edie grabbed her mother's arm and tried to yank her to the door. She of course didn't move at all.

'I hate this place,' she said. 'I'm going to go get Edie her tea. She shouldn't be alone. It's getting dark. And I want to go see her, see how she's doing.'

She turned to the door, pausing to scoop up her bag.

The door slammed shut.

And a slightly bored voice said:

'Ah, but it's so much more fun in the dark, don't you find?'

43

DARKNESS INVINCIBLE

The moment George stepped off the parapet of the riverwalk and out into the empty air, the falling snow stopped tumbling to the water below and started to land on the invisible surface of the Impossible Bridge all around him.

It felt weird as his leading foot felt unexpectedly solid ground where his eyes saw nothing but a long drop, but by the time his other foot touched down the few snowflakes that had already landed were ghosting an outline of solidity beneath him.

'Right,' he said.

He took a last look back. Ariel was standing on one foot in mid-air, her filmy clothing fluttering about her in the gentle breeze that seemed to blow everywhere she did. She raised a hand and gave him a surprisingly wide smile.

'Well done, boy, for much more is always lost by fleeing fate than facing it. I wish you well, whatever the outcome.'

'Thanks,' he said. 'I think.'

I AM YOUR WORST FEAR. WILL YOU FACE ME? boomed the Dark Knight, in a voice like a thunderclap.

George felt the vibrations of sound hit him head on as he kept walking forward. He kept going because he knew something the Darkness clearly didn't: his worst fear had been about his dad. He had worried that he'd died thinking George had meant the last angry words he'd flung at him, unaware they were to be their last words, that he'd died thinking George didn't love him. He'd lived with the fear that this had somehow been responsible for his dad's death. But he'd faced that fear when he stood the Gunner's watch on the memorial. He'd faced it and it had evaporated.

So now he decided that he'd feel frightened but just not show it. And as he moved forward it seemed to be working. He heard his dad's voice saying sometimes you just had to walk the walk, even when it was the last thing you felt like doing, and how it actually helped, because once your feet started walking your heart and your brain had no choice but to follow. He hadn't understood it then, but now he was doing it, he knew exactly what it meant.

'Yes,' he said.

ARE YOU READY TO FACE YOUR FEAR? repeated the Knight as George walked right up to the lance.

And then there was no chance to turn around because he was too close, and he had stepped past the tip of the lance, reaching for the horse's head.

'Yeah,' he said. 'But why's my fear hiding?'

And though his flesh crawled at what his good hand was doing, he plunged his fingers into the eyeholes, through the dark smoke curling out of them, and took a firm grip. He looked up into the eye-slits of the Dark Knight's helmet, and tried to clear his mind as he felt with his hand. The hand tingled as it had when he mended Spout's wing, only this time he was not feeling for the place where sundered stone fragments wished to rejoin. He was feeling for the flaws in the metal, the places the welding was weakest. He felt the heat in his hand radiate through the outer sheets of metal. The

269

Knight must have felt it too, because he tried to back up the horse.

WHAT ARE YOU DOING, BOY? he roared.

'Using a making hand to mar,' said George. 'Like this.'

And he closed his eyes, felt the flaw in the welding, and with the next toll of the bell he flexed his muscles and ripped the armoured front clean off the face of the Dark Horse within.

'HA!'

There was the sound of a great invisible host roaring in approval and smashing their weapons against their shields like a thunderclap, followed a beat later by a crack of lightning. And in the lightning George saw the Black Knight had not ridden alone. Rather he had ridden as the Last Knight of the Cnihtengild had ridden before the Darkness took him over and filled the hollow shell of the man and horse with the blackness of the Night Mare.

Unknown to itself the Black Knight had ridden with all the Knights of the Cnihtengild, the phantom band of war-scarred horsemen now ranged on each side of the Impossible Bridge.

The Black Knight saw them at the same time, and reined his horse backwards towards the City shore. As they reversed the Darkness smoked forward in wisps leaking from the exposed inner void of the horse's skull.

NOW YOU DIE, screamed the Darkness. NOW THE LIGHT GOES OUT.

And he kicked the charger forward, the sharp lance-point barrelling in through the big flakes of falling snow, straight towards George's heart.

The bell tolled again, and in the flash that came with it he saw the Cnihtengild. And he saw every battle-hardened face and hacked-about helmet was looking at him, not the Black Knight, to see if he would stand.

What they didn't know was that he had passed the moment when he would let himself run.

He'd taken the leap of faith.

All that remained, he thought, was the landing.

He braced one leg at an angle behind himself, twisting his hips so that his chest remained head on to the Knight.

Death whistled towards the core of his being, his heart pounding in time with the horse's hoofbeats.

And in the moment before impact he realized he had never, ever felt so calm.

This was it.

In what felt like a life spent running, this was the Great Unavoidable.

And as he faced it, he abruptly stopped feeling alone.

He stopped feeling like a lonely boy of thirteen summers.

He felt older, much older, almost ancient, and stronger than any one person could ever be.

He felt the great weight of every earlier George, every Chapman, every mother, every father down the long centuries who had lived before him and struggled and made and endured to bring their line to this point in the world, and they were all somehow standing with him, their shoulders to his.

It was as if that long line of dead men had shouted a great 'Yes!', and stamped their feet in approval as he straightened his back and hacked his heel into the ground.

And then it was over.

His stone arm snapped up and caught the tip of

the lance dead centre in the open palm of his outspread hand.

The impact and the forward momentum of the horse and rider jarred the breath out of him and jolted him so badly that his jaw jumped and he bit the side of his tongue by mistake. It slammed him at least twenty feet, but he kept his leg braced and kept his footing. A great pile of snow built up behind his foot as it snowploughed backwards.

And then the horse stopped.

George looked up.

'That it?' he said, and spat a thin twist of blood into the snow at his side.

The tip of the lance had fused into the stone of his hand.

He looked along the long length of the great spear into the black eyes smoking out of the Knight's helmet.

'Now. You want me to tell you about *your* fear? Because I can.'

The Knight tried to jerk his lance free, but George closed his open fingers into a fist that gripped it like a vice.

'I can feel your fear. You need a shape. You have no form to exist in within our world, so you need a shape, because without it you would be nothing, and you know what?'

He spat sideways without breaking eye contact, so he missed the second red star that bloomed in the snow as his spittle hit it.

'I've been frightened of a lot of things, too many things in fact. But even I can't figure out why I should be afraid of nothing.'

I AM NOT NOTHING. I AM EVERYTHING,

screamed the Darkness leaking out of the horse's torn headpiece.

'No,' said George, thinking of the Stone Corpse. 'You're not everything. You're just fear and pain and evil. And that isn't everything. I mean, it may be where you come from, but not here. In this world everything balances: like for like, ill for ill, good for evil, and for every Dragon . . .? Guess who?'

And with that he bent the tip of the lance into a right-angle, and jerked the Knight, who was trying to back-pedal the horse, forward and right out of his saddle.

'HA!'

The bell tolled, and the Cnihtengild moved as one, engulfing the Black Knight. And as the bell continued to toll, in the accompanying flashes George saw them hacking and ripping at the fallen Knight. He heard the Darkness shrieking in rage and then something like terror, and he felt the lance gripped in his stone fist begin to shake more and more as less and less of the Darkness was left with a place to be.

The Cnihtengild were ripping great panels off the black shape, and throwing them aside. As they did so the Darkness lost its form and twisted and flowed into the remaining sections of statue, desperately seeking a way to stop dissipating.

It flowed into the arm holding the lance, then on into the hand. The metal bulged and buckled as too much Darkness tried to find a shape within too little space, and then it swelled into the thin lance, bulging and twisting it as it tried to ram itself further inside it so that it writhed and fattened like a snake. The Cnihtengild tore the metal plates of the arm apart, and wrenched open the hand, so that for an instant the Darkness flared and leaked out of the end of the lance like some exotic bloom. Then George felt the pain in his hand explode, as the Darkness forced itself from the lance tip into his arm.

In the instant of shock he stared at the Darkness entering the white limestone fist, trying to find fissures and veins in which it could hide and take form, and he knew exactly why the last vein had been made of this stone and no other. It was exactly the same white gritty limestone as that of the London Stone, the Stone where he had refused to make a sacrifice, the Stone where he had chosen the Hard Way. He choked out a savage bullet of laughter through the pain coursing up his arm with the Darkness.

'Come on then!' he gasped.

The Darkness couldn't flow fast enough through the narrow tip embedded in his hand. In a flash of light, as the bell tolled he saw one of the Cnihtengild swing the savagely nicked blade of a great battleaxe down on the lance, severing it in the middle.

Darkness poured out and writhed in the air, like a many-headed hydra, each blind tentacle swirling about, trying to find somewhere to be, to take shape in.

'Come on!' sobbed George as a new and sharp pain tore across his chest and arm, and the stone kicked and buckled beneath his clothes with a horrid life all of its own. And then there was a tremendous ripping noise as the shoulder ripped out of his shirt and the two coats he was wearing, and the stone that had spread across his chest began to unfurl and peel back like an answering bloom to the Dark flower at the other end of the arm and lance that connected them.

The pain was like an enormous plaster that had been stitched to his skin being slowly pulled off. It was too acute for him to even cry out in protest as he watched the stone flare off his shoulder into matching tendrils that reached out to the Darkness beyond.

He just stared open-mouthed, his whole body trembling in shock as the stone and the Darkness met and whirled around each other, like two strange sea creatures, a black and a white squid twisting and squirming around each other in a titanic struggle for supremacy.

There was a final ripping noise and a jerk of excruciating agony, and then the Darkness and the stone were wrestling horribly on the ground as he backed away, shaking with the knowledge that the stone arm had been ripped off.

He knew he couldn't survive that.

And then he felt the last thing he expected. A small warm hand slipped into his and squeezed. It squeezed the right hand, the one he was sure had been ripped off. He looked down and saw his own hand, red and raw from where the stone had unpeeled itself, but flesh and blood. And in it a golden hand.

'Good, boy,' whispered a voice in his ear, and as he tried to look at the source of the warm breath making all the hairs on his neck suddenly and inexplicably stand to attention, she was gone in a flash of gold, soaring into the sky above the struggling stone and Darkness.

The stone jerked and snapped and then inexorably tightened round the Darkness, squeezing it within itself. It was, in the end, an uneven fight, because the Darkness needed a shape more than it needed to win, because if it had destroyed the stone it would have been left without a way or a place to be. There was a final wrench and the last thin tendrils died back into the evolving shape of the stone, and all there was left to see was the white limestone twisting and flexing into the shape it had adopted before flaying itself free of George's body. And then all was still on the snow-covered bridge, and George stood panting, looking down at a stone arm lying at his feet, surrounded by the discarded plates of armour that had once been the last Knight of the Cnihtengild, and the dead body of the Duke's horse. All the darkness had left the statues, and the jumbled fragments of glass-inlaid surcoat once more blazed clear blue every which way out into the air around them, so that he appeared to be standing in a thicket of lights as he bent down and picked up the arm.

The bell had ceased to toll, but in the glow from the Last Knight's armour he could see the ghost band of the Cnihtengild panting with their exertion, resting on their saddlebows, looking at him.

'Take the horse back to its plinth and then take the Knight and *his* horse home,' he said, pointing at the shattered fragments of the statues. 'The Darkness that took them over wasn't their fault.'

Ariel dropped out of the sky and looked quizzically at him.

'He deserves to live to fight another day,' said George.

'HA!' roared the Cnihtengild. And he thought he saw them raise their weapons in salute, and then he definitely saw them dismounting and picking up the fragments of armour.

'Good,' he said, feeling the weight of the stone arm in his hand was almost more than he had the energy left to carry even the short way back to the chariot.

'It was fated,' said Ariel.

'Maybe,' said George, climbing back over the wall on to the Embankment. 'But this isn't over, is it? There's the

Ice Devil, and he looks like a bigger problem altogether.'

'I am a mere Agent of Fate. That's not my job,' shrugged Ariel.

'Yeah,' he said, climbing into the chariot and feeling the cold biting into his one bare arm, making him feel strangely lopsided. It was a good feeling, he reckoned, given that it meant he still had two flesh and blood arms.

'No,' he said, placing the stone arm at his feet and picking up the reins. 'It's mine.'

And with a crack of the reins he was off, galloping along the walkway, heading for Trafalgar Square and what he knew in his bones was going to be, however it turned out, the last battle.

44

WALKER ON
THE BEACH

Edie was frozen in horror, jammed against the beach hut wall, locked into the darkest room of her nightmare. The only light was the one burning from her mother's earring. And in that light Edie saw a tall figure standing with his back to the door, tendrils of greasy hair escaping from a hoodie worn under a long green coat.

It was the Walker.

Her fists clenched and she stepped in front of her mother.

'Stop him,' she said, eyes flicking to the Gunner.

'If I could,' he said, pain in his eyes. 'I'd stop his clock once and for all. But I can't. We can't.'

'What a charming earring,' smiled the Walker.

Edie's mother was very still, like an animal that knows danger has arrived and it will have only one chance to make its escape. She suddenly looked very sober.

'Thanks,' she said, swallowing. 'I've got to go . . .'

'No, really,' the Walker said, stepping forward, and starting to circle her. 'Just a simple piece of sea-glass, and yet it has such . . . life in it.'

Edie knew what happened next. She'd seen it in harsh, terrifying flashes when she'd glinted it what seemed a lifetime ago, before she'd been chased by the stepfather and dealt with him and run away to London. She'd seen the Walker circling her mother, wheedling, teasing and then bullying and threatening. She'd seen him mocking her for not even knowing what she was. She'd seen the stepfather sitting and watching and giggling at it all. And then she'd seen him leap to keep the door locked when her mother made her last desperate break for freedom and sanity.

The struggle she'd seen as he tripped her and she fought to escape them both was fierce and brutal and – as measured in real time – quite short. To Edie it had seemed to go on for ever. She didn't watch it again, not the way she had when she glinted it.

This time she was in it.

As her mother ran for the door, Edie dived between her and the Walker, trying to block him. He slid past without noticing her. When she regained her balance she sprung for him, her fists glancing off his face, her throttling hands glissading round his neck without being able to crush it. Edie fought with every ounce of her strength. She fought hard and she fought silent, the way a born street-brawler fights, wasting no energy on noise, using every last fragment in the struggle. She kicked, she bit, she scratched, she gouged and she punched the unbreakable force-field so many times that her fists just got numb, way on the other side of pain.

But all she managed to do was exhaust herself.

The scream, when it came, was her mother's, as the Walker ripped the earring clear and held it high in his exultant fist. Edie sobbed and once again threw herself between the Walker and her mother.

There was no need. Now he had the stone, he stepped calmly back.

'Marvellous,' he panted, eyes bright, oblivious to the three scratches her mother had raked diagonally across his face, from forehead to ear as he gazed hungrily at the fire in the glass. 'Such a tiny fragment, yet such vigour within.'

Edie's mother scrambled to the locked door and tried to tear it open.

'Oh you can't go,' he said, as eerily polite as a host at a tea-party. 'Please. Dear lady. You mustn't go yet. I haven't told you what you are. I haven't told you what you've lost. It's quite the best part . . .'

The door bounced behind her as she staggered out on to the promenade and ran for her life.

The Walker didn't chase her. He shrugged, shook his head and returned to his contemplation of the stone.

'. . . No hurry. I have all the time in the world.'

Edie ran out of the door, on to the promenade. Her mother was sprinting away already fifty metres ahead. As she started to follow, the Gunner caught up and gripped her shoulders.

'Let go!' shouted Edie.

He lifted her in the air, her legs bicycling as she tried to run after her mother.

'You can't follow her, love. You can't help her, you can't change what happens. Look at you, look at how you've hurt yourself trying.'

Edie stopped struggling. She knew he was right.

The Gunner put her down. She was shaking with the shock and backwash of adrenalin from the one-sided fight. Her knuckles were split, her hair hung wild and there was a graze weeping on her cheekbone where she'd bounced off the rough brickwork of the beach hut.

'I just . . .' she began.

'Don't speak. Be still for a while,' said the soldier. 'Just be.'

She looked out to sea. He followed her eyes.

'It's a great calm, all that water,' he said. 'I've never seen the sea till now. It's calmer than the river.'

She stumbled over the edge of the promenade and dropped on to the loose shingle with a jolt. She crunched over to the wooden groyne, pulled her fur coat tightly round her and sat against it, eyes fixed on the gentle heave of the sea-swell in the middle distance.

She heard a louder crunch and footsteps approaching, and she felt the thud against the groyne as the bronze man sat down next to her. After a while there was a flutter next to her ear and then a weight on her shoulder as the Raven dropped in to perch on her, but she didn't react to that either.

And for a long time they sat like that, all staring out to sea while her heartbeat returned to normal and she stopped shaking.

Something grey and big-winged flapped slowly along the line of the shore, too far away to identify.

She knew she couldn't sit there for ever.

'He took her heart stone,' said the Gunner.

She nodded, eyes still fixed on the sea.

'He took her heart stone,' she agreed with a sniff. 'After that, must have been when she went loony. Went for my stepdad with the potato peeler.'

A flicker of satisfaction snuck on to her face at the memory, and then was gone.

'They took her away. She didn't come back.'

She scooped up a handful of small pebbles and let them drop to the beach one by one. The Gunner watched with her as they bounced and skittered across the jumble of stones beside them.

When her hand was empty she looked at him. Her

eyes were now dry, and her chin had regained its stubborn jut.

'She died?' said the Gunner softly.

Edie nodded. 'She killed herself.'

She shovelled her hand into the beach at her side, but this time she kept her hand closed round the wet gravel she dug out. The Gunner watched her knuckles whiten on it, though her voice remained calm.

'I'm not meant to know that bit. But he told me. My stepdad. One night. Drunk. He "thought I should know".'

The Gunner leant over and very gently his large bronze hands unwrapped her fingers. She didn't resist as he turned her hand over and let the clenched handful of gravel drop away.

'So why can't you forgive her?' he asked gently.

Edie took a big breath and held it while her body burnt all the oxygen in it. Then she exhaled.

'Because she was meant to look after me. But she left me. With him. She took the easy way out. And left me the hard way . . . ow!'

The Raven pecked her hard on the ear.

'Why'd he . . . OW!!'

The Raven did it again.

'He doesn't agree with you,' smiled the soldier, and stood up. He offered her a hand, and hauled her to her feet.

'Well, he doesn't know everything, does he?' Edie said, eyeing the bird with dislike as she rubbed her ear.

'No,' agreed the Gunner. 'Just everything that happened. And I think he knows something else that he wants to show you, and all.'

Edie turned and looked at the beach hut. The door

was now closed again, the memory locked away behind a rusting padlock. It looked as innocent and shabby as the other doors either side of it.

'What else can there be?' she said. 'Nothing can be worse than that.'

The Raven clacked its beak and looked at the Gunner behind Edie's back.

The Gunner shook his head.

45

HARE BELL

The Ice Murk made it almost impossible to move forward in any coherent direction, but the Queen of America and Shack were making progress by only moving in the direction of the noise the Queen had heard. They stayed in contact by each holding on to the shaggy coat of the buffalo at their side. In the grey fog the white stone of the Queen and her beast glowed a little, so that she was just able to track the dragon's trail in front of her.

As they trudged through the ever deeper snow Shack was able to hear the noise more and more clearly as his muffled ears caught up with the more finely tuned hearing of the warrior Queen.

It was people crying and shouting, a general lamentation that held more sorrow than fear. It was a sound of resignation, not of desperation, and there were more female voices mixed through it than there were men's.

And then they blinked in surprise as they walked unexpectedly out of the Murk and into one of the great avenues of open air that cut through the miasma in deep straight gullies like firebreaks in a dense forest.

They looked right and left, and saw with relief that the dragon's tracks led along the break, keeping out of the Murk.

'What is this?' said Shack, pointing right and left along the clear cut of clean air.

'Lines of power,' said the Queen.

'Of course,' said Shack. 'The ley lines.'

People who think London is a great shambolic mishmash of twisting streets that have grown up piecemeal over time are right, but only partially so. There are lines that underpin the apparent random shape of the City, and always have done. If you took a map of the City and drew lines connecting the major churches you would begin to see how many lie in a straight line. A straight line between three churches could be coincidence. A straight line between four or five or six is something else entirely. When you add in the even older holy wells and sacred springs and find them on the same lines, it's possible that there is a more ancient grid of power running under the City streets. And if you look beyond the city along those lines, you might find they cut through even more ancient stone circles and strangely hallowed hilltop sites in the island beyond.

These are the old lines of power, forgotten by everyone who crosses them every day just as the London Stone is, lines that are however still so powerful that the Ice Murk made no impression on them.

The voices were much clearer now, as if the clean-cut sides of the Murk canyon they were in were channelling them, like the long nave of a dark cathedral.

'Come on,' said Shack, jogging forward. 'There's something moving over there.'

The lines of power don't of course run neatly along the road plan of the city, and what was ahead of them was a harsh and complicated façade of a medium-rise office complex. The tracks led up some steps, and they had to dip into the murk and follow the wall of the building by touch until they turned a corner and broke back out into the clean air beyond. And when they did, they saw they were in the inner square of the Broadgate Centre, a blocky modern piazza whose normal starkness was softened by the snow.

The snow on the ground was not a virgin blanket of white. It was churned up in great chunks that bore witness to the great fight that must have taken place on it.

The Queen of Time was lying broken-winged at the edge of the piazza, a golden splash of colour in the middle of a ring of dark statues ranged round her in a protective perimeter. They were a group of spits, made to look like tired office workers. Clean scrapes of bronze showing through their normally matt surface showed where they had fallen on the dragons and tried to rescue the Queen from their ripping talons.

It was they who were doing the keening and lamenting.

'She's still breathing,' said an almost faceless male figure as Shack ran past him and the Queen of America slid to one knee beside the Queen of Time.

'Not for long,' she grunted. 'Put her on buffalo. We ride for the maker boy. Maker boy maybe can heal. It's only chance. Can be no turn o' day if she dies.'

There was an urgency in her voice that made the big polar explorer immediately reach down and slide his hands round the golden body of the fallen Queen and lift her gently, her shattered wings hanging loose, her hair tumbled in disarray over the gouges torn through her clothes into the body beneath.

'Got her,' he said, carrying her carefully through the Office Workers towards the waiting buffalo. 'How will you get to the boy through this Murk?'

The Queen of America ran past him to the other side of the square, where there was a statue of a sinewy hare leaping past a giant bell that was tipped on its side.

'Brother jackrabbit,' she shouted. 'Brother jackrabbit knows the secret ways through the City.'

And she swung her tomahawk and clanged the bell, and as she did so the hare sprang into life and raced in a circuit of the square, like something getting up speed.

In the silence that followed as the bell's noise died away, the only sound left was the sound of its feet circling them in the deadening snow-pack, and a distant sound of more voices crying. Shack cocked an ear as the Queen of America jumped up on the buffalo on which he had gently placed the other golden Queen.

'Ice man,' she said. 'What are you doing?'

'I think,' he said carefully, 'I think I should go and see what those girls are crying about.'

The Queen looked in the direction of the noise, which had been cloaked by the lamentations of the Office Workers.

'Sound of grief comes from Holy Well,' she said, pointing. 'Cannot be a good thing if the Holy Well is open.'

'Maybe so,' said Shack. 'But someone should go and see anyway.' And with that he raised his hand in farewell, and turned away, trudging off into the unknown snow waste on his own.

The Queen of America looked after him for a short beat, and then put a restraining hand on the gold body in front of her.

'We go,' she said. 'Follow jackrabbit . . .'

And the hare stopped its increasingly desperate circuits of the square and ran straight into the side of the Ice Murk, and the buffalo plunged into a gallop following the bobbing tail of the hare that blazed white in the gloom beyond.

And in a moment the Murk had swallowed them too.

46

DIVERS

Two things struck George as he swung the chariot up and on to Blackfriars Bridge. The first was that he was going to have to find another way to cross back on to the north side of the river, because the sheer massif of the Ice Murk had already spread west past the other end of the bridge. If he kept on he'd just barrel right into the middle of it and be irretrievably lost.

The second thing he noticed was the activity on the bridge. The Queen, Boadicea, was leaning over the edge shouting and pointing, with the unmistakable air of someone ordering a group of people about. There was a metal sack at her feet and as George approached first one then another figure flew up from the river below and clung on to the other side of the bridge wall talking to her and nodding and shaking their heads.

One of the airborne spits was a winged pilot, in World War Two gear, wearing a flying helmet and a life-jacket. His arms were attached to his wings, making him look more like a crucifix than an angel as he hung in the air talking animatedly with the Queen and the other figure. The other spit was recognizable as a Perseus – semi-clad with a feathered helmet and winged sandals, he was gesticulating with an aggressively curved sword at something below. The one thing they had in common, apart from the fact they could both, in their different ways, fly, was that they were both dripping wet.

The Queen turned as George approached.

'Boy,' she said without ceremony or a hint of surprise – or pleasure – at the fact he had come back at all from his ordeal. 'We cannot find it.'

'But chin up, old man, we're still looking!' smiled the Pilot and dropped off the edge of the bridge.

'Yes,' said the Perseus, his teeth chattering despite a wide grin, 'but I was not made for these cold northern waters.'

And with that he flipped backwards in a perfect back-dive. George jumped off the chariot and ran to the edge, just in time to see the two spits hit the river below and disappear.

There was a big barge moored in the middle of the river, and on it one of the sailor statues, the Bosun, was standing amid a ramshackle collection of stones and objects that were wet and caked in silt. As George watched a great bronze Dolphin leapt out of the water, trailing a laughing bronze Boy who held on to its fin as the creature arched high over the Bosun. He dropped another stone on to the deck next to him, and then Boy and Dolphin disappeared in another splash on the far side of the barge.

Jack Tar was standing in a small boat that the sailors had obviously commandeered from one of the large boats permanently moored on the embankment, hauling at a rope as he dragged the riverbed below with the anchor that, as George stared, broke clear of the water with half a rusted bicycle attached to it.

'We're doing everything we can,' said the Queen, as first the Perseus and then the Pilot burst out of the river, each gasping for breath and carrying assorted pieces of junk in their hands. They flew to the barge and dropped them next to the Bosun, who quickly sifted through them and shook his head.

'They can't find the mirror down there. They're pulling stuff out at random and hoping,' she said. 'We don't know what else to do. But we're not giving up.'

George knew he couldn't really feel more than a vague Dark presence out there. He knew that to find the mirror required someone who was an expert at feeling the power hidden within stones.

'We need Edie,' he said. 'Edie can feel its presence.'

He remembered what she had told him about why the Walker had kidnapped her to sift through his collection of black stones, looking for the one he could make into a Black Mirror. He knew without needing to think how or why he knew it that this was a job for her and no other.

'Where the hell is she?' he said, scanning the cityscape stretched all around him. 'If we can't find Edie, everything is lost.'

It was at that instant, as his gaze swept across the river on the other side of the bridge towards the east that he saw them. Flying fast and low, hugging the wavelets on the river's surface, a solid phalanx of ten ice-covered taints, inbound like silvery missiles.

47

ASYLUM

The smell hit Edie as soon as she stepped out of the mirror: the sharp piney-chemical spike of disinfectant cut with the sour reek of stale cigarettes was as unappealingly institutional as the queasy green corridor walls stretching away on either side of them.

The Gunner held out a steadying hand and for a moment, as she acclimatized, they stood there watching the Raven flap slowly away from them down the long corridor, his black wings doubled in the reflection on the shiny floor below, like a shadow that flew just a beat behind him.

'Are you all right?' said the Gunner.

'Let's go,' she said tightly, setting off after the bird who as always seemed to know exactly where they should be going.

As she followed other details began to filter into her consciousness. All the windows were barred with wire mesh, thickly painted the same colour as the walls. All the barred windows Edie had ever seen were barred on the outside to stop people getting in. These were different. On these windows the mesh was on the inside of the windows, protecting the glass. Stopping people getting out.

A stocky nurse pushed a squeaky-wheeled trolley loaded with medication past them, the brightly coloured pills rattling cheerily in their neatly ranked plastic cups as she went.

The Raven hovered above her head unseen while she punched a code into a keypad on the door at the end of the corridor. As soon as the door was opened the Raven flew in ahead of her, and Edie and the Gunner slipped after it as she turned to negotiate the trolley through behind her.

It was a big hospital day room. Patients were scattered around the plastic chairs, most of which were arranged in a jumbled half-circle in front of a ceiling-mounted television. The television was showing nothing but a bright rectangle of white noise, the tiny white and black flecks fizzing into a grey electric blur as an electrician in a boiler-suit and tool-belt stood on a chair checking the connections at the back.

Most of the patients – in pyjamas and dressing gowns – were sitting and watching it anyway.

A man sat at a table playing chess. With himself. And only a black rook on the board. Beyond him a woman stood in the corner, face jammed into the angle of the wall, slowly stepping from one foot to the other, one thin white hand twining blindly behind her back, doggedly going nowhere.

'It's an asylum,' said the Gunner, telling Edie what she already knew.

The electrician sucked his teeth in a disappointed snap of his tongue, got down off the chair and walked past them to a door in the wall. He pulled out a key and unlocked it.

The nurse with the trolley rolled her eyes at him as she passed.

'Have you not got it fixed yet?'

'I'm going on the roof. Must be the aerial. Those winds . . .' he said, opening the door.

Edie saw the stairs leading upwards beyond it.

'Well, mind you lock the door behind you,' said the nurse, stopping by a lone patient in a pale-lemon dressing gown sitting on a chair looking away from the TV, her face hidden by a long sweep of dark aubergine hair.

'You don't want to turn round and find any of this lot have decided to follow you on to the roof. He doesn't need any little helpers, right, Sue?'

It was Edie's mother. She turned her attention to the woman handing her a little disposable cup. Then she looked at the door and the stairs, face blank with lack of interest.

'Right,' she agreed, taking her cupful of bright pills and then swallowing them while the nurse waited and then ticked her name off a list.

'Lovely jubbly,' smiled the nurse brightly.

Edie's mother's face froze, and she pushed back in her chair so hard the foam padding whooshed air in protest.

'What are you doing here?' she gasped at someone behind the nurse.

The nurse turned and saw nothing but a blank wall.

'Who are you talking to?' she asked, turning back to her.

Edie's mother stretched out a long accusing finger, shaking with emotion.

'Him.'

The nurse looked again and saw nothing.

'There's no one there, Sue.'

Except there was.

It was the Walker. He had just stepped out of one of his hand-held mirrors and was carefully snapping them back together and pocketing them.

'She can't see me. Not unless I let her,' he drawled, stepping forward and waving his hand in front of the nurse's face. She didn't react at all, just looked at Edie's mother and wrote something on her chart.

'You just stay there, Sue. Doctor might come and have a little chat in a while, yeah?' said the nurse. 'Best just stay there for now. There's nothing to worry about, love.'

And off she jangled with her trolley. Edie's mother was still crammed back in her seat, her hands white-knuckling on the arm rests.

The Walker stroked his beard and looked at her.

'What do you want?' she croaked.

'What do I want?' he smiled, rolling his eyes as if theatrically bored by everything and everyone. 'I would like things to be easier. In the early days it was easier. There were fewer people, spread across a much simpler world. It was not hard to find you.'

'To find me?' she gulped, eyes switching left and right, looking for somewhere to run, or someone to help her.

Edie couldn't take it. She launched herself at the Walker. Once more she just slid off him, tumbling round his body and landing painfully on the floor. The Gunner stepped across the room and restrained her as she tried to launch herself back into the attack.

'No,' he said firmly, gripping her arm. 'No more of that. You'll just hurt yourself more.'

The Walker shook his head at her mother.

'Not to find you. To find such as you. Glints. They knew who they were, and others knew they were different, even if they were unaware of the exact nature of that difference. The hostile called them witches and burnt

295

them, the needy called them wise-women and asked for their help. Everyone knew who they were, even if only the glints themselves knew *what* they were. And they'd pass on that knowledge to younger women who had the gift, daughters and the like . . .'

And Edie watched as the Walker explained to her mother exactly what a glint was. And it was painful to witness the realization spreading across her mother's face as she understood that however crazy the message was or how frightening the messenger, it was all true.

Edie remembered how when it was explained to her she too had instantly felt the truth and rightness of it. And now she was seeing the same thing dawn on her mother.

'So I've had this ability, this "gift" all the time?' said her mum, twisting the tie of her pale-yellow dressing gown tightly round her fingers and pulling so tight that they whitened with lack of blood.

'Yes.'

She took a moment to watch all the carefully arranged dominoes of her life as she had misunderstood it tip over one at a time in a long chain that snaked, Edie knew, all the way back to the seven-year-old version of herself glinting the plague pit.

'And I wasn't mad,' she said, staring at her feet, but seeing something different entirely. 'Not ever. I was seeing things. Real things. Not imagining them.'

'Yes,' shrugged the Walker.

She bit her lip and looked up at him, shaking her head in disbelief at her predicament. She spoke very slowly as the last domino fell with a click like a door locking.

'And now I know that I wasn't mad, that I've never been mad – I'm in here.'

'Ironic, is it not? Though not for long, I feel, if that is any solace . . .' He grinned easily. 'You have the gift, but you no longer have the stone. Without a heart stone you will, really, go mad. You feel it, don't you? That sense of things coming unstitched, of the fragile mooring that held you on the earth slowly working loose?'

Edie's mother stared at him, her leg starting to jig up and down with the tension building in her.

'What do you want?' she drymouthed.

He reached in his pocket and held up the earring. Her eyes devoured it and the fire blazing inside.

'Such a small stone,' he tutted. 'Scarcely worth my trouble.'

'So give it back,' she said, swallowing.

'You have a daughter.'

Edie's mother went very still again, just as she had in the beach hut, like an animal sensing danger. She said nothing.

'Does she . . . have a stone?' he asked casually.

She shook her head emphatically.

'She's not like me.'

The Walker's hand shot out and gripped her chin.

'She's just like you.'

Edie gasped and stepped forward. The Gunner's hand fell on her shoulder and squeezed it in comfort. Tears of frustration welled behind her eyes at her inability to talk to her mother, to help her, to just touch her, even for an instant.

'In the old days mothers handed the knowledge of the gift to their daughters, just as they had been handed it by their own mothers,' the Walker continued, again sounding slightly bored by what he was saying. 'A clear line of communication and tradition reaching back to the dawn of time itself. Somehow, perhaps even because of my activities, these lines have been cut.'

Edie thought of the bagful of heart stones that the Gunner had brought from the Walker's underground cell. The stones that had warmed and brought her back to life. She thought of how many there had been, and how many lives that meant the Walker had destroyed to collect them, a life for each one. She shuddered.

'And it's been so very much harder for me, labouring as I do in these latter days, to find glints now that they no longer know who they are.'

'Poor you,' said Edie's mother.

Edie smiled at the contempt she put into the two words. She knew how scared she was. She'd been that close, too close to the Walker. And yet her mother was finding a way to fight back even though she had no way of winning.

'I'm not insensitive,' the Walker replied, squatting in front of her, eyeball to eyeball. 'I can see it must be painful for you now, knowing what you do, that you cannot pass that knowledge on to your daughter in the old way. You must be sorely vexed that she will go through a wasted life like your own, not knowing what she is, not understanding she's a glint, thinking she's mad.'

'I'll tell her,' she said.

'No. I don't think you'll tell her in time. Unless . . .'

'Unless?'

The terrible spark of hope that the one word brought to her mother's eye was painful to see. Edie knew the Walker never let anything get away. She knew his 'unless' was a viciously barbed trap waiting for her mother to step in it.

He stood up and stretched. His manner was all

the more menacing because of the careless way he issued his threats, always on appearing to be on the edge of yawning.

'She has a stone.'

He spoke to the ceiling with a studied lack of interest.

Edie's mother said nothing. There was a sudden jolt of sound from across the room as the television kicked back into life, the white noise being replaced by the early evening news. The other patients mumbled in approval and sat back to stare at the colourful images jerking across the screen above them. Edie's mother's eyes flicked to the screen and then to the locked door across the hall. Then she swallowed and looked at the Walker again.

In the window behind him beyond the safety mesh and the glass, the sun was beginning to set, smearing red across the evening sky, so that the Walker appeared to be framed in blood.

'She has a much larger stone than this pea of yours. He has seen it. Your "friend". He has told me of it.'

'I'll kill him,' she said, very calmly and with absolute conviction.

'What you do to him is no concern of mine, though I do not imagine you will achieve the opportunity before your mind goes. Your daughter has a stone. We have looked for it. But we cannot find it.'

Edie had a memory flash: her and her mother and an old biscuit tin. They were burying it in the scrap of woods just behind the house, in a hollow beneath an overhanging laurel bush. It was a place Edie liked when she was smaller, a sort of den in the woods. Her mother used to come and sit with her with a Thermos of tomato soup some days and tell stories.

On the good days.

And on one good day they'd seen something on TV about digging up history and decided they would bury the battered biscuit tin full of things that were precious, for the future.

'My time capsule,' Edie breathed. 'I put it in my time capsule . . .'

'What?' said the Gunner.

'Doesn't matter,' said Edie.

But it did. In her mind's eye she saw the clods of earth spattering down on the biscuit tin lid as they buried it, and though it was only a biscuit tin, it felt for a moment as if she was remembering a coffin being put in the ground. Her mother's coffin. The one she'd never seen. The one she'd never been allowed to see.

'I didn't tell her,' she whispered. 'She doesn't know where it is. We put in stuff and then we put in a secret envelope each . . . He's going to kill her because I didn't tell her where I hid it!'

'Not a bit of this is your fault,' rumbled the Gunner. 'Not a crumb.'

The Walker suddenly switched positions and sat on the chair next to her mother. He patted her hand companionably. She pulled it away as if she'd been stung. His smile didn't falter, but he slowly pulled the dagger from the sheath at his side and laid it across his knees.

'I'll make you a deal. You tell me where the girl hides it, and I'll let you live.'

'Or?' whispered her mother, eyes fixed on the dagger.

'Or I ask her myself,' he hissed, looking at the sunset reflecting off the flat planes of the blade.

Edie's mother licked her lips. There was a squeal as the door the workman had disappeared through opened. Her eyes twitched sideways towards it and back to the Walker.

'So. That's the deal. You let me live if I give you my daughter's stone?'

'I am not an unreasonable man . . .'

Without warning, Edie's mother jerked out of her chair and ran. She ran, but not in panic. The moment she exploded out of her chair it was clear to Edie what she was doing. She'd seen the TV go back on. She knew the electrician would be coming back off the roof. And she timed her run perfectly. She was also clear-headed enough to keep hold of the chair arm as she burst out of it, dragging it in front of the Walker, buying her a fraction of a second's advantage as he became entangled in it.

As he crashed to the ground, Edie felt a swoop of hope and just for a moment dared to think the inexplicable and the impossible both at once: this is it, this is where she cheats death.

She barged past the shocked electrician, sending him flying across the floor. Edie sprinted after her, the Gunner on her heels, as she raced up the narrow staircase towards the roof and freedom.

48

AMBUSH

The Perseus and the Pilot never saw what hit them.

The ice-sheathed taints howled in at zero feet, straight through the arches beneath the bridge and slammed into them at the very moment they burst back into the air from the bottom of the river. They had scarcely begun to gasp for a breath before it was knocked out of them by the impact.

The Bosun and Jack Tar did have a couple of seconds to react, because George's first action on seeing the phalanx of taints flickering across the river towards them had been to shout a warning. The Perseus and the Pilot had been underwater, and had not known what danger awaited them as they surfaced.

The Perseus was hit so hard that his sword went flying. The Pilot was knocked head over heels by a gargoyle that smacked straight into his face and hooked on with ferocious tenacity, snarling and biting at him.

Though they had been taken by surprise, they immediately fought back. The Perseus punched and kicked at his two assailants as they tried to bite him out of the air. All the taints had the same gryphon shape, with an eagle's wings and head and front talons, and a lion's body and hindquarters. Their bodies were stunted, but this just seemed to make them more manoeuvrable and powerful in the air. They fought in pairs, which made the fight that followed uneven and consequently short and viciously final.

The Pilot managed to tear one assailant off his face, only to have its partner gouge its talons into his wings and latch its screaming beak back on to his head. The whirling threesome slammed into the sheer wall of the embankment, knocking the Pilot senseless for just long enough for the second gryphon to rip off one of his wings and start tearing at his chest. With only one wing and two attackers, it wasn't long before the Pilot just stopped moving and hung there, draped over the river wall as the gryphons pecked at his lifeless body.

Jack Tar – having the advantage of hearing George's warning shout – had managed to duck the first of his attackers and swing the anchor at the end of a short length of rope with enough hurried accuracy that although the anchor missed the jinking taint, the thin anchor-chain snarled in its wings, and as it stuttered in mid-air and tried to twist free, the anchor swung round its neck and hit it in the face, dropping it into the water.

Having escaped immediate annihilation, Jack Tar didn't hang around in his exposed boat for a moment longer. Instead he jumped from the boat to the barge, hitting the hollow metal hull with a clang like Big Ben sounding, and scrambled up to join the Bosun. He got there in time to rip a gryphon from his shipmate's back and stomp it to trash with his heavy sea boots, and then he and the Bosun fought back to back as two taints whirled and snarled about them.

The Perseus had managed to pull one of his attackers off, and kicked the other one into it as it fell. While the two taints disentangled, he took advantage of the brief respite to run through the air towards the bridge. The feathers on his sandals whirred as he sprinted towards

George and the Queen. He slammed into the edge of the bridge and reached a desperate hand over the scarred stone lintel.

'My bag!' he shouted.

'Look out!' shouted the Queen and George as one, seeing the icy gryphon shrieking in behind him.

'My bag!' he yelled again, his hand stretching to the limit of his reach.

The gryphon slammed into his kidneys so hard that all the air was punched out of him and his eyes rolled back in his head.

'Out the way, boy!' shouted the Queen, hefting her spear.

George didn't get out of the way. He was already lunging towards the gryphon's wildly flapping wings. He caught one wingtip, then the other, and without a second's conscious thought, slammed them together. The gryphon squealed in outrage, but George closed his eyes and felt the heat in his hands, and the momentary awareness of the granular structure of the stone wings they were pinioning together.

And then he simply fused stone wingtip to stone wingtip and wrenched the gryphon off the Perseus.

The gryphon struggled to free its locked wingtips and flap, but couldn't do anything except plunge straight down, shrieking, into the black current below.

George reached a hand out, but there was a horribly abrupt jerking impact as two taints flew back round the bridge arches and hit the Perseus' dangling feet, tearing him off the bridge and into the air. As he dangled upside down above the barge, each one gripped a foot and flew in a different direction.

George looked away, but he heard the Queen gasp in

horror, and then the noise of the spit's body clanging down on to the barge.

The Bosun and Jack Tar were trying to fight their way to a metal hatch in the deck. The gryphons circled them slashing and biting, two of them actually standing on the hatch, blocking their way to safety.

When all seemed lost, all of a sudden the waters burst beside the barge and the Boy rode the Dolphin high out of the water, battering one of the gryphons off the hatch and throwing something to the ground at the sailor's feet.

George saw in a flash that it was the Perseus's sword.

The Bosun grabbed it and slashed right and left in a fury, cutting his way to the hatch.

'Come on, Jack!' he roared. 'Let's live to fight another day!'

He cut the gryphon standing guard clean in half, and kicked his way on to the hatch. He stood over it as Jack Tar dived down and ripped it open. The Bosun tumbled in and Jack Tar leapt after him, fast, but not fast enough to stop one gryphon diving in with them. The hatch clanged shut, and there was a muffled eagle-shriek from inside.

The Boy and the Dolphin surfaced and looked up at the Queen and George.

'Save yourselves!' shouted George, and without a second to spare they plunged deep into the river and disappeared as the Dolphin sounded deep and powered away from the scene of the massacre.

The Queen grabbed George's arm and hurled him into the chariot.

'We must go, boy, now!'

She threw Perseus's bag in after him and leapt aboard,

cracking the reins over the backs of horses that needed no second telling. They lurched into a gallop and the chariot careened off the bridge in a whirlwind of snow.

'It is no longer safe to be out here alone! From now on there is only safety in numbers,' yelled the Queen into the slipstream. 'And we may already be too late to reach that safety.'

George stared backwards, waiting for the pursuing gryphons, and thought two things.

Yes they were maybe too late.

And whether or not that was so, Edie was out there alone.

It wasn't just that he was desperately worried for her safety. He was worried for everyone's survival.

Because without her ability to sense the Black Mirror, all was lost.

49

A MATTER OF
DEATH AND LIFE

Edie and the Gunner were right behind Edie's
mother as she scrambled up the stairs and burst
through an outer door on to a flat, gravel-covered
roof. They just got on to it before she grabbed the outer
edge of the flapping door and slammed it shut. There
was a bolt on the outside of the door which she
rammed home.

Then she ran to the edge of the roof. There was
a sheer drop down to the car park in front of the hospital.

They watched as she dashed round the rectangular
perimeter, looking for a safe way down. They saw the
realization grow on her that she was trapped up here.

They heard the increasingly urgent banging on the
locked roof door, the distant sound of an emergency
bell ringing, and the muffled shouts of the nurse calling
her name.

They saw her turn and see the eye-twisting horror of
the Walker stepping out of a small round hand mirror
right behind her. She stumbled back in shock, falling on
to the sharp gravel.

The Walker looked down at her as he pocketed the
mirrors again and calmly drew his dagger.

'What are you going to do?' He wagged the blade at
her. 'I promise you, if you do not tell me where your
daughter's heart stone is I will split you open like a bag of

peas and you will die right here on this roof.'

She closed her hand on a fistful of gravel and staggered back to her feet.

'No. You will not go near my daughter.' Her voice was raw but steady. She stood in a crouch, ready to run in either direction if he came for her.

'I will do what I wish, this is your last opportunity. There is no more chance of you thwarting me in this than there is of these stones not hitting the ground below.' The Walker turned slightly and scuffed some roof-gravel over the edge behind him. 'I am as unavoidable as gravity itself. So tell me, where does the brat hide her stone?'

'Her name is Edie,' she said, her voice catching with pride as she stood taller, squaring her shoulders and looked him right in the eye. 'And I won't tell you one damn thing that would harm her.'

He yawned, studiously unimpressed.

'So you will not get off this roof alive.'

'Then neither of us will,' she said, throwing the handful of gravel at his eyes with a sharp jerk of her hand.

In the moment where he raised his hand to shield his eyes, she exploded into motion, sprinting straight at him.

Time slowed for Edie as she realized in horror what her mother was going to do and the price she was going to pay. She heard herself shouting 'Mum!' in a shriek that seemed to go on for ever, but her mother couldn't hear her.

All the wear and tear that the years and the drink – and the worrying that she was mad – had put on her fell away, and with her long hair flying behind her and the fire in her eyes, her face was, in this one last moment, fierce and focused as a lioness defending its cub.

She looked again like the mother Edie now

remembered only in her dreams.

The Walker slashed at her with the dagger, but she ducked her head and threw herself into a horizontal dive.

Edie saw the blade cut an arc in the air, reflecting the rosy light from the setting sun. It scythed over her mother's head, just missing her. The Walker staggered with the impetus of the mistimed blow, and so was off balance as Edie's mother hit him in a solid flying tackle, just below his waist. His body bent in the middle and his feet flew up off the roof. His hands bicycled sideways grabbing for a handhold in the empty air beyond the roof's edge.

The only sound was a strangled 'NO!' which jerked out of his mouth as he twisted and looked at the gulf of air below them.

And then they were gone.

Edie and the Gunner were left staring at the sun, now a red hole in the sky where her mother had sacrificed herself in taking the Walker off the roof.

'She didn't know that he can't die,' said the Gunner with great sadness.

Edie ran for the edge, but before she could get close enough to look over and see anything of her mother's body, his hand snapped out and yanked her back, so abruptly that her feet also left the ground.

He held her to his chest while she struggled to free herself and spoke softly into her ear.

'You may be born to pull the past from stones and see terrible stuff someone your age shouldn't have to see, but there are some images you *don't* need to carry in your head.'

The Raven perched on the parapet and looked over at what Edie could not see.

Her mother was spread-eagled on the tarmac below, one leg bent under the other, arms wide, almost as if she had been crucified on the parking lot. Her eyes stared sightlessly at the sky above, her face framed in the outflung fan of her hair. As people hurried towards her, one figure walked in the opposite direction, not looking back.

It was the Walker.

'I want to see how it ended!' hissed Edie, struggling against the bronze arm holding her in place.

'You saw how it ended,' said the Gunner softly, his voice rumbling so low in his chest that she could feel the vibrations in her back where she was crushed against him. 'You saw all that matters.'

He continued to speak into her ear, very calmly.

'It ended with your mother flying. She flew through the air, into the sunset. She was fighting for you. Just like she fought to bring you safe into this world and gave you your first breath, so she fought for you with her last. She fought to save you from him. She died with nothing in her but that fierce love of you.' The Gunner's voice was low and raw. He cleared his throat. 'And death is a terrible and final thing, Edie girl, but there's many worse ways to die than with love in your heart. And that's all you need to know. There is nothing you can see down there that is a truer or a finer end than that, and that's the God's honest truth of it.'

'It's my right to see it!' she protested, voice shaking. 'It's my right!'

'It is,' he said simply, and let her go. She stood alone and free on the gravel roof as he stepped back. 'Just like it is your right *not* to see it. Just as it is your right to choose whether the last image you carry of her is as a living creature or a dead shell, her body broken, but not her spirit.'

'It's my right,' Edie repeated.

The Gunner said no more.

Neither he nor the Raven looked at Edie as she stood there, the evening wind blowing her hair across her face and flapping the black fur coat around her ankles. She was poised between stepping forward and retreating, and the breeze seemed to rock her as her whole body remained balanced on the balls of her feet.

And then she just sat down and pulled her knees to her chest. She muttered something.

'What?' said the Gunner.

She raised her head, eyes bright with tears. 'The Sphinx lied! All this time I thought this was about finding her alive! I mean I knew she was dead, then I found her stone, and it stayed lit, and then the Sphinxes, the Sphinxes lied . . .!'

'Sphinxes don't lie,' he said sadly.

'But I thought she lived! I thought she was alive!' Edie hacked her heel into the gravel, sending it skittering across the roof. 'I thought . . . I thought I would get to hold her again. I thought she would hold me. Even just one more time, just once . . .'

She shuddered and dropped her head back into the hollow between her knees and her chest, her long hair tented over her face.

The Gunner put a hand on her shoulder and just left it there. He said nothing, just letting the solid weight of his hand ballast Edie as the gusts of emotion billowed through her.

When the sun had dropped halfway below the horizon and Edie's shoulder had almost completely stopped shuddering, the Raven hopped over and looked up at her. Then it pecked her shoe, but not hard. Almost companionably.

She sniffed and pushed aside the dark curtain of her hair.

'I thought she was alive. And I knew it was impossible, but I still had this crazy stupid hope that I would just hold her.'

The Raven clacked its beak.

'She is,' said the Gunner. 'And you do. Those we love never truly leave us. We carry them in us for ever. Her love will ride in your heart throughout your life and beyond . . .'

'How can it live beyond?' said Edie flatly. 'That's all magic rubbish . . .'

'It's not magic, girl. Or if it is, it's just the ordinary magic of being human. You'll carry her love and add it to your own, and one day you will pass it on to your own children, who will send it forward in time to theirs, long after you're gone. That's the glory and pain of being human, the curse and the blessing of life,' he said, stroking her hair with the care of someone comforting a wild animal that may bolt at any moment. 'Though I reckon it's more blessing than pain.'

Edie stared at the sunset now reddening the horizon and took a deep breath. She felt cleansed by it, so she took another one.

'She didn't commit suicide,' she said, exhaling.

'No,' agreed the Gunner.

'And she wasn't mad.'

'No.'

'And she went down fighting.'

'To the last,' he said.

'And that's what she gave me,' she said to the final sliver of sun blinking out of sight below the scarlet edge of the world. 'That rides with me too.'

Silence followed as the reds bled from the sky and the night started to roll in. She took another deep, deep breath and set her jaw before turning. The Raven flapped on to her shoulder and clacked into her ear. And she realized with a strange lack of surprise that she could understand it.

'Exactly,' she said. 'There's a fight going in London . . .'

She looked at the Gunner. Eyes dry.

'. . . so what the hell am I doing here?'

The Gunner pulled the two discs of glass from his pocket and grinned back at her.

'That's my girl.'

50

AN UNEXPECTED ALLY

The gryphons didn't seem to be following George and the Queen as the chariot raced along the river towards the looming sweep of Waterloo Bridge and the concrete bunker buildings that squatted theatrically beside it. George kept expecting the taints to suddenly accelerate into view behind them, so he stayed facing backwards holding the Queen's spear at the ready for just such an eventuality.

Something rolled against his leg, and he twisted round on reflex, but it was only the Perseus's bag that the Queen had thrown in the chariot next to the stone arm. He reached down and steadied it.

'Don't open that,' snapped the Queen.

'I'm just stopping it falling out!' he shouted back.

She reached back with her foot and pushed the bag forward against the inner wall of the chariot in front of her, treading on it to keep it in place. 'Just don't open it,' she said.

George scanned the sky behind him. The hairs on his neck were suddenly prickling upright, but the sky was empty, though he could have sworn that he heard something like wing-flaps in the sky. He took a deep breath and told himself that he was getting jumpy.

'Why not?' he said, as the Queen pulled on the reins, sending the horses hard right up the slope of the approach road to the bridge proper.

She never got to answer, because at that point the

four gryphons that had obviously been pacing them, low down and out of sight on the other side of the river wall, bounced up and over the parapet and yammered into the attack, eagle beaks snapping and shrieking as they came.

'Go!' yelled George, and heard the Queen snap the reins behind him. The chariot picked up speed, but nowhere near enough to outrun the ice-sheathed taints, who slipped through the sky towards them with a bullet-like velocity.

Once more they fought in pairs, and as George stabbed the lance at the first one that came at his face, its partner dipped in and pecked at something behind him. George missed with the lance as the attacker flipped its wing and sheered off at the last moment. He saw the other as a blur on the edge of his vision, and turned expecting to see it ripping at the Queen's exposed back. Instead he saw its talons closing on the stone arm at her feet.

'No!' he shouted, and without time to reverse the spear in his hands, slammed the blunt end of the haft into the back of its neck with all the strength he could muster. It squawked in outrage, and then turned to snap at him. He pulled back the spear-haft and punched it into the gaping beak, right down the throat of the creature. Then he swivelled violently, pitchforking the gagging taint off the back of the chariot. It hit its partner just as it swooped in to the rescue, and the two gryphons were, for a moment, a whirling, snapping ball of ice and stone in the sky as they tried to disentangle from each other, before depth-charging into the snow behind in a great cloud of powder.

He staggered to keep his footing on the bucking chariot, which lurched badly sideways as the Queen crested the approach road to the bridge.

'George!' she shouted. He turned to see the third gryphon had flown in from the side and was taloning the stone arm away. George stomped his boot into the side of the gryphon's head, buying himself just enough time to get his balance and retrieve the arm, which he did by grabbing its hand in his hand. As the gryphon darted in again he swung the stone arm like a club, knocking the taint into the snow just ahead of the chariot.

The gryphon made the fatal mistake of raising its head to shriek at him in protest before launching itself into the counter-attack an instant too late to avoid the whirling scimitar blade on the chariot wheel which smithereened it into a savage hail of ice-shards and stone fragments.

George rammed the stone arm into the space between the front wall of the chariot and the bag. 'They're trying to get the stone arm!' he shouted. 'They're trying to free the Darkness.'

The Queen nodded and put her foot on it to keep it from rolling out.

'Behind you . . .'

He looked up to see that the three remaining gryphons were jinking into the attack. He stabbed at the leading one with the lance, and missed. The second one darted in, and he jabbed at it, only to have the third one attack as he was at the limit of his thrust.

It didn't attack *him*, but grabbed the shaft of the spear instead, yanking it hard. It slipped out of his hand, but he managed to regain a grip only a foot from the end, which was almost worse than useless, because he had no way of controlling the spear at all, and it pulled once more, almost hoisting him off the back of the chariot altogether.

The second gryphon rejoined the attack, and the two taints working together managed to easily twist and wrench the smooth pole out of his hands.

'They got the lance!' he shouted as the third one screeched and threw itself at his face once more.

He felt its talons scrape past his cheekbone and a sharp pain in his ear. Without thinking he punched his open palm into the chest of the creature. Despite the jarring impact he gripped on and as he felt the heat flare in his hand, he had a deep and instantaneous impression of the flawed and grainy stone that the taint had been carved from. Again without conscious thought he sent the heat in his hand into the flaws and between the grainy matrices of the rock, and as he twisted his grip he saw the taint wheel upside down in his grasp, and then disintegrate into three separate parts that spun into the snow behind them.

The moment the stone fragments came to bits in his hand, he felt a wave of tiredness like a physical blow. He looked down at his hand.

'OK,' he said, breathing hard. 'OK.'

'Not OK,' said the Queen shortly. 'Not OK at all.'

He looked back and saw what she had seen. The chariot was going too fast to get a good count, but nine or ten gryphons had bounced up and over the side of the bridge and were sweeping in at an angle to join the two remaining ones behind them.

'GO!' he shouted.

'They're not the problem,' she shouted back. 'Look ahead!'

He tore his eyes off the phalanx of shrieking gryphons accelerating towards them and looked ahead, over the plunging heads of the horses.

The end of the bridge was seventy long metres away, but not only was there no way they would make the other side of the river before the incoming gryphons tore into them, there was no safety there in any case.

There was worse than no safety.

There were two figures blocking their way.

The floor of the chariot was still lurching up and down so his vision was blurred. One of the figures was indistinct, but the other one was unmistakeable.

It was a taint, and not just any taint.

A dragon.

Here I am again, thought George.

Between a rock and a hard place.

'Only one thing to do!' he shouted. 'Keep going straight ahead.'

'I know,' said the Queen, smiling fiercely and snapping the reins hard. 'Keep them off my back as long as you can.'

The horses must have sensed this was the end of the chase, or maybe it was because a light wind had blown some of the snow off the top surface of the bridge so that it was less deep, but whatever the reason, they picked up speed as they hit the down slope, so that the taints didn't catch them quite as fast as George feared, but closed up in a solid menacing formation right behind them.

George heard a muffled *WHOOMF* from the dragon ahead of them, but he didn't dare look round for fear one of the gryphons would put on a sudden burst of speed and grab him. His shoulders tensed and he ducked down, hoping the front prow of the chariot would give some protection from the fireball he knew must be hosing towards them.

'Boy!' called the Queen, her hand reaching back and feeling for his shoulder.

'Ram it!' shouted George, out of ideas. 'Just ram it.'

The Queen laughed, a wild and raw sound, so unexpected that George had a quick look behind him. 'No need,' she whooped. 'They're opening the gate.'

George's quick look turned into a long one. He was unable to look away from the sight now blocking the end of the bridge.

It was a wall of fire; not just any fire, but a bright multicoloured fire he had seen before. It was the wildfire of the true dragon, the Temple Bar Dragon. And the wall was no ordinary wall. It was the fiery recreation of the old Temple Bar gate to the City that the dragon had blown across George's path once a lifetime ago, or so it seemed. It rose in twisting spirals in front of his eyes, an elegant gatehouse on top of a broad double-gate that opened as they galloped towards it, just wide enough to let them through. And on the other side George saw the Railwayman beckoning them urgently.

'I don't . . .' began George.

'Nor do I,' laughed the Queen, cracking the reins one last time.

George spun and looked at the intent, furious line of gryphon-faces straining to catch up with them, four, now three, now two metres behind.

And then there was a flash of light as the Queen stampeded her horses through the gate and the whole gatehouse flashed past on either side of them, and then he saw the double-doors slam shut like the gates of hell, cutting off any view of their pursuers.

The gates bucked and jumped with the impact of the chasing taints slamming into the other side, and then as the Queen reined in, something bright and white snarled over George's head and landed in front of the gates, and tore them open.

It was the Temple Bar Dragon, stoked up to a white heat of fury.

It jerked the gates open and looked at the twitching, stunned bodies of the gryphons lying in the snow beyond, where they had knocked themselves senseless. One unlucky gryphon shook its head, trying to clear it and saw the dragon looking down. The gryphon opened its beak to shriek defiance, but the dragon just incinerated it with a blast of fire that jetted from its mouth like a hose. It swept the flames across all the figures until they were no more than featureless half-melted blobs of rock, scarcely recognizable as what they had once been.

And then it turned and looked at George.

He knew it was looking at him and no one else because it coughed something that might have been a small and spark-enhanced laugh, and then very delicately traced a sign in the air, a mark that hung between them in thin slashes of fire for a full five seconds before blinking out.

George looked down at his hand, where the same mark had been slashed by the same talon. He held it up and showed it to the dragon.

'Thanks,' he said. And then because his brain was still catching up after their headlong flight he added. 'But I thought you were a taint . . .'

The dragon just bowed its head, very slightly.

'Dragon. Save. City. Must,' it said, the words sharp and disparate. 'Maker. Save. City. Can.'

Well . . .' began George.

'So. Dragon. Maker. Save,' it finished.

'It was old Dictionary talked it round,' said the Railwayman, as the Queen reached down a hand and pulled him up on to the chariot. 'Said he and the dragon had always had the love of London in common. He said that they'd spent so many years looking at one another in the long hours of the night and talking about it that they were, in their own way, if not mates, sort of neighbours, like. Dictionary understood this chap's been made to defend the city. And as you can see he's already been in a barney with some of the other dragons what didn't have as strong a sense of their purpose as him. So he didn't take much talking round at all, if you follow.'

George saw the dragon cooling in front of him, the white heat flushing down to red and then pink and then back to a deep burnished grey in front of his eyes. And now that the bright glare of the heat was off him, he saw the rent in the dragon's wing and the half-torn-off ear.

'We must get going . . .' began the Queen, but George jumped off the back of the chariot, and without thinking why he was doing it, or how, he crossed to the dragon and reached up a hand. The dragon bowed its head, and he felt the torn ear. It was no warmer than a dog's ear now, and unexpectedly soft to the touch. He gently pushed it back into place, closing the tear, and then he closed his eyes too, and felt the metal beneath his touch. Where stone was granular, the metal was more like a fluid, as if he could feel the molten state that had flown into the mould.

'What's he doing?' asked the Railwayman.

'Man's work,' said the Queen. And then she nodded at the wall of Ice Murk visible over the rooftops. 'And we must be on our way, for there shall be more need of healing before this is over. Come, George.'

George opened his eyes and saw he had mended the dragon's ear. It shook its head like a dog does, just to make sure everything is attached, and then it smiled, as much as a dragon can. It looked at the Queen as George went to work mending its wings.

'We. Both. Come.'

51

THE HIGH ADMIRAL

Edie and the Gunner had followed the Raven into the mirror held in the Gunner's hand. They staggered out of the sunset light on the hospital roof and back into the dimly lit interior of the Black Friar's pub to find the Friar kneeling in front of one mirror with a candle held right against the glass, while Little Tragedy did the same on the other side of the arch. Edie's breath plumed and her teeth started chattering as soon as her feet hit the carpet. The interior of the pub was now well below freezing, enveloped deep within the Ice Murk. As soon as Edie breathed in the piercingly cold air burnt her lungs and she instantly felt the hairs in her nostril freeze up.

'Thank God!' breathed the monk. 'You must go now! You cannot live long in here, we are mired in the Murk and the fire itself can scarce find purchase on this all-consuming cold.'

'Trafalgar Square,' said the Gunner, throwing an arm round Edie, who was already beginning to shake, despite her fur coat.

It wasn't hard to see how close they were to having been stuck in the mirrors, as the glass was clouded by ice rime everywhere except where it was right next to the candle's heat.

The Friar reached above his head and twisted the great rings of mosaic in the ceiling.

As the Raven came to perch on her shoulder and clacked in her ear, Edie understood he was switching the mirrors' destinations from 'When' to 'Where'.

'Go now, and Godspeed,' bellowed the Friar. 'Come and find us when this is over.'

'What?' squeaked Little Tragedy. 'Come find us? Why? We shall be all right, shan't we? Old Black? We shall be right as rain, yeah?'

'We shall find out,' shrugged the Friar. 'This has never happened before. We shall stay put. As Guardian I cannot leave.'

The Gunner nodded at him.

'Be lucky, chum,' he smiled, and pulled Edie into the mirror.

'Th-th-thanks,' stuttered Edie as she looked back. It was so cold she was getting a brain-freeze just breathing, and she thought her teeth might just shatter like fine porcelain as they clattered together uncontrollably in her shivering jaw.

They fell into the blackness.

The Friar bent to pick up the candle that he'd left propped against the mirror, and then looked up as something brushed quickly past him. Whatever it was moved so fast that its slipstream guttered the candle in passing, and it blinked out, unable to fight off the surrounding cold. The Friar tutted and reached backwards.

'The matches . . .' he said and then turned to find no reply, and no Little Tragedy either, just a lone candle and a box of matches on the floor in front of the other mirror, too far away to keep the frost from crazing over the last teardrop-shaped patch of clear mirror. He realized only then what had brushed past him and followed the others into the mirrors.

'You imp,' said the Friar sadly, and sat cross-legged between the two mirrors, scraping slowly at the matchbox with fingers that were now starting to shake badly.

The first thing Edie saw when they tumbled out of the mirrors was that they were in another pub. The second thing she saw was that it was thankfully light outside. And then the Gunner opened the doors and the third thing she saw was the square beyond.

Trafalgar Square was of course covered in snow, but what was most striking was how crowded it was.

Spits were spread right across the great piazza, from the top, where they lined the balustrades along the terrace outside the classical portico of the National Gallery, right down to the traffic island facing Admiralty Arch and the long sweep of open avenue leading to the palace beyond.

'Wow,' she said.

The Gunner blew out his cheeks and exhaled in wonder. 'That,' he said, 'is quite something. I never knew there was so many of us.'

'Gack,' said something that bounded towards them from the side. They turned to see Spout bobbing and smiling at them. Then he flapped to the top of a grey pillar and waved his wing at the centre of the crowd at the lower end of the piazza next to the foot of the tall column.

'Eigengang!' he screeched. 'Eigengang. Goung gint! Gear. Gook gear!'

And he jabbed his wing emphatically downwards at Edie and the Gunner as they walked out of the shadow of the pub door.

'Eigeng—' Spout began, bouncing up and down in barely controlled excitement, only to stop abruptly as something white trickled down his forehead. His eyes rolled up to find the Raven perched nonchalantly between his ears, adjusting its feathers, before squinnying a second splatter on to the cat-gargoyle's head.

'I think he thinks you should calm down,' said the Gunner, looking up. Spout hissed and shook himself. The Raven floated off into the air and coasted behind Edie as she hurried towards the boy running up the square towards her.

Although she of course knew who he was the moment she laid eyes on him, there was something about him that had changed. She couldn't figure out exactly what it was, but he not only looked older but he seemed to carry himself completely differently, taller, like he wasn't trying to hide or somehow excuse his height or the breadth of his shoulders any more.

What it was, she realized, was that he was no longer turned in on himself, hunched around an apology for what he was. Even his face looked different with his hair now pushed back out of his eyes, so different that she could scarcely remember the worried and regretful boy she had taken such a firm dislike to so long ago on the parking ramp to the garage under the park. It was also the look in his eyes. He still looked worried, but it was a capable worry. It was the worry of someone who was dealing with something bigger than himself.

'Edie!' shouted George, raising a hand. 'We need you. We've got a dragon, but we need you!'

And as she walked towards him, oblivious to the interested glances of the forest of spits of all shapes and sizes she was passing through, George in turn was struck by the change in Edie. The Raven on her shoulder was one thing, but he'd seen that before. He'd seen the confident stride and the jutting jaw too. What he hadn't really seen was this smile. It was easy and unforced, and matched by a level look in her eyes that was both straight and just tinged with enough of a sparkle of humour at the back of it to make his stomach flip.

Thank God you're OK, he thought. But what he said was: 'What took you so long?'

She pointed at his bare arm. 'What happened to your sleeve?'

They stood there and, with interruptions from the Gunner and the Queen, and occasionally Spout, they quickly brought each other up to date with their adventures. George told her that the High Admiral had been watching the City ever since dawn had broken, and that he was sure the taints had all congregated on Tower 42, the black skyscraper in the distance, turning it into a citadel in the sky. He had used his telescope and seen a figure pacing the icy battlements which he did not recognize. They both agreed this must be the Ice Devil. George omitted to tell her that the Admiral had remarked how from certain angles the figure, though larger, had reminded him of the Walker.

As George explained about the ambush at the river and how they had been unable to find the mirror, Edie saw the Queen looking at her. Something passed between them that was beyond words. The light in Edie's eyes dimmed a bit as George rolled on, but by the time he had explained about the Temple Bar Dragon, and pointed out where it was now perched next to the High Admiral on the top of the column, she had taken a deep breath and combed her fingers back through her hair and was doing something to it behind her head.

George looked down from the dragon to see her face

unguarded by the normal shifting curtains of hair, and just as she had seen the rightness of his face now that she could see all of it, so he smiled despite himself as he saw her face clearly.

'What?' she growled.

'Nothing,' he said. 'What are you doing?'

'What does it look like?' she said. 'Plaiting this mess. If I've got to get wet and look for this mirror I'm not going to need my hair in my eyes, am I?'

He flashed the memory of her drowning face in the ice-hole, a long flag of dark hair slashed across her white face like a strip of seaweed, and he understood the courage it took for her to make light about what she was going to have to do.

'No,' he said. 'You're not. You know what else you don't need?'

'What?' she said, bridling.

'Guts,' he said, clapping her on the arm. 'I reckon you've got them to spare.'

'Enemy ahead!' came a ringing seaman's bellow from above. 'Prepare to repel boarders!'

The High Admiral, a tall stone figure in a cocked hat worn broadside on, was pointing his sword to the east.

'The sky's black with the devils!'

The Queen gripped Edie's arm.

'We must go now!'

Suddenly there was no time for goodbyes as Edie ran and jumped up into the chariot next to her.

'Spout!' shouted George. 'Go with them. Look after them. Keep an eye on the sky.'

'Gack,' croaked the cat gargoyle, and spread its wings.

'Edie,' shouted George as the Queen urged her horses into motion. 'Good luck.'

'I'll find it,' she called back. 'You just try and stay alive long enough to work out how we're going to get up there to use it!'

'OK,' he yelled to the disappearing chariot and her hand raised in farewell.

'Or just stay alive,' she said quietly and turned to steady herself on the front wall of the chariot as the Queen recklessly flung her horses straight down the steps heading for the river.

52

FIRST WAVE

As George had told Edie, the High Admiral had been watching the City since first light. He had seen the blank grey escarpment of the Ice Murk spreading inexorably across the horizon to the east. It had widened and seemed to grow taller as it approached as remorselessly as bad weather rolling in across the sea.

He had noted that the one building that remained visible in the City was not only the tallest, but seemed to be at the dead centre of the blooming cloud. He had spent the day scanning it with his telescope, and as the rest of the spits had poured into square below, had shouted down and kept them updated with what he could see from his lookout position atop the column. He commanded a great view from his lofty eyrie, which was just one of the reasons why this sailor with one empty sleeve pinned to his much bemedalled frock coat was known as the High Admiral.

The one good eye he had left had seen many strange things, but what he seemed to be seeing on top of the distant dark tower was something new. Though most of them had arrived under cover of darkness, he saw the last few winged spits coasting in at dawn and joining the rookery of gargoyles and other grotesque flying creatures that had blossomed around the building's rim, changing its sleek silhouette into something lumpy and unwholesomely organic-looking, like a blighting fungus. He'd seen the slow cascade of icy air falling off the top of the building down into the Ice Murk below, and as a sailor he'd known enough about how weather works to see that this confirmed his suspicion: the dark tower was the centre of the cold blight afflicting the City and spreading towards the rest of London.

He'd seen the strange elongated figure of the Ice Devil striding back and forth along the icy battlements of his citadel, and he'd watched the occasional patrols of gargoyles that had detached from the battlements and gone off on who knows what business throughout the day. He'd also seen enough of the Ice Devil to be reminded, at certain angles, of the Walker. But the most disturbing thing he had seen was the Ice Devil when it stopped pacing and just stood still.

In those moments the High Admiral, a man whose visible wounds attested to how little he cared for his personal safety in battle, felt the unfamiliar twinge of fear. The reason he felt this unaccustomed sensation was this: he was pretty sure that just as he was looking at the Ice Devil, so the Ice Devil was looking straight back at him. And the Ice Devil's gaze was almost palpable in its malign intensity.

All that had been the most disturbing thing until now.

Now the flying taints were peeling off the side of the black tower and spiralling into a winged maelstrom that circled the Ice Devil. Next the Ice Devil gesticulated with his arms, and the spiral flattened into a disc whose thin edge became a storm-front that thickened and grew as it headed straight towards him.

It was at this point that he had hailed the spits below and warned them to prepare to repel boarders.

He turned to the Temple Bar Dragon who was perched awkwardly next to him, looking in the same direction.

'You'd better get below. There'll be hard pounding before this is over.'

The dragon just looked at him, raised an eyebrow, then turned back to look at the approaching cloud of taints.

'Pound. Them. Shall. I,' it spat. And as it spoke the Admiral could feel the heat building up in the scaly body next to him.

'My. City. Ice. Cloud. Swallow. Not. For. Ever,' it continued harshly, tendrils of smoke starting to curl out of its reddening eyes. 'My. City. Free. Made. Free. Born. Free. Stay. Free.'

'Can't say fairer than that,' admitted the Admiral, putting his telescope away and drawing his sword. 'But if you get in the way or set anything on fire up here you'll have to find somewhere else to fight.'

All across the square below the spits were ready, spread behind every balustrade or fountain edge they could find, waiting for the attack.

The Gunner joined George behind one of the four massive bronze lions at the foot of the column.

'You just keep your head down,' he said.

'Why haven't these lions come alive?' asked George, nodding at the great bulk next to them.

'No one knows exactly,' said the Gunner. 'But they never have. Some say they're made wrong, others that they have one purpose, and they won't come alive until it's their time to fulfil it. That's why they're known as the Last Lions.'

'What purpose?' asked George.

'Don't know. Some say there's something under this column that they're defending, others that they only come alive when the land's at its deepest peril or some mumbo-jumbo like that. Me?'

He rapped the butt of his pistol on the side of the lion with a clang.

'Me, I think they're just lazy, like all cats is.'

And before George could ask another question the sky did indeed seem to go black as a cloud of airborne taints poured over the rooftops in a howling avalanche of fangs and claws and talons.

Battles don't have much sense or shape, not when you're stuck in the middle of them. If you're high above them there are patterns that can be discerned as the struggling masses attack and retreat. You can see power flowing and whirling back and forth as the forces feint and dodge and stand fast in their turn. You can even, if asked afterwards, draw neat diagrams that appear to make a clean and clinical sense of the bewildering chaos and carnage that it actually is for the person stuck in the middle of it.

When you're in the middle of a battle, with your boots on the ground, you're lucky if you notice anything beyond your immediate vicinity. In fact most of the time you're lucky if your boots are on the ground. In George's case it was his knees and then his chest as the Gunner kept pushing him out of the way of a succession of diving and snapping taints. He crouched against the lion, wanting to fight, but knowing he had to keep guard of the Darkness trapped in the stone arm that he was clutching tightly. The Gunner shot a gargoyle out of the sky in front of George's face and shook his head in frustration.

'It's that damn stone arm of yours!' he shouted. 'It's like wasps and a bloody jam pot. Here . . .!'

He unclipped the groundsheet he normally wore as

an improvised cape round his shoulders and threw it down to George.

'Wrap it up. If they don't keep seeing it we'll have it easier,' he yelled, and was then hit by two small taints at once.

The taints each fastened on to one of his arms and ripped them sideways, exposing his chest to a third one that slammed into him. Before George could leap to his aid the Gunner had head-butted the taint as it tried to bite his face – ramming the sharp edge of his steel helmet into its beak and shattering it. The force of the blow snapped his chinstrap, and as the helmet tumbled off the back of his head and the taint fell off his chest he roared in anger and clapped his two outflung hands together, clattering the two smaller spits into each other in a shattering impact.

They fell to the ground and he put a bullet in the one he had head-butted, and then turned to finish off the other two. Nothing remained of them except ice fragments.

'That's a bit queer,' he said, 'where's the bloody stone?'

Another taint whirled to the ground and pancaked across the flagstones in a smoking mass between them, taking his mind off the strangeness of the ice taints who had no stone body. He nodded at George who had been narrowly missed by the crashed taint.

'Keep your head down, son,' he grinned. 'It's gonna get hotter before this is over.'

The Gunner looked strangely younger without his helmet. His hair stuck up in an unruly tuft above the shorter sides. He scraped his fingers through it and scanned the piazza for the next threat.

The Officer came tumbling over the top of the lion

and landed with a crash next to George, trying to throttle a stone pterodactyl that in its turn was straining to rip his throat out with its fanged beak. The Officer's pistol swung wildly around on the end of its lanyard.

'George, my gun, if you'd be so kind . . .' he gasped.

George leapt forward and grabbed for the swinging weapon. The pterodactyl snapped at his hands, but he got them round the oversized pistol and jammed the barrel into the creature's chest, pulling the trigger. The hammer clicked noisily, but there was no accompanying explosion or bullet.

'Ah,' said the Officer.

George just dropped the gun and grabbed the pterodactyl's beak without thinking much. He felt the heat in his hands and the loose particulate molecules deep in the stone. He swivelled his hands round the two halves of the beak, and as he did so he felt a granular smearing as he wiped one set of molecules into another, joining the top part to the lower, gagging the surprised taint so that its saucer eyes widened and bulged even larger.

It dropped to the ground and hopped around, furiously but ineffectually tearing at its beak with the talons on the end of its wings, trying to open what was now one piece of stone. It was almost comical in its rage. The Officer looked at George with a new respect.

'That is some trick you've got there.'

George nodded. The Officer looked at the hopping pterodactyl.

'Seems almost a shame to—'

BLAM. The Gunner blew its head off.

'Not to me it don't,' he grunted. 'Behind you . . .'

Two taints were swooping in, their eyes fixed on the

bundle that George was wrapping in the cape. The Officer leapt on one and clubbed at it with the pistol he had hurriedly reversed in his hand. The Gunner shot the other one three times before it died, so close to George that its body knocked him flying.

The battle was of course a series of small fights just like this, all rolled into one giant maelstrom of violence. What George couldn't see was that the taints were beginning to isolate and pick off groups of spits at the edges of the square, and having surrounded them, attack from all sides and destroy them before looking for the next vulnerable pocket of men. The king who had smacked the Lionheart on the helmet was in one of these pockets, slashing and hacking with a thin ornamental sword while the six spits around him were torn to pieces, and then the taints swarmed him, the force of their attack ripping him up and out of the saddle. There was a series of terrible breaking noises, and then they dropped him into one of the two fountains, where his broken body hit with a tremendous splash and explosion of broken ice, and then lay still, his curly wig splayed alongside his cropped head suddenly looking less like an elaborate hairpiece than an exhausted yet faithful spaniel.

The taints howled off and joined another attack that was boiling around the empty plinth, where the Euston Mob were fighting back to back.

George had seen the king's body tumbling into the fountain and had felt sick at the impact it had made, but an instant later another attack had blurred past and he was backed into the lion's side by the Officer and the Gunner who had obviously decided they could protect him best by shielding him with their bodies. For several minutes all George could see of the fight were fragments snatched between the gaps in the two broad backs. And then, although the sounds of gunfire and shrieking and yelling all around were deafening, the Admiral's voice cut through them from above.

'To the sky! Look to the sky!'

George jerked his head upwards, and saw for the first time how the battle was being fought in the air above his head. The Temple Bar Dragon had been firing gouts of wildfire at the airborne taints. These multicoloured airbursts hung in the air and faded into skeins of smoke that overhung the battle below. Through the smoke looking east George saw immediately what the Admiral was shouting about.

Four struggling figures were being carried off by teams of larger taints, their greatcoats flapping as they twisted and fought to free themselves.

'It's the Euston Mob,' breathed the Gunner.

George stared in horror as one of the soldiers dropped his rifle. A taint unhooked from his arm and dived straight down, catching the gun before it fell to the ground.

'What the hell did it do that for?' said the Gunner. 'Why'd it catch the gun?'

The taints carried their struggling victims out of sight over the top of St Martin's church. And almost as if this was a signal, the taints that remained behind disengaged and poured out of the square in their wake. In less than one minute the whole echoing piazza was silent except for the moans and cries of the hurt. George looked up to see the Lionheart looking down at them, showing his teeth in a wide battle-drunk smile. 'I did not know London held so many taints,' he laughed, 'but we saw them off, by God!'

'It doesn't, and we didn't,' said the Gunner, looking at the Officer. 'I killed two that weren't stone to my knowledge, maybe others.'

'What do you mean?' said the Lionheart.

'Something is making taints out of ice,' said the Officer. 'Copying them.'

'Nonsense,' laughed the Lionheart.

'He's right,' said George.

'All the more for me to kill, if they dare to come back,' snorted the Lionheart, riding off.

'They'll come back,' said the Gunner.

'Why would they take the Euston Mob?' said George, remembering with a sharp pang how the four soldiers had saved him only the night before, how he had sat with them and enjoyed their easy company.

'I don't know,' replied the Officer. 'But I don't like the way they took care to keep that gun. It was only our guns that saved us this time.'

George looked round at the shattered bodies strewn across the piazza. If this wasn't the finish then he worried about what that would look like. Surely it could not be worse. 'I shouldn't have brought the arm here,' he said, feeling desperately sad and guilty. 'None of this . . .'

'Nonsense, boy. There's no other place in the world you should have brought it if not here, for where else could you defend it from those who would free it?' rumbled the bear-like man in the overcoat.

George looked at him.

'George. This is Bulldog. Bulldog – George,' said the Gunner. 'He knows a thing or two about keeping on scrapping when all looks lost.'

'Pleasure,' nodded Bulldog, looking a little bit like a gangster as he smiled round the cigar in his mouth.

"Though if you're feeling guilty, try working out how we can use these mirrors of yours against that thing on top of the tower.'

'If Edie manages to find them that is,' added the Officer. 'And think fast, because I don't know if we can survive another attack.'

53

THE OLD GROWLER

There was no time for ceremony when the Queen got Edie to the riverbank by Blackfriars. She'd had to drop back over Waterloo Bridge and take her to the south side of the river, and this had taken extra time as well as distance. They could hear from the shouting and crackle of gunfire that drifted across the river that the battle was continuing, and though neither of them said it, they both understood that their failure to get the mirrors and return them to the square in time might make all the fighting pointless.

'Where are your daughters?' Edie had asked in her one attempt at conversation.

'They went to look for you,' answered the Queen shortly.

She didn't need to say anything more. Edie looked at the side of her face as she whipped the horses forward, and saw all the worry that she wasn't voicing.

When they arrived just upstream of the bridge, the Bosun and Jack Tar were again on the deck of the barge, throwing the anchor out and dragging it in again, and the Boy and the Dolphin were hard at work in the water beside them. Of the gryphons there was no sign, and the sailors shouted across the water that they had left once the Queen and George had gone.

The Pilot was still lifelessly bent backwards over the river wall on the other side of the water, and when Edie asked about it, the Queen gave her an abrupt and unadorned answer. For the second time Edie wondered if the Queen was angry with her, worried for her daughters, or trying not to show that she was worried about the outcome of the struggle facing them all with the Ice Devil.

She decided it was all three, got out of the chariot and stripped off her fur coat. Then she sat on the edge and yanked off her boots. The Raven eyed her quizzically, and then jerked its head with the follow-me gesture she was beginning to recognize. She walked through the snow to the edge of the river, not worrying about how soaked her socks were getting, in the sure and horribly certain knowledge that she was about to get them a lot wetter and colder any moment now.

The Raven curved down over the river's surface, and then stopped, in mid-air.

Edie looked from it to the bridge and back again.

'Yes,' said the Queen. 'That's about right.'

Edie felt the Queen's hand on her shoulder.

'The Raven remembers everything. It is there that the Walker disappeared, there that he left the mirrors on the ice, there that they will have sunk into the water once the ice melted,' said the Queen.

'So I'll search along that line, from there downstream, I suppose, in case they got swept along,' said Edie, trying to sound nonchalant about a horror she had no idea how to face.

'Yes,' agreed the Queen. 'Though I feel that objects of such Dark power do not drift. Rather they pin the world beneath their awful weight.'

Somehow this talk of awful weights was not helping Edie get into a particularly optimistic frame of mind about the upcoming ordeal. She knew if she started to think about what she was about to do, she might not do it, so she just peeled off the two sweaters she was wearing and turned to the Queen. 'Right,' she said, 'I can hold my breath for about a minute. Maybe a bit longer. So. How are we going to do this?'

There followed a fast consultation between the shore and the barge. While this went on, Spout looped overhead, watching the surrounding skies, on gryphon watch. After a few minutes Jack Tar whistled him down, and explained to him what the plan was.

'Gack,' said Spout, nodding.

'Gack indeed, me old china,' said Jack Tar. 'Take a hold of the glint and ferry her over, would you?'

The plan was as simple as it was terrifying.

There was no time for finesse.

Edie was to be tied to the Dolphin.

They decided the best thing to do was to rope her underneath it, so she could reach down to the riverbed and retrieve the mirrors, and would be able to direct it left or right by reaching back and pulling on the relevant fin.

'Like steering a bicycle. With your hands behind your back,' explained Jack Tar not particularly helpfully.

Tapping it three times in a row would mean she was running out of air.

The Bosun and the Boy worked with the Dolphin as it came out of the water and lay on the back of the small boat so that they could work a rig of ropes around it, while Spout came and gently lifted Edie across to join them.

Edie didn't know what to say to the Queen, but she felt a knot of emotion as she looked back at her while Spout carried her over the water.

'I'm sure your daughters will be fine,' shouted Edie.

The Queen smiled briefly and nodded. 'As I am sure that you will come through this ordeal. Andraste guards you, and you have too much fire in you to be quenched even by as great and timeless a river as this old growler before us,' she shouted back.

The old growler flowing beneath Edie's feet looked cold and deadly as gunmetal. The current seemed to twist past with a silent growl, pitched too low for human hearing, but there all the same, right on the edge of her consciousness.

Then the little boat was below her, and she was dropped into the waiting hands of the sailors, who lifted her on to the harness. She could feel the soft surface of the Dolphin at her back, and when she reached for the flippers experimentally it twitched each one in turn, and clicked and whistled in greeting.

'Hi,' said Edie.

'He would never harm you,' said a laughter-filled voice at her ear, and she turned her head to see the tousled head of the Dolphin's Boy smiling encouragingly at her, upside down. 'And besides, I shall swim with you both. We play in this river every night, so it holds no fears for us.'

Maybe it was because he looked so like another little boy, one who had betrayed her to the Walker, or maybe it was because that betrayal had led to a drowning that meant this river did hold fears for her, but Edie, instead of feeling calmed by this, felt instant panic to the point where she was about to forget to breathe. She felt the ropes the sailors were tying round her chest and middle and arms were going to kill her.

There was only one way out.

'OK,' she said shortly. 'Let's do this now.'

And she started purposefully taking deep breaths, hyperventilating to cram her lungs with all the oxygen she knew she was going to need the moment she hit the water.

The cold nearly made her breathe out all of the carefully hoarded air in a single shocked outbreath. She kept her mouth closed and just screamed on the inside, behind her tightly clenched teeth.

There were bubbles all around her, and then darkness as the Dolphin swam straight to the bottom of the river beneath the hovering Raven. Edie knew she had to reach out, clear her brain, and stop worrying about things like the excruciating pressure in her ears or drowning in the knifing cold. She needed to feel the dark pulse of the obsidian mirrors, but the moment she tried not to think about drowning, she thought of nothing else.

She felt the powerful flex of the Dolphin's belly behind her, and heard a high-pitched keeking and clacking. She didn't need to speak Dolphin to know it was asking her where to go.

She had no idea.

This was not going to work.

This was going to get her killed.

She reached her hands blindly forward, but felt nothing as the Dolphin slowly skated along the unseen floor of the river. And then her lungs began to burn with oxygen starvation, and she tapped the fin three times.

Edie burst into the air with a rasping breath, unaware in her desperation that the Dolphin had controlled its ascent and was now standing on its tail so that she could breathe.

'Did you get it?' shouted the Bosun.

Edie just shook her head.

Not only did she not get it but there was no way anyone in the world could make her go down there again.

No one.

Ever.

Only now she was back in the air did the wall she had put up between her and her memories of dying by drowning tumble down. The cold desperate horror came flooding over them and engulfed her, obliterating everything else as it came.

'One more time . . .' she gasped, sucking in air.

No one could make her go into the water again.

No one except herself.

And then she trapped a giant lungful in her chest, tapped the Dolphin's fin, and plunged into the deadly cold one more time.

54

GROUND ASSAULT

The second wave didn't come from the air.

Not at first.

The first assault came boiling out of the side-streets and approach roads. All the wingless taints, the strange and the fantastical sculptures of London charged in at ground level. They came ripping and tearing and screaming, and they all launched their attack at the same moment. They had obviously worked their way all round the square while the spits had been distracted by the earlier aerial engagement. The attack came on every side, hopping and running and slithering into the shocked ranks of the spits with bewildering speed.

Because the onslaught roared in through the snow, the fight was even harder to keep track of as the assailants kicked up their own ice cloud as they came, but George had more time to try and make sense of it because he was in the centre of the square at the foot of the column, so not immediately involved in the fighting. Despite this it was still just a great, terrifyingly brutal mess.

Wingless gargoyles and snakes and lizards fought side by side with unformed or grotesquely exaggerated human figures. He saw two tall male humanoids with smoothed off features and blank heads, one rustier than the other, flailing into the middle of a group of spits on the outer edge of the west fountain.

'They're almost human,' he said.

'Yeah,' replied the Gunner at his shoulder. He shot the rusty one in the chest. 'It's the "almost" that makes 'em so angry.'

The pair of the downed taint raised its eyeless head and looked across the intervening space, zeroing in on its twin's killer.

The Gunner flipped open his revolver and reloaded. The Lionheart tumbled past, hacking at a stone lizard that had knocked him out of his saddle. The impact made the Gunner drop the bullets he was loading. He knelt to pick them out of the snow, scowling at the humanoid that was sprinting towards him, furiously knocking aside any spit or taint that got in its way. George could hear a muffled scream inside it, like a bell resonating around its hollow interior as it found that its maker had made it without a mouth to let the rage out.

'Bugger,' said the Gunner, his hands scrabbling in the snow as the gap between them closed with alarming rapidity.

'Don't worry,' said the Officer, stepping in front of the Gunner and raising his pistol. 'I've got him.'

And then there was the sound of a shot and the Officer twisted and looked at them in shock, the back of his head blown open.

George and the Gunner had a second of complete horror in which they watched the Officer drop in his tracks. And then George looked up and saw the faceless man-taint leaping at the Gunner. And in that moment George felt something under his hand, and realized it was the edge of the Gunner's helmet, and with a massive despairing twist of his muscles he jerked it off the ground and spun it at the attacker like a giant flying disc.

It hissed through the air and took the taint's head off at the neck.

The body stumbled forward and dropped to the ground. George saw the hollow core through the neck hole.

'George . . .?' said the Gunner.

'I don't know,' he replied quickly, knowing what the Gunner was going to ask him and looking down at his hands, which felt unusually hot again. 'I don't know how I did that.'

'No,' said the Gunner, slamming him back into the side of the lion as something cracked flatly past his ear. 'I meant: get down.'

He jerked his thumb over his head at the rooftops hidden beyond the steep protecting bulk of the lion's torso. 'I meant they've got bloody guns.'

They stared at each other, then at the lifeless corpse of the Officer. And then they both inched their heads up the smooth flank of the motionless lion and peered carefully over the top.

'How the hell do taints know how to use guns, let alone bloody get hold of them . . .?' began the Gunner.

They saw the snipers on the roof at the same time.

'Oh no,' breathed the Gunner. 'That's not right. You can't do that . . .'

The Euston Mob were ranged along the parapet of the building, greatcoats snapping in the wind that had just kicked up in answer to the storm raging through the square below.

They were firing into the spits, picking them off one by one.

But the eyes that squinted along the gunsights were not the eyes of the soldiers. Those eyes stared sightlessly from the heads that had been torn partially off the bodies and now hung off their necks. Gargoyle heads were stuck on in their place: snarling stone heads welded to the ripped open neck stumps with thick collars of ice.

55

THE DEATH OF WATER

Nobody says second time lucky.

That was the thought that plunged with Edie to the bottom of the river.

It's never the second time.

Third time is always the charm.

The thought, she knew, was killing her. It was bouncing round her brain, obscuring everything else she might be doing, telling her she was going to fail. It was drowning her like a block of lead chained round her neck. She wasn't just fighting the water, she was fighting herself, and she knew she was a tough and ungiving opponent.

She just couldn't clear her mind and think about anything except the cold and the pressure and the fact she was running out of air.

The pulse of Dark power came at her at exactly the same moment that the light came on. For the first instant she didn't know what it was, and then she knew exactly.

The pulse was the mirrors.

The light was her sea-glass heart stone blazing a warning through the material of her jeans pocket, through the thick silty water of the river bottom, through the Darkness itself.

The light said second time lucky.

Second time the charm.

The light also said danger.

She reached her hand towards the pulse of Darkness ahead of her.

The danger coiled out of the clay bed of the river and wrapped a thin tentacle round her wrist.

She felt it before she saw it, because she was looking ahead into the wall of water on the edge of the light-bloom from her warning stone. She looked down and saw the feeler made of clay coiling tightly around her arm. And next to it she saw the edge of Darkness, and knew it was the side of one of the mirrors.

Without thinking she grabbed the mirror with her free hand, knowing if she didn't she might pass it a thousand times and never see its narrow profile again. And because the mirror that had broken in two had had the original shape of a hand mirror, Edie found she had gripped it by the half-handle that remained. Again, almost without thought, she scythed the Black Mirror through the clay tentacle, so that it had severed and dissolved into the water before her conscious mind had begun to process the horror it was.

And then the Dolphin pulled her off the riverbed, and she burst upwards and out of the river into the sharp air, the mirror half clamped in her fist, this time screaming in a breath as the Dolphin rolled on its back and the Boy swam up to her and loosened the knots tying her to its belly. Then rough stone hands reached gently down and lifted her on to the boat by the barge, and she managed to control the shaking and override the bone-shattering cold that had frozen her to the core and chatter out one despairing cry.

'No! I only got one!'

The sailors looked down at her.

'I have to go back,' she sobbed.

The tentacle of clay burst out of the water like a small waterspout.

The end waved right and left, as if looking for something, but there was no eye in the blunt tip of the thing. Instead it grew a crown of nubby fingers that twisted and writhed into longer and thinner tentacles before her shocked eyes.

In the instant before it sensed her Edie saw the glistening surface of the main arm twisting with river-stones and other bits of waterborne garbage that were forming themselves into thick veins and corded sinews.

The many-fingered hand at the top of the arm bent towards her, and she saw the grinding maw that had opened in its palm, a great mouth lined with broken bottles and torn and shredded cans that chomped against each other hungrily.

And then life happened very quickly as death struck.

The tentacle reared back like a snake and then lunged.

The grinding mouth slammed at her and there was nowhere to hide, no time to even get to her feet or roll out of the way. And then a grey blur of stone hit her and she couldn't breathe and she was lifted above the river, ready to be plunged down to her last icy doom. And she heard the tentacle gripping her say:

'Gack.'

She looked down and realized it was not the tentacle that had grabbed her, but Spout, who had seen the danger and snatched her to freedom.

Before she exhaled in relief, Edie looked down at the arm pinioned to her side. Her fist still white-knuckled on the Black Mirror.

Edie breathed.

Spout flew across and circled above the Queen. The Raven lofted off the wall and rose to meet them.

'What the hell is that?' Edie said to herself, staring at

352

the tentacled mud still sinuously coiling and searching for her above the river's surface.

The Raven clacked its beak.

'Unmade Things?' said Edie, teeth chattering. 'What do Unmade Things want with me?'

It was George who had aroused the hunger of Unmade Things, George who had been attacked by a similar loamy tentacle in the underpass two, or was it three long nights ago?

She was losing count.

She was losing her grip.

Losing everything except the mirror half gripped in her fist and the sense that things were wrong and getting more wrong by the second.

George had aroused the hunger of Unmade Things because he was a maker.

Edie wasn't.

Her stomach lurched as Spout dropped out of the sky and grabbed a bundle the Queen was holding up to him. It was her fur coat and her clothes.

'Go!' shouted the Queen. 'Just go!'

'Eigengang,' agreed the gargoyle. 'Go Eigengang!'

And before Edie could speak, the Raven and Spout had wheeled in the air and were flying full tilt back across the river.

Towards the sound of the guns.

56

DIVIDE AND CONQUER

'You can't just turn a spit into a taint!' exploded the Gunner.

'What about Spout?' shouted George. 'I did it the other way round, didn't I?'

A bullet spanged off the spine of the lion behind them and ricocheted across the square over the heads of the fighting statues.

George's eye followed the whirring noise and came to stop on a giant taint, wading through the spits, slashing left and right with a huge weapon like a double-ended spear. It was in fact a pair of enormous geometrical dividers, but it wasn't the weapon that got George's attention. It was the taint itself, and the jerky disjointed way it walked and moved. It reminded him of the GridMan. Its naked figure was constructed of connected lumps, as if someone had taken a band-saw to a muscular and well-proportioned body and cut it into awkward chunks before sticking them together again, leaving wide gaps between the reassembled parts. The parts almost moved together, but were just out of sync enough to make your eyes hurt. His eyes blinked a half second apart, and when he shouted the two sides of his mouth seemed to fight each other.

'Maker!' he bellowed, twirling the dividers round his head. 'I have come to measure your span and weigh the Darkness you have stolen!'

'It's the Newton,' said the Gunner. 'I thought he was

one of us. Been spending too much time up St Pancras way next to that rookery of taints, I expect.'

He dealt with his disappointment by emptying his pistol into the advancing giant. Each bullet hit a different section of the body, and each section spun on its axis, like a bewildering 3-D fruit machine, but the figure kept on striding towards them through the carnage.

'Right,' the Gunner said, reloading fast. 'Don't let him get that bloody arm, eh?'

There was no one between them and the Newton now. The Gunner flashed George a smile.

'Been a pleasure, son,' he said.

'No!' shouted George.

'It's what I do,' said the Gunner. 'There's a bullet with everyone's name on it somewhere. I've told you before, thing is not to worry about it and live while you can, because sure as guns, no one's got a guarantee on tomorrow. Be lucky.'

And with that he snapped his pistol back together, clapped George on the shoulder, and ran straight at the Newton, firing as he went.

'Save the boy!' he roared. 'Everyone round the boy!'

This time each one of the bullets he fired hit the same spot – the Newton's right eye. The section of head containing it was blown loose, but before he got to fire the sixth and final shot there was no more time, and the snarling taint had stabbed the end of his sharpened dividers in a savage blow that sparked like a grinding wheel as it caught the Gunner halfway between belt-buckle and heart.

George heard the impact, and the 'oof' of surprise it punched out of the Gunner. He saw him stop dead as the Newton jarred to a halt and shook itself before turning its one remaining eye on the Gunner and then George.

'I am the Unstoppable Force!' it roared in a high croaking voice, twisting the point in the Gunner's wound.

The screeching noise was the one made by metal on metal, but to George it sounded like the Gunner's dying scream. He rushed forward, only to be grabbed from behind and held tight.

'No, boy,' growled Bulldog, holding him low to the ground as he struggled to run the twenty feet to his dying friend.

The Lionheart leapt his horse over their heads and swung his great double-handed battle-sword with one arm, cleanly severing the dividers.

The Gunner staggered back, still impaled on the freed end. The Newton whirled the dividers so the remaining point speared the Lionheart through the shoulder, yanking him off his horse and lifting him high above his head.

'Have at you, fiend!' shouted the Lionheart, his battle-frenzy undimmed as he swung the sword at the arm lifting him.

The Newton simply ripped the sword out of his hand and took his head off with it in one angry backhanded swipe.

The head was immediately buried in the snow, but the crown bounced off a balustrade and landed at George's feet.

'That's how a king goes,' said Bulldog. 'Worse luck.'

The Newton shook the Lionheart's body off his spear-point and took one step towards George. Bulldog shoved himself in front of George.

'When he gets me, you run like blazes,' he said.

But the Newton stopped dead.

It couldn't walk forward.

Its other foot was impaled to the ground.

There was a distant sound of approaching thunder, and the noise of a high-pitched whooping, but George barely registered it because he didn't have time to worry about whatever fresh wave of taints was about to engulf them.

He was transfixed by the fragment of life and death in front of him.

The Newton roared in pain and frustration as it turned its remaining eye to see what had happened on its blind side.

The Gunner had pulled the broken dividers out of the wound in his torso and used the last moment of his strength to shank it through the Newton's foot, down into the stone beneath the snow. Pinning him to the spot.

He fell back and sat there, splay-legged and scrabbling for the pistol on the end of its lanyard.

'Unstoppable force?' he spat. Breathing hard. 'Immoveable object more like.'

And he fired his sixth and last bullet into the Newton's enraged eye, blinding him.

'Behind you,' he coughed, and then his back crumpled and he pitched forward lifelessly into the snow.

57

NO RETREAT,
NO SURRENDER

The Newton didn't look backwards as the Gunner fell. His attention was taken by something bounding past him, something that he struck at on instinct. It was the hare and it shrieked as it wriggled off the end of his spear and ran on.

Because of this he never saw the source of the thundering noise approaching from behind him as the Queen of America stampeded off the top layer of the square in an huge eruption of snow. Which was a shame, because a buffalo does not leap very often, and there are few people who have seen one fly through the air with such intense velocity. It landed without stumbling, and George saw the flash of gold from something lain across its shoulders in front of the warrior girl riding it.

'They got her!' he yelled exultantly, but before anyone could ask who had got whom, the buffalo charged into the back of the Newton's knees, knocking his feet from under him.

The Queen of America bent low as the Newton tumbled back over her head, and then the buffalo slid to a halt in front of George, and the limp body of the Queen of Time slithered off its hump and landed at his feet.

'You mend!' she barked, then the buffalo spun round and she charged the Newton once more just as it was trying to raise itself off the ground. She speared it in one ear and out the other, and then leapt off the buffalo. She ran up to the giant taint, ripped her lance free and stabbed it again and again. It twitched and jerked and then lay still.

She jumped on to the Newton's chest and speared it one more time, right where its heart would be. 'Stay dead, windigo,' she hissed, spitting contemptuously into the blank unmoving bullet hole in its eye.

And then as she turned to answer George's smile, a bullet from the rooftop knocked her leg out from under her and she tumbled off the giant taint and landed across the Gunner's legs.

And the very last thing the Gunner did was grab her and fold her in his arms, twisting to shield her with his body so that the last three bullets caught him in the back and didn't hit her.

It all happened so quickly and matter-of-factly that it was over and the Gunner had sacrificed himself before George could even shout 'No!'. The word died in his mouth, unsaid, and he staggered towards his fallen friend in an instantly numb daze, as if the horror and the loss was just too much for his brain to process. He couldn't believe what his eyes had just told him. He couldn't believe the Gunner was dying, was going to be as dead and as gone as his father, as everyone who—

Bulldog grabbed George and ran him across the few feet to the base of the column. He shoved him behind it, away from the snipers on the roof, and then he turned and shouted across the square in a voice deep and ominous as a thunderclap.

'To me! To me!! Everyone to me and form a square! Form a square!'

'Why?' said George, looking around for a weapon to pick up off the ground.

Across the square the isolated groups of spits, although drastically reduced in number from the crowd who had flooded the piazza earlier, started to fight their way through the taints towards the base of the column.

'Why form a square?' repeated George, who had found a discarded sword and was looking hungrily about for a taint to bury it in to avenge the Gunner.

'Because it's who we are, boy. We fight better when our back's to a wall, and when there is not even a wall we fight the best of all, because there is no better buttress than the back of the man behind you, the man who is fighting for you in his turn,' laughed the big man, reloading his rifle with practised movements that made him look like a much younger version of himself.

It had got suddenly quieter. The reason was that the taints had retreated. As the spits fought their way to the centre of the square to make their stand, the taints had not followed. Instead they disengaged and moved in the opposite direction, melting away to the edges of the piazza, and then dissolving into the shadows of the surrounding streets.

George's immediate fear was that they were leaving because one of them had somehow crept through and snatched the stone arm and the Darkness within, but when he looked down he saw the bundle was still there, wrapped in the Gunner's cape.

Involuntarily his eyes swept up and across the square, and found the one body that really mattered. The Queen of America had rolled out from under the Gunner and was dragging him towards the base of the column, hobbling as she did so.

'This should be good, the taints all going, shouldn't it?' said George, itching to break cover and help, but held firmly in place by Bulldog who was chewing on a cigar he had retrieved from his pocket.

'Yes,' he said, though George noticed it sounded like 'Yesh'.

'But it isn't, is it?' said George.

'No,' he replied.

'Taints ho!' bellowed the Admiral from above.

Something swept in behind the last remaining taints, the grotesquely altered former spits of the Euston Mob. For an instant all the guns on that side of the square pointed at the incoming shape. And then George who had peered round the corner despite the attempts of his protector to stop him shouted.

'Don't fire! It's Edie!'

And the Euston Mob turned as one, the upside-down heads of the former soldiers bobbling on the end of the bronze flaps where they had been decapitated, and the replacement gargoyle heads snarled and spat in anger as they tried to aim their guns, but they were too slow and Spout was gliding in too fast. His wide-stretched wings hit them all and swept them off the rooftops to crash down the front of the tall building where they slammed into the railings below and moved no more.

There was a ragged cheer from the dense square of spits grouped round the base of the column as Spout followed them down at a slower pace, flaring his wings and dropping a wet and shivering Edie at George's side, tossing her bundle of coat and clothes to the ground and pointed excitedly at the rooftops.

'Gaints, Eigengang, genny gaints!'

Edie ripped off her wet top and folded herself into her coat in one fast move, hugging it round herself. 'We saw a lot of taints flying this way. They'll be here any minute!'

she stuttered through her chattering teeth.

The Queen of America laid the Gunner's body against the column. Edie gasped and stumbled over to him, arriving at the same time as George.

'No!' she said, her hand clapping over the wound in his chest, as if she could stop the life flowing out of it. George was on the other side, looking at the three bullet holes across the back.

The Gunner's eyes half opened.

'S'all right. It's just dying. Be fine.' And they flickered shut again.

'It will be all right,' she said urgently, not caring about the tear running down her face. 'George! It'll be all right, won't it? I mean we'll just put him on his pedestal and he'll get better at turn o' day like spits do, right?'

'If time is out of joint, we don't know if there'll be a proper turn o' day,' said Bulldog. 'I think unless time flows normally, dead means dead.'

'George!' shouted Edie. 'He can't die. We can't lose him. He's . . .'

The importance of what the Gunner had become to her choked her into silence.

'I know,' said George. 'He feels like family to me too . . .'

'But . . .' she began.

'Shut up and let me see if I can do this,' he said, closing his eyes. 'Let me see if I can heal him.'

And right there in the middle of the square he placed his hands on the three bullet holes and felt the damage and the rents in the metal, and he felt how the bronze had cooled in the mould, and how it wanted to be, how it had been before the bullets smashed into it, and his hands were hot, and he was so concentrated that he never noticed Edie staring at her hand on the front of the Gunner, and as the wounds mended and sealed on the back, he never knew that the hole under Edie's hand, the one he didn't think about in the heat of the moment, had also healed.

'Blimey,' said the Gunner, opening his eyes and sitting up. 'And there was me thinking I'd have a nice kip and wake up when you two had all this sorted.' He reached a hand over his shoulder and felt the smoothed-off scars of the bullet wounds. And then he looked at Edie and the one wound she had healed.

She shook her head warningly.

'No rest for the wicked,' she said darkly, almost managing to hide the smile of relief.

She picked up her boots and busied herself pulling them on, struggling with the leather against her wet feet. And as the other spits clustered round the Gunner and looked at his healed scars in quiet wonder, George told her what the Stone Corpse had said to him about how they could defeat the Ice Devil and force him back through the Black Mirrors.

'Black Mirror,' said Edie gloomily, her eyes darting around the sky. 'I only got one. I failed. One mirror's not enough.'

'We just break it and use the two quarters,' said George. 'That'll still be bigger than the little mirrors the Walker used to use.'

Edie didn't look convinced. He carried on and told her the obscure rhyme that he had been given.

'As the dragon marked your hand, so a dragon shall be your tool, for flames taint and ice have fanned only spit and fire can cool?' repeated Edie. 'You sure you weren't talking to a Sphinx?'

'That's what I said,' he replied, shaking his head. 'I've still got no clue as to what it means. Then it said: "To see the fires of darkness fade'll need all the light glint and maker made"– I mean, I'm a maker and you're a glint, but what light have we made?'

'Don't know,' she said.

And before they could continue, the sky darkened again and there was a roar from the surrounding streets, and the taints attacked from the air and the ground at the same time.

And then they were too busy altogether.

58

LAST STAND

This time the fighting was more intense, but the spits did better, because they were tightly bunched in a square round the base of the column. This enabled them to concentrate their firepower, and made it harder to pick them off one by one.

George missed the first wave of the attack because he was bent over the Queen of Time, trying to mend her as fast as he could. It was exhausting work, and he began to realize that every time he healed a gash or smoothed out a hole, it took something from him. He was putting himself into his work, literally, bit by bit.

By the time the attack retreated, he felt washed out.

He looked up to find Edie looking at him with an angry scowl.

'What?' he said.

'Well, I reckon the first answer is about using the Temple Bar Dragon to make something, I mean, that's all I can think of, yeah? I mean since he turns out to be the only dragon we have on our side.'

'Sure,' he said, looking up at the creature that had dropped into the square and had been flaming taints as they attacked, acting like a kind of living artillery piece. 'Sure, that's what I thought.'

'But that answer you got from this Stone Corpse thingy,' she continued, voice tight with frustration. 'That answer is *just* like the Sphinx! What does spit and fire mean?'

'Sorry?' said Bulldog, removing his well-chewed cigar as he turned to look at them, his plundered rifle held casually over one shoulder.

'Just a riddle,' said George. 'Like a crossword.'

'Ah,' he said, replacing the cigar. 'I thought you said Spitfire. Would be a lovely thing to have right now . . .'

And he turned away to watch the sky.

Realization hit George like a bucket of cold water.

'No,' he said. 'Yes. Of course. That's what it means . . .'

He flashed the memory of the Stone Corpse whirling slowly in front of him and saying: 'You carry the answer with you . . . you always have.'

He jerked his hand into his pocket, hoping against hope that in the turmoil of the last few days he still had the thing, the thing he always carried with him. He knew he'd had it to get back into his flat, before the Walker came for him and he'd had to make a sudden exit out the back . . . and then he felt the reassuring jagged edge of the house-keys, and then the smooth, curving elegance of the miniature brass key-ring they were attached to.

George looked at Edie. Edie looked at George. They both looked up at the dragon who was watching the sky above.

'Excuse me,' said George, pulling out the key-ring and holding it in front of the dragon's nose. 'Do you think if you made one of these, it would fly?'

'What. It. Is?' asked the Dragon, turning to have a closer look.

'A plane,' said George. Turning to Edie with a smile.

Her face was white.

She was staring at the key-ring and the little brass

Spitfire twirling in the air at the end of his fingers.

'What?' said George. 'You look like you've seen a ghost.'

'I have,' she said, her mouth dry. 'Where did you get that key-ring?'

'This?' he said. 'My dad made it for me. He had one just like it.'

'Your dad?' she gasped.

And then, because her brain seemed to have suddenly gone into overdrive and shut down all non-essential functions like remembering to stay standing up, she abruptly sat down.

'Edie girl . . .' began the Gunner.

'No,' she said.

'The bloke on the bridge. With your mum. The one she . . . That was his key-ring . . .'

'I know.' She swallowed hard.

The Gunner reached out a hand and grasped her arm gently but very firmly.

'If we were wrong. If he was what you first thought. If he *was* your . . .'

She shook her head. The implications were too big for her to process.

'Not now,' she pleaded. 'I can't.'

'You have to,' said the Gunner. 'And yeah. You can. You're made of special stuff. That's always been obvious. But how special?'

Her eyes were welling up as she looked at him, wordlessly shaking her head. It was just too complicated and too full of hope for someone used to travelling roads that ended in disappointment to trust.

'If you were made by a glint and a maker? I don't know if that's ever happened, right? I don't know. But I reckon you'd be something more than special, wouldn't you?'

Edie's eyes darted at George and then back to the Gunner.

'Please,' she said. 'We don't know.'

The Gunner's hand went to the scar on his chest, the almost invisible streak of fresh and untarnished bronze where Edie's hands had smoothed the wound and healed him. He leant in and whispered in her ear.

'It ain't just the boy who's got maker's hands, is it?'

Edie the oddball. Edie the loony. Edie the killer. Edie the always-alone turned and looked at George, and wondered if the size of the new possibilities she was taking on board meant her head would explode before her heart burst.

'What?' asked George. 'What are you whispering about? What did glint and maker make?'

'Edie,' said the Gunner. 'Tell him. Maybe that's why this all happened. Maybe that's why you saw him and ran after him. Maybe that's why he broke the dragon's head, to find you. Maybe it's why we all found each other.'

Once again Edie felt herself drowning in 'maybes'.

'Maybe none of this was ever an accident. Like the Queen said, the world balances accounts,' the Gunner finished.

'Edie,' said George, with an increasingly dangerous look in his eye. 'What did glint and maker make?'

Edie's hand went where it always did when she had to face a danger she couldn't quite see. It found the smoothed edges of her heart stone, and as her thumb coasted over the familiar sea-tumbled lines, she felt the heat and pulled it out of her pocket. It was blazing light, brighter and more powerful than she had ever seen. And she had never seen so many kinds of light. For the first time instead of its normal warning blaze it had a full rainbow of colours blasting out of it in a constantly changing glare that was as bright and twisting as the dragon's wildfire.

Edie laughed in surprise and wonder.

'This. They made this! My mum, the glint, and your dad, the maker, we saw them. Before I was born. Before you were born. And they made something. They took this bottle and filled it with hope and love and good stuff and if you laugh I will knock your bloody head sideways . . .' she said, bridling at the smile that had kindled on the side of his mouth. 'And they threw it into the river and it washed up on a beach and later, much later, I found this broken bit of it, and it became my heart stone. And . . .'

Her heart really was much too full to go on.

'And what?' asked George.

'And if that bloody Ice Devil is another creature of Darkness, then that light is the very weapon we need,' said Bulldog. 'And if he remains on his high citadel and won't come down to fight, then you will have to go to him. Up there. So.'

'So?' said Edie and George as one.

'So. We. Spitfire. Make,' said a very dragony voice behind them. They turned to see the Temple Bar Dragon standing over them. his talons kneading a ball of pure wildfire like a lump of clay.

'OK,' said George carefully, and he held up the key-ring. 'They look like this.'

'Ha,' said the dragon.

'Ha?' said Edie.

'I believe he knows what a Spitfire looks like, my

dear,' said Bulldog. 'As any of us do who lived through the Blitz and the Battle of Britain.'

The dragon turned to the centre of the square.

'Make. Room.'

59

SPIT FIRE

The Temple Bar Dragon closed its eyes, as if remembering something. As it stood there its greyhound chest swelled and the heat from its fire-crop built up so fast that by the time it was ready to make the Spitfire its scales had paled from charcoal dark to ash grey to radiant white, matching the white heat stored inside.

As it ramped up the intensity of the banked wildfire, the spits had not been idle. The Gunner and the bald man in the coat had organized them into a bigger square to accommodate the space the dragon was to use.

'Bad news,' said the Gunner. 'No one's got many rounds left.'

'You're running out of bullets?' said George in amazement. 'I thought you just . . .'

'We got what we carry. Once they're gone. We're done,' answered the Gunner tightly. He climbed on the back leg of one of the unmoving lions.

'Right,' he shouted. 'Listen up. We're outnumbered. We haven't got much more ammo. And unless these two kids and Snakey over here can pull it out of the hat, we probably can't win . . .'

'Which has never been a reason to stop fighting,' growled Bulldog at his side.

'Which has never been a reason to stop fighting,' repeated the Gunner. 'So it's going to be close work, lads, cold steel, bare hands and devil take the 'indmost!'

There was no great cheer to greet his words, just an

approving grumble and the businesslike sound of metal on metal as bayonets were fixed and swords were drawn. George looked along the line of the square and saw weapons bristling along its length like an angry porcupine. He was shocked by how reduced the number of spits was from the great crowd that had ringed Cleopatra's Needle earlier.

'So few,' he said under his breath, and then he felt the bald man's hand on his shoulder. He looked up. 'Do you think we can win?'

The great bulldog face crinkled into a fleeting smile as he pointed his cigar toward the east.

'I don't know where that hellish thing up there was spawned, but I do know where every damn person in this square comes from,' he growled, stabbing his cigar down at the snow-covered ground he stood on. 'Right here. And there's an old saying. Whatever the world dishes out . . . London can take it.'

The dragon spat fire into the hollow rectangle behind the men's backs. And while he blew and made, it was hard for anyone to keep watch on the skies as the twisting ropes of many-coloured wildfire hit the snow and spiralled and fizzed into shape, as if filling up an invisible mould in the shape of an elegant fighter-plane of a bygone era.

First two chubby wheels hissed out of the snow, and then the fire spread up the undercarriage legs and billowed out, pancaking along the sweeping shark's curves of the underbelly, slowly spreading fore and aft and side to side in a rough cross shape, as first the fuselage and then the two wings became distinct. The wildfire licked up and over on itself, tracing the graceful leading edges of the wings and curving round the perfect shallow sweep of the rear profile, outlining the flaps and then meeting other flames rolling down the steep sides of the long fuselage. Flames spiralled up and round the sharp nose cone and spun into the two whirling blades of the propeller. A long wave of flame blew off the distinctly visible cowlings in the backdraught and curved up and over the cockpit and then raced towards the tail, which they traced up and down and left and right, before dropping back into the snow with a light pop as they finished the entire plane by bulging out the surprisingly small tail-wheel.

'Wow,' said George.

There it stood. A perfect Spitfire, made from wildfire that smeared and coalesced across the surface in a constantly moving approximation of Second World War camouflage done in infinitely brighter and more surprising colours.

'Wow.' And then because he didn't want to look stupid by saying 'wow' again he said: 'My dad would have loved this.'

'Yeah,' said Edie. 'Mine too.' And then, before the Gunner caught her eye, 'How does it fly?'

'I. Fly,' creaked the dragon, and simply walked into the flame shape and spread its wings within the Spitfire's.

'What next?' said Edie, rather unnerved by the way the plane's flame canopy had just slid back.

'I reckon I should break that mirror,' said George. And he reached for it, put his hands on either side, and tried to feel the flaws and break it along one of them.

Two bad things happened.

Firstly he couldn't find any flaws or break the mirror, no matter how hard he tried.

And secondly the taints howled into the attack.

373

60

THE HIGH CITADEL

As the world became noisy and violent and complicated around them, George bent over the Black Mirror and tried to snap it.

'Come on,' shouted the Gunner. 'You need to be gone!'

And then he turned and shot a flying gryphon that was trying to snatch the bundled Stone Arm out from under his heavy boot.

'Come on, George,' said Edie. 'They can't hold out for ever.'

'I can't break it,' he said, straining so hard he thought his wrists would snap before the mirror did. 'I can normally feel the granules inside, the flaws in the stone, and I can break it along them.'

'Look, maybe if we both try,' she said, gripping the mirror with him.

'Edie, I don't think—' he began and then stopped, aware the heat in his hands had just doubled.

A stone pterodactyl hit the ground next to them, spraying them with beak-fragments. Edie was concentrating so hard she didn't even notice the chip that flew past her cheek, leaving a thin ribbon of blood in its wake.

'Yeah,' she said. 'Of course you can't find any flaws, I mean, feel it. It's not really stone, is it? It's more sort of . . . flowy. It's glass.'

'Edie,' he said, realizing what was happening. 'You can feel that too?

The mirror snapped in half.

'There we go,' she said in satisfaction. 'Yeah. I guess I can.'

'Time to go,' said the Gunner, throwing George the stone arm and then reaching up and tearing a screaming gargoyle right out of the air and stomping it to shards. 'GO!'

And then adrenalin did the strange thing for both George and Edie of making time go both fast and simultaneously slow – there was a lot happening in a confined space but they seemed to run in a dream, so that they avoided the flailing limbs and shattered weapons slashing around them, and leapt up on to the shining wing and into the cockpit. The dragon roared and the propeller sped up in answer, and the way ahead was blurred by a slight shimmer and they saw a line of backs, which was the outer edge of the square.

'Oh no . . .' said Edie.

There was a large creature standing four-square in their way on the other side of the line. A massive and angry taint, bigger than the Spitfire. A Sphinx.

'. . . roadblock.'

There was a crash and a shudder as something landed right in front of them. There was a moment of invisibility as the propeller whirled the snow that the impact had kicked up back over the canopy, and then they saw it was the High Admiral.

'I am the Sphinx, the great and mighty enigma of Egypt,' growled the giant head on the lion's body.

'Then this bids fair to be a most unhappy engagement for you,' said the Admiral, bowing coldly. 'For I am the Victor of the Nile, and this square of land is my damned quarterdeck.'

And then as the Sphinx roared so loudly that his hat was blown clean off his head, he roared right back and charged into a headlong attack, hurdling the swipe of the Sphinx's foreleg and swinging his heavy sword with all the power in his one remaining arm so that it split the Sphinx's head-dress. The two sides fell away as the wounded creature pounced on him.

The Admiral jabbed the sword into the paw that was trying to rip him open, but then it was torn away as the second – good – Sphinx burst out of a side-street and hit her sister broadside on, knocking her over and clearing the way ahead.

'GO!' shouted George, seeing the opening, and then the plane leapt forward and the square broke apart just long enough for it to roll towards Admiralty Arch, the taints ahead of it diving out of the way of its brutally spinning propeller. Edie and George felt their stomachs being left behind in the square as the Spitfire roared under the arch, along the Mall and lifted into the air with a sudden and vigorous jerk that banked into a tight right turn over St James's and then went upside down as the dragon barrel-rolled once, accelerating towards the Ice Murk and the high citadel beyond.

George was filled with a deep thrill of elation at the speed and the power all around him in the plane. He looked at Edie.

'OK,' she said. 'Wow.'

A phalanx of gargoyles broke off the tower and headed for them, as straight and merciless as missiles.

'George?'

'Straight at 'em,' he replied, hoping the dragon below them would hear, and then it was too late to worry, as a second unseen group of gargoyles dropped on them out of the sun, and the Spitfire spun and rolled and jinked as, one after the other, the taints tried to tear and bite chunks out of it to get at George and Edie.

And then they were all on its tail and it was screaming for the heavens to avoid them. And because they flew relentlessly after it, it looped all the way round and came up behind them, and then the dragon's wildfire cannoned out from within the plane and the attackers dropped from the sky as they accelerated through the smoke left behind as they fell.

The Ice Devil howled in fury as they passed over him, and slashed a misshapen hand at them as he roared:

KILL IT AND BRING THE OTHER DARKNESS TO ME.

The flared outer lip of the citadel it had built for itself exploded outwards in all directions as the remaining gargoyles unhooked and took to the sky in a shower of snow and icicles. From the silvery sheen on a lot of them George could see the Ice Devil had been making his own copies of the existing ones, which explained why the cloud of attackers they were now buzzing through was so thick.

'We can't . . .' he began, and then the Spitfire tipped on one wing and flew a tight circle round the top of the tower, howling through the air as it went. There were bumps as it hit taints left and right, but it kept on circling in what seemed like ever tightening rings. The bumping and the buffeting got less and less as they chased their own tail round the tower, and the sky got lighter. This wasn't because they were clearing it of taints, but because the Spitfire was trailing wildfire as it went, building a flaming cone that rose around the citadel.

George, looking across the inner void of the cone saw

the opposing curve of fire and remembered how the dragon had trapped him inside a fiery tornado when it had marked his hand, and how he had been unable to escape it. His hand twinged and he looked down and saw the scar. And then he knew what they had to do.

He reached in his pocket and tapped Edie on the shoulder. She was staring open-mouthed at the whirlfire cone they were screaming around.

'You take one half. I take the other half. Get on either side and point them at each other. That'll open the portal,' he shouted.

He would grab the Ice Devil and plunge it through the mirror. If that meant losing his hand, perhaps that was what was meant by the Stone Corpse's prophecy. He had been hoping that trapping the other Darkness in his stone arm would have covered that, but in the absence of a better plan, this was all he could think of. It seemed like a suitably savage end to his ordeal.

'How do we get down there?' she yelled back. 'Oh.'

The plane was slowing, and as it slowed she noticed it had been thinning out as the wildfire it had been made of had smeared itself into the sloping tornado they were on the inside of.

As they slid down the side the canopy slid open, and then the Spitfire tipped and bucked and decanted them on to the top of the tower, facing the Ice Devil.

'Save. City,' roared the dragon. And as they looked around, George realized it was on the outside of the cone, keeping it spinning, in the same way it had done the last time he had seen it conjure the wild whirlfire.

They were on their own.

With the Ice Devil.

'Tell you what,' said George carefully, getting to his

feet clutching the stone arm in one hand and the fragment of Black Mirror in the other and edging right, 'you don't have to be a glint to feel the Darkness in that thing.'

'In him,' said Edie, edging left. 'Definitely a him.'

The Ice Devil could sense the other power trapped in the stone arm. It was so heady that it made it laugh.

GIVE.

It held out its hand.

'Sort of looks like the Walker,' said Edie, still curving round the edge of the roof in the opposite direction to George. 'If you'd put him through a mangle.'

'Well, there's a nice thought,' said George. He was uncomfortably aware that the stone arm was flexing and reaching its fingers towards its brother Darkness.

GIVE FAST OR DIE SLOWLY!

George swallowed and stopped moving.

'Edie?'

'Gotcha,' she said, stopping and slipping the mirror out of the end of her sleeve.

George threw the stone arm on the ground in front of him.

'There,' he said. 'There it is.'

The Ice Devil strode forward with eye-blurring speed and reached for the arm.

'Now!' yelled George.

And he and Edie angled the front faces of their fragments of Black Mirror at each other as the Ice Devil stepped between them.

There was a snapping noise, and the mirrors jumped in their hands as they found each other and the reflections locked them together. And in between them, as if trapped in a force-field, the Ice Devil was spun and frozen, one hand reaching forward, the other reaching back, each hand being pulled into a different mirror.

'Got him,' shouted Edie exultantly. 'Easy!'

The Ice Devil shrieked so loud their ears rang with pain, and then it pulled its hands closer together.

Edie and George kept a tight grip on their mirrors, but each saw with horror that the Ice Devil was pulling them towards him by the rope of invisible forces connected to whatever lay on the other side of the mirrors.

'Or he's got us,' gritted George, staring in shock at the furrow his feet were making in the snow as he tried to resist the inexorable pull.

'Edie,' he yelled. 'Your sea-glass!'

'What?' she said, all her energy on not letting the mirror rip clear of her fingers.

'If it's what glint and maker made, we need to see if it does something, because I'm out of ideas.'

She clamped down on the mirror with one hand, freeing the other to scrabble the sea-glass out of her pocket.

It was so hot that she almost dropped it. But she knew she mustn't, so she rode the pain and tried to ignore the smell of burning.

Then she turned it towards the Ice Devil and it flared so suddenly that the pain was too much and her involuntary reflexes took over, and she dropped it.

And the world once more went fast/slow as she saw the last hope tumble towards the ground and heard the Ice Devil roar. And then there was a flash from behind her as something splashed through the wall of fire and flapped past her. A white bird, an owl, gently plucked the tumbling fragment of light from the air and carried it straight towards the Ice Devil. The Ice Devil opened his mouth to roar it to smithereens, but the bird flew slowly straight through the middle of his chest, in one side and out the other as if he was made of nothing.

Which of course he was.

Nothing but ice crystals and the Outer Darkness and the inhuman terror which has no form in this world other than what we give it.

'Andraste,' breathed Edie.

The owl flew relentlessly on, disappearing out the other side of the cone of whirlfire.

But what it left behind in the rapidly dissolving body of the Ice Devil was the scorching, all-melting heat of Edie's stone heart.

The ice melted, and the Ice Devil had no form, and as it searched blindly for a way to be, shrieking in terror, it found a Darkness it recognized and reached for it. The Darkness on the other side of the Black Mirror in George's hand.

There was an enormous explosion of noise, loud as worlds colliding, which in a way they were.

And then the heart stone flashed white as an atomic ground zero, and the mirrors leapt in their hands as the Ice Devil was sucked back into the unknowable Dark. And because the world balances accounts, and matches every exit with an entrance, just as the Ice Devil popped out of this world, a small package popped back in the other direction, and went whirling disorientedly over the edge of the tower, so fast and so unexpectedly that George and Edie, blinded by the light, missed it.

And then they were both violently jerked across the tower towards each other, as the mirrors slammed together like super-magnets.

They untangled themselves and found that the

mirrors had again become unstuck.

George looked down at the fragment in his hand. It was no longer the blackest thing he had ever seen. He showed it to Edie.

She lifted hers. They were identical. It was white.

'Snap,' she said, blank with the shock and relief of success.

All around them the cone of fire was dropping away, revealing a clear sky and a very happy-looking dragon.

'Good. You. Are. Both,' it said simply. 'Saved. All. All. Debted.'

And it dropped away, heading back to Temple Bar.

George stared at Edie.

'What's that?' he said, getting up and pointing at her other hand.

'The stone burnt me,' she said, reaching up and letting him pull her to her feet. She showed him the jagged scar burnt on her hand.

And he turned his own palm upwards to look at the same maker's mark on his palm.

'Double snap,' he said. 'Edie . . .'

'Yeah,' she said. 'So. There's something I think we need to talk about . . .'

She didn't know how to begin, largely because she still wasn't admitting what she thought about it. So she tried to buy a bit more time.

'How are we going to get down?'

'Gack,' said a voice from behind her.

61

TWIST IN THE TAIL

They stood on the edge of the tower and looked out over the city. The Murk was as gone as the Ice Devil that had spawned it. George carried the stone arm, and Edie had retrieved her heart stone from the centre of the roof. Spout stood beside them.

'George,' said Edie. 'It's quiet.'

He nodded.

'I can't hear the guns.'

'Yeah,' he said, ears straining for any distant sound the wind might bring them. 'I think the battle's over.'

'Gack,' confirmed Spout.

Here and there George could see what he first took for birds returning to the empty skies, and then he saw they were taints, flying back to their perches.

'It's all over,' said Edie.

'Not quite,' he said, hefting the stone arm. 'I've got a couple of things to do. First we need to put this back in the London Stone where it can't do any more harm. Then I've got to go and mend the little dragon I broke. Then . . .'

'Then it's all over.'

'No,' he grinned. 'Then it begins.'

Edie looked a question at him.

'You think all *this* was impossible, try and figure out how we explain you to my mum.'

She looked away, her eyes skating over the strangely peaceful city below.

'We don't have to,' she said.

'Yeah we do,' said George. 'And we will. She's not entirely normal herself.'

'What do you mean?' she said, bridling.

'Nothing,' he replied. 'You'll see. Don't be so touchy.'

'I'm not,' she sniffed. 'And I'm not some lost puppy that needs a home.'

'No,' he agreed. 'But you've got one anyway.'

They didn't say much else. Not right then. And because Spout could only carry one of them at a time, they didn't fly straight to the London Stone either. Instead they just let him ferry them to the foot of the tower, and walked through the empty City, while he flew back to Trafalgar Square with news of what had happened.

'They're not going to understand him,' said Edie. 'It's not like he talks very well.'

'He'll do fine,' said George, nodding at the black Raven that had looped overhead and had joined Spout on his journey west.

As they headed off towards Cannon Street through the snow-clogged wilderness of the City, they really didn't talk much at all. Partly it was because they didn't want to disturb the silence around them, partly it was because they both had so much to say that they didn't know how to start, but mainly it was because they were both as tired as they had ever been, and now the adrenalin and the fear had gone, they felt all of it at once.

'What was that?' said George.

Edie had stopped dead and was peering down a side street, suddenly tense again, like an animal poised to run for its lie.

'I saw something,' she said. 'At least I think I did . . .'

George looked down the empty street and saw nothing.

'Saw what?'

He walked into the side-street and looked down its length.

'There's nothing here, Edie. Not even footprints.'

He was so sure, and his certainly was so reassuring that she let herself relax. She hadn't seen anything properly, just a brief dark blur caught with the tail of her eye as she passed, something random that her mind had cobbled into a false impression that looked like Little Tragedy ducking out of sight.

'Yeah,' she said. 'Sorry. I'm just still jumpy.'

'Me too,' he said. 'And tired. More than tired really . . .'

'Chinstrapped,' she said, straightening up. 'Come on. And we should walk on the pavements. In case time starts suddenly.'

She pointed at the frozen traffic all around them.

'Getting run over would be a pretty stupid way to end this.'

George didn't say anything, but he did switch carrying the stone arm from one shoulder to the other as he stepped off the road and on to the pavement. He was so exhausted that it just seemed to get heavier with every step.

And then they heard wheels and horses and saw the Queen turning her chariot into the street ahead of them. The Gunner rode beside her, still helmet-less. They were both smiling.

'Well,' said the Queen.

'Yeah,' said the Gunner, hoisting first Edie and then George on to the chariot and slapping them both on the back. 'That was something.'

'Why hasn't time started again?' asked Edie.

'The Queen of Time has to get back to her plinth, see to the Clock of the World,' replied the Gunner. 'The Clocker and her'll see to it. Don't you worry.'

'We're not,' said George. 'It's peaceful like this.'

'Besides,' continued the Gunner, 'them what are left in the square've got a lot of dead spits to get back on their plinths before turn o' day. There's no hurry.'

'Have your daughters come back?' asked Edie quietly.

The Queen shook her head.

'The Queen of America has gone to look for them. She usually finds anything she starts to track. And they are big girls. They can look after themselves. I am not worried.'

Edie looked at the Queen, but all she got was the side of her face and a tight smile. She decided not to pursue the question for now, but she noticed that the Queen was a great leader, but a surprisingly bad liar.

And again, because there was so much to say, they all remained silent as the Queen drove them to London Stone.

There were two figures already there when they arrived.

The Old Soldier and the Young Soldier were standing looking at the sword and the hand and the frozen gout of metal that had once been the Duke, trying to work out how to remove it from the Stone.

'We don't know what to do,' said the young one.

'I do,' said George, jumping off the chariot, and walking over to have a look, followed by the Queen and the Gunner. He knelt in front of the Stone and reached out. His fingers felt the thin crack in the limestone block that the Duke had kept open.

'I can get the stone arm and we can widen this crack and put the old Darkness back in and seal it up . . .'

'Where have you two dozy beggars been?' asked the Gunner.

'We got lost in the Murk,' said the old one.

'We thought we'd try and get old Hooky, what's left of him, back on 'is plinth.'

'So that, come turn o' day, he's get better . . .' explained the Young Soldier.

'Nothing gets better,' said a dry voice from behind them, a voice shot through with malice and satisfaction. 'Not ever. Not really. Certainly not for any of you . . .'

George was the first to turn.

It was the Walker.

He held Edie tightly round the neck, the thin straight blade of his dagger pressed to her jugular, so nearly cutting it that George could see every pulse bulge the vein against the sharp metal edge.

Edie stood still as a statue. She didn't look scared. She looked angry, angry with herself for letting her guard down, angry for believing she of all people might actually deserve a happy ending to her ordeal, angriest of all for letting the Walker creep up behind her and trap her again.

'You shouldn't have come,' said a thin urchin's voice from the right. 'You really shouldn't have come. Not here. Not now . . .'

Little Tragedy stepped out from a doorway to one side, shaking his head. It was probably just melting snow, but there was water running down his cheeks.

'I *did* see you,' said Edie. 'Stupid. Of course . . .'

She should have trusted her first instinct. She'd relaxed and believed again, just for a moment, that she might just be allowed a happy ending, even a temporary one. She hadn't been jumpy and imagining things. She'd been right. And now it was all wrong. She looked at George.

George didn't waste time trying to figure out how the Walker had returned, though it was in the end simply because the world likes balance: in the same way that the Ice Devil had entered this world by filling the space displaced by the Walker, so when the Ice Devil returned to the Outer Darkness it was his body that had been spat back out of the mirrors and fallen off the roof unseen by George and Edie.

Just because the world likes balance doesn't mean that the weights and the counterweights are always good ones.

George didn't worry about that. He put all his energy into trying to work out how to keep that knife from cutting into the fragile pulse pumping in Edie's neck.

Little Tragedy walked past him, towards the Walker. He was holding something down by his side, slightly behind his back, something shiny.

'No,' he said. 'You shouldn't have come here, because it's the first place he'd look, innit? And now he's got you again, and I'm sorry he got you the first time . . .'

It was the Walker who realized it first. It was the Walker who saw the moisture on the boy's bronze cheekbone was real tears, and knew that the catch in the voice was crying, and it was the Walker who understood, just fatally too soon, that Little Tragedy was going to try and rescue Edie.

'Get back!' he shrieked, pointing the dagger at him.

'No,' said Little Tragedy, and leapt for him.

The shiny thing he had been holding at his side was a gin bottle he must have taken from the Black Friar's pub. He moved surprisngly fast, and got his wiry little body between the dagger and Edie. He grabbed the Walker's wrist with one hand, keeping the blade away from her as he smashed the bottle on the side of the Walker's head with the other.

'Leave her alone!' he yelled.

It almost worked. But the Walker hacked Tragedy's legs from under him with a brutal kick, and as the boy fell, they all saw the speed with which the Walker freed his knife hand and slashed the blade through the falling figure in a movement that was almost balletic in its elegance and power.

Before Edie could make even one step away from the Walker he had the knife back at her throat, and Tragedy was sprawled at her feet, looking in horror at the terrible wound that had almost cut him in half.

'Look,' he said, his eyes dimming. 'Look. I'm hollow. I knew it. I ain't . . . there's no . . .'

'Stop your whining,' spat the Walker, and kicked him so hard that his torso hinged back off his legs and sprawled on its back in the snow.

George saw Tragedy staring at him in shock, upside down.

'I told you I was made wrong . . . nothing in there. No heart . . .'

And then his eyes rolled back and he died.

'Poor little bugger had heart in the end,' growled the Gunner.

'Oh, do shut up your sentimental clap-trap,' hissed the Walker, seemingly oblivious to the damage Little Tragedy's attack had done to the side of his head. 'Where is this stone arm you say has the Darkness in it? I would enjoy having the Darkness in my power for a change, I'm sure I could encourage it to lift my curse. I imagine we could even enter into a more beneficial partnership.'

'I'll see you in hell first,' said the Gunner.

'You will all do exactly what I tell you or I shall open his smooth little neck and we shall all see the colour of her blood on this white, white snow,' smiled the Walker. 'Where is this stone arm?'

George looked at Edie. She tore her eyes from Little Tragedy's broken body at her feet.

'It's OK,' she said. 'Whatever you do. It's OK.'

'Go and get it for me, boy,' said the Walker, licking his lips as if he could already taste the power he was about to get control of. 'Give me the Darkness and I will let the girl go free.'

George spared a quick look at Tragedy's lifeless eyes.

'All right.' He nodded.

'Wait,' said the Queen.

'You can't trust him,' agreed the Gunner.

'Have you got a better plan?' said George, looking at them both. He could see they didn't. They looked as frozen by this as he felt. And so he knew what he had to do.

'Don't,' said Edie.

'I'm not going to watch him kill you just to keep himself amused,' George said flatly. 'Not amused.'

'Very sensible,' spat the Walker. 'Go get it, boy.'

And George turned and walked past the shocked faces of the Gunner and the Queen and over to the chariot. He and down. And he reached behind the front wall and hoisted out a bundle and walked across to the Walker.

'Don't hurt her,' he said, his voice trembling a fraction. 'Please don't hurt her.'

'George,' pleaded Edie. 'Don't . . .'

'Just don't hurt her,' repeated George, the tremble growing as he avoided Edie's eyes. He looked like the frightened boy she had seen from the very beginning. He looked tired and beaten. 'Really. There are better ways to keep yourself amused.'

'Of course I won't hurt her,' lied the Walker. 'Not if you give me the bundle and stop your whining . . .'

He reached for the bundle. George let him have it.

And as the Walker scrabbled the wrapping open, George straightened up and looked her right in the eye, all the trembling and illusion of weakness suddenly gone.

'Edie,' he said. 'You know how you never do anything anyone tells you?'

She looked straight back at him.

'Close your eyes.'

And she did.

The Walker laughed as he unwrapped the bundle.

And the sudden shriek of terror with which he greeted the contents was cut off as abruptly as it had begun, frozen on his snarling lips as they and the rest of him instantly turned to stone.

The glare of the Gorgon's head that George had handed him instead of the bundle with the arm in it literally petrified the Walker, changing flesh and blood into a rough granite, greasy and crazed with flaws.

'It's the Medusa, isn't it?' said Edie, her eyes still shut. 'Not "amused". Medusa.'

'Yup,' said George as the Gunner stepped across and covered the Medusa's head again. 'The Sphinx told me to remember that riddle.'

The Queen met his gaze and smiled.

'I'm glad you did,' she said.

And then Edie opened her eyes and twisted out from the Walker's grip, and they all stood and looked at him. He had been turned into a grotesque statue, eyes ripped wide with horror, mouth rictussed into a scream, long coat dramatically whipped back as if blasted by a great and sudden wind, his naked fear and weakness immortalized in stone for all the world to see.

'I'm not much of one for poetry,' said the Gunner. 'But that's the kind of justice I like.'

'The world balances stuff out,' said George. 'Let's get this finished.'

Then he and Edie walked back to the chariot and got the other bundle, containing the stone arm. And while the spits watched they worked quietly together, freeing the sword from the Stone, and pulling the crack wide enough to put the arm in, and then closing the Stone back up around it, so that the London Stone looked as it always had and always would.

And if it were a bit bigger in the days to come, no one would notice, because no one ever saw what was important about it anyway, if they ever noticed it at all.

'He, um . . .' began Edie.

'Yeah,' said George, standing decisively and pulling her to her feet. 'Absolutely.'

The Gunner and the Queen and the two soldiers watched George and Edie work on the broken boy. And because they were not close enough, they didn't see the small shape that George saw Edie's fingers outline on the inside of the boy's chest before they closed him up and made the join smooth with their hands.

'I know,' she said quietly, seeing his smile,

'sentimental clap-trap. You're smiling because you think I'm being stupid. But he tried to save me. And yeah, I know none of them have really got them. But it'll mean something to him, because he cared about not having one.'

'They may not have them that we could see if we cut them open, but they've got them where it counts,' said George. 'And you know why I think that is?'

'Why?' she said.

'It's what my dad used to say: if you're going to make anything good, anything worthwhile, you have to put your heart in it. That's why I'm smiling. Not because I think it's stupid. Because you knew that without being told.'

And once more he hoisted her to her feet, and they stretched and looked around them.

'What are we going to do with that?' said Edie, nodding at the new statue of the walker.

'Leave him to rot,' said the Gunner.

'No,' said George. 'I think everyone should enjoy this. Bring him.'

'Where?' said Edie.

'I know just the place,' said George. And as the Gunner loaded the Walker's statue on the chariot, they handed Little Tragedy and the remains of the Duke to the two soldiers, who carried them away with a smile, promising to get them back on their plinths by turn o' day.

'So. You are both master makers,' said the Queen quietly, sounding impressed for the first time ever. 'That has never happened.'

'No,' grinned the Gunner. 'Mind you, there's a lot of that about.'

'How can that be?' the Queen said, looking from one to the other.

And as they rode slowly back through the snow, Edie told her. And when she got to the bit about seeing her mother and George's father on the bridge, she stopped the horses and looked hard at them both.

'So you think this man, this man who was George's father, is your father too?'

Edie looked at George.

'Feels about right, yeah,' she said carefully.

He gave her a complicated look, as if saying it out loud had jerked things on to a level he hadn't quite got a handle on yet. Probably because he hadn't known it was there in the first place.

As they walked on to Trafalgar Square they passed other spits returning to their plinths, often carrying the broken bodies of others who had fallen in the great battle so that they could be healed by turn o' day when it came.

At Trafalgar Square they picked up a chariot load of shattered bodies that needed to be taken in the direction they were going. They saw that some spits were returning for a second load and were now carrying dead taints as well. This was because Bulldog had persuaded them that most of the malice in them had been whipped up to an unaccustomed frenzy by the Darkness and the Ice Devil, and that London would be a drearier place without them.

Edie caught George looking from the Walker's statue in the chariot to the empty plinth on the north-west corner of the piazza.

'George . . .' she began, realizing what he had in mind.

'Why not?' he said. 'Every victory needs a monument.'

'He'd hate it,' she said, grinning slowly. 'Everyone seeing him scared and beaten . . .'

And in no time George organized a chain of spits to pass the Walker from one to the other and up on to the empty plinth, and they all stood for a moment, enjoying the sight.

Then the Gunner hoisted the lifeless body of the Officer on to his shoulders, and George and Edie walked between him and the Queen, who led her horses on foot.

'What are we going to do now?' asked Edie as they walked along The Mall.

'We're going to the Natural History Museum. I'm going to mend the carving I broke,' George replied. 'And then we're going home.'

'George . . .' said Edie.

There was so much that was impossible about the last sentence that he'd said that she didn't know where to begin. She just ran right out of words and shook her head.

'I know,' he said. 'But after everything we've done, everything we've seen, everything that's impossible, explaining you to my mum is only going to be . . . difficult.'

And he looped his arm companionably over her shoulder. She let it ride for a couple of steps.

'What's that?' she said.

'My arm,' replied George. 'Get used to it.'

And he left it there.

And as they and the Queen and the Gunner walked together into the west, and the sun ahead of them lowered into an increasingly golden sky, time started again, not in a jerk, but slowly: the snow seemed to melt away gently before their eyes and as the whiteness disappeared from everything the colour bloomed back into the City around them, like spring returning. Movement began as people slowly appeared again in this layer of London. First they faded back in slow motion, almost like animated watercolours of themselves, pale opaque ghosts that slowly became denser and richer as they passed.

'George,' said Edie. 'The Black Mirrors turned white.'

'Yes,' he replied. 'I was thinking about that.'

'The Black Mirrors led to the Outer Darkness,' she said. 'What do you think happens if you go through the white mirrors?'

'I don't know,' he said, yawning. Edie saw it and caught the yawn herself.

And it seemed the most natural thing in the world when George looked down and saw that she had snaked her arm easily round his waist.

The Gunner grinned and stole a look at the Queen over their heads. The Queen raised an eyebrow, the merest hint of an answering smile twitching the side of her mouth before she got it under control as they all walked together into the bustling life and colour that was returning to warm the stone heart of the City.

THE END

ACKNOWLEDGEMENTS

Just as George and Edie might not have found their way safely to the end of their journey without the help of a strong mentor like the Gunner, I wouldn't have got their story into print like this without the help of my own extraordinary friend and guide Kate Jones. Kate was without doubt one of the all-time good guys, someone who got the joke (and greeted it with a gurgling and deeply infectious laugh). She had a really great mind with an even bigger heart. She died with terrible suddenness just as I was setting off on the third leg of this trilogy, and I still find it hard to write about her in the past tense. So, Kate, I'm going to use the present tense, not just out of denial, but because you are in my heart as I write, as you're in the hearts of so many of the large tribe of your friends and colleagues: I owe you more than I could ever repay, for which – now and for ever – thank you.

I am also very grateful for the good-humoured and painstaking care taken by everyone at Hachette, especially my excellent editor Anne McNeil who, along with Rachel Wade, helped me to get out of my own way more times than I am comfortable remembering.

As I began, so I end: Mum and Dad, thank you again for all you've given me, especially for passing on the love of stories. Jack and Ari: these books are for you both. I hope you go out into the world and find the magic all around you. It's just a matter of looking with an open heart.

And finally, Domenica: thanks for everything, especially for being the magic that I found.

Don't miss *Stoneheart* by Charlie Fletcher, the first story about George and Edie lost in unLondon . . .

Deep in the City something had been woken, something so old and so ordinary that people had been walking past it for centuries without giving it a second look . . .

When George breaks a small dragon carving from the Natural History Museum he finds himself plunged into a world he can't understand; racing for survival in a city where sculptures and stone carvings move and fight, where it's impossible to know who to trust and where nothing is what it seems . . .

Shortlisted for the Branford Boase Award.
Longlisted for the Carnegie Award.

Don't miss *Ironhand* by Charlie Fletcher, the first story about George and Edie lost in unLondon . . .

'Edie,' said George, 'we're going to do this together. I'll be right there with you. Anything, anyone trying to get you is going to have to come past me first.'

But when George makes his promise he is not aware that high on the rooftops an unseen gargoyle is watcing them hungrily, quivering with anticipation for the moment when it will unfold its stone wings and pounce.

The thing on the roof knows that nothing is over; nothing is finished.